NO OTHER LOVE

A Novel By Divine G

Also by Divine G

Novels:
Baby Doll (Published by Q-Boro Books)
Money-Grip (Published by Street Knowledge Publishing)
Money-Grip 2 (Published by Createspace)
Enigma of Love (Published by Divine G Entertainment)
The Canarsie Connection (Published by Divine G Entertainment)

Short Stories:
Averted Hearts (appearing in *The Game*, published by Triple Crown Publications)

Stage Plays:
Peak-Zone (appearing in *Exiled Voices, Portals of Discovery*, published by New England College Press)

NO OTHER LOVE ®

ISBN-10: 1940765099
ISBN-13: 978-1-940765-09-9
Createspace Edition

Paperback & ebook editions published by Divine G Entertainment
Written by: Divine G
Edited by John "Divine G" Whitfield
Cover layout/Design by Divine G Entertainment

For information contact:
Divine G Entertainment
Website: http://www.divinegentertainment.com
Email: divinegentertainment@gmail.com

Dedication

This novel is dedicated to the numerous family members, friends and associates who were very instrumental in helping me to get this novel written, edited and published. The list of supporters is so huge and extensive, I am very apprehensive about attempting to mention names, because from past experience, if anyone is inadvertently left out and feels he or she should have been mentioned, it creates a lot of bad feelings. So, this time, I am taking the safe road by sending out a universal dedication to all those who played a part in the success of this novel, without itemizing each individual name. If you were there, by my side, had my back, and was supportive, then you are the person I am referring to when I send out this dedication. This novel is dedicated to you for being there when times got extremely rough, rocky and raw. Once again, thanks for all the support, love and understanding.

CHAPTER # 1

Dinasia Whitman sat at her desk, reading and taking notes from a chapter in her biology textbook, which dealt with amoebas and their evolutionary process.

She suddenly heard the sound of keys jingling. Her head nervously rose from the pages. Dinasia sat her pencil down and focused her attention on the noise that came from down the hall, right outside her bedroom she shared with her foster sister, Valerie. Her pretty little baby doll face, and those enchanting brown eyes, no longer had their youthful, playful like aura.

Seconds later, someone entered the fourth floor Project apartment.

Dinasia glanced at the alarm clock on the nightstand beside the bunk bed. Her heart rate increased when she saw it was a quarter to eleven. "Oh no," the unconscious mumble escaped from her lips. She quickly turned to see if the bedroom door was locked. When she saw none of the locks were activated, she frantically shot out of her chair and raced to the door.

Her five foot two inches, one hundred and five pound slender frame moved gracefully across the room. She was dressed in a purple sweat suit, and dangling from her neck was a leather necklace, which had a matching medallion with "Super Ninja" written in yellow letters.

After slamming the sliding bolt lock into place and turning the knob lock button, she sighed and went back to the desk.

Dinasia picked up where she left off.

Thump! Thump!

The sudden, excessively hard knock on the door caused Dinasia to spring into a standing position, dropping her book to the floor.

"Open up this damn door, girl!" Kirk Shepard slurred, his beer belly wobbling as he tilted the bottle of Wild Irish Rose red wine up to his lips and took a huge gulp. The cheap wine bubbled in his stomach. Ever since he left the corner with his drinking partners, after the liquor store closed, the alcohol had been telling him he had to treat himself to a piece of this pretty young thing tonight.

"Go away!" Dinasia shouted, trying to make her squeaky, childish sounding voice appear threatening, but failed miserably at the attempt. "I'm warning you--"

"Come on now! Barbara and Valerie's upstairs . . . All I wanna do is show you how to be a real woman." He giggled, violently rattled the doorknob and banged harder on the door.

Dinasia hastily went to the top bunk and snatched the huge carving knife from under her pillow. The way she stood in the ready position, waving the weapon, she looked like a Zulu Warrior Princess. No one would've believed she was seventeen years old. Growing up parentless in the New York State Foster Care System had its way of enhancing such inborn survival attributes, and Dinasia was no exception to the rule. But her heart still raced nervously in her chest, despite her constant exposure to these rape attempts.

This time it would be worse because she could hear it in his voice. He was pissie drunk, and when he got that way, he became insanely bold. "Kirk, leave me the hell alone! I'm tryin' to study. I got a test tomorrow and I--"

"What'd you say, I just lick on it a little. I promise you, you'll like it." The thought of how sweet her young juices would taste made him drool. He wiped his mouth with the sleeve of his dirty navy blue jacket.

As Dinasia dragged her bookshelf in front of the door, she shouted. "I got my knife and I swear to God I'll cut your ass again if you come in here! Now, leave me the fuck alone!"

This made Kirk stop and think. He instantly caught a flashback of the time when Dinasia cut his hand. He looked at the six-inch scar in the palm of his hand and the alcohol took control of his mind. "You bitch!" He mumbled under his breath as the rage, mixed with drunken delirium, mounted. He began kicking the door with the sole of his worn-out black work boots, wobbling about intemperately.

2

When the thunderous banging started, Dinasia felt the knot of anxiety in her stomach transformed into a hysterical fear. Each time her Foster Uncle Kirk kicked the door the walls trembled violently, causing her to wince while making a flinching involuntary sound similar to someone being poked with a lit cigarette.

This fear wasn't entirely linked to this rape attempt, since she'd learned how to handle the knife quite well. The root of her anxiety was the possible involvement of the police. If a neighbor called the cops, and the law got involved, she would be sent back to the institution, away from Tislam, and that scared her more than anything.   This catch 22 predicament was the reason why she never reported the numerous other rape attempts to the police.

Dinasia took long deep breaths when she saw the doorframe started to give under the grueling force of the pounding. With the knife trembling in her right hand, Dinasia braced herself for the inevitable.

Suddenly, the door crashed open, flinging the bookshelf out of the way as if it was made of papier-mâché. Books were scattered all over the room.

She saw Kirk standing in the doorway with the bottle of wine in his hand, huffing and puffing with exhaustion, looking like a deranged bull that just ran a two mile sprint. The pungent aroma of the cheap embalming fluid like wine was the next thing to attack her senses. The odor was so penetrating it smelled like he had bathed in the stuff. Kirk stammered rapidly towards her.

While jabbing the knife at the air, she shouted. "Don't come near me, you--"

Kirk faked like he was going to toss some of the wine in Dinasia's face. When she ducked to the right, he timed his next toss of the bottle so perfectly a river of red wine splashed her dead in the face.

Dinasia screamed as the burning, stinging sensation in her eyes registered. She also screamed because she knew without being able to see it was impossible to defend herself. Swinging the knife wildly, with both

3

eyes shut tight, she felt a blow to the head that buckled her knees. Stumbling backwards, she tried to open her eyes. The scorching sensation made her change her mind.

She shrieked when she felt her wrist being viciously twisted. A couple of her knuckles cracked as the knife fell from her grip. The fear of what was about to come next created a blinding urgency inside of her. The terror-stricken feeling was identical to the emotion that a cornered wild animal experience upon realizing it was trapped and death was only seconds away. She kicked, punched, scratched and even tried to bite at anything that touched her.

Suddenly, the wind was knocked clean out of her by a blow to the stomach, which took her straight to the floor. After two additional kicks to her side, and a solid punch to the side of her head, she couldn't breath. Her head started spinning and she felt like she was hurled into a dream. Through a partially conscious mind, Dinasia felt Kirk turn her onto her back, forced her legs open and got on top of her. The weight of his body made her feel like she was being smothered to death and she struggled to get air into her lungs. He grab both her wrists with one of his huge hands and pin them to the floor over her head, restricting her ability to gorge his eyes out of his head. His free hand began fondling her.

Oh, God no! Please don't let this happen to me! Dinasia heard her inner voice cry out as she struggled desperately to get a bearing on her punch-drunk mind. She had to think of a fast way to get out of this, and judging from all circumstances, an escape didn't look very likely. Kirk was twice her size, she was weaponless, her foster mother and sister were upstairs smoking crack, she was hanging onto consciousness by a string, and her head was still spinning with pain and dread.

The tears of frustration flowed because if her foster brother, Prince, hadn't gone away to college this drunken, alcoholic, dope fiend, slime bucket would've never tried this to her. When she felt Kirk trying to pull her sweat-pants down, Dinasia spoke softly. "Okay, okay, I'll do it. Let me take 'em off."

4

"That's the oldest trick in the book. If I let your hands go, you'll start actin' up." He tugged harder at her sweat-pants, causing them to slide down to her knees. His hand went for the panties.

She started squirming. "No, no!" she screamed. "I promise I won't act up." She continued thrashing, squirming and kicking frantically. "Let me do it!"

Kirk giggled because her sudden violent movement really excited him. When he felt her pubic hairs, his shaft started throbbing. His breathing escalated and his blood began to boil. Instead of pulling her panties down, he ripped them off in two swift jerks. He guided his hand down to her vagina and began his perverted massage.

Dinasia felt nauseous when he began touching her down there. After she saw him sniff his fingers and then started licking them greedily, the nausea turned into the urge to spit in his face.

When he began hastily unfastening his pants, Dinasia knew if she didn't do something within the next couple of seconds, she might be counting her last days on this planet. Kirk shot drugs and didn't believe in condoms during his many episodes of promiscuous sex, which she knew made him a prime candidate for exposure to HIV, the virus that causes AIDS.

Dinasia started breathing hard, pretending to be sexually excited. "Kiss me first, Kirk, please." She said sensuously. "It'll make me wet. You like it wet, don't you?"

"Ahh, yeah baby, you like this shit don't you? I knew you was a little freak on the down low." He puckered up his lips as he guided his mouth towards hers.

Dinasia felt a surge of energy come from an unknown reserve inside her soul. The thought of dying from a disease such as AIDS created a fear that produced a willpower that was beyond this world. With every bit of strength she could muster, Dinasia head-butted him on the bridge of his nose while simultaneously turning her body.

Kirk hollered explosively.

Dinasia wrenched her hands free without difficulty because both of Kirk's hands involuntarily went up to his bloody nose. She shoved him aside, sprung to her feet, pulled up her sweat-pants, and kicked Kirk in his head.

As Kirk made an effort to get up, Dinasia looked around desperately for something to use to stop this drunken maniac. After only two seconds into her terrified search, she saw an excellent object. She raced over to the dresser, picked up the twelve-inch television and smashed it on his head. Upon impact, there was a small explosion as electrical sparks, glass and plastic flew everywhere.

Dinasia ran towards the door, but when she jumped over Kirk, her foot made contact with his shoulder, which caused her to trip and fall face first. She blunted the impact of the fall with both of her hands. "EHHH!!" She moaned loudly from the sharp pain that shot up her left arm. The source of the injury was the wrist and there was no doubt in her mind it was sprain.

As she scrambled back to her feet, clutching her wrist, Dinasia noticed Kirk was now on his hands and knees crawling towards the desk with his back to her. She saw the perfect way to put out his fire. She charged at him and kicked him square in the behind, making extra certain her foot impacted with Kirk's testicles.

The loud cry Kirk released instantly told her she would die if he somehow managed to get his hands on her. The ear-twisting holler also told her this apartment could no longer be a home for her under any circumstance, unless she wanted to die a miserable and expedient death, of course.

As Kirk laid in a fetal position, moaning and groaning while clutching his crotch, Dinasia almost tripped over the bookshelf as she ran out the room. As she was retrieving her coat from the hallway closet next to the kitchen, she heard something behind her.

She turned and saw Kirk crawling out of the room, muttering curse words a mile a minute. "Don't run now," he said as he tried to stand; then he shouted. "I'm gonna kill you, bitch!" But the pain brought him back to his knees.

Dinasia put on her brown ski-coat and raced out of the apartment. She went straight to the staircase and ran downstairs two steps at a time. She was hoping and praying her best friend Keisha Anderson could help her. When she reached the ground floor and opened the outer door of the Project building, the February night cold made her realize she should've snatched up some extra clothing.

"Come here, you bitch!! Don't you run from me!!" Uncle Kirk yelled down the stairs, just as Dinasia stepped out of the building. A brittle cold gush of wind touched her way down to the bone and brought tears to her eyes as she headed down the street.

*   *   *   *

Shateek Davis was behind the wheel of the brand spankin' new cranberry colored 1994 Accra RL, cruising down Blake Avenue. He was bobbing his head to the bangin' beat of Biggie Smalls' "One More Chance." Dressed in an expensive tan wool sweater, brown jeans and a raccoon fur coat lying on the side, his high yellow complexion and sleek curly hair made him look like a cross between Gregory Abbott and Malcolm X.

But unlike the usual pretty boy type, Shateek had a vicious knuckle game and a no nonsense attitude and temper to match. On top of that, one of his brothers was the biggest drug dealer on this side of Brooklyn, the oldest was a police sergeant with New York's Finest while his mom and dad were the owners of a multi-chain franchise and Shateek was the baby of the family who was spoiled rotten on a proceduralized basis.

The heat in the car was turned up so high his rollin' partner Trigger had a two inch crack on the passenger window. Trigger was almost the complete opposite of Shateek. His rough neck, scary and hard facial features along with his bulky, tank like body was extremely intimidating, but in actuality, he was easy going, and was always inaccurately prejudged as a troublemaker.

In the back seat, Watch Dog was sipping on a tall can of Ballantine Ale, and he was short, dark and partially handsome. He rightfully earned the title as the "quiet storm" since talking wasn't something he did very well in light of the speech impairment that made him sound as stupid as a drunk, retarded republican on acid laced crack. So, wisely, he let his action do the talking in most situations.

The three of them had just come from the pool hall over on Logan Street and were calling it a wrap for the night. Shateek glanced at his 14-carat gold plated watch and saw it was ten after eleven o'clock. As he turned onto Linden Boulevard, heading for the Pink House Projects to drop off Trigger and Watch Dog, he stopped moving to the beat and started beating himself up mentally because he knew he should've been home at least an hour ago. He still hadn't done his homework assignment for Ms. Lewis's social studies class, nor did he even take a peek at his biology notes for tomorrow's test. Now he would be up until one o'clock trying to get his shit together.

With his eyes on the road, Shateek saw a girl in a brown ski-coat up ahead, on his right side; her back was to him and she was walking very fast. He could even see her hourglass shape through the coat she wore. In light of the fact it was 20 degrees with a wind chill factor of 2 below zero, and extremely too late for a sister with such a juicy booty to be out on these dangerous streets, the young lady definitely got Shateek's attention. He noticed Trigger saw her as well. As he drove pass, Shateek tried to get a look at the girl's face without any luck.

"Yo, hold up!" Trigger said as he turned the volume knob on the CD player all the way down. "That looks like that girl that got you strung out, Sha. I think her name is Shanasia, Rahasia, or some shit like that."

It was Dinasia, Shateek realized and immediately applied pressure to the breaks while double parking next to an old black Volvo. He quickly put the gear in park, hit the electric window button and pulled the passenger window all the way down. The agonizing cold shot inside the car and attacked their faces.

"Dinasia!" Shateek shouted across Trigger just as she walked pass the car. When she kept walking without answering, Shateek realized she never saw this car before because it was his brother's newest ride. He hastily opened his door and got out. "Yo, Dinasia it's me, Shateek."

Dinasia stopped and turned. "Hey, Shateek, how you doing?" A surge of relief cascaded over her mind and body since she wasn't in the mood to deal with any more drama.

"Come here," Shateek said as he walked towards her. He felt his heart turn to silly putty because Dinasia was the only girl he had ever truly wanted, but couldn't get. "What you doin' out here this time of night?"

"I'm on my way to Keisha's house and--"

"What the hell happened to your face!?" Shateek eased close enough to see the traces of blood on her chin. Then he saw the swelling on her cheek and the rage brewed in the pit of his stomach. His demeanor became stern and dangerous like. "Don't tell me Tislam been beatin' on you."

She sucked her teeth. "Now, you know Tislam ain't into that." Shivering uncontrollably, she glanced at Trigger when the music was suddenly turned up inside the car.

"Come on, get in the car. I'll drive you there." he was about to head back to the car, but she didn't move.

"I can walk the rest of the way; it's only about ten more blocks." She saw Watch Dog was the other person in the car with Trigger. Boy did she truly dislike both of these losers. Plus, she knew Shateek wanted to get with her and she didn't want to start leading him on or causing him to get brain locked into any wrong ideas. Her heart was Tislam's and Tislam's only. She was about to walk away, but Shateek gently grabbed her arm and held her in place.

"It's freezing out here, Dinasia. Plus, you know how crazy these streets are at this time of night. And look at you. You're trembling." He wanted to embrace her, comfort her, and most of all, find out who did this to her pretty little face so he could break the motherfucker's legs, arms and all other limbs.

9

Shateek let go of her arm. "Come on now, as much as me and you be kickin' it in biology class and during lunch period, I thought we was mad cool? Ain't we peeps?" He noticed she was cutting her eyes at Trigger and Watch Dog, as the two rocked their heads to the pounding bass. "Don't worry about them; I'm just giving them a ride home. And if you want," he paused with a comical facial expression. "I'll kick 'em out right here. That's my word, just say the word."

Dinasia giggled. She loved Shateek's crazy sense of humor and got a thrill out of how some of the toughest hard nose guys were afraid of him. She never saw or heard of fine looking guys being able to intimidate the rough looking ones until she met Shateek. She wanted to insist on walking the rest of the way, but deep down she knew she needed a ride; ten blocks was too long of a distance to be walking in this cruel and vicious cold, especially since she wasn't properly dressed. A sudden angry gust of wind lashed at her back and shoved her a couple inches closer to Shateek. "Okay, you can take me there."

"You want me to kick 'em out?" Shateek said seriously, heading for the car as she followed.

"Of course not," she said.

Shateek pulled open the passenger door and initially said nothing to Trigger, who looked up at him stupidly. After a moment he said, "What the fuck you want, an invitation or somethin'? Get'cha Bozo ass in the back."

"It's all right, Shateek," Dinasia chimed in. "I'll get in the back."

"Picture that," Shateek said to her as Trigger eased into the back with Watch Dog. He smiled at Dinasia as she sat in the seat. That funny feeling he got whenever she was in his midst increased significantly. He wasn't normally a sucker for love, but Dinasia was different. The first day he laid eyes on her, he wanted her and been on a mission to win her heart ever since. He closed the door, went around to the driver side, got in and pulled off.

During the short ride, Shateek said very little until after he dropped off Trigger and Watch Dog. They both lived in the same Projects as

Dinasia, but on the far side, about four blocks away from her building on Crescent Street.

Shateek already had an idea what the situation was with Dinasia's injuries, and since he lived at an extremely high pitch of emotions—especially for those he harbored a strong liking for—he couldn't resist the urge to meddle into her business. It shattered his heart to see Dinasia holding her wrist, trying to pretend she wasn't in pain. "Dinasia who did this to you?"

Dinasia never told anyone else besides Keisha about Kirk's rape attempts and suddenly felt awkward when she contemplated telling Shateek what happened. During numerous lunch breaks at school, she and Shateek had talked about all sorts of things, and he even shared a lot of his personal business with her. She now felt like she was acting unfairly by not doing the same. Her anger told her to tell him, but her conscience insisted she not do it.

She knew Shateek would probably do something quite vicious to Kirk. His eyes had that mean, deadly serious look. For the sake of maintaining the brotherly love she had for Prince, and because she wouldn't be able to live with herself if her conduct was the cause of harm to another human being—even involving a scum bag such as Kirk—she held back. "I don't wanna talk about it, Shateek. It's a family thing. I don't put my family business out on the street like that."

Shateek nodded his head, realizing she had just told him everything he needed to know in order to figure out who did this to her. "I can respect that. But . . . like I said before, if you ever need someone to talk to, a shoulder to lean on, or if you need anything handled . . . that includes money, whatever, I'll be there for you, Dinasia."

There was a long movement of silence while Shateek observed Dinasia looking out the window. His yearning to win her heart uncapped an eruption of sudden memories. All those vicious rumors he heard flooded his mind. Months ago, after hearing about Dinasia being attacked by Kirk, Shateek did his own investigation, which lead him to more gossip.

Now, as he glanced at her through the corner of his eye, Shateek realized the rumors were indeed true. He was furious and had to focus in order not to reveal this anger to Dinasia. He wondered what's the best way to punish ole dope fiend Kirk for tryin' to violate my future wife?

Then, suddenly, Shateek realized he might be able to kill two birds with one stone. With a wicked smile trying to come to life, he thought hard about the idea and realized it might just work.

For the past eight years, he'd been trying to come up with a way to get Tislam out of the picture. Everything he tried up to this point failed miserably. As long as Tislam was on the scene, Shateek knew Dinasia would never allow her love for him to become true love in the man and woman, husband and wife sense. He was deeply mesmerized by Dinasia's undying devotion and loyalty to Tislam, and his jealousy was about to skirt the edges of sheer hatred. The three fights he had with Tislam—two of which he loss—did nothing but make his emotions even more compelling.

He wanted Dinasia so bad, he even contemplated murder on many occasions, but now with this new idea brewing inside his head, he could feel it was going to finally work. The intricacies of the plan percolated powerfully in his mind and the step-by-step details slowly began to fall in place.

Shateek smiled as he stopped the car about two houses from Keisha's. The private houses that lined the block were noticeably well kept and had middle class written all over them.

"Thank you, Shateek. I really appreciate the ride." She opened the door and got out. When she saw Shateek get out as well, she said, "I'm okay now, I can handle it from here."

"Once you're safely inside, then I'll break out."

She saw Shateek wasn't taking no for an answer and so she shrugged her shoulders, and headed for the house. She opened the gate and tiptoed towards the back. All the lights were out since Keisha's mother was strict about going to bed early. She went to the basement window where Keisha slept and tapped on the window very lightly.

After waiting a minute, she tapped again. She was on the verge of panicking. What was she gonna do if She couldn't get inside? She tapped a little harder. When the first floor lights were suddenly turned on, Dinasia quickly tiptoed around the corner since she knew it was Keisha's moms. After waiting a couple of minutes, she peek around the corner and noticed the first floor light was turned off.

As she headed back to the basement window, Dinasia heard the door open. Paralysis instantly gripped her whole body since she just knew Keisha's moms caught her. She turned and saw Keisha.

"Come on, girl." Keisha whispered while waving for Dinasia to come to her. The oversized green night coat made her pudgy and pleasingly plump body look thin and petite. "Hurry up, it's cold out here."

Dinasia quickly entered.

After Keisha patched up her wounds, and the two got comfortable, Dinasia finished explaining how Kirk attempted to rape her once again.

"Dinasia," Keisha's sympathetic, sleepy eyes were truly pained. "You gotta do something to stop that creep . . . If you don't, he'll keep doing this to you. Hell, he might even kill you in the process . . . If I were you, I'd tell Tislam and let him whip the living shit out of him."

Dinasia enthusiastically shook her head no. "You know Tislam got a crazy temper. He wouldn't just hurt Kirk; he'll probably kill him for doing something like this to me. I would never create a situation that would cause Tislam to hurt himself or anyone else for that matter. Not only that." She sighed because what she was about to say made her feel silly after all the pain and suffering she'd been through. "I wouldn't wanna see Kirk dead. It's the drugs that's making him act crazy. Before he started getting high, he never acted like this. If anything, the man needs help."

Keisha burst out laughing, which brought a confused expression to Dinasia's face. Through sniffles, Keisha spoke. "You said you don't wanna see him dead? That's kinda hard to tell with you busting him in the head with a damn television."

They both laughed.

Keisha brought her laughter under control. "You're a better woman than I am because if that motherfucker tried that with me, I'd have that nigga's ass either in jail or six feet under . . . And your crack-head moms deserve even worse. You told her what Kirk is doing, and she threatened to send you back to the institution is just plain evil. She ain't nothin' but a wicked bitch. Whether she's on drugs or not, that shit is foul."

Short pause.

Dinasia felt drained and chronically depressed just being reminded of the fact she had no real family. One would think, after spending a lifetime without a family, she would be used to it by now. But, the truth was, she needed that sense of family in order to feel like a part of the human race. "You're right. But that don't stop the world from turning. Right now, I'm focusing on finishing these last four months, graduate and put that scholarship I won to full use."

"And it's a damn shame your crack-head sister is acting like she don't know this shit is going on either, especially after she walked in on one of the incidents . . .This shit got me tight as hell because they know Kirk is a fuckin' pervert and they could stop it if they wanted to."

"That's exactly why I can't go back to that house. The way Kirk screamed when I kicked him in the nuts, I think he'll kill me if I ever go back there. I need to stay here for a while. Can you help me?"

Keisha smiled. "Girl, we ain't best friends for nothing. Of course you can stay, but how are we gonna hide you from my moms? Sooner or later she's bound to catch on."

Dinasia had already structured a plan during her trip here and quickly explained the scheme to Keisha.

"Girl, I see why you wanna major in psychology. With that shrewd ass attitude of yours, you picked the right future occupation because you got one helluva sneaky mind."

They both giggled.

"I think it'll work." Keisha caressed her shoulder. "Let's go for it, girl."

CHAPTER # 2

Tislam Parker was pulled out of the daydream when the A Train conductor announced Euclid Avenue was the next stop. He had been imagining how lovely it was going to be on the cruise he and Dinasia planned to take after they both graduated high school in a couple of months. He stood sluggishly and forced his medium size physique towards the sliding doors. It was a little after four o'clock and the train was almost filled to capacity.

He eased pass the straphangers and could smell the strong odor of garlic, which seemed to come from the breath of just about everyone on the train. When he reached the doors, Tislam saw his reflection in the glass window plate. The image told him he needed a break.

Going to school and working part-time afterwards at a trunk loading dock in Queens had begun to take its toil. The bags under his eyes made his naturally pleasing and dignified facial features look aged and visibly worn-down. But his light brown skin complexion contrasted with his meticulously groomed high top fade continued to give him the look of elegance and self-assuredness. At only seventeen and five-sixths years of age, he looked a little older and conducted himself as if he was three times that number.

When the sliding doors opened, he briskly stepped off the train and put his hands in the pockets of his black bubble Northface, heading towards the token booth. He caressed the 16 shot 9mm Ruger, and the weight of the gun made him feel safe and secured.

After exiting the Euclid Avenue station while heading down the Street, Tislam began to imagine Dinasia's face when she surprisingly saw him. He took a day off work just to see her and since they hadn't seen each other for a week and a half, his emotions were revved. He actually wanted to meet Dinasia at her High School (Maxwell High) over on Pennsylvania Avenue, but in order to accomplish that he would have had to cut his last class, which was general science. The SAT's were only weeks away, and

16

if the teachers were telling the truth, everything taught these last couple of months would, in someway, appear on the tests.

"If you miss a class," he remembered Ms. Barrington say, "you will miss out on something of extreme importance on the SATs."

Unlike most high school students, Tislam didn't hate school. Certain aspects of school he did, of course, despise; like getting up in the morning, having to put up with open and flagrant racist teachers, the one-sided and often false and racist information the American educational system force fed its students, the violence and rampant drug use, and so on. But nevertheless, the whole process of constant learning and expansion of the mind had an addictive effect on him, and it showed in his grades and perfect attendance.

Learning was the love of his life, second only to his love for Dinasia. His foster family (the Burtons) proudly looked upon him as a dream child, primarily because he was a young Black male living in America, who had some discipline and enough intelligence not to fall for the many traps constantly being set by the system.

As Tislam turned the corner of Logan Street, the phone call he got at work yesterday from Dinasia telling him not to come visit her this Saturday, suddenly entered his mind. The same tension he felt upon hearing this heart-breaking news resurfaced. She had never canceled one of their Saturday get-togethers before, and the reason she gave for doing this had a strong ring of insincerity to it. She said that she and Keisha were invited to a party at Keisha's cousin's house, and Mrs. Anderson, Keisha's moms, would be there with them, which was the reason why he couldn't attend the party.

He could tell there was something bothering Dinasia. Since he grew up with her in the institution and knew her so well, he could almost tap straight into her emotions, reading and interpreting them with profound clarity. Dinasia sounded upset, shaky and unsure.

He also sensed she was hiding something from him due to the unsteadiness in her voice, which completely compelled his decision to take a day off work and pay her a surprise visit.

Ten minutes later, Tislam saw the Pink House Projects come into view. He increased his pace. As he neared Dinasia's building, he noticed an approaching red colored car suddenly slowed down to a crawl.

When the car was right upon him, he saw Shateek looking at him piercingly from behind the wheel. He felt a growing anxiety in the pit of his stomach, and as usual, an eruption of memories was uncapped. The three fist fights he had with this "trouble making, piss colored punk", re-enacted themselves in his mind. Also Shateek was the reason he was forced to carry a gun.

After being robbed at gunpoint on three occasions, while on his way home from visiting Dinasia—during the last robbery he was pistol whipped, and force to flee barefooted and partially naked—he vowed to never get caught out there in that fashion again. Although he knew for certain he didn't have it in him to shoot anyone, but he also was aware of the universal fear that guns bestowed upon people.

"All you gotta do is show those stick-up kids you're packin' a burner and that'll stop them cold in their tracks," Tislam remembered a guy named Squirrel said to him when he purchased the gun while they were in their home room class at Jackson High in Queens. Tislam agreed totally with Squirrel's common-sense analogy.

But on the other hand, Tislam was definitely not the docile, punk type that would run from or duck a fight. A lifetime spent in the New York State Foster care system, where he was forced to fight or settle for daily abuse, obviously had its way of hardening him mentally and physically.

Also, his self taught skills in the martial arts, Tai Chi in particular, put him in a frame of mind that made him obsessed with winning his fights, since he very rarely loss any. In fact, as Tislam grew older, he thought of the experience at the institution as a blessing in disguise.

"God bless the child who can hold its own!" was Tislam's golden rule. He couldn't think of any better quote that fit his situation, and so he utilized this saying in his approach towards just about everything he did in life.

Tislam watched the car cruise out of sight and he continued on his way. He entered Dinasia's building, got on the elevator and was surprised when his nose wasn't assaulted by the smell of urine.

He got off on the fourth floor and went to apartment 4D. Knocking lightly on the door, he felt his usual anger come to life. He wanted to take Dinasia away from all of this confusion, but there were so many stumbling blocks.   Tislam knocked again, this time slightly harder.

"I'm comin'! Hold your fuckin' horses." he heard Valerie shout from a distance, approaching the door. "Who is it?"

"It's Tislam."

She unbolted the three locks, opened the door and stuck her worn-out, skeleton looking head out the door. "Dinasia ain't here. And what the hell you knockin' on this door like you ain't got no damn sense."

Tislam ignored her remarks. "You know where she's at?"

"Give me five dollars and I'll tell you." Valerie smiled, displaying yellowish brown teeth.

"I already told you, Valerie, I'm not gonna help you kill yourself with them drugs--"

"Fuck you! You just a cheap, stingy ass bastard! That's all it is!"

Tislam sighed hard. "Did she say she was going to Keisha's house or the library?"

"I don't know. She ain't been home in two days. I thought she ran away to live with your ole sorry ass. And if you see her before I do, tell her I said she's gonna pay me for tearin' up the room before she left and make sure you let her know . . ."

Tislam headed for the elevator while Valerie was still complaining about her room being messed up. Hearing that Dinasia hadn't returned home for two days, and her room was left in disarray, filled his whole body with a rush of anxiety.

When he thought the elevator was taking too long, Tislam raced down the stairs.   He knew she had to be at Keisha's house, and he suddenly felt the urge to run. His mind started rapidly putting the pieces together and his gut instinct told him there was something wrong.

Tislam barreled out of the building, breathing hard and stopped when he saw Shateek, Trigger and Watch Dog standing near the benches. They were apparently waiting for him. As they walked towards him, he put both hands in his pockets, gripped the 9mm firmly as he made a violent effort to pull himself together.

"Well, well," Shateek said, stopping about ten feet from Tislam and then folding his arms, with Trigger and Watch Dog on either side of him. "Now what do we have here."

Tislam sighed extremely hard. "I ain't got time for your little bitch games." He started to walk pass them and stopped abruptly when Watch Dog displayed a gun. With his hand still on the weapon, he took a few steps back while slowly and inconspicuously maneuvering the 9mm, pointing it at Watch Dog through the coat.

Shateek saw the bulge and the movement of Tislam's right hand in his coat pocket. He'd been hoping Tislam would eventually strap-up sooner or later, and he smiled because now they could proceed with the next part of the plan. *So far, so good*, he thought smilingly. "Check this out, Tislam." He tried to sound friendly and non-confrontational. "I didn't come here to fuck with you, man. I just thought it's only right you know what's going on with your girl, Dinasia." He paused, searching for a certain facial response. When he saw it he continued. "How could you call yourself a man while standin' around lettin' your girl get raped?"

"And by some dirty dick, dope-fiend motherfucker at that." Trigger added.

Tislam's knees almost gave under the weight of his body. Shateek and Trigger's remarks jolted him in the same fashion as that of a hard slap to the face with spiked gloves. He suddenly had difficulty breathing and couldn't conceal the hurting sensations that dominated his mind, body and soul.

Shateek giggled. "Don't front like you don't know what the fuck's going on, nigga. Her Uncle Kirk been in them drawls for the longest, and I know she told you . . . And if she didn't tell you, that thang thang of hers should've. What? Your equipment is so inadequate you can't tell when somebody's been messin' around in your cookie jar?"

Trigger and Watch Dog burst out laughing.

Shateek cut into the laughter. "I know this ain't any of my business, but, ah, it just turns my fuckin' stomach when I lay eyes on a coward, pathetic, weak ass potato chip nigga like you!"

The laughter erupted again.

Tislam was trembling with rage, breathing hard while a sheet of perspiration materialized on his forehead, despite the freezing cold. When he saw the laughter had caused Watch Dog to point the gun downward, Tislam pulled the 9mm. "Raise up!" he shouted. "Put the gun down! I said put it down!" With his eyes wide and wild looking, he started grandstanding, not having to pretend to be crazed by the mixture of rage, anger and a desire to pull the trigger.

Watch Dog dropped the gun. It hit the pavement, making a clinking sound.

Tislam quickly approached the three. "I'm tired of you frontin' on me, Sha! I ain't your punchin' bag, motherfucker! . . . Back up!" When the three didn't move he shouted while jabbing the gun at them. "I said back the fuck up!"

When the three stepped backwards with their hands still raised, Tislam quickly scooped up Watch Dog's automatic. He hit the release button for the clip and the metal container made a similar clinking sound as that of the gun when it struck the pavement. Tislam flung the gun towards the patch of grass on the side of them, picked up the clip and pocketed it.

Tislam stared Shateek dead in the eyes. "Why we gotta always go through this kid shit every time you see me, Shateek? . . . Huh? . . . I ain't got a beef with you, Bro. And as you can see, if I did, your monkey ass would be dead." He saw the twisted smirk on Shateek's face and it made him extremely nervous because it looked like Shateek was truly enjoying this whole ordeal. There was something else in that warped evil grin that was incomprehensible to the naked eye, but detectable by the instinctual vibes. It made a small chill travel down Tislam's spine.

Just before Tislam turned to walk away, he said, "You better raised the fuck up off me . . . Keep pushing me, man, and I might give you what you're apparently beggin' for." He hesitated slightly. "Play with fire long enough and you're bound to get burnt." He quickly walked away as he stuffed the 9mm back in his pocket, over-anxious to get to Dinasia. He felt the urge to run, but fought the feeling.

When Tislam was about twenty yards away, Shateek pulled a 44 Magnum from his waist and carefully aimed at Tislam's back. He spoke to Trigger and Watch Dog. "Should I blaze him and put an end to this?"

"Yeah, let it ride!" Trigger said jubilantly.

Watch Dog shook his head no. "T--Too many W--witnesses."

Shateek laughed because he knew damn well he wasn't stupid enough to shoot a man in the back in broad daylight. Nor did he have any intentions of, or even a desire to, shoot or kill Tislam. That would be too easy, far too easy. And not to mention, outright uncreative and totally detrimental to the thoroughly thought out plan.

As Watch Dog went to fetch the automatic, Shateek put the 44 Magnum back in his waist and headed for the car with Trigger in hot pursuit.

CHAPTER # 3

"Dinasia!?" Keisha rushed into the room where Dinasia was doing her English homework. "You ain't gonna believe who's at the door." She looked sincerely disturbed.

Dinasia's heart jumped. The first thing came to mind was the foster care people had come to take her back to the institution. "Is it for me?" As she rose from the desk, she saw Keisha nod her head yes. Her legs felt like spaghetti. "Who is it!?"

"It's Tislam. And boy does he look upset."

Dinasia sighed with partial relief. As she headed for the door, a new anxiety surfaced because Tislam wasn't supposed to be here, and her wounds were still visible. Most of all, she was caught off guard since she hadn't formulated a story to explain the injuries. "Did you let him in?"

"Yeah, he's upstairs in the living room." Keisha followed Dinasia as she headed for the stairs. "Don't forget, my moms will be home any minute. So you better make it quick."

Dinasia rushed up the carpet-covered steps, which led to the first floor. When she saw Tislam standing near the door, she went to him with a smile on her face. She saw his eyebrows suddenly crunched together. The expression was a mixture of confusion and anger, apparently caused by the sight of her arm in the sling. Her instinct told her there was going to be sparks and explosions flying no matter what she told him.

"Dinasia!" his mouth hung open and the pain almost made his eyes water. "What happened!?" he said softly, while rushing towards her, meeting her halfway. He embraced and kissed her tenderly. He intended to hold his head and pretend as if he didn't know what was going on, but the temptation to vent his anger was just too much. Then through clinched teeth he muttered. "When did he do this to you? Why didn't you tell me?"

"Tislam, please calm down," she felt something hard and heavy in his coat pocket bump into her side. She was hoping it wasn't what she thought it was. "Don't worry, it's really nothin'." She tiptoed and kissed his cheek.

23

"What!?" he decided in that moment he would kill Kirk as sure as shit stinks. "It's nothing?! . . . Look at your face, your arm." He sighed hard and then drew a deep breath. He struggled to calm himself down. Even the sight of the Super Ninja necklace around Dinasia's neck couldn't tame the rage. "We got some serious talkin' to do. I don't think this is the place for it. Let's go down to the pizza shop."

Dinasia saw that look in his eyes and knew he was about to enter a blind rage. "I'll get dress." she turned and headed for the stairs.

As Dinasia got dressed, Tislam's comments puzzled her. Why would he ask "when" did "he" do this? How could he know? And most of all, how could he know it was a "he" that did this to her? She never told him or anyone else besides Keisha. Maybe he went to the apartment and somebody told him? She searched for an explanation and then realized even if he did go to the apartment, no one knew Kirk attacked her the other night since she mentioned it to no one. She was wrecking her brains trying to figure out who told him, and finally she just gave up, realizing she was going to find out the deal soon enough.

Five minutes later, she returned to the living room dressed in some of Keisha's much too large clothing and they exited the house.

On the way to the pizza shop, Dinasia noticed Tislam hadn't said a word. She saw his facial and bodily gestures had a look of deep sadness that would change to anger and then fluctuated back and forth between the two emotions. They entered the pizza shop on the Sutter Avenue near Lincoln Avenue (which was also a restaurant with dozens of booths where customers ate the meals they purchased). They took a seat in an empty booth in the back. A Hip Hop tune by Tupac hummed from the Jukebox.

"You want something to eat?" Tislam asked.

"I'm not hungry," She was searching his eyes to see if he knew.

"So, what happened, Dinasia? Why you didn't tell me you left home?"

She again wondered how much of it he was aware of. Staring at him in an unwavering fashion, Dinasia couldn't make a determination based on the look in his eyes. But his initial comments upon seeing her replayed themselves inside her head. The truth would be the safest approach, whether it would hurt him or not. "Tislam, before I tell you anything." She paused. "You gotta promise me you won't let your temper get the best of you."

Tislam stared at her without saying a word for several seconds. The clouds of burning hot steam rolled off his body. "Dinasia, I thought we promised to never lie to each other? No matter what the issue is? I kept my end of the agreement. Why can't you?"

Dinasia was about to engage him in a debate because she never lied to him in an evil sense of the word. But then she realized a lie was a lie, no matter who uttered it or why it was uttered. "If I told you the truth, you would've went out and done something crazy . . . Now promise me you won't start acting crazy."

"I can't do that . . . Because if it's what I think it is, there's gonna be hell to pay. I couldn't live with myself if I did nothing." His eyes felt watery every time he stared at the bruises on Dinasia's face. When Shateek and Trigger's comments reappeared, dancing erratically in his mind, a small moan slipped through his lips.

Dinasia saw in his eyes there was no way to make him commit to such a promise. He was the most stubbornness man in the world. Once his mind was made up, there was a better chance of turning shit into gold than there was of changing his position on a matter. "So, what did you hear?" She figured if she had to tell him what happened, she might as well see if there was a way to downplay the impact of the blow to his heart and ego.

"I heard that motherfucker Kirk's been forcing you to do the wild thang . . ."

Dinasia was startled because the cat was out of the bag and was about to wreck havoc. The whole truth and nothing but the truth was the only thing that could follow. "He tried to rape me a couple of times without any success." She paused. "Who--how did you find this--"

"That's totally irrelevant." Tislam said calmly. "I wanna hear it all. Everything, from beginning to end."

Dinasia hesitated as her anxiety fused into a mild form of terror and distress. She reluctantly told him about the twelve times Kirk attempted to rape her, and how each time she warded off the attacks with a knife and the karate stuff he had taught her. She also explained why she told no one other than Keisha.

WHAM!

Tislam slammed his hand on the table. "And when the hell was you gonna tell me!!" The sudden outburst startled everyone in the place, including a couple standing near the threshold, leading to the rest room area.

Dinasia saw a tear drip from Tislam's left eye. In that moment, she was literally scared to death. Tislam in this state of mind was like a nuclear bomb in the hands of Saddam Hussein (it was destine to explode). She had to calm him down quickly or else he might become suicidally dangerous.

"I'm gonna kill that motherfucker." Tislam whispered venomously. "That nigga just signed his death certificate."

"Listen to me, Tislam. Calm down and stop talking crazy. I told you he never got--"

"That ain't the point! He knows how much I love you, and for him to even entertain the thought of trying--"

"The man is a dope addict. It's the drugs. People under the influence of that stuff will--"

"I don't care! Maybe a bullet to the head is what he needs to take him out of his misery. And I'm gonna help him out with his death wish."

Short pause.

"So that heavy thing in your coat pocket is a gun?" she asked worriedly.

"That's right." His mannerism was now becoming less intense because his mind was entering its plotting mode.

"What the hell do you need a gun for?" Dinasia was more shocked than upset.

"For protection." It suddenly dawned on him, he never told her about the three times he was robbed. His mind made the connection, comparing her and his situations, and suddenly felt odd and extremely uncomfortable. He paused while his conscience screamed 'hypocrite! What's good for the goose is good for the gander!' Another voice in his head insisted he was justified because he never actually lied to her, while her lie wasn't justified because she did actually lie. Plus, she could've gotten herself killed.

"We all know what guns represent," Dinasia reached across the table and caressed his hands. "You don't need that thing, Tislam. All the statistics we've talked about and how guns are responsible for killing so many--"

"May I remind you, guns don't kill people, people kill people . . . You know I'm not a violent person, Dinasia. I become violent only when I'm protecting myself against violence inflicted upon me or the ones I love. At one time I honestly never thought I could shoot someone, but now, after finding this out, I realized I can do it. And do it I will!"

Dinasia saw he was dead serious and realized extreme measures were the only possible way to make him rationalize. "If you do something stupid, I'll leave you, Tislam . . . Life is too precious and murder is an unforgivable sin . . . How could I continue to love you, knowing you premeditatedly snuffed out the life of another human being? I couldn't do it no matter what you believed you were doing it for . . . If you believe in our oath we made to each other that there will be 'no other love', you will stop this foolishness because if you kill Kirk, it'll not only hurt you, but it will destroy our relationship. Even if you don't get caught, I'll know and my conscience won't let me live a single day in peace. You're starting to make me think our vow meant nothing to you!" She paused, realizing the last comment about the vow brought a pain-stricken expression to Tislam's face.

Dinasia's next words were stated slowly and deliberately. "I love you more than life itself, but I will leave you if you kill him."

There was a long sullen silence.

As Tislam was hurled into a deep, penetrating silence, Dinasia looked on, feeling bad she had to accuse Tislam of not being sincere about their vow. She could remember the events leading up to that day as if it was yesterday. As usual, the mere mentioning of their vow caused her mind to respond as if it was on autopilot. Suddenly, the mental images of how they met, and how the vow came about, danced in her third eye like a video recording. Thrusted into a daydream, her mind visualized the following:

The date was May 16, 1984 and the place was the Jermain Lunsford Child Care Institute in upstate New York. Dinasia Whitman was seven years old, and was with her best friend, Julie Robinson. They were strolling along in the huge field in the back of the institute, picking dandelions and other colorful flowers to bring back to their dollhouse.

Dinasia glanced over her shoulder and smiled when she saw the little boy who always followed them around whenever they played in the field. He was standing about ten yards away, near a large Oak tree, and as usual, he just stood there staring and smiling at them. Dinasia often wondered who was he staring at the most, her or Julie, and wanted him to look at her more because she thought he was cute.

Suddenly, from behind, Dinasia heard the rapid movement of many feet running towards them. She turned and her eyes grew wide when she saw the five boys running towards them. "Let's get out of here! It's Dontie and his friends."

Dinasia ran as fast as she could and noticed Julie had managed to get ahead of her. She hated Dontie and his friends because, from her perspective, "they were the worst trouble makers and bullies in the world." Up ahead, Dinasia noticed Julie stopped abruptly. When she saw four other boys coming straight at them, Dinasia realized they were trapped. The boys had strategically boxed them in.

A minute later, Dinasia noticed the nine boys were all over them; grabbing, squeezing and fondling all of her and Julie's private parts. Dinasia felt her stomach turned with disgust while the boys joyfully laughed, teased and wouldn't stop despite her and Julie's screams. Dinasia kicked, punched and scratched at the boys, but they kept coming. After she and Julie were knocked to the ground, four of the boys held their hands and feet while the others continued their unrelenting fondling mission.

Seconds after she fell to the grass, Dinasia saw the little boy who followed them around running towards them. She just knew he was about to join the other boys. This broke her little heart because she thought he was a nice guy. When she saw the boy flying kicked one of their attackers, and then started punching and kicking the others in the same fashion as the karate men in the movies she saw on Saturday afternoon, a wave of joyfully relief swept over her. She smiled triumphantly when they let go of her and Julie, and began surrounding the little boy, who looked much smaller than all of the bullies. When three of the boys ran away, Dontie called them names, like "cowards," "pussies", and "fags."

Dinasia and Julie stood on the sideline giggling joyfully.

"Get 'em! Kick 'em!" Julie shouted excitedly, cheering the little karate fighter on.

The fight resumed with an explosion. There were all sorts of punches, and only a few kicks thrown. The six remaining boys wisely rushed towards the little boy at the same time, and he was powerless against the force of so many. But he fought valiantly, each and every step of the way, never once giving up.

Dinasia became scared for the boy when she saw blood pouring from his nose and mouth while he was on the ground being repeatedly stomped and kicked. "Stop it!" she jumped in the fight, shoving some of the boys away. "You leave him alone! You're killing him!"

When Dontie turned with angry clenched fists and was about to strike Dinasia, the little boy sprung to his feet and kicked Dontie in the head so hard with a round-house kick, Dontie went straight to the ground. With his arms and legs sprawled out, looking like a small letter X, it wasn't hard to realize Dontie was knocked out cold.

The other boys were confused and panic-stricken because now their leader had fallen. One of the boys began slapping Dontie's face, and when he responded by mumbling something none of them could understand, they scooped him up. Two of the boys wrapped an arm of Dontie's around their necks and fled with their partially unconscious comrade.

Dinasia saw the little boy was so exhausted, he collapsed and was now sitting on the ground with his arms wrapped around his knees tucked closely to his chest, breathing extremely hard.

Dinasia went to him as Julie followed. That's when she discovered his name was Tislam Parker. After they cleaned and patched him up, the three of them talked. Dinasia felt bad for Julie because Tislam rejected her bold advances towards him and told her point blank: "I don't want you, I wanted Dinasia." Blushing profusely, Dinasia accepted Tislam's offer to be her boyfriend. From that day on, she and Tislam became literally inseparable.

A year later, in the summer of 1985, the Institute had its annual summer picnic. That year, a carnival was hired and one of the supervisors, Bob Baker, (who was once a D.J.), rented some professional audio equipment and furnished the music for the two day fun-filled event. This was a moment in both Dinasia and Tislam's lives they would never forget.

From the moment the sun rose, Dinasia and Tislam played games, rode the amusement rides, and ate every piece of junk food they could get their hands on. They had so much fun, their heads felt like they were going to explode from a pleasure over-load. All throughout these two days of mind-boggling fun, D.J. Baker played one record 80% of the time, and by the middle of the second day, Dinasia and Tislam learnt all the lyrics to the song "I Love Your Smile" by Rashon and Amina. They both fell completely in love with this R&B, Hip Hop style melody.

As a result of the lyrics of this song, Dinasia came up with the idea that she and Tislam should make an oath, promise and a never-ending vow that for as long as they live, they will always be together. Sitting at a bench near the cotton candy booth, she told Tislam they should swear that they will love each other forever, never leave each other, and most of all, there will be no other love in either of their lives, no matter what happened, even if they were separated.

"Yeah, I like that!" Tislam said happily, raising his right hand and placing his left on his heart. "I agree and promise forever to love you, Dinasia."

"No, you gotta do it and say it like this," Dinasia raised her right hand and put the other on her chest. "I swear for the rest of my life, me and Tislam will be together forever and there will be 'no other love.'" She put her hands down. "We can make this our secret code word and we'll call it, 'No Other Love.'"

"It's the words right out of the song," He began singing the ending part of the record where mention is made of the comment "no other love."

"Come on," Dinasia shook Tislam's leg, stopping him from singing. "You have to do the promise the way I did it."

Tislam quickly obeyed and afterwards he cheered excitedly. "Yeah!" He leaned over and was about to kiss Dinasia on the cheek, but she turned and kissed him on the lips.

The two held the kiss for ten seconds. When they finished, they cut their eyes at each other blushingly.

"Hey!" Tislam said suddenly. "I got an idea! Why don't we make our pact more real like the way blood brothers do when they cut their hands and put 'em together . . . You can't have a real promise without doing something more than just saying it. There's gotta be something else."

"You're right," Dinasia nodded. "It's like when people get married there's gotta be a ring and then afterwards they, ah . . ."

"They do the nasty! You see? There gotta be something else . . . I can give you my Super Ninja necklace." He hastily began taking off the necklace he purchased for ten 25-cent stamps from an ad in a Kung Fu Kid comic book.

"No, I can't take that," she grabbed his hand, trying to stop him from taking the necklace off. "It's your lucky charm, remember?"

He shook loose of her embrace. "Well, it's yours now." He put it over her head and onto her neck.

They sat silently for a couple of seconds, smiling and acting their age.

"I guess now we gotta do the nasty," Dinasia said shyly. "And then we'll be married forever and ever . . . Do you know how to do it?"

"Yeah, I think so. Jocko told me how to do it. He said the boy sticks his thang in the girl's belly button and after he pees in it then they finished."

Dinasia burst out laughing. She had once read a porno book she found lying around in the prohibited section of the Institute's library and saw what the naked people were doing. "Come on, let's go inside." She scooted off the bench.

Tislam grabbed Dinasia's hand as they approached the building. Moments later, they consummated their vows, despite not having the faintest idea of what they were doing.

A voice roused Dinasia from her reverie; it was the voice of Keisha and the tone of it dissolved the smile on her face like butter on a red-hot skillet. Keisha sounded terrified. It took Dinasia a moment to snatch her mind completely out of the daydream. "What's wrong?"

"Kirk came by my house and my moms--"

Tislam shot out of his seat and headed towards the exit.

"Tislam, no!" Dinasia tried to grab his arm, but it was wrenched away. She glanced over at Keisha with fire in her eyes. Her anger began to boil. The urge to slap Keisha into the next century was extremely strong.

32

"Why you didn't pull me to the side to tell me something like that!?" She ignored Keisha's comment as she ran after Tislam.

CHAPTER # 4

Dinasia sat in the far right corner of the Maxwell High cafeteria, nibbling on a soggy peanut butter and jelly sandwich. The lunch hall was half filled and the rap songs that played over the speakers created a mood that was tranquil and harmonious. Even the awful smelling soup of the day seeping from the cafeteria kitchen didn't bother her as usual. She glanced at her watch and wondered what was taking Keisha so long?

The episode with Tislam three days ago still had her stressed. After convincing Tislam not to do anything to Kirk, they talked until 8:30 and Tislam had to leave. His promise not to get into a conflict with Kirk appeared to be sincere, but after being with Tislam for practically all of her life, she knew how hotheaded and sporadic he could get when dealing with issues of the heart.

As she thought about Tislam's several other adamant promises, (one of which was to obtain an apartment for them within the next six months), she saw Shateek enter the cafeteria. She saw him scanning the hall and knew he was looking for her. Within seconds he found her and approached.

"What's up, Dinasia?" Shateek had on his best smile.

"How yah doin', Sha?" she glanced around at the jealous eyes on the faces of the other females in the hall.

"You know the day won't be worth living if I don't hang with you for a few." He sat across from her. "What's that you eating?" He stuck his head out to see what it was, even though he smelled the peanut butter. "Ah, come on." He sprung to his feet. "I'll be right back--"

"I'm all right, Shateek. Don't go wasting your money. I'm full."

Shateek sat back down with a reluctant gesture.

Dinasia reached inside her satchel. "And why did you put this in my bag?" She sat the two fifty dollars bills on the table, and slid them towards him. "Please, Shateek, will you stop this. I told you I can't take money from you."

"Why not?" He said softly. "You can use a few extra dollars . . . I'm just trying to be a true friend to you, and I can't understand why you won't let me do something as simple as that . . . Friends are supposed to help each other at times in need. With you going through that little thing with your family and all, I figured I'd try to help out a little."

"I appreciate your concern, but believe me, I'm all right. After all the hell I've been through during my life, this is petty stuff."

Shateek stared her in the eyes and felt that blown away feeling he got whenever he imagined riding off into the sunset with Dinasia as his number one girl. He had a serious Jones for strong, chocolate colored, super fine, and mentally sharp sisters. And since Dinasia was the epitome of that type of Black woman, she was a dream girl in his eyes. "Did I ever tell you, you're the epitome of a strong Black Queen like Nefertiti and Nzinga, and that's why you shouldn't have to struggle the rest of your life? . . . You know what Dinasia?" He paused for a long moment, wondering should he try talking her into becoming his girl again.

Long pause.

Dinasia hated to be primed for a question and then left hanging, waiting as the suspense increased. "Well, let's hear it."

Shateek sighed as he fiddled with the two fifty dollar bills. "Listen, Dinasia. I—I--. . ." He hated when his emotions got in the way of him formulating his words. "I know I've said this before, but I'm gonna say it again . . . I wanna get with you, Dinasia. I want you to be my girl, my woman, my wife, my everything . . . I've never met a woman in my life who I wanna be with as much as I wanna be with you . . . I can get us an apartment right this minute. Check it out." he began reaching into his pocket. "I got over ten thou--"

"Wait a minute, Shateek. I know you got money. I know about your family business, and I know about your brother Shabazz. But I'm—I . . . I told you I'm in love with Tislam . . .You're a kind, beautiful person, I enjoy your company and I'm glad to have you as a friend. But, we can only be friends and nothing more." She paused. "I'm engaged to Tislam and we're getting married this summer after we graduate. Sorry, Shateek I hope . . ."

Married!? Shateek heard a terror-stricken voice in his head reiterate the word as Dinasia continued talking. If he had been standing at the moment she said, "married", his knees would've buckled upon hearing this dreaded news. His facial expression almost gave him away, but he quickly got himself under control. "Well, how that saying goes?" He smiled sarcastically. "You can't fault a fella for trying."

"I don't know what you see in me anyway," Dinasia continued. "I'm just a poor sista from the PJ's tryin' to survive in this mean ole world, who's in love with a guy I've been with almost all my life . . .There's a lot of fine sisters running around here, and damn near all of them are feeling you." She suddenly saw Keisha enter the cafeteria and headed towards them, looking happier than usual.

"Sorry, I'm late," Keisha said as she sat next to Dinasia. "I had to go to the counselor's office. Hey Shateek, what's up, man?"

"Hey Keisha, how ya doin'?"

Keisha spoke excitedly. "I got that stuff--"

"Don't worry about that," Shateek stood, grabbing and pocketing the bills. "I'll talk to you about that later." As he was about to head towards the entrance, he turned and said, "I'll talk to you in biology class, Dinasia." He gave her a playful wink of the eye and a broad smile in an attempt to mask his mixed emotions.

"See you then," Dinasia waited until Shateek walked out of the cafeteria, and then said to Keisha. "What stuff you got? What's going on?"

"Oh, it's nothing," she suddenly realized Shateek specifically told her not to mention anything to Dinasia. Now she felt awkwardly uncomfortable. "It was um . . . uh . . . believe me, girl, it's nothing."

Dinasia had an idea what it was the minute Keisha opened her mouth. "What? Did he give you some money?" She saw Keisha quickly shake her head no with a nervous looking facial expression. The response told her everything she needed to know. "So he gave you some money, claiming it was to help me out . . . You ain't gotta lie to me."

"All right, all right, he gave me a few dollars to help replace some of the food I'm sneaking to you everyday. If he didn't do that, we would've been caught by--"

"Knock it off, Keisha," Dinasia sighed, picked up the last portion of her sandwich and stuffed it in her mouth. "I've been buying my own food with the money I got from Tislam . . . But if it makes you happy, you can take Sha's money. But I won't."

"Girl, that man loves you," Keisha said in a sassy tone of voice. "You better wake up and smell the scent of that mint, child. That man got money drippin' outta his ass and he's riding your bra strap like a crazy dog in heat. And if I were you, I'd get with Shateek." She began counting off descriptions on her fingers. "He's fine as hell, he don't fuck with drugs, he ain't no street corner bum, he ain't the type to run around sticking his dick in everything that moves and therefore he's disease free and he's going to College. Where you gonna find a Black man around here with all that going for himself and head over hills for you at the same time? Shit, you need to stop trying to live in that fantasy world of yours. Those childhood romance dreams are just what they are: Illusions and delusions, kid fairy tales that come true only in the movies and romance novels. Tislam's a nice guy, but he don't have the financial ability to give you the things you need in order to . . ."

As Keisha talked on and on, Dinasia said nothing, realizing she wasn't in the mood for another one of those long drawn out debates about money and how gold digging is supposed to be socially and morally acceptable in this society. Then a little voice in her head reminded her that without money in this capitalistic world, you are going no place real fast.

*   *   *   *

Later that evening, Shateek, Trigger and Watch Dog were at their regular hang out, shooting a game of pool when Trigger saw a rough-neck enter the pool hall.

"Yo, that's the guy, right there," Trigger was about to take a shot and stood from the pool table as Shateek and Watch Dog's heads turned.

"Don't forget what I told you." Shateek said to Trigger. "Act like it's coming from you, not me, all right? And keep the price down as much as possible."

"I got it, I got it." Trigger said as he sat his cue stick down and approached this pudgy rough neck looking guy dressed in an army fatigue jacket. "Yo, Stony! What's up, son?" He shook his hand and they gave each other a strong embrace. "Come on over here, I got a proposal for you. You still like making easy money?"

"Name me one mufucka out here, that don't," Stony smiled, taking advantage of the opportunity to show-off his two gold front teeth.

Ten minutes later, Trigger gave Stony a hi-five and walked back over to Shateek and Watch Dog as Stony left the pool hall.

Shateek leaned against the table with his arms folded. "So, what's the deal? Can he do it?"

"Yeah, he can do it. He ain't go for the first price. The second one he was cool with. But, he says it's gonna take sometime to set it up correctly." Trigger picked up the cue stick, ready to resume the game.

Shateek sighed and his impatience took over. "How much time is he talkin'?"

"He said about a month or two," Trigger said, cueing up the ball.

"God damn!" Shateek began racking up the pool balls. "What the fuck he think we tryin' to do? Assassinate the President or something?"

"If we gonna do it right, it's gonna take time." Trigger hit the cue ball into the other pool balls, creating a crackling explosion upon impact. None of the balls dropped into a pocket. "Shit." He muttered angrily.

Shateek positioned his cue stick, taking aim. "Six ball in the corner pocket." He cracked the cue ball and accomplished his prediction.

Suddenly, Watch Dog spoke. "D--Do you really think he'll s—s--shoot him?" He was speaking to no one in particular.

"Bet your black ass he will." Trigger said as Shateek continued knocking balls into the pockets. "Money makes the world go around, and with Sha kicking out all that cheddar, I can't see how it won't work."

Shateek stood from the aim with a smile. "He'll do it. And we'll fix it to where he'll have no choice in the matter."

CHAPTER # 5

Stony sat in the blue Ford Explorer waiting for Tislam to come out of the Euclid Avenue train station. He was parked a block away and had his eyes locked on the corner. The date was March 25th and he was glad it had only taken a little over a month to get the run underway.

He looked at his wristwatch. It was ten after seven. A half hour flew by so fast Stony tapped his watch to make sure it was working correctly. His nervous tension increased as he wondered if Tislam changed his mind about visiting Dinasia tonight.

It was a beautiful, clear spring night; light jacket weather. Stony was dressed in his army fatigue jacket, black jeans and Timberland boots; this particular attire was called his work uniform. The quarter moon rose on Stony's left hand side, gradually inching its way over the rooftops of the East New York tenement buildings. With the radio on Hot 97, barely loud enough to be heard, Stony suddenly saw a group of people walk out of the station. He scooped up his compact binoculars and put them to his eyes.

It was him.

Stony hastily got out of the Jeep and followed Tislam as he headed down the block in the opposite direction from where Stony's Jeep was parked.

*   *   *   *

Tislam felt in a good mood this evening and was happily humming the melody to Red Man's "Time 4 Sum Aksion." The exhilarating cloud of joy he floated on had its roots in the fact he had some good news to share with Dinasia. Dressed in a brown baseball jacket, a matching cap, dark blue jeans, and the 9mm tucked in his waist, he bopped along imagining Dinasia's face when he told her he got them an apartment out in Jamaica Queens.

His foster mom and dad worked a miracle for him when he told them what Dinasia was going through, and what he was trying to accomplish. There were stipulations that would have to be met, of course, but the way

Tislam felt, he would've sold his soul to the devil if it meant saving his precious Dinasia from even an iota of pain and suffering.

Plus, Tislam's foster parents (Jeffrey and Amy Burton) remembered the several times Tislam escaped from the Institute just to see Dinasia, and knew if Tislam didn't find a legitimate way to obtain an apartment for Dinasia, he could possibly be forced into utilizing desperate, illicit measures to acquire money. The Burton family was well aware of the drug epidemic and how so many beautiful young Black men destroyed their lives chasing that fast money and they had no intentions of letting that happen to Tislam. A considerable portion of their savings was laid on the line to fulfill the financial obligations for the apartment, but they sincerely believed Tislam would pay it back as he vehemently promised he would do so.

As Tislam was about to turn the corner, he heard someone calling his name. He turned and saw a man in a green army jacket rapidly approaching. Instinctively his hand went for the 9mm.

"Yoh Tislam! It's me, Stony."

A couple of seconds later Tislam saw it really was Stony. "Hey, Bro, don't be creeping up on me like that. What's wrong with you, man?" He said smilingly since the good mood still had him light headed with happiness.

They shook hands and hugged each other.

"Check it out, Tis. I hate to be the one to tell you this," He sighed, pretending to be upset by what he was about to reveal. "But, I gotta put you on point cause me and you is mad cool . . . Something just jumped off out in the Projects. Dinasia went out there and Kirk ran up on her again--"

"When did this happen!?" Tislam's eyes were bulging. "Is she hurt!?"

"I think so, and since me and you are--"

Tislam took off down the street, the surge of anxiety taking full control of his response. As he ran, Tislam turned and shouted. "Good lookin' out, Stony!"

As Stony smilingly watched Tislam's figure turn into a dim shadow, he mumbled to himself: "That was easier than I thought it would be. It's a crying shame how these niggas get all pussy whipped and totally twisted over these chicken head broads with greedy fuckin' fingers all up in a brother's pockets." He turned and ran back to the Jeep.

*   *   *

Kirk Shepard sat on the bench in front of his building, wolfing down the second bottle of the four bottles of Night Train wine that Stony bought him two hours ago. He was thoroughly juiced up and hyped up because he had a pocket full of money he had also received from Stony.

As his head spun from the cheap wine, Kirk tried to remember the instructions Stony gave him and realized he forgot what he was supposed to do after he beat the living shit out of Tislam.

After working his drunken mind at full capacity for a straight minute, it all came back to him like a mystical tidal-wave crashing onto the shore of a streaming hot beach. *He wants me to take the fake gun from him. Yeah, that's what he said. And he's gonna hit me off some kinda proper!* Kirk giggled, taking another swig. *How much did he say he'll give me if I get that toy gun?* His mind relapsed back into its massively confused state.

Whatever the price was, Kirk did remember it was enough to get him excited, and so he swept the issue to the back of his mind as another problem pulled complete focus. Prince came home from college yesterday for spring vacation and was raising hell because Dinasia wasn't home when he arrived. Kirk knew if Prince saw him and Tislam fighting he would not only interfere with him completing his mission, but was bound to talk to Tislam, and find out. He, Barbara and Valerie lied to him when they told him Dinasia was sent back to the Institute.

Before Kirk could ponder the situation any further, he saw a blurry image of a person approaching. As he squinted his eyes, he realized it was Tislam. He sprung to his feet. The alcohol rushed to his head like the force of a cannon explosion. He clumsily kicked a fresh bottle of wine and it jettisoned across the pavement, shattering and unleashing its contents.

"Shit! God-damn it!" He muttered under his breath and instantly re-focused his rage at the loss of the wine, blaming it on Tislam for popping up on the scene out of nowhere.

He stumbled towards Tislam with his teeth and fists clenched.

Tislam saw Kirk headed directly towards him. His anger increased ten-folds. *How dare this bastard act like he really wants some drama.* The rage was at boiling point. When he was ten yards away from Kirk, Tislam shouted. "What the fuck you did to Dinasia!? You fuckin' drunken son of a bitch!" He pulled the gun and was surprised when Kirk didn't respond in a terrified fashion.

Kirk charged at Tislam with his head down, apparently intending to ram into Tislam, but he went stumbling to the pavement when Tislam sidestepped the awkward tackle maneuver. Kirk slowly got up and stupidly tried the same thing again, with the same results. This time Tislam was about to unleash a vicious wave of solid kicks to Kirk's rear-end.

"Tislam! What's wrong with you, man!"

The voice of Prince stopped Tislam just as he was about to let go of the kick. Tislam looked up and saw Prince running towards him, while Kirk was slowly getting up off the ground.

Prince helped Kirk into a standing position. His glance went to the gun in Tislam's hand and then rose to his eyes. "What the fuck are you doing with a gun, Tis? What's this? You trying to be a thug now? And what the fuck are you beating up on--"

Kirk charged at Tislam again, but this time he collided into him. Quickly grabbing hold of Tislam's clothing, Kirk body slammed him to the concrete.

Just as Kirk was about to stomp Tislam's face, Prince aggressively pulled him away. "Chill Kirk!"

Tislam sprung to his feet with the gun pointed at both Kirk and Prince. "Do that shit again and I'll blast your ass!"

Prince raised his hands in the air, speaking softly while slowly walking towards Tislam. "Relax, Tislam! Put the gun down. You're making a scene, baby bro. Look around you. You got people all in their windows."

Tislam looked around and noticed at least four different windows were loaded with spectators and then it suddenly dawned on him. Someone probably called the police by now. His anxiety grew rapidly. Then, suddenly, his attention was rudely snatched back to the two when Kirk tried to rush towards him again, but Prince grabbed hold of him.

Tislam pointed the gun at them angrily. "You better calm his ass down or else he's--"

BOW! BOW!

The two shots startled Tislam so viciously he instantly dropped to the ground. He almost lost hold of the gun, thinking it had somehow discharged. Then he realized the shots came from behind him. As Tislam's frantic mind tried to determine what was happening, he looked up and saw Prince clutching his chest while stumbling backwards, falling hard to the pavement. Tislam hysterically turned to see who it was that fired the shots and saw someone dressed in dark clothing running away.

"You shot my nephew!" Kirk cried as he went to Prince and kneeled beside him. With his hands pressing down on Prince's chest, apparently trying to stop the waterfall of blood that squirted from his body and onto the pavement, he started screaming as the tears began to flow. "You killed him, you motherfucker! Somebody call an ambulance!"

As Tislam nervously stood on trembling legs, he suddenly heard sirens. When he looked at the windows he noticed people were yelling out of their apartments; saying things like "Oh shit, he shot him", "call the cops" and "Is he dead?"

Tislam's terror-stricken mind stumbled all over itself. "I—I--it wasn't me. I didn't shoot him. It was, it was . . . " He suddenly realized Kirk was too drunk to notice where the shots came from, and all the people in those windows would obviously think he fired the shots because his gun was pointed at Prince and Kirk at the precise moment the stranger shot Prince. And since the people in the windows couldn't see this guy because he was hidden behind the corner of the building, Tislam knew they would assume he did it.

The sirens grew louder.

Tislam's mind was now thinking strictly escape. His instinct to get away took control. He frantically tucked the gun in his waist and ran in the same direction as the shooter.

CHAPTER # 6

Dinasia sat on the bus on her way to school, devastated by the news. Tislam had shot and killed Prince last night in the Projects. Keisha sat next to her with a helpless look on her face, feeding her napkins for the tears that dripped freely. Dinasia had been crying ever since she saw the blue homicide Detective car on the sidewalk in front of her foster family's Project building.

This morning, as Dinasia and Keisha waited at the bus stop, on their way to school, Valerie approached them and told Dinasia what had happen, but didn't know all the specific details. At first, Dinasia thought Valerie was playing some kind of vicious trick on her, since her mind simply refused to believe such a dreadful thing could possibly happen. She and Keisha got on the bus, made a pit stop at the Projects, and after seeing the D.T.'s car, Dinasia waited around until she saw someone from the building. A lady named Jody Edison exited the building and told Dinasia what had happened.

The people on the bus stared at Dinasia with sad expressions as she dabbed at her eyes and sniffled profusely. Why she chose to go to school in this twisted state of mind, she knew didn't make sense because there was no way she would be able to concentrate on anything. The real reason she put herself through the trouble was because this was the countdown to graduation and even one absence would destroy her perfect attendance record.

Five minutes later, the bus came to a stop across the street from Maxwell High School. They got off the bus.

As Dinasia headed towards the entrance with Keisha along side of her, she saw Shateek leaning up against his car with his arms folded.

Shateek saw the pain vibrating all through Dinasia's body and he felt bad for her. "Dinasia, we need to talk. Hi ya doing, Keisha?"

"What's up, Sha," Keisha released a strained smiled.

46

Dinasia gazed at him for a couple of seconds before speaking. "I can't talk now, Shateek. I'm already late for my first class. Meet me at the lunch hall." She walked away and entered the building, heading straight to English class in room 207, while Keisha went to room 315 (Geometry class).

Dinasia walked through the door and went to her seat. She was so emotionally distressed she made no attempt to explain to Mr. Jerome why she was late for class.

Mr. Jerome stopped in mid-sentence when he saw Dinasia's eyes were blood-shot red as if she'd been doing some heavy crying. He was about to inquire, but remembered teacher's etiquette prohibited discussion of delicate matters in the presence of the entire class. "Miss Whitman, I would like to see you after class." He resumed his discussion on the basic mechanics of writing College level essays.

Dinasia didn't completely hear what Mr. Jerome said to her because she'd already picked an area on the wall and just stared at it as her mind tried desperately to find logic in what had happened. Her eyes were locked on the poster, which said, "Drugs Kill!" There was a picture of a skeleton sitting at a table cheering on a kid with a crack pipe in his mouth. Her imagination replaced the statement "Drugs Kill!" with "Guns kill!" and saw an image of Tislam blazing away at Prince. She shook loose of the mental picture while forcing back the tears. She hated to appear weak in the eyes of others, but the pain was just too much and the tears seem to force their way out from under her eyelids.

With a jaw-clenching struggle she got the waterfall under control. The image of Prince and Tislam materialized in her head and wouldn't leave. She just couldn't fix her mind to believe the only two male figures in her life that she'd loved as much as she loved herself were taken from her in one single night. One lost forever to the grave and the other to the Criminal Justice system, which is nothing more than a sophisticated way of re-naming and disguising slavery. The only questions, which loomed heavily in her mind, were why? And how did this happen?

When the bell rang, Dinasia headed for the door.

"Excuse me, Dinasia," Mr. Jerome moved quickly towards her. "I would like to have a word with you."

"Please, Mr. Jerome, I mean no disrespect to you, but right now I am not in the frame of mind to talk to anyone." She turned and left as Mr. Jerome spoke to her back.

Dinasia went to her Algebra class in room 321 and did the same as in English class; blanked out everything in her surroundings and stayed in deep thought. During her next class (Physical health) nothing changed. Afterwards, she was on her way to lunch hall.

As she walked down the corridor, feeling the dozens of eyes upon her, Dinasia realized Shateek would most likely know the details about the incident. The urge to talk with him increased with every step that drew her closer to the lunch hall.

When she entered the Cafeteria, Dinasia was surprised to see Shateek was already there. He was sitting in their usual section and had meals stacked on the table. Dinasia noticed a pained expression on Shateek's face as he stared off into space. She approached.

Shateek turned and was snatched from the daydream when he saw Dinasia. He stood, gently took her book bag, laid it to the side and guided her to the seat. "So how are you holding up?" He sat down across from her. When she didn't respond, he tried another approach. "You'll feel a lot better if you eat something." He began unwrapping the food. "I got us some turkey and cheese heroes, some steamin' hot vegetable soup, some blue berry pie, and--"

"Do you know the details?" Dinasia stared at Shateek unblinkingly. "I wanna know how it happened?"

After pausing for a moment he said, "Yes, I saw the whole incident." Silence.

"So what happened?" She insisted.

"I think we should eat fir--"

"I wanna know right now!"

"Okay, okay," he sighed hard, pretending to make an effort to gather his thoughts. "Well . . . Last night around eight o'clock, I saw Tislam walking towards your building. He looked real upset about somethin'. Then I saw Kirk get up off the bench and rush towards Tislam like he wanted to fight. Tislam pulled a gun and busted Kirk in the head with it. Then Prince rushed out the building just as Tislam was about to stomp Kirk out. Tislam chilled out, listening to whatever Prince was saying to him. Then Kirk rushed and grabbed Tislam and threw him to the ground. When Tislam got back up, Prince said something to him. That's when Tislam shot him twice in the chest and then ran off."

She shook her head as if to say that wasn't possible. "That don't make sense. Tislam liked Prince too much to do something like that to him. Tislam would never use that gun on anyone. He had it only to scare--"

"I'm not the only one who saw him shoot Prince. You got the whole Harper family on the third floor, most of the Mosleys saw it and that Spanish man on the fifth floor . . . I'm sorry, Dinasia. I know you wanna believe he didn't do it, but there were mad crazy people looking out their windows when it jumped off." He sighed hard. "There's something else, but, I--I didn't want to tell you this and . . . Forget it, it's really nothing."

"No! Tell me! I wanna know!" she demanded.

"Alright. This guy out there named Shaka told me Tislam was planning to shoot Prince because of a money beef they had a couple of months ago."

"That's not true!" She said forcefully. "Tislam and Prince never had any kind of beef, much less over mon--" She suddenly remembered the incident where Prince borrowed twenty dollars from Tislam and never paid it back. The revelation left her speechless and flung her into a silent cocoon. But Tislam wasn't upset about that. And he told Prince to keep that "chump change" and even made a joke out of the issue, claiming as long as Prince owed him money "he'd never go broke." But then again, Tislam had a way of harboring grudges, and didn't always show his animosity or rivalry. She knew Tislam's greatest strength resided in his tenacity and steady, relentless drive to accomplish something he set out to do, and she pitied the fool who provoked his vow of vengeance. If he killed Prince over something as petty as twenty dollar debt, she would never, ever as long as she lived, forgive him.

"Dinasia, you alright?" Shateek saw she was thinking of something connected to the money and realized he should monopolize off of the situation. "The way Tislam shot Prince, there definitely was some kind of beef between them."

Dinasia saw the unwavering seriousness in Shateek's mannerism and it shattered her hopes that Tislam may have done it by accident. She felt devastated. "Of all people, how could this happen to Prince?" she mumbled, speaking more to herself than to Shateek.

BLAM!!

Dinasia suddenly pounded on the table with the ball of her fist, startling Shateek. "Do you realize Prince made a complete 360 degree change in his life!? He went from a drug dealing, gun tooting, strong arm enforcer with a street thug mentality to a full fledge college honor student with A grades all across the board!" She laid her head on her folded arms on the table and sobbed. "And after all that, now he's dead!" she felt a growing hatred for Tislam that scared her because she never thought she could experience a sincere abhorrence towards him.

A minute later, Keisha rushed over to the table. "Dinasia!"

Dinasia's head sprung up. When she saw Keisha's petrified face, she knew it was something extremely serious. "What is it now?"

Keisha hastily sat next to Dinasia. "I think those security guards over there are looking for you." She nodded her head at the two school security guards on the far side of the cafeteria; one of them had a picture in his hand comparing it to the faces of every student they came across.

"Listen to me, Dinasia," Shateek said excitedly. "It's probably the police. They're in the Deans office and they're gonna question you about the shooting--"

"Why they wanna see me!?" Dinasia's eyes were wide with fear. She began wiping her eyes, trying to compose herself. "I don't have anything to do with--"

"Apparently they found out you were going out with Tislam," Shateek continued. "This is a murder and they're gonna check everything moving. The way you handle this is to say as little as possible because they're experts at flipping the things you say," he saw the guards were now heading towards their table and began speaking faster while lowering his voice to a whisper. "Since you're not an adult they supposed to question you in the presence of your parents. Make sure you ask for a lawyer if--"

"Excuse me, Ms. Dinasia Whitman," One of the guards said. "Please come with us. The Dean wants to see you in his office."

Dinasia stood and instantly noticed her knees were knocking as she walked towards the entrance. She looked back and saw Shateek and Keisha were following, but she knew they wouldn't be there with her during this interrogation.

A minute later she and the two security guards entered Mr. Crowe's Office. The first thing she saw was the two Detectives dressed in business suits and trench coats.

"Hello, Ms. Whitman," The white cop stuck his hand out. "My name is Detective Coluncci."

Dinasia shook his hand and was surprised by the hard sandpaper like feeling. She'd always thought DTs sat behind desks and never did much physical labor that would cause the development of calluses. The other DT introduced himself as "Detective Adams", and she saw he was a red bone black man with the type of soft hands she'd expected a DT to have.

"Dinasia," Mr. Crowe said as he put his arm around her shoulder and escorted her to a seat. "These gentlemen would like to have a word with you concerning your foster brother's death. Are you up to it?" After Dinasia nodded her head, he continued. "I can imagine how you feel right now, but they need to talk to you. I'll remain with you throughout the interview. Or, if you would like, I could make arrangements to have your legal guardian here?"

"No, that won't be necessary," Dinasia said quickly, knowing that would make matters worse.

"She's all yours," Mr. Crowe said to the Detectives. "I'll just have a seat over here at my desk."

Both Detectives pulled up chairs and sat across from Dinasia. Detective Coluncci pulled a small pad and pen from his inner breast pocket while Detective Adams spoke. "We're gonna try to do this as smoothly and quickly as possible. First,

is Tislam Parker your boyfriend?"

"Yes he is."

Detective Adams continued, "Are you aware that he is suspected of shooting your brother, Paul?"

Dinasia nodded her head.

"Where were you at the time of the shooting?"

"I was at my friend's house. Keisha Anderson."

"When was the last time you seen or spoke to Tislam?"

"Last week was the last time I saw him. I spoke with him over the phone about three or four days ago."

"How long have you and Tislam been dating?"

Dinasia was about to blurt out the answer and suddenly realized it would sound unbelievable. She wondered should she embellish the facts some. After a moment she decided to be straight up. "We been together ever since we were seven years old."

Coluncci looked up from his pad. "Seven years old?" He shifted through the pages of his pad and read something. "So, you both were living at the Jermain Lunsford Child Care Institute?"

She nodded her head.

Detective Adams continued. "Did Paul and Tislam ever have any fights, arguments or was there any tension between them?"

"No. They were friends."

"Friends!?" Coluncci's thick eyebrows rose as he turned the pages in his notepad. "Do you know of any money problems they may have had?"

Dinasia suddenly felt a wave of anxiety in the pit of her stomach. Even though she was furious with what Tislam did to Prince, and felt the thin line between love and hate slowly disappearing, she still felt an odd urge to stay loyal to the man she once loved. Then the image of Prince's face popped inside her head, along with all the nice things he had done. The desire to remain loyal was instantly shattered. "Yeah, Prince owed him twenty dollars."

"What did Paul borrow the money for?" Adams asked.

"Prince—I mean Paul needed carfare to get back to College and Tislam lent him the money."

"Was Tislam upset about not getting his money back?"

"No."

"Did you and Paul have any recent fights?"

"No. Me and Paul never had any fights."

"Do you know of any reason why Tislam would wanna hurt Paul?"

"No."

"Did you ever see Tislam with a gun?"

She was about to say yes, but something touched her heart. The sudden vibe made her feel as if she was about to inflict a devastating blow upon Tislam. She was angry with Tislam, and knew she could never forgive him for what he did to Prince, but the thought of hurting him disturbed her greatly. Plus, if she told them Tislam had a gun, it would be considered straight out snitching; one of the most unforgivable violations and a cardinal sin in the hood. Her chaotic mind was jammed tight with confusion and indecisiveness. Her tongue felt like it was literally tied in knots.

"Excuse me, Ms. Whitman, did you ever see Tislam with a gun?" Detective Adams instantly knew what the answer was, since her hesitation and facial expressions told it all.

Dinasia sighed hard. "No."

Short pause.

Staring hard at Dinasia, Detective Adams spoke in an impatient and slightly hostile tone. "Are you aware, young lady, that lying during this interview is a criminal offense?"

Detective Coluncci added in the same tone. "It's called obstructing justice and it's a felony punishable by imprisonment and a fine. Now, we're gonna try this one more time and we want a truthful answer."

Mr. Crowe sprung to his feet. "She answered your question." He came from behind his desk. "And why are you threatening her? I don't take too kindly to intimidation tactics geared at students under my supervision." He saw Dinasia was upset by the Detectives' remarks. "I'm sorry gentlemen, but I'm terminating this interview."

"Hey! Wait a minute," Detective Coluncci said, "we have more questions."

Mr. Crowe ignored the comment as he went to the door and yelled to one of the security guards. "Mr. Sanchez. Ms. Whitman is finished." He turned and spoke to Dinasia. "Do you wanna go home for the day or go to your next class?"

Dinasia stood and headed for the door. "I'm going to my next class." Just as she was about to step beyond the threshold, she glanced back at the two Detectives. A nervous tension erupted when she saw the evil looking smirks on their faces, which said: "Run all you want, but you can't hide, young lady."

As she headed towards the staircase, with the guard on her heels, a little voice inside her head scolded her for lying. Then, another voice, the one deep inside her subconscious, reminded her that a person is innocent until proven guilty and even Tislam was entitled to that benefit of the doubt.

CHAPTER # 7

Tislam stood silently in the alleyway of the house across the street from Keisha's house with his eyes glued to the second floor bedroom window. He was anxiously waiting for the lights to go out. It was twenty minutes after ten o'clock and he couldn't understand why Mrs. Anderson wasn't sound asleep by now? He had to see Dinasia; he had talk to her, caress her and let her know the truth.

At this moment, there was nothing in the world he wanted more than to hear Dinasia's soft, sensuous voice say to him she understood and would be beside him every step of the way during this crisis. Talking to himself had now become a standard operating procedure. *I didn't do anything and I know she'll believe me if only I could just talk to her*, he was pouting desperately.

The mere thought of Dinasia thinking he killed her brother terrified him more than the rumors of what went on at Rikers Island. If she believed he did it, there was no doubt she would leave him. And he didn't believe he could live a single day without his precious Dinasia. The expectation that he could lose her as a result of this situation brought tears to his eyes every time the thought crossed his mind.

For the past three days, that crazy voice in the back of his head kept saying: "You're losing her. If you don't hurry up and get to her, it'll be too late." At times, he could feel he had already lost her, almost as if they were communicating through telepathy.

Immediately after the incident, Tislam went straight home and told his family what happened. They instantly insisted he turn himself in and tell the authorities what happened. But Tislam told them he had to talk to Dinasia first. When his dad became upset and accused Dinasia of being the reason why his life was now turned upside down, Tislam was on the verge of cursing him out. With a struggle, he held his tongue. His dad's sudden anger initially confused and agitated him, and only after Tislam realized his dad was just venting, he calmed down enough to listen to the advice he had to offer. With Jeffrey, Amy and Allen all on his back, pleading for him to go to the police, Tislam fled with nowhere to go.

He decided to hide out in the South Jamaica Houses AKA 40 Projects, several blocks from his home. The following day, he called his moms and found out the police came to the house, and as he suspected, they thought he did the shooting.

On the roof top of a seven story Project building on 109th Avenue, Tislam slept in the roof stairwell, and with the money he saved up, he bought himself some food and drink. When there was a need to use the bathroom for the purpose of making a crap, he relieved himself at the gas station a couple of blocks away.

During school hours, he stayed hidden. At night, he snuck out to Brooklyn, dressed in a makeshift disguise, and hung around Keisha's house, hoping to see Dinasia. Yesterday, he was about to go to the basement window, but the family in the house across the street where he currently hid, saw him and he was forced to hastily disperse from the area. The urge to immediately go back and try it again was very strong, but his rational mind told him tomorrow was another day.

Tislam stared at Mrs. Anderson's window so long every time he closed his eyes he could still see the image in his mind as if it was engraved on the back of his eyelids. Then, suddenly, the bedroom light went out. Tislam winced with pleasure and glanced at his watch. He had to hold fast for a couple of minutes to make absolutely sure Mrs. Anderson was asleep.

Five minutes later, he couldn't wait any longer and headed across the street. The nervous pounding of his heart echoed in his ears. Although the street was deserted, he suddenly got the strange, uncanny feeling like he was being watched. He hastily scanned the vicinity and saw nothing. He was certain there were no undercover cops because he searched the area before he decided to hide across the street. But then he remembered seeing the same three cars popping up every so often, and he again wondered if they were the police? *Nah, I doubt it*, he thought as he continued across the street.

When he was several feet from the gate, he saw a car turn on to the block, the two headlights rapidly heading towards him. Tislam increased his pace, swiftly entered the gate and crouched behind a bunch of naked bushes as the blue station wagon cruised by.

He waited a couple of seconds and went to the basement window. The faint sound of the TV could be heard. Pulling in a nervous breath of air, he tapped on the window very lightly and then waited.

About a minute later, he tried it again while whispering Dinasia's name.

Worn-out with fear, grief and now a terrifying frustration, he tried it again.

Nothing.

Just as he was about to knock harder on the glass, a dim light was turned on. He almost burst into tears of joy.

As he braced himself for Dinasia's face to appear in the window, he noticed something moved on his right side. At about the same moment, he also heard rapid footsteps on his left. His heart almost jumped clean out of his chest when he turned and realized it was the police coming at him from both directions.

"PUT YOUR HANDS UP!!--DON'T MOVE!!--GET 'EM UP! GET 'EM UP!!" The overlapping shouts and screams from the dozen plain clothe officers with guns pointed were loud enough to wake the dead.

Tislam quickly complied as he choked back the urge to run.

Moments earlier, Dinasia was lying on the floor in a sleeping bag on the side of Keisha's bed, watching the ten o'clock news. The sleeping bag was in a position, which concealed her from the view of anyone who entered the room. Keisha was fast asleep.

She suddenly thought she heard something. Her attention was drawn from the TV. When there were no immediate follow-up noises, she re-focused on the TV.

A couple of seconds later, Dinasia heard the same noise again. This time she struggled to determine what it was and where it came from. It occurred again, and she was able to determine it was a tapping sound and possibly a whisper. She pulled herself into a sitting position.

After waiting a long moment, Dinasia got up and turned on the night lamp, realizing the tapping and whispers apparently came from the window. *Tislam! It's Tislam*, she thought as she approached the window. Just as Dinasia was about to lift the window blinds, loud screams and shouts shattered the evening silence.

"PUT YOUR HANDS UP!!--DON'T MOVE!! . . .

Dinasia flinched, jumping back from the window as if gunshots were being fired at her. She turned and saw Keisha was rudely awakened, her face and eyes drenched with deep sleep. Dinasia panicked and raced for the door as if her legs took full control over her body. She knew Tislam would run and try any possible attempt to escape. She had to calm him down or else the police would kill him. Her mind was instantly flooded with the horrifying images of the countless dead black men who were maliciously gunned down by racist trigger happy cops within the New York City Police Department. The thought of Tislam dying merely because of who he was—a young black man—made her respond as if she had a barn-fire under her behind.

Dinasia frantically unlocked the door, snatched it open and bolted out inside. "Don't hurt him, please!"

Two of the cops were so startled they nervously spun around, pointing their weapons at Dinasia. When they saw who it was, they relaxed.

"Dinasia!" Tislam shouted. He was being dragged towards an unmarked patrol car, now kicking and screaming because he heard Dinasia's voice. The handcuffs felt like they were cutting through his skin.

"Please, I gotta talk to you, Dinasia! I didn't do it! I didn't do it! If you give me a chance to talk to you I'll--"

Tislam was tossed inside the car and the door slammed behind him, cutting off the rest of his comment.

Seconds later, he was whisked away as Dinasia stood staring. Tislam's comments tumbled about inside her mind. The voice of Mrs. Anderson talking to one of the Detectives caused a surge of electrifying anxiety to rush through Dinasia's body. She turned and made eye contact with Mrs. Anderson. In shock, Dinasia re-entered the basement and saw Keisha was so distraught by the fact they were caught, she just sat on her bed with her elbows propped on her knees, shoulders sagging, head down, looking like a defeated prize fighter refusing to go back in the ring for another round.

"I told you he was gonna come here," Keisha hissed, shaking her head in disbelief. "Now, we're both fucked! I'll probably be on punishment for the next four years."

Dinasia began packing her bags because she knew Mrs. Anderson wasn't trying to hear anything. She played no games and was probably one of the strictest ladies in the neighborhood. "I'm sorry, Keisha. I thought he would know the police was staking out your house. I honestly didn't think he would take a crazy chance like that."

"You know damn well the way you got Tislam strung-out he was bound to come here!" Keisha laid back on the bed and cupped her hands behind her head, staring at the ceiling, waiting for her moms to burst into the room hollering and screaming. Keisha knew she was definitely going to ground her and hoped and prayed she would at least let her go to the prom. If only the police hadn't made such a big deal out of this, with all those police cars all over the damn place, and all that screaming and yelling, she might've been able to talk her way out of this.

"Keisha!" Mrs. Anderson barged into the room. "What the hell did you think you were doing!!!"

Mrs. Anderson shouted and screamed for five straight minutes, lecturing them on everything from disrespect to the things she did when she was their age. She concluded with a direct order that Dinasia "take her behind back home", and Keisha was "grounded for two months without TV, Internet, phone or radio." Just before walking out the door, Mrs. Anderson said to Dinasia. "Have all your belongings ready within the next five minutes. I'm putting you in a cab and sending you home."

After Keisha was sure her moms was out of hearing range, she closed the room door and said to Dinasia. "Are you going back?"

"Like I told you before, I'm never going back there. I don't care if I have to sleep on a park bench and eat out of trash cans, I ain't going back."

"You should go stay with Shateek. He's got his own crib. And child he is strung out on you. I'll call him right now, he should--"

"No," Dinasia grabbed Keisha as she headed for the phone. "I can't do that. I don't--I--I'm not feeling Shateek in that way. I like him as a friend, not as a boyfriend."

"Listen here, Dinasia," Keisha crossed her arms impatiently. "You need to stop this little Miss goodie two shoe mission you on. You ain't got nowhere to go, so swallow your pride and go to him. As fine and rich as he is, you can learn to love him in a matter of days. Shit, even minutes or seconds, if you just let ya self go. Now, I'm gonna call him and tell--"

"I said no, Keisha!"

Keisha stopped and stared pitifully at Dinasia. "Well, have it your way. I would like to know where you gonna go, if you're not going back home?"

Dinasia sighed hard, deep in thought. After a moment, she said, "I'll figure something out."

Five minutes later, the horn of the cab was heard. Lugging three shopping bags filled with her worldly belongings, Dinasia said good night to Keisha and got in the cab. Mrs. Anderson instructed the cab driver to "take her to 855 Crescent Street in the Pink House Projects." She gave the

Arab looking man a five-dollar bill and told him to keep the change. The taxi did a U turn and disappeared down the block.

*   *   *

Keisha anxiously watched her mother go upstairs to her bedroom and closed the door. She then tiptoed to the kitchen phone and dialed Shateek's number. On the fourth ring, someone picked up and said, "Hello."

"May I speak to Shateek?" She whispered.

"Speaking."

"You ain't gonna believe this, Sha. My mother kicked Dinasia out after the police caught Tislam when he came here to see her. I don't--"

"Where did she go!?" Shateek's voice rose several notches. "How long ago did she leave?"

"Five minutes ago. My moms put her in a cab and sent her back home, but she told me she ain't going back there. I think she's gonna roam the streets. I told her to go to you--"

"Thanks, Keisha! I gotta catch her!" He hung up the phone and within two minutes he was in his car heading for the Pink House Projects.

*   *   *

"You can let me out here," Dinasia said to the cab driver. "I'll walk the rest of the way."

"I'm sorry, ma'am, I can't do that. The lady instructed me to drop you off on Crescent Street and that's what I intend to do."

Dinasia wanted to argue with the cabby, but quickly changed her mind when she remembered there were sick taxi drivers in this city, who were just as dangerous as any other deranged criminal lurking in the shadows.

When the cab pulled in front of her Project building, she got out and headed down Crescent Street, on her way to the A line Train station. She decided to go to the women's shelter in downtown Brooklyn over on Fulton Street. Times would be extremely rough these next couple of months, but at least she would have a place to lay her head and food in her stomach, she repeatedly told herself in an effort to build her courage.

61

Strolling down Crescent Street, Dinasia noticed the streets were a little too deserted. It was springtime and normally there were sprinkles of people roaming the streets, but not tonight for some odd reason. The quietness made her extremely nervous because this was the perfect condition for a mugging.

No sooner than she thought that dreadful thought, she saw two thug looking men with their pants hanging off their behinds, turn the corner and head towards her. One of the men was extremely tall while the other was medium built with a muscular physique, who probably just got home from prison, she surmised.

Dinasia was about to turn around and haul ass the other way, but she stopped herself when she remembered predators almost always fed off of the fear of their potential victims. Where the hell did she hear that from? Did that make sense? At the moment, her adrenaline-ridden mind was as cluttered as Fred Sanford's junkyard during an economic boom, and it was apparent no answers were forthcoming. If there were any truth to the saying, she would soon find out. Breathing deeply in an attempt to tame her nervousness, she poked her chest out, held her head up high, and continued walking straight towards them.

As Dinasia passed in between the two, one of her shopping bags brushed against the muscular guy and the tall one spoke. "Hey, pretty young thang, do you got the time?"

Without looking back, Dinasia said, "No, I don't." A couple of seconds later, she heard footsteps in back of her and this time she did look back.

They were following her.

Anxiety gripped Dinasia's stomach as she increased her pace, only seconds from bursting into a full fledge run. When she heard her pursuers running footsteps, she started running as well. With shopping bags flapping in the wind, she turned the nearest corner and didn't realize it was Blake Avenue, and the other end of the street was sealed off due to construction. By the time she saw the warning and dead-end street signs it was too late. Dinasia stopped and turned around with terror racing through her from head to toe.

"Just give us the stuff in the bags," The muscular guy said, breathing hard. "And we won't hurt you."

With a switchblade in his hand, the tall guy added. "We want all the money too."

"Take all of it," Dinasia sat the three bags down and stepped away from them, praying and searching desperately for an opportunity to run pass the two. "All the money is in the blue bag. Please, don't hurt me."

The muscular guy started rummaging through the bags while the tall guy approached Dinasia with a crazy, teasing smile on his face. Toying with the knife, the tall guy said, "I could sure use a shot of some jelly because the way all that junk in yo trunk was jigglin', it damn sure can't be jam." He giggled.

A chill shot through Dinasia's body as she backed away. They were going to rape her, she realized. She couldn't believe this was happening and thought she was in a dream. *Here we go again*, that voice in her head said. *Why is this happening me!?* Was she some kind of magnetic that attracted perverted fucking freaks?! *Why me, why me!? T*hat voice in her head cried.

Before Dinasia could get a firm grip on her thunderstruck mind, she tripped and fell backwards, hitting the pavement hard when her foot stepped in a deep hole in the ground.

In a blink of an eye, Dinasia felt the tall man's hand locked tightly around her neck, hoisting her onto her feet. She tried to scream without success as she was being dragged away towards what looked like an alleyway. Kicking, scratching and thrashing wildly, Dinasia successfully knocked over one garbage can and managed to rip the jacket sleeve of the tall man who had a death hold on her neck. The sensation of suffocation was strong and her eyes bulged out of her head. *You're killing me*, she wanted to say, but her throat and voice box were out of commission. She suddenly became dizzy, weak in the knees and extremely sleepy. Her lungs screamed for air.

Then, suddenly, she sensed the muscular guy was trying to unfasten her pants. Dinasia kneed him in the face. He shrieked. She instantly regretted she did that because the tall guy applied more pressure to the neck squeeze. She could've sworn she heard and felt her wind pipe make a crunching sound. The excruciating pain caused her legs to collapse completely. She fell lifelessly to the ground with the neck hold still in place.

WHAM!!--EHHHH!!--WHAM!!--WHAM!--AAHHHHHH!!--WHAM! . . .

Dinasia heard agonizing screams just as the tall guy let go of her neck. She instantly went into a coughing spell as her body shot into a fetal position. The sounds of pain drenched yells and shrieks filled her cloudy, oxygen-deprived mind. It also sounded like a hard object was repeatedly hitting another object, similar to the impact sound a baseball bat makes when coming in contact with a ball.

As Dinasia got the coughing under control, she heard someone softly utter her name and felt herself being scooped up off of the ground.

It was Shateek.

"Are you hurt?" Shateek's voice was saturated with terror. He ran out of the alleyway with Dinasia in his arms.

"My throat," She said hoarsely, barely above a whisper. The bouncing motion caused by Shateek's running with her in his arms had a strong awakening effect on her mind.

"Can you stand on your own? I gotta open the car door." He slowly put her down as she nodded her head.

As Dinasia sat in the passenger seat, pulling in deep, hard breaths of air, she turned and saw Shateek had a crowbar in his hand. He tossed it in the back. It made a hard thumping sound when it landed.

Then Shateek ran down the street. *Where is he going?* Dinasia sat up in the seat and watched him gather all her belongings scattered in the street, quickly stuffing them in the bags. When he found just about everything, he raced back to the car, placed the bags in the back, jumped in the driver's seat and spun off.

Shateek spoke excitedly. "Are you hurt? You need to go to the hospital!?"

"No, I'm okay. My throat's a little sore, that's all."

He sighed with sheer relief.

Dinasia glanced at Shateek and saw there was blood on his hand. "You're injured. Is it a deep cut?"

"It ain't mine." He said, without taking his eyes off the road.

"What did you do to them? I hope you didn't kill them." She couldn't imagine being an accomplice to murder.

"Them ole hard headed ass niggas ain't gonna die . . . even though they deserve to . . . They're gonna wake up with some vicious headaches and a couple of busted up arms and knee caps, but they won't die, so calm yourself down . . . What the hell are you doing out here this time of night anyway? I told you these streets are dangerous. And where do you think you're going with all these bags?"

"Keisha's moms kicked me out. Tislam came to her house and the cops arrested him. Mrs. Anderson blew a gasket when she found out I was staying there. I'm going to the women's Shelter over on Fulton Avenue. You can drop me off at the Euclid Avenue train station."

"What are you? buggin' out? Imagine me takin' you to a shelter when I got my own crib . . . I'm takin' you home with me and I'm not--"

"I can't do that Shateek." Dinasia said firmly.

Parked in front of Shateek's house, Dinasia remained adamant about going to the women's shelter, and after a twenty minute back and forth debate, Shateek reluctantly gave in to her wishes. During the ride to the shelter, Shateek continued his hard-pressed effort to persuade Dinasia to change her mind. Nothing he said altered her position, but he did talk her into "borrowing" two hundred dollars from him so she could buy herself an outfit to wear at Prince's Funeral Services scheduled for Thursday. She also agreed to allow him to pick her up for school and drop her back off at the shelter afterwards.

Before exiting the car, Dinasia hesitated, wondering should she do it. She was truly grateful Shateek saved her from those two freaks and all the other helpful things he'd done for her, and wanted to let him know how she felt. "Shateek, thank you." She slid over and gave Shateek a soft and tender kiss on the lips, which lasted only three seconds, but felt like twenty minutes to Shateek. Dinasia gathered her bags and headed towards the front door of the shelter.

As Shateek sat staring at Dinasia enter the shelter, while in an exotic and sensual daze, he smilingly thought, *I'm almost there. Just a few more maneuvers and she'll be all mine.*

CHAPTER # 8

Four days later.

Dinasia stood in a long line of visitors, waiting to enter the visiting room of the C-74 House of Detention for Adolescents. She was amazed at how huge the whole Rikers Island was, and was also aggravated by the large crowds of rude people that shoved, pushed, bumped into her and stepped on her toes without saying "excuse me" or "sorry."

In these last few days, She'd made some drastic changes in her attitude and approach towards life and struggled not to lash out violently at these ill-mannered folks.

Dinasia never thought she would experience a hell worse than the foster care system, but upon entering the women's shelter, she realized that place was it. At first, things seemed bearable. She sincerely thought she could put up with it for a short while, but then things changed overnight. All sorts of crazy things started happening; someone was stealing her clothes, food and even her schoolbooks, and the other women displayed a strong hostility towards her.

It was like she woke up into a twilight zone TV program. Her emotions were so highly tuned and chaotically mixed up, she felt like she was becoming chronically depressed and on the verge of losing control. Prince's funeral two days ago was the coup de grace blow that crumbled her broken heart into pulverized dust and began pushing her completely over the edge. During the services, she felt dehydrated and knew it was because of the loss of so much water due to her constant crying.

Yesterday morning, after she woke up and discovered her shoes and all other footwear were missing, she'd decided to stop being a wimp and an excessively humble person. All that Mr. nice guy shit was out the window. She was a natural born fighter and was also aware of the fact people did things to others only when those others allowed it and put up with it. Something snapped inside her and she vowed in that moment to take no shit from nobody else ever again.

Dinasia literally had to beat flames out of a woman named Sheila after she found a pair of her sneakers hidden under the woman's bed. Immediately after the fight, she decided to go to Rikers Island to have a talk with Tislam to find out why the hell he destroyed his life and hers as well. She'd come to the conclusion that he was the root of all this current pain, suffering and misery in her life. She had to find a way to vent her anger or else she would explode from the built up rage that percolated with a furious intensity. They had so many wonderful plans, and as far as she was concerned, Tislam had some helluva explaining to do for fucking up those beautiful dreams.

By the time Dinasia reached the processing window, she had steam and fury rolling off her body. She still couldn't believe the correction officers were a thousand times more disrespectful than the visitors. Three times she had to bite down on her lip in order not to curse out these arrogant, pee brain, and petty minded creeps. If stupidity had a face to it, the pictures of these fools would've been it, she'd concluded as she headed for the section she was instructed to sit, which was row seven, seat number four. The small plastic table and two matching chairs looked worn and too small for even adolescents. It was apparent this was harassment at its best.

She sat in the hard plastic chair, waiting and looking at all the stressed out faces of the black, brown, red, yellow, and a very small number of white folks.

Five minutes later, Dinasia saw Tislam come out from behind a huge electric gate, dressed in a gray colored jumpsuit. He looked terrible. She didn't know if she should remain mad at him or to feel sorry for him. When they made eye contact, she saw Tislam was about to run to her, but he constrained his excitement. He walked towards her with an extremely fast pace.

"Dinasia!" Tislam was almost to tears with joy. When he reached her, he hugged and tried to kiss her on the lips, but Dinasia angrily turned her face.

"Hey you!" The guard in the far corner shouted angrily at Tislam. "Take a seat!"

Tislam sat down. His eyes searched desperately for the Super Ninja necklace and saw it wasn't around her neck. Terror gripped him. "What happened to the necklace?"

"What do you think?" Dinasia said in a snotty tone of voice. "I'm not wearing something from a person I ain't dealing with."

"Dinasia, please, you gotta believe me, I didn't do it. The way it went down, I think somebody's setting me up or—"

"How's that possible when there's at least eight people saying they saw you shoot Prince."

"Just hear me out for a second and you'll see what I mean when I say it was a set up." He told Dinasia everything that happened from the moment Stony told him about her being attacked by Kirk, up to the part where he fled the scene.

"And you expect me to believe that bullshit lame story?!" Dinasia felt herself becoming more upset with Tislam by the seconds.

"But it's the truth! You know I would never lie to you. And I damn sure wouldn't lie about something as serious as this. I need your help, Dinasia. The D.A. is thinking about seeking the death penalty. They're about to kill me for something I didn't--"

"You should've thought about all this before you started carrying that gun around. I told you time and time again that guns destroy people's lives. If you didn't have that damn gun, you couldn't have shot Prince or put your--"

"I told you, I didn't do it!" Tislam shouted, startling Dinasia.

"I didn't put you here, so don't take it out on me. You said you wanted to see me and now I'm here . . . You know how much I loved Prince, Tislam . . . You say you didn't do it, but I'm gonna be honest with you Tislam because that's one thing we agreed to always do with each other . . . I don't believe you . . . I think your temper finally got the best of you, and now you're regretting it. I told you if you killed someone I would leave you! You didn't just kill someone; you killed two of my best friends. You and Prince were the only people in this world I loved as much as I love myself and now that's all gone." She paused, struggling to hold back the tears, sniffling. "Your attitude and temper, and that damn gun has taken you away from me and--and I hate you for that!" She gritted her teeth, completely shoving away the urge to cry, replacing it with a hard penetrating stare.

Tislam's whole world was shattered. He was hoping and praying she would believe him, but that wasn't going to be the case. Looking at all the facts he tried to tell himself if he were in her shoes he probably would've felt the same way. *Hold up! I can't lie to myself like that!* If this was on the flip side and Dinasia said she didn't do it, he would've believed her even if there were ten million eyewitnesses and the Pope swore on a stack of golden Bibles. *This shit ain't right!* His anger began to reach a boil. "How could you do this to me, Dinasia? You're flippin' on me! Whatever happened to our no other love vow? Remember we said we would never--"

"That ain't got shit to do with you spazzin' out and killing someone, especially after I warned you not--"

"Would you stop saying I killed Prince! What the fuck is wrong with your god-damn ears! After all these years we've been together, and the first fuckin' sign of turmoil, and already you're about to jump ship on me . . . I don't believe you're doing this shit. What? You don't have faith in me anymore? Dinasia, I would die for you at the drop of a fuckin' hat and now you acting like--"

"Stop yellin' at me!" Dinasia wanted to reach across the table and slap his face. "I didn't come up here to argue with you!"

"So, what did you come here for? Because if you love me, you would believe what I'm telling you. You acting all upset, but I'm the one who should be upset! . . . You making me think all these years we been together was a one-sided relationship. If I didn't love you, do you think I would've done all those crazy things for you? What about those two times I escaped from the Institute just to see you after the Shepards adopted you?

Remember how I found a way to get adopted by the Burton family just so we could be close to each other? And don't forget how I visited you constantly, never once missing a beat, even at times when I was sick or injured? . . . That's pure love, Dinasia, and when people love at that magnitude, they don't lie to each other. Now, tell me, Dinasia, does all that count for something?"

No response.

Tislam was too charged up with anger to stop now. "If you was a real woman that kept your word, you wouldn't be here creating unnecessary conflict by not believing me. You would help me without question and would--"

"You arrogant, self righteous, manipulative bastard!" Dinasia stood up abruptly, pointing her finger at Tislam while talking. "How dare you try to flip this shit on me! You killed my brother and now you want me to take your side? That shit won't happen in a million years! When you killed Prince, you killed us!" She headed for the processing room.

"Dinasia! Please don't leave," Tislam grabbed her arm, but it was wrenched away. "Please, Dinasia! Don't leave!" He tried to chase after her, but the guards pounced on him and began dragging him towards the electric gate.

When she reached the door leading to the processing area, Dinasia turned and shouted at Tislam. "And don't you ever call or write me as long as you live!"

"No, Dinasia! DON'T DO THIS!!"

CHAPTER # 9

Shateek pulled the car into the parking space across the street from the shelter.

"Thanks, Shateek," Dinasia was about to get out of the car.

Shateek cleared his throat loudly.

Dinasia's hand stopped on the door lever. With a smile she turned and saw Shateek's lips puckered up. "I see I done started something." She scooted over and kissed Shateek. Her mind spun with delight. The warmth circulating through her body was getting stronger each time she engaged in this little affectionate ritual. She didn't want to admit it, but she knew she was falling for Shateek. It wasn't love yet, she was sure of that. However, with Keisha pissing in her ear daily, along with these particular tender moments, she realized she was gradually feeling that sensation in her heart she equated with love.

Dinasia pulled from the long kiss and composed herself. "I'll see you tomorrow." She exited the car.

Shateek smilingly watched Dinasia cross the street and waved at her as she entered the shelter. He glanced at his watch, started the car and pulled from the curb. Five minutes later, he saw a group of women standing on a corner in front of a grocery store. When he recognized Sheila, he double-parked the car.

Sheila saw the car, ran across the street, got in on the passenger side and spoke happily. "Shateek, what's happenin' man?" Shelia's crack craving was so strong she felt all her senses were turned up to full volume.

"So, what's going on?" Shateek said impatiently. "It don't look like she budged one bit. She should be stressed out of her mind by now."

"If you don't want us to rough her up a little, you just gonna have to hold tight. I don't know how much longer I can go for her hittin' on me and not being able to stomp the shit out of her little hot ass--"

"I saw a bruise on her face," Shateek reached over and grabbed Sheila by the neck. "Did one of you bitches touch her!?"

"No!" Sheila shrieked in terror, clutching at Shateek's hand around her neck. "We didn't do nothing to her."

Shateek shoved Sheila into the door. "If you hurt her, or put one fuckin' scar on her, I'll make you miserable motherfuckers disappear. You hear me!?"

Sheila nodded frightfully. "Look what she did to my face, Shateek." She positioned her cheek for Shateek to see the bluish bruise and a scratch. "Even after she did this, I still didn't touch her . . . I should get extra for a scar like this, Shateek."

Shateek stared at her for a moment and then said, "You been out in the streets fuckin' and suckin' everything movin' for less than crumbs and you ain't been beefin' about that. Don't try to front on me like you some kinda bitch that deserves to be treated like a Queen. You getting paid top dollar already . . . You know what? Get the fuck outta my car. There's a thousand bitches out here that would--"

"No, I'm sorry Shateek, I take it back. I didn't mean it. I just need a few extra dollars to buy my son a birthday gift, but if it's making you upset then forget it. I'm sorry, I was just trippin'."

Shateek knew the little tricks crack-heads used to provoke sympathy and to get extra money from people they called Vics. "If your son needs anything, I'll personally take him shopping. In the meantime, this is what I want you to do." It took Shateek two minutes to explain his plan and all the consequences if she didn't follow his instructions.

Sheila agreed with the scheme whole-heartedly, since she really didn't have much of a choice.

*   *   *   *

Tislam was in the shower working up a good soap lather all over his body. He had on his sneakers and boxer shorts and could hear the three booty bandits lurking around in the bathroom, apparently scheming on how they were going to run up on him. With two shanks (homemade knives) tied to his wrists, Tislam rinsed the soap off his body and waited for the first fool to rush inside the shower.

73

Through the fungus infested plastic shower curtain, he saw the three figures moving about. These three oversized bullies had raped two new jacks already, and it turned Tislam's stomach inside out because the correction officers pretended not to hear the screams. Tislam had been taking birdbaths ever since he been on the block, but after the visit with Dinasia he decided to take a shower with hopes that these fools would try to do something stupid to him.

After the tragic situation on the visit, Tislam decided to commit suicide. Twice he gathered some bed sheets, tied them to the shower stall and then around his neck. Just as he was about to jump, something inside of him wouldn't let him do it. He then made himself a razor and was seconds from slitting his wrist, but again, that strange force from within wouldn't allow it. He concluded, he wasn't the suicidal type and knew no matter what he did, he personally wouldn't be able to do it. That's when he decided to make someone else do it for him.

After officially losing Dinasia, Tislam felt he had nothing else to live for. By provoking these booty bandits, Tislam figured he could use himself as a vehicle of justice, and end his miserable life in the process.

These three particular inmates possessed store bought knives, and had no gripes about using them. Tislam hated bullies, and especially despised men who took advantage of weak and helpless men only for the sake of humiliating them. Any man that would use the misery of others to boost his own warped and twisted ego deserved no mercy when the can of whip ass was opened. Tislam had a nice little trick for these particular bandits because surviving in a hostile institutional environment was nothing new to him. He was well experienced with handling bullies, especially the ones that made the mistake of assuming they automatically had the upper hand.

"Yo, shorty!" The booty bandit, who had two missing front teeth said to Tislam as he banged on the stall with a metal object (a pipe). "That's my shower. You didn't ask me could you use it."

"You been in the block long enough to know better," The fat Latino bandit said, standing beside the missing teeth inmate. "I hope you know that's gonna cost you a case of raw hide."

Tislam turned the water off, got the two shanks ready, turned and faced the shower curtain and said, "My name ain't shorty. It's Tislam."

"What kinda name is that?" The other bandit, who wore a do rag and an ear ring in his left ear said, "What are you, one of them 5 percenters? You one of them peace gods, or somethin'? If you are, you in the wrong cell block, dog."

Tislam was tired of all this talking, and since his adrenaline had reached its peak point, it was show time. "Yo, listen here. Get the fuck away from the shower, so I can get dressed. And if you don't like what the fuck I said, you can--"

The three booty bandits burst out laughing.

They laughed so hard and long, Tislam noticed it was contagious. He started laughing along with them.

Then, suddenly, the plastic shower curtain was ripped away from the stall. As fast as a blink of an eye, Tislam jabbed the missing teeth bandit in the face, just below the left eye. The ear-shattering scream scared the other two into a retreat state of mind. But Tislam was far from finished. He rushed out of the shower, grabbed the fat Latino guy and stabbed him twice in the stomach.

As the guy wearing the do-rag scrambled to his feet, after tripping over the missing tooth bandit, he was brandishing a hunting knife twice the size of Tislam's shank. Before approaching do-rag, Tislam stabbed missing tooth two more times as he tried to get up. But this time Tislam blessed him with two solid body shots. The blood squirted from the wounds and profusely poured from his body.

Tislam was filled with rage as he slowly moved towards the guy wearing the do-rag. When Tislam saw the nervous gestures of this coward rapist, it made him even more outraged. He felt a surge of joy at the thought of how it would feel when he stabbed this low life bastard into a permanent sleep. The fury raging through his heart, mind and soul caused by the loss of his only love sparked a surge of anger that was making his head spin with pure rage.

The thunderous sound of the riot squad materialized and Tislam knew if he was going to get a piece of this particular booty bandit, he would have to move quickly. He heard the other two bandits making noises as if they were trying to get up. Tislam ignored them, assuming they were incapacitated. Tislam was about to charge at do-rag.

WHAM!--EHHHHH!!

Tislam screamed when he felt the blade of a shank sliced through the lower section of his back. It felt like the knife cut through his back, went through his whole body and came out of his stomach. As Tislam collapsed to the floor due to a rapid loss of energy, he felt a strong wave of terrifying heat swarmed over his body. Under normal circumstances, Tislam would've never given his back to an enemy while in the heat of combat, unless that opponent was no longer a threat, but his anger and reckless disregard for his own life clouded his judgment. As the realization of defeat sunk in, he cursed himself for not listening to his first instinct, which was to go back and finish them off.

As his mind became fuzzy, and the riot squad crashed through the bathroom door, Tislam saw a picture of Dinasia in his third eye and he smiled. He felt himself fading rapidly into a deep sleep, while the blood oozed from his body. Then, suddenly, Tislam saw another vision that made him realize he didn't really want to die. But a scary premonition which shook his pillars was reaching way down into the inner-most part of his soul, assuring him that he fucked up, and did so big time.

CHAPTER # 10

"Get up! Get your ass up!"

Dinasia pulled herself from the deep sleep when she heard the voice, and felt her arm being rudely nudged. When her vision came into focus, she saw four women standing over her. With a burst of energy, she tried to jump out of the bed, but the arm and leg restraints stopped her flat. Her mind instantly went into a terror-stricken panic because something was covering her mouth and her hands and feet were tied to the bedpost. She mumbled angrily, jerking wildly, trying to break free from the ropes.

"Calm your ass down, girl!" Sheila said as she pulled a hypodermic needle from her dirty Adidas jacket pocket. The syringe part of the needle contained a blood colored substance. "Dinasia." She said with a wicked tone as she sat on the bed. "We need to have a nice little talk."

"Mmmmmmuuummmm!!" Dinasia mumbled, and if she could have been heard she would've said, "Get this shit off of me, you crack-head bitch!"

"I'm gonna get right to the point," Sheila continued, "No pulling punches and shit . . . You're not welcome here. We want you to pack your shit and leave today. If you try that super woman shit with us again, we're gonna lace you up with a case of AIDS."

Dinasia's eyes suddenly grew wide causing her tormentors to giggle.

Sheila continued. "Yeah, that's right, this is HIV infected blood and we're gonna inject your ass with it if you don't leave."

Ramonica saw Dinasia's fear and knew this was the the perfect opportunity to grandstand, knowing it would only help the situation. "Fuck this bitch! Let's inject her ass anyway. Give me that fuckin' needle, I'll stick her ass."

Sheila played along. "Wait, wait! As long as she leaves, there won't be a need to inject her . . . Dinasia, are you gonna pack your shit and leave?"

Dinasia frantically nodded her head.

"And if we cut you loose," Ramonica said, "are you gonna start acting crazy? Huh? If you do I'll personally stick the shit out of your ass. You promise not to act up?"

Dinasia never stopped nodding. In fact, right about now, she would've agreed to just about anything.

Shelia said, "We want you out of here this morning, and if you tell anybody about this, we'll send somebody to creep up on you and stick you dead in the ass." She waved the needle near Dinasia's face, arms, chest and stomach while the teasing smile grew larger. "When that boyfriend of yours pick you up this morning, that's the last time we ever wanna see you! You hear me?"

Dinasia nodded as the tears of rage erupted from her eyes. These weren't the standard tears of pain, but the ones of hate and hopelessness that could cause people to snap.

"Cut her loose," Sheila said to the other women and they obeyed.

When the masking tape was ripped from her mouth, Dinasia released an abrupt moan. After the ropes were cut, and the women stepped away from her, Dinasia rose from the bed and went straight to work packing her belongings. She didn't know whether to be grateful, angry or scared. But there was one thing she was certain of, and that was she wanted to get away from this place as quickly as possible.

As she flung and tossed her things into the suitcases, Dinasia wondered where she was going to go. It didn't take long for her to realize there was nowhere to go. The shelter in the Bronx was the only other shelter left in the city that was accepting new homeless people, but it was too far. Going back to the Pink House Projects to live with her foster family was out of the question, and she had no other friends besides Shateek willing to take her in.

That obviously meant there was only one place: Shateek's crib. She'd thought about giving it a try on a couple of occasions and actually thought it might not be all that bad after all. Plus, she knew his nose was wide open for her.   Since there were no other options, and she didn't have a man anymore, she figured it couldn't hurt to give it a try.

Fifteen minutes later, she exited the shelter, carrying her two huge suitcases. After waiting out front for five minutes, Shateek pulled up.

Shateek lit up with mind-tingling joy when he saw Dinasia carrying her bags. *It's about Goddamn time*, he beamed happily to himself as he got out of the car and rush towards Dinasia. "What happened!?" He looked truly surprised. "You all right? What're you doing with your bags?" He scooped up the suitcases and headed for the trunk of the car.

"I can't stay here anymore," Dinasia said as she got in the car. After Shateek put the suitcases in the trunk, and got back behind the wheel, she decided to test the waters before she went with the obvious course of action in response to this predicament. She sighed and said. "When I get out of school, I need you to drive me to the Bronx. I'm gonna stay at that shelter."

A shock wave of sheer disbelief almost caused Shateek to completely lose control of his composure. He sighed hard, struggling to maintain his calmness. "Dinasia, are you serious? There's no way we'll be able to make it to and from the Bronx for you to go to school. It's mathematically impossible. Listen, Dinasia." he was desperately searching for the rights words. "Please boo, you gotta be realistic here . . .

As Shateek rattled on and on, trying to sound like an old wise man with a ton of worldly knowledge, Dinasia giggled inwardly because she loved to see him engage in his fast talking antics. After he went on for about two straight minutes, pleading with her to move in with him, Dinasia spoke. "You know something? I gotta admit; you're right. It definitely makes a lot of sense."

"So you'll stay with me?" Shateek tried to sound calm, but the attempt didn't work quite well.

Dinasia paused. "Yes, I'll stay with you, but only if you agree to my stipulations."

"Stipulations?" Shateek squinted his eyes in confusion and really wanted to say: *What the hell is this, a court proceeding or something?* But he was too close to a win to start creating bumps in the road to victory. "Okay. All right. You name it, you got it."

It took Dinasia five minutes to explain all her terms, all the material things she needed, and all the miscellaneous rules of the relationship.

Shateek burst out laughing. "I see you been mapping this thing out thoroughly. So, in other words, you wanna wear the pants and I gotta put on the skirt."

They both laughed.

"It's not too late to turn back," Dinasia said.

"Girl, as hard as I been tryin' to get with you, shit, I'm libel to agree to you plugging my ass up with one of them Tampons, if it'll win your heart."

They laughed explosively as Shateek pulled the car onto the roadway.

As Dinasia savored the wonderful euphoric sensation caused by the re-igniting of their laughter, she felt herself falling fast, descending so swiftly in love, the feeling made her realize she should've made this decision a long time ago.

CHAPTER # 11

Five years later.

Dinasia rolled over in bed as her eyes slowly opened. She saw the alarm clock on the nightstand said it was a quarter to six. Scooting from under the covers and into a sitting position, she let loose a huge stretch. She reached over, disengaged the alarm button and noticed she felt refreshed and well rested despite going to bed an hour later than her usual ten o'clock self-imposed curfew.

She stood and was about to awaken Shateek, but remembered there was a half an hour left before he had to get up. Her first stop was the bathroom and then the kitchen to get the herbal tea brewing.

Proceeding down the spiral Victorian style staircase covered with an expensive beige colored carpeting that matched the elegant wallpaper, Dinasia realized the issue she was thinking about just before she went to bed last night suddenly came back to her with unusual clarity.

Next week was their first wedding anniversary, and from the way Shateek was acting it appeared he forgotten. All week long she'd been giving him hints of all sorts, and each time he responded in a way that indicated the wedding date was totally non-existent in his mind. His behavior baffled her and all sorts of crazy things started running through her mind. *Is he cheatin' on me? Is the fire in our relationship losing its spark? Am I doing something wrong? Is there any reason why he would forget something as important as this date? Or could it be he's up to something?*

As Dinasia entered the huge kitchen (that was just recently renovated with country style cabinets and matching table and chairs made of a rare oak wood), she struggled with these questions and instantly shot all of them down. There were no signs of Shateek messing around; their sexual affairs were not only exotic and thoroughly erotic, but were toe twisting, back scratchingly good; she was on top of her business as a wife, friend, lover and psychological advisor, and Shateek never forgot any other important dates like birthdays and even the day she moved in with him just before they graduated from high school. Plus, they had just purchased this two hundred and fifty thousand dollar home on Spring Fall street in Nassau County, which was said to be one of Long Island's most well respected upper middle class sections in the region.

She sighed hard because it was nothing short of sheer insanity to believe they're marriage was in a state of turmoil. She pushed the whole issue to the back of her mind and focused on this morning's routine.

After Dinasia sipped down a cup of Golden-seal tea, and prepared Shateek a bowl of Farina mixed with an assortment of organic fruits, she woke up her husband. As he ate and got ready for work, she went to their exercise room in the basement and commenced with her one-hour workout routine that consisted of aerobics, sit-ups, deep knee bends, biking, pushups and pull-ups.

Shateek was once her workout partner, but due to a severely pulled muscle in his right shoulder, their private Doctor (Dr. Randall) instructed him not to do any strenuous activities and specifically forbid any exercise until further notice. The injury had no affect on his ability to go to work since Shateek was the owner of a construction company he built from the ground up—along with a little financial assistance from various family members—after he graduated from Brooklyn Technical College with a Bachelors degree in architectural science and business management.

Dinasia glanced at the clock on the gym wall and super-setted her last four sets of sit-ups. She was a true health fanatic and was proud to admit it. Her strict low fat, high fiber diet and her obsession with alternative medicine were just a speck in a cosmos of natural healing treatments ranging from herbal and vitamin therapy to Homeopathy and acupuncture.

As she headed for the shower, she realized she felt like ten million dollars! She couldn't understand why so many people didn't see the obvious health benefits involved in living a natural life style? These people would alter their views if they were aware of all the glaring dangers involving the use of traditional medicines. She was suddenly reminded of the numerous documented cases where the so-called health system killed its patients, and how the discovery compelled her to deal with no other doctor besides one involved in natural healing.

If she didn't honestly believe she had a spiritual connection and obligation to people in need of social guidance and services, she would've became a doctor in the field of natural healing. After four years at Brooklyn College, and acquiring a Bachelors degree in psychology, sociology and behavioral science while currently holding a supervisory position at the Queens County Social Services Department, Dinasia still felt internally dissatisfied and often thought it was because she hadn't pursued a career in natural medicine. At least that's what she sincerely wanted to believe was the root of her internal dissatisfaction.

Deep down, she knew it was something far more delicate than a mere career decision, and tried hard to pretend it had nothing to do with the drastic change in her life during the last year of high school. Lying to herself wasn't something she did quite well. The source she suspected was Tislam and the shattered dreams that were forever lost as a result of the tragic incident. Tislam was so deeply connected to her inner-most being, there was no way she would get him out of her system with just a snap of a finger. But the fact that he killed her brother was a driving force that made the transition possible.

Just before the trial, Tislam was often in her dreams, which made her wonder how he was holding up. Each time this reverie appeared, she shoved the mental images away, trying to convince herself she hated him, but that strong spiteful emotion was a force that wasn't within her character and the endeavor never worked. After she heard about Tislam being severely stabbed while on Rikers Island, she wanted to visit him, but Shateek and Keisha talked her out of it.

When the jury found Tislam guilty and the judge sentenced him to 30 years to life imprisonment, thus, legally rendering him a convicted murderer of her brother, Dinasia noticed the feelings for Tislam finally started to fade, and as of this date, he was just an old nagging memory that was tucked away in the back of her mind, which came to life whenever she saw or heard something that distinctly reminded her of him. Other than that, and much to her surprise, he was out of her system enough for her to enjoy life with Shateek.

As the soothing warm water sprinkled over her muscular and pleasingly voluptuous body, Dinasia heard Shateek enter the bathroom.

"Dinasia," he said. "I wanna ask you something."

"You sure picked the fine time to wanna get into a discussion. Ain't it time for you to leave."

"It's not gonna take that long." He paused, feeling himself becoming horny. The mere thought of being in the presence of her unclothed body was enough to get his blood pumping. He glanced at his watch to see if he had enough time to run up in the shower and get off a quickie. When he saw he was already behind schedule, he shoved the thought out of his head. "Listen, I just got off the phone with Shabazz . . . I want you to meet me at his house when you get off work this evening, he and Charmaine invited us to this dinner party they're having--"

"Shateek, you know I hate going over there. You remember what happened the last time at one of those little dinner parties of theirs."

"Yes, I remember, but that won't happen again. Believe me," He bit down on his lip, holding back the laughter. The argument (more like a ranking contest) between Dinasia and Charmaine was the most comical quarrel he'd ever seen. Dinasia and Charmaine were like fire and water; two substances that didn't get along together no matter what the conditions were. "Your girl Keisha's gonna be there. It's a celebration for the opening of a new store and you know Shabazz'll rise hell if we're not there."

"Another one of those stores, huh?" She knew what type of store he was talking about and it amazed her how Shabazz was able to disguise his illicit activities without anyone noticing. If she hadn't known his history, she would've thought he was a legitimate businessman. "All right, but don't get upset when I get on some anti-social stuff."

"I got enough spirit for the both of us, plus some more. Hey, let me get some sugar before I break out," Shateek said as he slid the shower curtain aside.

They kissed.

Shateek relished the touch of her wanting lips as if they were as sweet and delicious as a milk chocolate candy bar. Before he knew it, his hormones were raging out of control. He gently pulled from the kiss, his breathing accelerated, his joint rock hard. "Ahh shit. Now look what we done went and did?" He quickly started getting undressed.

"What are you doing?" Dinasia said smilingly and felt she'd done something naughty because she knew her 'get it while it's hot kiss' would provoke this sort of response. "You're gonna be late for work."

"So what, when you're the boss," Shateek excitedly tossed his clothing to the floor. "You can barge in at anytime you want and can't no body say a damn thing." He stepped in the shower butt naked with only his black dress socks on.

They kissed passionately as their bodies rubbed against each other in a slippery rhythmic fashion.

"Didn't you get enough last night?" Dinasia asked through the kiss.

"How Barry White said it? Can't get enough of your love, baby." He guided himself inside of her. It was ecstasy as always.

Dinasia was about to ask Shateek point blank what was up with their anniversary, but changed her mind when Shateek touched her gee spot in such a delicate and unique way, it activated electrical sparks all throughout her whole body.

*   *   *   *

Tislam pulled the collar of his green state-issued coat up against the late September breeze. As he circled the F and G Block yard of the Green Haven Correctional Facility, an inmate wearing wire framed glasses and sporting a neatly trimmed goatee by the name of Cheops was along side of him. They spoke to each other, their voices in a low tone just above a whisper.

"He's coming to the gym tonight," Cheops said. "Spade talked to his man and from the way it looks, he's rocked to sleep."

Tislam said nothing for a long moment, in deep thought. "How much did you say this hit is worth?"

"A face scar is two hundred dollars. If we send him out with stab wounds, it goes to five. If he goes to the outside hospital with major injuries, it's a thousand. They don't want him dead at the moment. They want him to suffer some first. So if we kill him, we get nothing."

Tislam sighed loudly. He hated this type of hit. In fact, he despised doing any kind of hits. Although 99.9% of all the cats that got it deserved it, this wasn't what Tislam was all about and was fully aware this was his way of letting off some steam.

After he almost died from the stab wound, which required major surgery and a stay in the Rikers Island hospital for two months, he decided to live. This sudden change of heart was attributed to the vision he saw as he laid on that dirty jail house floor bleeding. It was a woman who looked just like him, and without moving her mouth, she told him to go back while pointing at something he couldn't make out, but his subconscious told him it was something awaiting him in the future. He never met his mother, but he knew that's who it was. It had to be. Tislam decided he wanted to live and to find out what the vision was referring to.

After he blew trial and was sentenced to 30 years to life, and sent to Green Haven Correctional Facility, he was devastated, walking around as if he was in a world of delirium and derangement. To make matters even worse, his foster mom and pop abandoned him. That didn't really surprise him at all because there was no blood link, and therefore, no obligation to provide life time support.

The minute Tislam arrived at Green Haven, a contract hit crew called "Happy Hits Incorporated", who heard of his little fiasco on Rikers Island, wanted him to join up with them. Tislam rejected the offer. The missing tooth and fat Latino booty bandits he stabbed on the Island had reputations that spanned across the whole New York State prison system, and when

Tislam defeated them, he developed a reputation of his own. Cheops, Spade, Flipper and Chico Rico tried daily to get him involved with them without any luck. Upon receiving a letter from Keisha informing him that Dinasia married Shateek, Tislam joined the hit crew.

For years, he wrote letters to Keisha and Dinasia's foster family in a desperate attempt to find out Dinasia's whereabouts, and to get a letter to her. He made this a weekly ritual and never received a response, except that one time from Keisha regarding Dinasia's marriage to one of his archenemies. When he received this letter, he began writing almost everyday until it caused Keisha and the Shepard family to file complaints with the police, who in turn contacted the prison authorities. The prison administration threatened to put Tislam in the box if he continued to write, and then monitored his outgoing mail, intercepting any correspondence addressed to Keisha or the Shepard family.

Two weeks ago, Tislam finally decided to throw in the towel. He finally recognized it was a useless pursuit of a dream that would never be. Dinasia was gone, his life was forever screwed and it was sheer stupidity to keep chasing Dinasia because all it was doing was making his life a living hell. It hurt beyond description, but he had to get on with his miserable life and let Dinasia get on with hers. Hurting Dinasia was something he didn't want to do and trying to pull her back to him under these circumstances was bound to hurt her, so he knew he had to pull back. This is why he figured if she was happily married, he couldn't be the one to cause her any pain by attempting to shatter that happiness. He vowed to never write her or anyone connected to her again.

Tislam was so adamant about his newfound energy and position, he wrote to his counselor and told him to avoid, intercept and disregard any and all contact by anyone who was not on his approved correspondence and visiting lists. Since there was no one on either of these listings, the obvious implication was that he wanted to cut himself off from the whole outside world. Even though he knew it didn't make much sense for him to go to this extreme because no one was going to write or visit him anyway, but it made him feel good; like he was in charge of something that affected his life and was taking action against the pain in his heart, and that, in and of itself, had a therapeutic effect on his battered spirit and will. It made him feel alive.

Unfortunately, Tislam didn't realize this meant the prison officials were now authorized to discard all incoming mail and to turn down any and all visits "without further notice to the inmate", which put him in a very, very precarious position.

"Yo, Tislam!" Cheops said when Tislam failed to respond to his question. He noticed Tislam was daydreaming again. "Wake up, man. You probably ain't hear a damn thing I said. How the hell can you daydream and walk at the same time?"

"Pardon me," Tislam headed towards a bench near the "Iron Gods" weight court. "Let's chill over here." He sat down on the bench and so did Cheops.

"I hope you ain't stressin' over that broad Dinasia again. I thought you said you was over that."

"She ain't no fuckin' broad," he said with an angry smirk. "So don't call her that. And for your information, I was mappin' out the hit on this clown inside my head."

"Well that's why I'm out here with you, to map this shit out. I'm gonna ask you again since you apparently didn't hear me . . . Flipper and Chico Rico think you should be the lead hitter on this one. We need that thousand dollars, and with you takin' the lead, we'll definitely get it. That'll be two hundred dollars each and only ten seconds of work. You with it?"

Tislam was surprised they wanted him to take the lead, but didn't show it. "What's your's and Spade's opinion on this? You know I ain't in to the business of pulling blows. So before you answer my question, I'm lettin' you know, I'm not gonna tone it down one single bit. If that motherfucker spazz out, I'm gonna take it to the limit."

Cheops smiled. "That's exactly why we all agreed you should be the lead."

Tislam didn't like the way Cheops said that. It sounded like there was something they weren't telling him. But the information he accumulated on their target told him this run wouldn't be any different from all the others. "Well I guess it's a done deal. I take the lead."

As they structured a step-by-step plan of action, Tislam realized he was getting a strange vibe and wondered should he ignore it? His ego was his guide and he swept the invading sensation away as if it was dirt being tucked under a rug.

CHAPTER # 12

At 7:35 p.m., Dinasia pulled her cranberry colored Mitsubishi into the driveway of Shabazz's five-car garage and parked behind a tan colored Ford Taurus. The ride from Queens to Westchester was so hectic this evening she was still suffering from gridlock stress. The garage was filled to capacity and six additional cars were parked in front of the driveway while several others were parked on the side and in front of the mansion.

Dinasia saw her husband's blue Cherokee Jeep and Keisha's red BMW as she got out of the car and headed towards the front door. As she approached, Dinasia could hear Luther Vandross's soft voice coming from the audio equipment inside the house. Her eyes danced about the elegant structure because every time she laid eyes on this million-dollar two-story mansion, she had to admit Shabazz knew how to enjoy life and how to squeeze it for everything it was worth. She rang the doorbell.

The door was snatched open.

"SURPRISE!"

Dinasia had a dumbfounded look on her face when she saw a mob of faces with party hats and drinks in their hands. With a smile, she instantly put the pieces together before the crowd shouted: "HAPPY ANNIVERSARY!"

Shateek rushed to her with a smile bigger than hers. "I got yah, didn't I!?" He gave her a soft kiss that lasted about ten seconds, while the crowd cheered and clapped their hands at the sight. After taking Dinasia's coat, Shateek escorted her to the table of food while speaking. "Since the date of our anniversary falls on a week day, I figured, it would be best to push the party up and surprise you at the same time. And this is a Friday, which is the appropriate day for a party. Get yourself something to eat and I'll be right back." He headed towards the kitchen.

As Dinasia fixed herself a big plate of food, selecting from a mass array of all sorts of seafood, raw vegetables, fruits and exotic salads, she saw Keisha on the other side of the room talking to her husband, Herbert. When they made eye contact, Keisha rushed over.

"Dinasia, how's my girl?" Keisha said as she hugged her. "So what's up? Just look at this. I know you're enjoying yourself."

Herbert, Keisha's wimpy husband, came over. "Hello, Dinasia." He extended his hand and she shook it. "Happy anniversary."

"Thank you, Herbert." Dinasia said. "I'm glad you guys showed up."

"We wouldn't miss this even if they paid us," Keisha said. "Excuse me, Herbert, I have to talk to Dinasia in private," She pulled Dinasia towards the patio as Herbert turned and headed for the bar, so glad he could now sneak himself a couple of solid shots of rum.

Dinasia sensed there was something wrong as they stepped outside. The night chill activated her senses. "Is everything all right?"

"Yeah, I just wanted to tell you." she paused. "Your foster uncle Kirk is in the hospital. They admitted him two days ago. Not that you really give a shit. I just wanted to let you know. I was searching through the database and I saw his name. You know, I went up there to see him, and that old nasty bastard had the nerve to make a pass at me. The man is dying of AIDS and is still flirting with every piece of pussy that crosses his path."

"Well, some people never learn. Ever since he got into them drugs, he was always that type," Dinasia was surprised she felt a slight pain in her heart. "I guess his life style is finally catching up with him . . . I'm truly sorry to hear that. Is there anything else?"

"No."

"Let's get back inside, it's cold out here." She led the way and Keisha followed.

The night was going somewhat smoother than Dinasia expected. Her and Charmaine didn't clash once, and even had a short friendly talk about childbearing. The gift opening session went extremely well and was the part Dinasia liked the most. Even though most of the things they received were useless or was stuff they would never use, nevertheless, she knew it was the thought that counted, and she loved everyone for not forgetting this wonderful day of their lives.

She felt extremely exhilarated. The mood was so highly charged, she even drank a couple glasses of Champagne. By 11:30 her head was spinning and she had to step outside for some fresh air.

Dinasia walked over to the pool. As she approached, she heard voices. It sounded like two men talking and laughing good-naturedly. They appeared to be on the other side of the six foot tall bushes that served as a sophisticated divider. The two were deeply into a conversation and Dinasia noticed it was Shateek's old buddies. Trigger and Watch Dog. When she heard Trigger mention Shateek's name, she decided to be nosy. She tiptoed over to the bushes and listened closely.

"I still don't know how Shateek pulled that shit off," Trigger said. "I thought he wanted Tislam to knock off Kirk. The way he rigged it up to make it look like Tislam killed Prince was some real swift shit, man."

"It's what you might call caught in the cross," Watch Dog said unwavering. After two years in a speech therapy class, his stuttering problem was under control and returned only when he became extremely upset or excited. "I doubt if Shateek wanted him to kill Prince. I think he was just in the wrong place at the wrong time."

Dinasia felt an explosive wave of wide-eyed disbelief. The shock engulfed her whole body. Her forehead was instantly bathed in perspiration despite the cool breeze. The bafflement was rapidly growing into something indescribable.

"You know something?" Trigger said. "This shit has been fucking with my head ever since it happened. When that guy started shooting at Prince, I could've sworn I saw Shateek look like he was more shocked than even I was. For a second, it looked like Sha didn't know what the hell was going on."

"That's because Shateek ain't no dummy, bet that shit. He's sharp on his toes like that. Any wise man would act like he didn't know what's going on. Murder ain't no lightweight crime. People who conspire to commit murder get just as much time as the dude pulling the trigger."

There was a long pause as the two sipped on their glasses of wine.

Trigger broke the silence. "You know something. It seems like the older I get the more I feel sorry for Tislam. I can't imagine spending the rest of my life in prison for some shit I didn't do. Boy, I know this shit got his ass stressed the fuck outta his mind."

"But . . . Home team gotta handle that shit." Watch Dog said. "I feel for him, but that's the way the ball bounces . . . At least we know Shateek definitely ain't complaining."

"And you know that shit," Trigger said.

Watch Dog took another swig of the wine and continued. "All that crazy shit Sha did to get with Dinasia," He paused while shaking his head. "Paying crack-head broads to play with the woman's head and all that craziness is just too much for me. Dinasia must got some right death defying pussy to have a motherfucker going crazy like that. That could never happen to the kid cause as far as I'm concern, ain't no bitch that bad."

Trigger laughed. "But you gotta admit one thing, big Sha ain't stop loving his Dinasia. He probably loves her more now than back in the day. At least he did keep it real with her, staying faithful with that one-woman shit. He damn sure didn't lie when he said she was gonna--"

SNAPP!

Dinasia inadvertently stepped on a twig. She hastily turned and quickly tiptoed away from the bushes while in a state of sheer shock and confusion. A white-hot rage was already spreading all over her body.

"There's somebody on the other side of these damn bushes." Trigger said, about to make a hole in the bushes so he could peek through, but changed his mind when he realized the bushes looked too well groomed to treat like any ordinary bushes.

When Dinasia heard Trigger's comment, she increased her pace, heading back to the house with full intentions of slapping the living shit out of Shateek. *That dirty bastard set this whole shit up?* She wiped a runaway tear away from her face. A hundred things flashed through her mind, and with each second that passed, her urge to do something terrible to Shateek grew rapidly. *How could he do something as wicked as put an innocent man in prison for a murder?*

Just before she was about to enter the house, Dinasia slowed her pace. Something in the back of her mind told her to calm down and think because making a scene wasn't going to do anything but make matters worse. Nor would it solve anything. She did a U turn and sat at the patio table next to the pool.

Dinasia drew deep breaths of air as her mind began to function in a rational fashion. She started analyzing the situation from different angles, searching for a way to handle this without scratching Shateek's eyes out of his head.

"Hey, Dinasia,"

Dinasia turned and saw it was Shabazz. He was thirty-four years old with a face that was smooth and cheerful. He looked older than his age, and his hair was not as curly as his baby brother's, but their eyes, nose and cheekbones were a perfect match. "How are you, Shabazz?"

'What are you doing out here without a jacket? I don't want you getting sick and driving my brother up the wall . . . You look upset, is everything all right?"

'I'm okay. I just needed a little fresh air. It's my allergies. This is hay-fever season, remember."

"Looks like you got a lot on your mind."

"Oh yes, there's a lot on my mind." At that moment, the way to deal with this whole thing suddenly came to her. Just looking at Shabazz and being reminded of how sneaky, shrewd and effective he was in the way he handled things turned on a bright light in her head.

Dinasia rose to her feet with a smile, looped her arm inside of Shabazz's and headed back inside the house. She spoke in a soft tone of voice. "There's so much on my mind, Shabazz, that I'm gonna have to find a way to unleash--ah, I mean unload all this stuff inside my head."

CHAPTER # 13

Tislam entered the gym and headed for the weight room. He saw Spade and Chico Rico over by the bleachers amongst a crowd of inmates getting ready to play a game of basketball. Tislam saw Spade's hand signal. *Good.* Everything was in place. This was Tislam's fifth hit, but his heart still pounded in his chest and the nervous tension in the pit of his stomach was there as well.

When Tislam entered the weight room, he saw Cheops and Flipper were in place. On the left side of the huge room, working out at the shoulder press machine was the target, Reggie Watson. He had on a red tank top shirt and black leather workout gloves. Tislam realized he now looked a lot bigger, more muscular.

The thought of what Reggie was in prison for resurfaced in Tislam's mind and it caused his anger mounting. Any person who would rape and kill a twelve-year-old child didn't deserve hospitalization as a punishment, but needed to be castrated. Cheops' people on the other side of the wall— the source of all the hits—wanted to play mind games with this perverted fucking freak. Tislam, on the other hand, didn't feel Reggie's proposed punishment was appropriate, and therefore, planned to implement what he thought would suffice; castration.

Tislam inconspicuously pulled the 9-inch shank while he was in back of Reggie, now moving rapidly towards the target.

"Reg!!" A prisoner on the other side of the room shouted.

All hell suddenly broke loose.

Cheops and Flipper pulled their shanks and both stabbed the guy who yelled to Reggie. After he fell to the floor, they made the other prisoners remain calm and not rush out of the gym. Spade was at the entrance of the gym and pushed two of the panic-stricken inmates back inside. They knew C.O. Hunt would turn the other cheek, but C.O. Garrison wouldn't because he wasn't on the take.

Meanwhile, Tislam charged at Reggie, stabbing and jabbing at him. Reggie went into a karate blocking routine, deflecting all of Tislam's carefully aimed body shots. Tislam's eyes squinted in confusion mixed with realization.

As Tislam was sizing up Reggie for another wave of stab attempts, his mind put the pieces together. *So this is why everybody wanted me to take the lead. This motherfucker knows the arts and they didn't think they could handle him.* Just throw ole crazy ass Tislam out on the front-line; test the waters with the new guy, huh? But he had a surprise for them because they didn't know he knew the arts as well.

Tislam never told any of his comrades about his past martial arts training and wanted to keep this ace in the hole hidden. But that wasn't gonna be possible because Tislam had no intentions of letting this run go to waste and he definitely wasn't going to let a child molester whip him.

Tislam unleashed a spinning roundhouse kick and caught Reggie in the head, dropping him to the floor. Reggie sprung back to his feet and kicked Tislam in the stomach, flinging him backwards.

"Hurry up, Tislam!" Spade shouted from the door. "Garrison is about to do his rounds!"

"Why y'all coming at me, man?" Reggie said, backing away from Tislam. "I ain't do nothing to you, man."

"Shut the fuck up, you fucking perverted coward!" Tislam kicked Reggie into the wall. "You like raping little helpless children, huh?" Tislam snapped kicked him in the face. The blow took Reggie down to the floor hard and fast.

"Wait! Wait!" Reggie raised the palms of his hands. "I didn't do it! I didn't do that to that kid! They set me up! I'm a scapegoat, man! I swear to God, I didn't do it, man!"

Tislam was about to plunge the knife in his chest, but Reggie's comment stopped him in his tracks. That plea sounded too sincere. Tislam could instantly identify with the feeling of being a scapegoat; he was the epitome of one. Plus, he vowed never to inflict harm on an innocent person. And since there were so many innocent black folks in prison nowadays, there was no way of telling by just looking at a person. If this guy could prove he didn't do it, Tislam was going to give him the benefit of the doubt.

"He's coming!" Spade said in a restrained, but excited whisper. "We gotta go, now! Come on!"

"Finish him, Tis!" Cheops shouted as he headed towards the entrance. "Do it! Now!"

As Cheops and Flipper rushed out of the gym, Tislam stepped away from Reggie and said, "If you're telling the truth, come to the yard tonight." Tislam tucked the shank in his waist while moving backward towards the entrance. "I'll listen, and if you're telling the truth, you'll be all right."

And with that Tislam disappeared out of the gym.

*　　*　　*　　*

That evening in the east-side yard.

Tislam stared at Reggie after he finished explaining all the outlandish things the police and D.A.'s office had done to him. Tislam looked over at Cheops and Chico Rico and saw their facial expressions said they weren't going to believe this guy no matter what he said. Tislam, on the other hand, knew if this guy was really a black community activist, everything he said was probably true. "And you think they did this to you because of your work in the community?"

"I'm absolutely certain that's the reason." Reggie wanted to start pacing, but controlled the urge. "Several years ago, I exposed three money schemes where various councilmen from the 23rd district were in cahoots with an organized crime family. They were stealing money from the community, and because of my endeavors, two of them were arrested and the scheme dismantled. Afterwards, I received several threatening phone calls from a mysterious person claiming I would pay for what I did. It's all here in these documents." He handed Tislam two thick folders.

Cheops snatched them. "How we know you ain't trying to play us," He opened the folder and started reading.

Chico Rico spoke as he stepped closer to Reggie. "Anybody can rig up a bunch of documents. And a motherfucker in your shoes would do anything about now to get this fire off his ass."

Silent pause.

Tislam felt Reggie was telling the truth, but knew the others would want more proof. "What else you got? You got anything else besides these documents?"

Reggie sighed. "I know this sounds crazy, but this is all the evidence I have to show I was set-up. In another month, my new lawyer is going to get a court order so my blood and the blood at the scene of the murder can be re-tested by a different lab. I assure you those results will exonerate me. Give me until then and you'll see. I'm innocent, man."

Tislam felt in his bones Reggie was telling the truth. Reggie would have to be the best actor in the world to provoke that much sincerity and convincing bodily gestures. Tislam decided to save him. "Check it out, Reggie, I'll get with you in a couple minutes. We need to talk in private." When Reggie gestured for the return of his folder Tislam continued. "Meet me by the pull-up bar. I'll bring the folders with me."

As Reggie walked away, Cheops spoke. "I see it in your face, Tislam. You believe this piece of shit. Why the fuck can't you see this nigga's tryin' to play us?"

"I don't think so," Tislam said calmly. "You know when black folks get involved in helping the community they become targets for shit like this. I think he's telling the truth. What's your opinion on this Chico?"

"No comment."

Cheops said, "I'll take that as you believe he's lying. That's two against one so far."

Tislam knew Cheops wasn't gonna give up an inch on this one since money was involved. They were hungry because they hadn't received a hit in two months, and so Tislam cut to the chase. "I say we hold off and see what happens with those tests." Tislam paused while scrutinizing Cheops' reaction. When he saw the smirk, he let his heart and gut instinct take control. "And even if I'm out voted . . . I'm gonna hold him down."

"Oh, so you're flippin' on family now?" Cheops said in a fatherly fashion. "Over some clown ass pervert you're gonna put your neck on the chopping block? Come on man, you know the rule, Tislam. Once we go this far with a hit, there's no turning back. My contacts ain't tryin' to hear it."

"Come on, Cheops, knock it off," Tislam said. "We called off a hit before and we can do the same with this one. You just letting your greed get the best of you--"

"This ain't about money!" Cheops said. "This is about keeping our word and our reputation right."

Tislam paused. "I'm in here for a murder I didn't do. I know what that man is going through. If you ain't never been in that type of predicament, you'll never know the feeling."

"But why put yourself in harms way?" Cheops said. "You don't even know this motherfucker. He could be a professional liar. My connects are gonna find out why we didn't hit this chump no matter what I say. Why put yourself and all of us in harms way for this guy?"

"Let's just say I gotta spiritual connection to people who are victims of circumstance. If we was really family, you would back me all the way on this one. Whatever you decide, my mind is made up. I'm not gonna let this guy get hurt and I'm gonna hold him down to the bitter end." Tislam took the folders from Cheops, turned and headed towards the pull-up bar.

Cheops smiled as he watched Tislam leave.

"So what's your prognosis on this, boss?" Chico Rico said, trying to make a joke out of the situation. "I told you Tislam got a lot of psychological luggage and skeletons in his closet. Bro is too fuckin' sensitive for this type of work."

"If I ain't like this kid," Cheops said as he headed towards the weight courts. "I would throw his ass to the wolves. Instead, I guess I'll throw him to the dogs."

CHAPTER # 14

Dinasia entered the library on 42nd Street and 5th Avenue and headed for the Directory. This establishment was the biggest library in New York City and probably the largest in the whole State of New York. She was searching for the Law Department or any section that would provide her with information on how to investigate a criminal case.

The date was November 3rd, and ever since that dreadful day in September when she overheard Trigger and Watch Dog talking about Tislam's unfortunate situation, she'd been on the move. From that moment on, she tried not to reveal to Shateek what she knew since she strategically decided to keep her endeavors secret, but the rage was truly overwhelming and would come out every so often.

She decided to get Tislam out of that place even if it took her the rest of her life. From her perspective, it was logical to assume if Tislam wasn't the actual gun man and people were looking out of their windows just before shots were fired, then someone had to see what really happened. Since Shateek's brother, Freddie Davis, at the time of the shooting was a police sergeant (now a Lieutenant), she knew facts and circumstances could've obviously been manipulated. She felt in her bones there were people out there who knew the truth and she intended to find them.

The following day after this mind-boggling discovery Dinasia made close to a hundred phone calls, trying desperately to find Tislam's whereabouts. She even called numerous lawyers. By the end of the day, she found out Tislam was in Green Haven and the chances of getting him freed at this late stage in the case didn't look good at all. All twenty lawyers she spoke to indicated the only way to create a half ass fighting chance of freeing Tislam was to find some irrefutable evidence of his innocence. When repeatedly asked, "Would these men you overheard discussing Mr. Parker's innocence be willing to come forth?" She told them all "I doubt that very seriously."

She knew Trigger and Watch Dog would never turn on Shateek. Even she oddly felt duty bound not to flip on her husband because she knew he did it only because he loved her. But she noticed she was gradually developing an emotion towards him that was similar to hatred, although not as blindingly strong. Her love for Tislam re-surfaced and began to grow with unusual and grueling force. The second she heard he was innocent, it was like an explosion of mixed emotions swarmed all over her body and made her feel faint.

The heart wrenching pain of knowing she didn't believe him was the most agonizing sensation of all the other nagging emotions. She broke down in tears every time that mental picture entered her head of Tislam being dragged off the Rikers Island visiting floor while screaming and pleading with her not to leave him. At such delicate moments she had to get far away from Shateek or else she would have killed him.

A different form of tears flowed when she searched her old trunk in the basement, which contained all her old things, and found the Super Ninja necklace. When she got a flashback of the day she was about to throw the necklace in the trash, and remembered how that powerful vibe and the voice in the back of her head wouldn't let her discard it, the feeling frightened her very deeply. She didn't believe in ESP (Extrasensory perception) or telepathy, but that mysterious force that made her hang on to the necklace must've had a clairvoyant origin. She put the necklace on and knew this time it would never come off again.

For a straight month she wrote Tislam a letter twice a week; each one was returned with a note from the prison instructing her not to write anymore. She visited once and was denied entry into the facility. When she was told by the guard at the front gate: "Until Mr. Parker signs a form lifting the bar on his visitation privileges, I advise you not to come here anymore", she started searching for other ways to get word to him and learned the hard way there were none.

Dinasia contacted Tislam's foster family and surprisingly discovered they cut him off. Then she searched the Internet, randomly selected a prisoner's name who was at Green Haven, wrote him, asking Mr. Clarence Rose 97A4167 to find and instruct Tislam to write her. When she received a letter from Clarence, she opened the letter with trembling hands, read it and tossed it in the trash because Clarence was trying to hit on her and claimed he didn't know Tislam and had no way of finding him. She tried the same thing with several other inmates with similar results. So far, she received no response from Tislam.

In a last ditch effort, she waited in the prison employee parking lot during shift change and tried to get a black Correction Officer to give Tislam a message. The CO was about to have her arrested for bribery, but she talked her way out of the situation.

As the days went by, she became more and more desperate.

Just last week she took a leave of absence from work in order to dedicate 100% of her time learning how to re-investigate Tislam's case. After hiring two private investigators, which produced nothing of any significance, she realized if this thing was going to get done the right way, it was going to take her doing it herself. She knew there was no one on this planet that would give all within his or her power and go the extra miles in the same fashion as she would, and therefore, she committed herself to this task without the slightest hesitation.

Looking at the huge directory on the wall near the security counter, Dinasia found what she was searching for. The Legal Department was on the second floor in the western region. Two minutes later, she stepped inside the law library. There were rolls of bookshelves, long tables with chairs all around them and several dozen people scattered about with their heads bowed while reading. Dinasia knew she was going to need some assistance finding what she needed and headed for one of the clerks, who wasn't helping someone else.

"Good afternoon," The clerk said; her smooth smile and aqua blue eyes made her look like she was born to be the nicest clerk in the City of New York. "May I help you?"

Dinasia smiled back. "Yes. I'm looking for some materials on how to investigate a criminal case."

"That would be in section number four, aisle eleven and twelve." She pointed towards her right. "It's located right behind this section, you can't miss it."

"Thank you," Dinasia followed the woman's instructions. When she saw each aisle looked almost as long as a City block, she sighed and went straight to work.

As she pulled books (reading the table of contents or the index and then putting them on the side if she thought they were good or putting others back on the shelf if they were rejected), she felt a profound sense of accomplishment. She knew it was nothing more than a psychological response to the subconscious belief she was in the process of altering a gross wrong.

When she accumulated a stack of nine good textbooks and instructor's manuals, she sat and began reading. After reading the first few chapters in an instructor's manual titled "Universal Investigatory Tactics" by Professor Dennis Thomas, who had Masters' degrees in Law Enforcement, Political Science and Constitutional Law, she was able to reduce her research time in half because there were limited tactics available at this stage in Tislam's case.

The most important assets to an investigator, she learned, were good credible witnesses. The availability of adequate financial resources was another crucial element to the effectiveness of an investigation, and now she was glad she didn't make waves with Shateek because she was going to finally drain his pockets dry. He complained constantly about her not enjoying all the money he was making, but that would change. She liked that idea of draining his pockets bone dry. The justice aspect of such a punishment could serve his ass just right. She smiled as she wrote down the pages in the book she intended to photocopy.

Next, she learned a series of other important techniques; how to conduct site visits, locating witnesses, developing contacts, fact gathering efforts, tactics for interviewing witnesses, and working with a theory of defense or approach in mind.

Within two hours she chose the sections in each book, photocopied them and then hit the shelves again until she came in contact with twenty-five textbooks, instructor's manuals, and other miscellaneous materials. Her book-researching endeavor was completed when she realized all other books were now repeating information she already possessed.

Next, she hit the Internet. An hour of surfing the World Wide Web and she was able to terminate her studies for the day, since she found nothing new. As she exited the library, on her way home, she knew the real work didn't even start yet because now she had to go home, read all the photocopied materials, and begin the process of committing this stuff to memory.

An hour and ten minutes later, Dinasia entered her home.

"That you, Dinasia?" Shateek shouted from the upstairs study room.

As she took off her coat and hung it in the closet, she wanted to say: "What the fuck you think? You trifling no hearted bastard!" But instead she simply said, "Yeah, it's me. Who else would it be?" She realized she had to work a little harder on her snotty attitude.

"You're late. Is everything all right?"

She heard him coming down the stairs and she went to the kitchen to prepare a quick bite to eat. Shateek was rapidly approaching, and just before he opened his mouth, she said with excessive force. "I'm not in the mood. I had a long day and I don't wanna talk about it." She saw Shateek was confused, but he said nothing else. He did an about face and disappeared back up the stairs.

After gobbling down two tuna fish sandwiches and a glass of fresh squeezed orange and pineapple juice, Dinasia went straight to work.

Upon entering her workroom, she noticed the strategically positioned chair was moved. She suspected Shateek was snooping around, trying to find out why all of a sudden she was so hostile towards him, but she couldn't prove it. The moving of her stuff confirmed her suspicion since her little trap apparently worked. He was prying into her business by prowling about. Her first reaction was to go upstairs and start a fight. After pondering the pros and cons of creating more tension, she constrained her urge to approach him.

She checked her safe and the locks on her file cabinets. They were intact. She sat down at her desk, read for two minutes and noticed her eyes felt like they were throbbing; even her neck muscles were sore. *A full body massage would sure be nice*, she muttered silently to herself. When she imagined herself receiving one of Shateek's famous alcohol rubdowns, she angrily shoved it away with a loud sigh.

By 12 o'clock she'd developed a solid plan of action, which would begin bright and early in the morning. Out of the four activities the re-canvassing of the Pink House Projects was the one that provoked the most anxiety. She yawned and forced herself to call it a night.

Gathering all her materials to be tucked away inside the safe, Dinasia wondered if there was anyone from the neighborhood who really saw what happened. And if so, would they be willing to cooperate?

As she headed out of the room, on her way to the bathroom to get ready for bed, she also wondered, was there a way to get her hands on a gun?

CHAPTER # 15

Tislam was sweeping his cell floor with a small hand broom when he heard the approaching footsteps. It was cell clean up time for his gallery. Since his cell was the last one on the gallery, and most prisoners knew the area was off limits, he stopped sweeping and stood up.

It was Reggie Watson.

"What up, Tislam?" Reggie said cheerfully. "I came to check you out before I leave. Tomorrow's the big day."

"How'd you get on this gallery? Ain't that ass-hole C.O. Jones working the O.I.C?"

"Yeah, but I had C.O. Garrison talk to him for me. You know damn well I wasn't gonna leave this place without kicking it with you one last time."

"We just kicked it a couple hours ago."

"Yeah, I know, but you know how that is man. I ain't never been the type of person who had a lot of friends in my life. So I guess I don't know how to act when it's time to say good-bye. Plus I gotta thank you for everything--"

"You already thanked me a thousand--I meant a million times already . . . Come on in and have a seat."

Reggie sat at the bottom of the bed while Tislam leaned up against the locker.

This was the first time Reggie ever seen Tislam's cell. He wasn't the least surprised when he saw dozens of pictures of Dinasia plastered on the cell walls. "So did you change your mind about trying to write her again?"

"Come on, Reg. I told you that's a long lost dream world." Tislam's whole demeanor changed when he stared at the 8 by 10 picture on his right hand side. Years ago when he was on Rikers Island, Tislam had his foster brother Allen send up all his pictures of Dinasia. When he got up-state, Tislam sent the pictures out to one of those photo labs and got them copied in all sizes.

Reggie felt a pain in his heart at the way Tislam looked when he spoke about Dinasia. "You never know, maybe if you drop her a line again--"

"Why would I keep opening a wound that's starting to heal?" Tislam didn't want to lash-out at Reggie, but if he kept up with the Dinasia issue, he was definitely going to let him have it. "She's happily married, probably got a kid on the way by now and . . ." He sat on the bed and sighed. "Please, Reg. Let's talk about something else, because if I start droppin' tears up in here like some kinda punk-ass cry-baby on a sensitize sucker for love mission, I'm gonna pound your gorilla looking ass out for bringing up this shit."

They both laughed.

"I don't know how you intend to do that without your crew." Reggie said smilingly. "You know my shit is tight right about now. I told you I been sharpening up my round house kicks."

"Keep talkin' that crazy shit and I'll sick Flipper on that ass." Tislam tried to keep the humor going. When he saw Reggie wasn't laughing, he stopped giggling. "Ahh, come on. It's a joke, man."

"You know I don't like that cat," Reggie selected his words carefully because Flipper and Tislam were extremely close. "The way that dude is always dissing me, trying to make me look like his bitch or something, I would love a one on one with his ass. If he wasn't your man, and wasn't down with Cheops, I'd lay one of these wicked flying kicks on his ass."

"As long as you packin' a butcher knife afterwards, you might live to talk about it. And even then there's a question of whether you'll use the damn thing correctly."

Short silent pause.

"I still wanna help you get a lawyer, Tis," Reggie said, changing the subject to a serious one, which was the actual reason he visited Tislam one last time. "But you gotta drop that restriction on--"

"Fuck that! I told you no!" Tislam said angrily. "I'm all right. What part you don't understand? I'm not gonna get my hopes all up just to be let down again. My case is nothing like yours. You were one of the lucky ones who had a DNA case."

"But giving up is not the way--"

"I said forget it!" Tislam's voice went down a notch or two. His eyes beamed with a vicious anger. There was a moment of silence, during which time Tislam was re-contemplating whether he should ask Reggie to do him a favor when he left tomorrow morning. It took only seconds to disregard the thought because he knew Reggie wasn't built for that type of activity. Then he said, "Let's talk about something else . . . Hey, I got this Kung Fu maneuver I wanted to show you. Come over here, let me show you . . ."

As Tislam explained the Kung Fu tactic, Reggie realized Tislam's pain was transmitted straight to his heart. That damn Dinasia fucked this brother's life up. If she only knew what she'd did to him when she abandoned him. The damage done to Tislam was permanent, and Reggie knew he was as good as dead because once the will to fight was gone the game was officially over. He wondered if his newfound anger towards Dinasia for what she'd done to Tislam was misdirected and had a rational basis?

When the ideas for implementing retribution re-entered Reggie's head, it made him pause because he still wasn't sure if the punishment he'd thought of was necessary.

*   *   *   *

Two days later.

Tislam, Spade and Flipper sat at a table in the back of the Auditorium watching TV. Their block (G-Block) had in-door Recreation for the night.

"You were right, Tis." Spade said through his strong southern accent. "It would've been kinda fucked up if we would've blazed that dude, Reggie." He shook his head, disbelievingly. "What got me fucked up is if he didn't have a new lawyer who was willing to get his DNA re-tested his ass would've been finished."

Flipper said, "Fuck that bitch ass nigga. That dude's a cold fuckin' coward. But I do have to admit, this is some real scary shit because that means the police and D.A. falsified his original test results." He redirected his attention back to the TV program, America's Funniest Home Videos.

"I'm just glad you two are independent thinkers." Tislam said. "If one of you would've voted with Cheops and Chico Rico, shit would've got real funky up in this piece."

Flipper was pulled back into the conversation. "You seriously was gonna hold Reggie down, huh?"

"No doubt about it," Tislam wondered if Flipper or Spade would've voted the other way if they weren't scheduled to see the Parole Board. He was about to ask them straight up, but decided to do it the diplomatic way; beat around the bush. Plus, he wanted them to do him a favor when they walked out the front door next week. They both made the Board and were built for the type of shit he wanted them to do. "What's the sense in being alive if you're not willing to stand for something that's right and exact?"

"Personally," Spade drawled. "I don't give a rat's ass about Scram Jones."

Flipper said, "And you know how I feel about that mothefucker."

"What made me vote the way I did," Spade continued, "was to prevent Cheops from sending a crew at you. Once I got wind of what went down, I knew if you lost the vote, your hard headed ass wasn't gonna pull back."

Flipper said, "Imagine if we would've let our crew fall to pieces because of a bullshit beef over some cat that ain't even down with us? The whole jail would've been callin' us a bunch of babblin' ass idiots if we would've went out like that." He paused, sighed and then continued. "And me and Spade damn sure couldn't afford to get into one of those no escape conflicts like that. If another click ran up on you, they would've had to run up on me and Spade as well. We brought you in and when we said it was one love, we meant that shit, baby pah."

That's what Tislam wanted to hear. He held back a smile. There was a saying called "one love" in the prison system, which had the same connotation as the "one for all, all for one" quote used by the Three Musketeers and when Tislam heard Flipper mentioned it, he knew the time was right. "You know something? You dudes are real brothers I never had." He tried to sound sentimental. "And that one love thang is something I take very seriously. And I hope it's an everlasting mutual promise from your standpoint. You guys are the best friends I ever had, and if I was leaving this place, you could bet your ass I would--"

"What is it, Tislam?" Flipper said, knowing he was buttering them up for something. "Stop jerking our chain and hit us with it."

"I need y'all to step to a few things for me when y'all leave next week and I--"

"Nigga you know we're there for you," Spade said, sounding like a hillbilly. "With that long drawn out song and dance about one love you just laid on us, makes me think you got doubts about us keeping it real when our feet touch New York."

"Hold up, hold up," Tislam said defensively. "I ain't insinuating nothing. All I'm doing is reminding you that we're homies for life . . . And I'm asking for a major favor."

"A major favor!?" Flipper said, making his voice sound like a Londonite with a decrepit British accent. "Why doesn't that quite surprise me?" He spoke directly to Spade. "My dear, Watson, I think he's got it. A case of the fuckin' please don't forget me syndrome."

They all laughed.

Spade spoke through his chuckles. "On the real ta real, tell us what you want and you got it?"

"As long as it ain't a genie," Flipper said. "Or three impossible wishes, I think we can firmly say whatever it is we can handle it."

Tislam slowly explained what he wanted, and as he spoke he noticed their facial expressions become stone like because they knew he was deadly serious when it came to this particular topic. They wouldn't dare play games with this delicate issue.

When Tislam finished speaking, Spade sighed and said, "I thought you were over this woman? I understand this is your childhood sweetheart and all, but what makes you think she's--"

"What the fuck is all that about!?" Tislam shouted as he rose to his feet, drawing attention to them, not caring who heard him. "Are you gonna do it or what!?"

"Of course we'll do it," Flipper said. "Now, calm your crazy strung out ass down."

"That's right," Spade reached over and pulled Tislam's arm, forcing him to sit back down. "It would be a pleasure to be of assistance to you, Tislam. We'll do the job so god-damn well, we'll make ghetto history. And that, my brother, ain't meant to be a fuckin' joke because I ain't laughin', smilin' or grinin'."

*   *   *   *

Dinasia knocked on the door of apartment number 3C in the building next to her foster family's building on Crescent Street. Dressed in a cheap blue goose down wind-breaker and wearing glasses, Dinasia hoped Ms. Tillman wouldn't recognize her. So far no one knew it was her.

"Who is it?" Ms. Tillman said as she looked through the peephole.

"Hello, Mrs. Tillman. My name is Cheryl Davis. I'm a law student at John Jay College and I'm doing research into a criminal case involving Paul Shepard. He was shot and killed approximately five years ago right out front of this building. I would like to know if I could ask you a few questions regarding that--"

"I'm sorry, but I know nothing about that incident."

"But your bedroom window faces the location where the shooting occurred." Dinasia persisted. "Your assistance could really help me with--"

"I'm sorry, I can't help you," Mrs. Tillman sounded impatient. "I wasn't home that night. I told the police this when they were investigating the case back then. Sorry, I can't help you. Good-bye."

"Thank you for your time, ma'am," Dinasia headed around the corner to 3E, Mrs. Rachel Morris's apartment.

Dinasia was hoping the Court files she read five days ago at the Kings County Supreme Court were wrong, but up to this point they weren't. The following day after reading all those textbooks on investigating a criminal case, she commenced with the three easy activities first. Her first stop was the Courthouse. She pulled all the files on Tislam's case classified as public records, which consisted of police reports, prosecution and defense motions, and the transcripts of the proceeding. It took her two whole days to read everything.

Afterwards, she went to the Kings County D.A.'s Office a block away from the courthouse and then across the Brooklyn Bridge to One Police Plaza in lower Manhattan, which was the main headquarters for the entire NYPD. Both visits were a complete waste of time since without a notarized authorization form from Tislam, giving her permission to handle his files, there was nothing either Agency could do to assist Dinasia with her request to view Tislam's records.

For the past two days, she'd been re-canvassing the apartments within the Pink House Projects. So far, the outcome was the same as that of the D.A. and Police Department visits. Yesterday, when she called it quits for the day, she started getting very nervous because there were only ten more apartments left that were in a position to see the shooting.

Just as Dinasia knocked on the door of 3E, the elevator door burst open. Her hand shot into her pocket and grasped the gun.

The weapon was a 25 automatic she purchased for a hundred and twenty dollars from a guy named Robert Sanchez, who worked at a pawnshop on Merrick Boulevard in Queens. Dinasia met Robert Sanchez when he came to the Social Service Agency seeking financial assistance, and she became his case worker. Three months later, he was back on his feet and no longer needed the Social Service Agency. He thanked Dinasia and insisted if she needed anything from the pawnshop to drop in anytime.

When Dinasia saw the three teenagers, her heart fluttered and a nervous perspiration instantly appeared on her forehead. Even her palm, which gripped the gun, started sweating, and she wondered should she pull the gun? Get the draw on these gang members before they pulled a gun on her? She heard about the gang problems in the Pink House Projects, and when these three teens started following her around, she suspected this would eventually happen.

"Hey, lady," The kid who wore a sheepskin coat and a matching hat said. "Is you a cop?"

A teenager who had on a blue wind-breaker said, "We don't like strangers comin' in our hood." The kid in the sheepskin coat elbowed him, and he suddenly realized he was talking too hastily.

Dinasia's mind raced. She wondered would it be wise to lie? If she told them she was a cop, would they leave her alone? Or would they attack her? Suddenly the images of cops being gunned down entered her mind and the indisputable fact the police was well hated in this community made her play it safe. "I'm a reporter doing an investigation on a shooting that occurred several years ba--"

Mrs. Rachel Morris opened her door. "Can I help you?" She peeked out her door to see who Dinasia was talking to and saw the three teens. "What are you doing, Johnny? Is everything all right, Miss?"

"Ahh, yes, yes everything's fine," Dinasia saw the three teens give her a menacing stare as they disappeared into the stairwell. With a smile Dinasia turned and saw Mrs. Morris still looked rather youthful for her age. Her streaks of gray filled her head, no longer unnoticeable only from a distance as they were five years ago.

"Well, what is it you want?" Mrs. Morris said. "Did you knock for any particular reason or was it to escape these bad ass, disrespectful kids?" She squinted her eyes as if she was trying to place Dinasia's face.

"Yes, I'm investigating a homicide that happened in front of this--"

"You're the Police?" Mrs. Morris sounded more distrustful than surprised.

"No, no, I'm a law student at John Jay College and I'm doing a final paper on the shooting death of Paul Shepard and I wanted to--"

"That's where I remember you from," Mrs. Morris said. "You're that foster child. The Shepard's foster child. Girl, I never forget a face. You sure look like you haven't aged much. Come on in."

After Dinasia entered, Mrs. Morris bolted the locks on the door and then escorted her to the living room. Mrs. Morris spoke with a kind smile. "It's sure a pleasure to see you, child. I never had the chance to tell you, but I always liked you. What's your name again?"

"Dinasia."

"Yes, that's right, I remember it now. That sure is a beautiful name, yes it is." She gestured for Dinasia to sit on the sofa while she sat in a matching arm chair. "So what made you go back to College? I heard you graduated and was supposed to be working somewhere in Queens?"

Dinasia knew now she had to come clean and since she never expected anyone to remember her, much less know what was going on in her life, she felt like she was caught off guard. "Actually, Mrs. Morris, I'm not a college student. I'm sorry for not being truthful up front, but I am investigating the shooting death of my foster brother, Prince--Ah, I mean Paul. I recently discovered the man who they have in prison for the murder is really innocent."

Mrs. Morris paused. "Is that the young man you were going out with?"

"Yes," Dinasia saw the sad, pained and nervous expression on Mrs. Morris face as if she was suddenly reminded of something terrible. When she began fiddling with her fingers, Dinasia was compelled to inquire. "Is everything all right, Mrs. Morris?"

Mrs. Morris frowned, making a weird facial expression similar to someone who just been bombarded with a mouthful of raw lemon juice. "So that means you seen the tape I guess. We wanted to do something," She started speaking fast, "but, but those men threatened us. I insisted we do something even though they would hurt or kill us. They told us if we went to the--"

"Please slow down, Mrs. Morris," Dinasia couldn't believe what she was hearing. "I don't understand what you're saying." However, enough was said for Dinasia to realize Mrs. Morris obviously knew something of extreme importance concerning the case. She struggled to control the wave of excitement that grabbed hold of her. "What men are you talking about? What tape? What do you mean by 'we'? Who else is there?"

Mrs. Morris realized she spoke too hastily because it was evident Dinasia knew nothing about what happened. She stood and walked to the window, looking out. "I'm sorry, I--I can't . . . I can't discuss it." She abruptly turned, facing Dinasia. "I have to ask you to leave. I can't get involved in this. Just forget I ever mentioned anything to you--"

"Mrs. Morris, please. You obviously know something." Dinasia stood, approaching Mrs. Morris. "You know the man who's in prison for that murder is innocent, don't you? You just mentioned a tape? What tape? Please tell me. Is it a tape of the shooting? Please Mrs. Morris you have to help--"

"Leave!" Mrs. Morris shouted as she rushed towards Dinasia and grabbed her arm. "Get out of my--"

"Please Mrs. Morris," Dinasia resisted Mrs. Morris's gentle pull on her arm. "If you are a woman of principle, who has morals and a heart you must--"

"Leave or I'll call the police!" she screamed belligerently as she let go of Dinasia's arm, heading for the door.

Dinasia reluctantly gave into Mrs. Morris's hysteria and slowly followed her to the door. She wanted to get on her knees and beg and plead with Mrs. Morris, but Dinasia saw she was too frantic and beyond the realm of reason. Dinasia could feel her mind gradually entering desperate territories. She stuffed her hand into her coat, grabbed the gun and just before pulling it out, the rational side of her mind told her to relax. With an effort, she let go of the gun.

When she stepped through the threshold and the door slammed behind her, Dinasia turned and just stood staring at the door speechless for a couple of seconds with a pitiful dumbfounded look on her face. She saw Mrs. Morris looking through the peephole. "Mrs. Morris, if you do nothing to help this man, you're just as guilty as all the others who did this to him." She remembered Mrs. Morris was a religious woman and hoped her next shot would hit its mark. "God will never forgive you if you continue to allow him to suffer. If you have it in your power to stop it, you're committing a sin if you turn a blind eye."

Short pause, silence.

A couple of seconds later, Dinasia heard Mrs. Morris walk away from the door.

Dinasia's heart dropped to the floor. As she turned and headed for the elevator, her energy to continue was sapped completely out of her. She wiped a tear away from her face. Her mind instantly started thinking of other ways to squeeze Mrs. Morris into telling her what she knew. She truly didn't want to resort to unscrupulous and extreme measures, but that particular inclination was rapidly disappearing.

*   *   *   *

After visiting his sister to lend her two hundred dollars, Trigger was on his way to his car. When he saw the woman who looked like Dinasia come out of 832, he squinted his eyes and hastily entered his vehicle. He found his binoculars and got a closer view.

"Oh shit!" he muttered when he saw it was Dinasia. The glasses and make-up she had on didn't do much for her as a disguise, but it did tell him she was doing something she had no business. When she turned the corner, Trigger started the car and followed. After he turned the corner, he double parked.

He watched her get in a blue car and pull away. From the numbers on the license plate, he determined it was a rental car. *Should I follow her or find out what she's doing out here?* he pondered as he stared at the back of

118

the car rapidly moving down the street. He decided to find out what the hell she was doing out here, and quickly parked his car.

Trigger got out and headed towards 832, looking for little Johnny Steele. He knew Johnny would know what she was doing in his building since the little squirt thought the building was his personal property.

Within fifteen minutes Trigger found Johnny, spoke with him in detail and discovered Dinasia was going from door to door asking people about the shooting death of Paul Shepard.

As he headed back to his car to get on the cellular phone, Trigger could already imagine Shateek hitting the ceiling when he heard this news.

CHAPTER # 16

At about the moment Dinasia drove away from the Pink House Projects, Tislam laid on his bunk reading the latest Divine G novel. Lately, he found it very difficult staying in his cell, and every time he entered it, he preoccupied his mind with an activity which took him to another place.

The 4 pm master-count was in progress, and in an effort to avoid thinking about what might be going on beyond the prison walls, and to stop trying to figure out why Flipper and Spade hadn't wrote him a letter despite their release almost a week ago, he resorted to fiction novel reading during these two hours in the cell. His neighbor, Jay Bone, had a whole selection of Divine G action novels and had been trying to get Tislam to check one of them out for the longest. Tislam finally read one four days ago and was now hooked like a heroin addict, running through a novel a day.

Tislam was so caught up in the story, he didn't realize the correction officer stopped in front of his cell and was talking to him. The C.O. tapped on the cell bars, causing Tislam to look up from the book.

"Name and number." The C.O. said, with an arm full of mail.

Tislam shot into a standing position. "Tislam Parker. 95A5197." He hadn't received mail in so long, he felt like a poverty stricken kid at Christmas time about to rip open a gift.

The C.O. set the letter on the cell bars and continued down the gallery delivering mail.

Tislam excitedly grabbed the letter. When he saw the name Raymond Murphy, he cheerfully said "Yes!" Thank goodness his counselor honored his request to terminate the correspondence block for mail only from the fictitious names Flipper and Spade would be using. As he opened the letter from Flipper, he sat on his bunk and began reading. He smiled when he got to the part he wanted to know. His smile gradually disappeared as he continued reading.

"Ahh, fuck!" Tislam hissed angrily. He stood and paced back and forth in the small cell like a caged Lion in desperate need of a shot of freedom. He wanted to kick and punch something or someone, but instead he flopped back down on the bunk and continued reading the rest of the letter, hoping he misinterpreted Flipper, or he would explain what the hell he meant by "it's gonna take a little more time than we expected."

*   *   *   *

The following morning Dinasia was back at it again. She drew a deep breath as she got out of her car and headed for 832 Crescent Street.

The whole night she tossed and turned in bed, and got only three hours of sleep. The thought of Mrs. Morris knowing something that could possibly help Tislam, and was refusing to reveal it was not only driving her crazy, but was also interfering with her ability to think of other avenues of investigation. She knew until she found out what exactly it was Mrs. Morris was concealing from her, she wouldn't be able to do anything else. The moment she awoke, Dinasia got dressed and was on her way back to Brooklyn.

As she walked towards the building, Dinasia glanced up at Mrs. Morris's third floor window. She saw the curtain move slightly. Could it have been the glare from the glass? Or were her eyes playing tricks on her? Since it was a cloudy day, she knew it wasn't the glare. Her anxiety was instantly turned up because the movement could be only one thing and she hoped and prayed Mrs. Morris wouldn't call the police before she got a chance to talk to her again.

While getting on the elevator, Dinasia reiterated her pre-planned speech inside her head. She looked at her watch and saw it was 8 o'clock. She got off the elevator and drew a deep breath while heading for the apartment. Just as she was about to knock on the door, it was snatched open, startling her almost into a frantic retreat.

"Come on in," Mrs. Morris whispered excitedly as she grabbed Dinasia's arm, pulling her inside the apartment.

Dinasia's eyes widened with surprise. The sudden change in attitude was truly frightening, but also pleasing at the same time.

"You were right," Mrs. Morris said, heading for the living room. "I always knew I had to do something." She and Dinasia sat in the same seating arrangement as that of the previous day. "I read the Bible last night, 1 Timothy Chapter 5, verse 9 through 10, dealing with the lists of widows and it said, 'No widow may be put on the list of widows unless she is over sixty, has been faithful to her husband, and is well known for her good deeds, such as . . . helping those in trouble and devoting herself to all kinds of good deeds.'" She paused. "And it's just down right sinful to stand by and let something like this continue."

Dinasia saw the woman was a little jittery. She wanted to tell her to relax, but she didn't want to break the flow of her dialogue.

"There was a videotape of the shooting."

Dinasia almost lost control of her cool and calm mannerism. The joy was truly mind shocking.

After a moment's pause, Mrs. Morris continued. "You remember Mrs. Elizabeth Daye who used to live upstairs on the fifth floor?" She waited until Dinasia nodded her head and then she continued. "She recorded the whole thing from the moment those two men started arguing. From the angle Liz was pointing the camera, she was able to pick up the other man who actually did the shooting. He was hiding behind 822. She even filmed him running from the scene and zoomed in on the man's face two good times . . .

Dinasia was itching to cut in and ask where was Mrs. Daye and was the tape still available, but she tamed her anxiousness, merely nodding her head agreeingly.

"She came straight to my apartment and we sat and watched it. And child, we could not believe our eyes." She paused, staring at the floor while shaking her head as if she was saying no.

Dinasia took advantage of the opportunity to slip in a question since she could see Mrs. Morris was reminiscing about the incident. "Do you know where Mrs. Daye is currently living?"

Mrs. Morris snapped out of her reverie and said, "That's the whole crazy thing about all this. After Liz gave the police a copy of the tape when they came around interviewing everyone, those men came to our apartments a couple days later. She decided to take that money from those men and move out of the Projects. We were very close, you know, and it shocked me when she wouldn't tell me where she was moving and just up and disappeared without even telling me anything . . . But, I really can't blame her because those men made it clear, they would kill us if we ever mentioned anything about that tape. They even offered me money to leave the Projects, but I refused. Liz took that money and ran, child."

"You said she gave them a copy of the tape? Are you sure it was a copy?"

"Yes," Mrs. Morris said, now staring Dinasia in the eyes. "She always made copies of everything she videotaped. That woman sat up in that window and videotaped everything that went on. I guess when you get old and lonely like us, you gotta find something to keep you going."

"But how do you know she kept copies?" Dinasia wanted a straightforward answer to relieve her anticipation.

"Because after she gave the police a copy, and before those men came to our apartments, we watched it again. Liz told me that tape was gonna be worth some big money in a few years; talkin' about how she was gonna hold on to a copy of the tape until things calm down some and how she was gonna sell it to one of those TV shows that showed real incidents. Knowing Liz, she probably already sold it to one of those TV stations."

After hearing all this, Dinasia heard enough to realize there was some hope for Tislam. Now, she was more than ready to leave in order to immediately begin her search for Mrs. Elizabeth Daye, but didn't want to appear rude and disrespectful, and so, she decided not to terminate the visit until Mrs. Morris burned herself out. Dinasia listened intently and resisted the temptation to give Mrs. Morris a hint by taking a peek at her watch.

A half hour later, Mrs. Morris realized she was hungry. "Hey, Dinasia, do you want something to eat?" She stood, heading for the kitchen without waiting for a response.

"Wait, wait, Mrs. Morris, I'm not hungry. I have to--"

"Don't be silly child, you look like you could use something to eat. I got all sorts of good stuff in here. Come on in here with me." She started pulling food items out of the refrigerator. "Did I tell you about old Mr. Canty on the third floor over in your old building? . . .

Dinasia smiled because it was apparent Mrs. Morris was suffering from a severe case of loneliness. She listened intently as Mrs. Morris cooked the food, and felt good she was able to give her some satisfaction by giving her some company. They ate an early lunch consisting of grilled cheese sandwiches, lettuce, cucumber and tomato salad, chicken noodle soup, herbal tea and blueberry muffins. Dinasia realized she started enjoying her little stay with her new found friend who'd just given her the best piece of information she probably would ever come across.

By 1 o'clock the visit came to an inevitable end. As Dinasia put on her coat, Mrs. Morris spoke. "There's one more thing I have to ask you . . . Those men weren't just talking. I hope you don't get me involved in a situation that's gonna get me killed. I understand we gotta do something to help that poor man in prison, but please be careful . . . for both our sake."

Dinasia was speechless because she had every intention of diving headlong into this thing without regard to Shateek and his friends. After a moment of silence, she spoke. "Mrs. Morris, believe me, I would never put you in harm's way. If anything develops that might jeopardize your safety, I'll use the utmost discretion before acting. And I'll personally find a way to protect you if anything happens that would require the need for your safety." She hugged Mrs. Morris, saw the sincere smile on her face, turned and headed for the door.

As Dinasia exited the building and headed for the rent office to see if they had information on Mrs. Elizabeth Daye's whereabouts, she saw the kid named Johnny and his two sidekicks. The penetrating stares on all three of their faces instantly made her ponder if she could really live up to those promises she gave Mrs. Morris?

CHAPTER # 17

With feet dragging, back and neck aching, and fatigue running wild throughout every muscle in her body, Dinasia got out of her car and headed towards the front door of her home. The time was 9:45, and all she could think of was jumping in bed.

As Dinasia strolled up the walkway, she saw through her side vision the strange car with the two figures inside suddenly drive away. She wondered who, what and why this car was parked in front of her home, and why did it drive off after she arrived? A nervous tension began to boil inside the pit of her stomach.

A wave of mixed emotions was now intermingled with her exhaustion. Joy, fear and bewilderment were the main ones. Provoking the joy was the fact she found out where Mrs. Daye lived. The two men were responsible for the fear, and all the lights turned out inside the house caused the bafflement. Since the sensation of victory was the more dominating force, and she was instantly able to come up with at least a half dozen harmless explanations for the presence of the two men in the car and the lights being turned out, the joyful feeling of accomplishment quickly took control as she unlocked the door and entered.

Dinasia hit the light switch and flinched when she saw a man sitting in a chair a couple feet from the door. She shrugged off the sudden shock when she saw it was Shateek sitting with one of his legs crossed over the other, looking highly upset.

Shateek looked at his watch and said, "Wow. What happened? Was it overtime? A flat tire? Ohh, I think I know what it was, you had to do some unexpected field work with one of your subjects?"

Dinasia wasn't in the mood for this sarcastic bullshit and was only seconds from exploding. After what he did to Tislam, she wanted to do something quite vicious to him and knew she couldn't get into an argument with him because it would get extremely physical. If it wasn't for the large sum of money she needed for all the things she would need to get Tislam out, she would've divorced this bastard the minute she found out he was responsible for the wrongful imprisonment. She sighed loudly. "You hit it right on the head. It was over-time." She headed up the stairs.

Shateek followed. "Dinasia, it's time you and I have a nice long talk." He wanted to tell her she was a goddamn liar because Keisha called and told him everything. About an hour and half ago, she told him Dinasia was trying to find the whereabouts of a woman named Mrs. Elizabeth Daye and wanted her to get her friend, Shirley Waters, who worked at the Social Security Office to find this woman's address. Shateek also knew Dinasia had taken a leave of absence from her job, and had developed a knack for lying with a straight face, something she couldn't do effectively until now. "We gotta talk, Dinasia."

Dinasia entered the bedroom and started undressing. "Not tonight, Shateek. I'm tired, I got a headache and I feel like I'm coming down with a cold or the flu . . . You know how I get when I'm sick."

"Fuck that!" Shateek shouted. "We need to talk now! For the last two months you been shutting me out of your life, and I wanna know what's going on?" He lied because he knew exactly what she was doing. His anger, fear and frustration ate away at him because she didn't realize what she was about to get herself into. His voice became soft and tender-like as he approached her. "What's wrong, Dinasia? What have I done? Please talk to me?"

Dinasia released an animated smirk. When she saw Shateek put on his little sad eyes gimmick, she wanted to slap the living shit out of him because she knew he was trying to butter her up and play on her emotions. But this time it wouldn't work. It would never work again. "Don't touch me, I mean it. I said I don't wanna talk." She brushed pass Shateek, heading for the bathroom.

As Dinasia soaked in the hot bath, she reflected back on all the things she went through just to find out Mrs. Daye's address and sighed loudly.

The Pink House rent office was a waste of time; the credit card bureau produced nothing; the Internet was useless and the phone company was a total squandering of precious energy. Reluctantly, Dinasia decided to seek Keisha's assistance. Keisha's friend, Shirley Waters, worked at the Social Security Office, and since Mrs. Daye was receiving SSI benefits, Dinasia knew Shirley could find her whereabouts. However, because of Keisha's habit of running her mouth around the wrong people, Dinasia told her she needed Mrs. Daye's address from Shirley in order to help a client get in contact with her long lost Aunt before the woman died of cancer. Keisha apparently went for this farfetched story without asking any questions, and that surprised Dinasia.

While waiting for Shirley to retrieve the information, Dinasia went back to the library on Fifth Avenue and researched video visual enhancing technology so if the copy of the videotape wasn't 100% clear, she would have a head start. At about 8 o'clock Dinasia's cellular phone rang, and Keisha told her the address. If it wasn't so late, and if she wasn't so exhausted, she would've drove out to Coney Island and visited Mrs. Daye immediately upon finding out the address.

Meanwhile, Shateek was fuming, pacing back and forth in the bedroom and then abruptly decided to leave the house. He raced down the stairs, snatched his coat and was on his way out the door. He got in his car, found the car phone and dialed a number. As he waited for the other party to pick up the line, he muttered to himself, "Woman do you realize you're about to open a can of worms that'll get you killed."

When the other party picked up, Shateek said, "It's me, Shateek." He sighed loudly. "Remember what I mentioned yesterday? . . . Yeah, that's it. Well, you can green light that . . . Yes, I'm sure. Don't ask any questions, just do it."

*   *   *   *

Elizabeth Daye was propelled out of her sleep when she heard the hard knock on the door. The first thing she did was turn on the lamp beside the bed, found her glasses, looked at the clock on the night-stand and couldn't believe someone was knocking on her door at this God forsaken hour. It's almost 3 a.m. in the morning for Christ sakes.

Liz's old and brittle bones snapped, crackled and popped as she got out of bed, found her slippers and robe, then headed for the door. "Who is it?" Liz said hoarsely.

"It's the police."

The petrifying anxiety stopped her cold in her tracks. She frantically turned and rushed back to her bedroom, found the 38 revolver in the top dresser draw, put it in her house coat pocket and went back to the door. "Is there a problem?" She looked through the peephole.

"Yes, there is, ma'am. We received a report from someone across the street indicating they saw a burglar tampering with your window, and I have to take a look at it."

Still looking through the peephole, Liz said, "Why can't you do this in the morning?" she noticing the white man looked like the stereo-typical plain-clothe cop. But she wasn't going to let them fool her. "I'm very old and I don't open my door at this time of night for anyone. I'll take a look at the window and tell you if anything's wrong, but I won't open--"

Liz hysterically pulled away from the peephole when she heard the sound of breaking glass. It came from the kitchen where the main fire escape was located. The noise was low, but loud enough to almost give Liz a heart attack and make her pull the gun from her pocket. She nervously tiptoed towards the kitchen.

Then, suddenly, all at the same time, the locks on the door behind her were being opened while the glass in the kitchen made a smashing sound. The door slammed open, but the chain lock restricted it from opening completely. With the gun in her hand, and her already faulty ticker about to burst, Liz frantically turned back and forth with jolting speed; trying to determine which way to go first; the door or the kitchen. Totally confused and scared to death, she looked like a lunatic spectator watching an accelerated tennis match.

When the door swung open and she saw the white man with a pair of wire cutters in his hand, Liz knew for certain these men weren't the police. She nervously took aim. Just as she was about to pull the trigger, she heard rapid footsteps behind her and then felt a very hard blow to the back of her head. The last thing she remembered was falling to the floor.

"Grandma dynamite was about to shoot me, you seen that?" The white man said to the brown skin black man. "Did you kill the bitch?"

The black guy kneeled down and put his fingers to the woman's neck. "Nah, she's still with us."

"Well in that case," The white guy reached inside the inner breast pocket of his coat and pulled out an electrical extension cord. "Step aside." He wrapped the cord around the old woman's neck and pulled until the veins in his neck swelled up, looking as if they were about to burst. He giggled as the woman thrashed desperately. About 40 seconds later she became perfectly motionless. He checked her wrist for a pulse. There was none. "She's gone." He stood and stretched.

"Let's find that god-damn tape and get the hell outta here." The black guy said as he headed for the bedroom while the white guy went into the living room.

CHAPTER # 18

The following morning, the two men who snuffed out Mrs. Daye sat waiting patiently in their green four door Ford Escort a block away from the murder scene. Every time they saw someone enter or exit 711 Seagate Avenue, they flung their binoculars to their eyes. It was 7:13 in the morning. They were upset because the temperature dropped to 19 degrees and were pissed off because they just got word none of the seven videotapes retrieved from Mrs. Daye's apartment had what they were looking for.

"Man, I'm telling you," The black guy said from the passenger seat. "This whole thing is a fuckin' wild goose chase. Probably ain't even a tape with that shit on it."

"So what?" The white guy said. "We gettin' paid for this shit regardless. If his paranoia is puttin' money in our pockets who are we to complain?"

"I ain't beefin' about the money. I just hate to do a job with a bunch of bullshit information. I like for things to be straight forward and clean cut."

"So what are you saying?" The white guy turned and looked at his partner. "Little Johnny lied when he said he over heard that old lady in the Projects telling Dinasia this old bag here had a copy of the tape?"

"Well, let's put it this way. That little bastard got two thousand dollars for that piece of information. For money like that, any motherfucker would claim he heard that conversation through a damn steel door, especially if he knows he got people believing him."

Five minutes later the black guy spoke. "There she goes." Through the binoculars he saw Dinasia come from around the corner, heading for the tenement building. "Looks like Johnny Steele was telling the truth after all."

With binoculars to his eyes as well, the white guy said, "Boy, this broad is definitely a show nuff busy body." He put the binoculars down and picked up the cellular, hastily dialing 911. "I didn't think she was gonna show." A couple of seconds later he spoke excitedly into the phone. "I wanna report a murder at 711 Seagate Avenue apartment 2D. It's a black woman wearing a brown coat who did it. She's still inside the apartment!" He hung up with a long smile on his face and leaned back, getting comfortable, already imagining the look on that broad's face when they dragged her ass out in cuffs.

*   *   *   *

Dinasia's eyes got wide with a mixture of surprise, fear and inquisitivity when Mrs. Daye's apartment door opened after she knocked on it. *This ain't right. Something's terribly wrong here. Run! Get away!* Her instinctive voice inside her head shouted. But her desire to get her hands on that tape was far stronger than any other emotion or inner voice. Her hand involuntarily went for the 25 automatic, caressing it, but not taking it out of her pocket.

"Mrs. Daye," Dinasia stuck her head inside the apartment. "Are you there? Mrs. Daye." She saw nothing looked out of the norm. The smell of moth balls was thick in the air; a typical fragrance for old folks, she thought as she stepped inside. "Hello. Mrs. Daye. Is anybody home?"

It was now evident no one was home. *Where could she be at this time of the morning?* Dinasia slowly moved towards the kitchen while scrutinizing her surroundings with hawk eye precision.

Ssscrraasshh . . . Sscrrasshh . . .

The scratching sound caused Dinasia to pull the gun. "Who's that? Mrs. Daye is that you?"

No response, but the scratching sound continued.

Dinasia followed the noise. She noticed it was coming from the back of the apartment, the bedroom. She slowly approached and entered the room. Scanning the room, she saw a Siamese cat scratching at the closet door. She put the gun back in her pocket. "Hey there, Kitty." Dinasia smiled as she went to the cat and picked it up. "Where's Mrs. Daye? You tryin' to get inside here?" She loved cats, and they got along with her just as well. "You wanna get inside here? Well, let's see what we got here." She opened the closet.

AAEERRHHHHH!!

Dinasia screamed, causing the cat to catapult itself from her embrace as she stumbled backwards. The dead body fell and crashed to the floor, making a loud thud upon impact.

A spell of mass hysteria instantly gripped her mind. Dinasia quickly began breathing very rapidly and deeply, saturating her mind with soothing oxygen. She saw the woman's face and hands looked bluish and were swollen to twice their normal size, which Dinasia knew was a tell-tale sign that the woman was dead. She also had that weird scary stiff look which brought chills down Dinasia's spine. She never saw a dead body before, and suddenly all those horror movies about dead people coming back to life and eating the living, flooded her mind. There was a short-lived urge to check for a pulse, as the fear knocked the thought clean out of her head.

Then, suddenly, she realized if she were to get caught inside this apartment with this dead body she would be considered the culprit. With panic-stricken vigor, she ran for the door and then stopped abruptly. *The videotape!* She had to find that tape. If she didn't get it now she might never get her hands on it. This place was going to be a crime scene without a doubt. She raced back to the bedroom.

Searching frantically, she realized if she intended to do a thorough job she would have to slow down and concentrate. *Where would she put a tape?* She repeatedly asked as she opened drawers, looked under everything in sight and began to realize there were no tapes here. She stopped for a moment with both hands on her hips, thinking hard. *Maybe she hid it somewhere else. Maybe it's not even here. Where would a person hide things and keep it safe all at the same time?*

The answer hit her with grueling force. Just as she frantically ran to the dresser where she remembered seeing a small box of keys moments ago, she heard commotion out front of the building; screeching car tires and men shouting excitedly. She snatched the lid off the top of the jewelry box and began stuffing keys inside her pocket.

BOW! BOW! BOW! BOW! BOW! . . . .

The massive gunfire startled every drop of energy out of Dinasia's body. Her knees buckled with trembling force as she hit the deck, believing she was being shot at. Instinctively, she quickly crawled to the bedroom window to see what was going on. The gunfire sounded like a war was in progress and it made her bladder feel weak.

When she saw the police cars and the officers firing their guns down the street from behind their vehicles, the paralyzing shock wouldn't let her move. *Run! Run! Run!* Her terror-stricken third eye hollered. With eyes bulging, mouth hung open and her brain locked so tight it could've put vice grips out of business, Dinasia tried to flee, but the enthralling fear and shock had a firm, unrelenting hold on her.

CHAPTER # 19

Cheops and Chico Rico were the last two of the group of thirty inmates from F-Block to enter the East side mess hall. As they waited in the slow moving line to pick up their trays of breakfast consisting of watery oatmeal, buttered bread, cold coffee and two glasses of powdered milk, they whispered among themselves.

Chico Rico spoke. "We can kick it now. Let's hear it, the suspense is killing me."

"You ain't gonna believe this shit." Cheops said. "C.O. Carol just hit me off with a kite this morning, and man this is some real rough shit." He shook his head as if the news was truly amazing.

Long pause.

Whispering excitedly, Chico Rico said, "What did the kite say? Was it from your peoples?"

"Who else would it be from? Yeah, it was my people . . . They put a tract out on guess who?"

"Cricket?" He saw Cheops shake his head no. "Danny Wop?" Again no. "Cee Cee?" Wrong again. "Ahhh, come on man, who?"

Cheops drew a deep breath. "Tislam." He saw the shocked and hurtful look on Chico Rico's face. "Here's the fucked up part. They want him dead . . . And the price tag is $250.000. A quarter mill."

"God-damn!" Chico Rico blurted loudly, with bug eyed shock written all over his face. He noticed his outburst drew some unwarranted attention, forcing him to quickly relax and re-compose himself. He waited about a minute before speaking. "I wonder what the hell he did to rack up some fire like that on his ass!?"

Cheops knew it had something to do with Tislam's case, but he vowed not to reveal what he knew to anyone. "I don't know. And don't particularly care. The kite also said it's a no refuse offer. If I turn it down, I fall with Tislam. I guess they feel whoever learns about this hit has to be

135

with it 100% or gets knocked out of the picture. One of those squeaky clean runs with no loose ends floating around."

"This is fucked up, Cheops," Chico Rico saw they were almost to the serving counter and started whispering a little faster. "Tis is family, man. There ain't no way you or I could gun him down face to face. It'll violate our code of--"

"I already thought that out," Cheops knew it was time to cut their conversation short, since the serving counter was right upon them. "We'll finish this at the table."

They retrieved their trays and sat at a table in the middle section of the messhall.

Cheops noticed a new prisoner sat at the table with him, Chico Rico and two other inmates. Cheops gave Chico Rico the eye, which said they couldn't talk in the presence of this new jack. They said nothing as they ate. Upon finishing, they lined up in single file, dumped their trays, exited the messhall and headed back to F-Block.

Cheops spoke when they were moving down the corridor. "How you feel about giving up 25 gees out of your cut?"

"What's that, a joke?" Chico Rico hated when Cheops asked stupid questions. "If we gettin' 100 gees just for making sure the gunners complete the job, it would be sheer madness to beef about something like that. This is the biggest pay off we'll ever see. What fool wouldn't be with it? . . . Who's the lucky crew?"

"The Crimson Cowboys."

"Good choice," Chico Rico nodded his head agreeingly. "A damn good choice."

*　　*　　*　　*

Dinasia ran towards the fence in back of the building as the car tires squealed and a few gunshots could still be heard. There was no other escape route and the closer she got to the fence the more she realized she couldn't get over it because it looked fifteen feet tall and had those spike looking things on the top.

136

She reached the fence and sighed with relief when she looked to her right and saw a swinging gate that was open which led to 37th street. Moving quickly, she went through the gate, peeked down the block, saw it was clear and hurried on her way. More police cars arrived, and as she looked back, she saw a few of the cops on foot running towards the front of the building she just left.

Whatever or whoever it was that caused the police to start shooting, she wanted to thank because if that hadn't happened she would've been caught inside that apartment.

Moments ago, after she pulled herself out of the debilitating shock, Dinasia raced down the stairs from the apartment. Just as she was about to exit the building through the back door, she heard a cop, who just entered the front door tell another cop "the transmission said it was 2D." The sudden revelation that a few seconds later and she would've been caught in that apartment made it even more apparent that if the police hadn't been diverted, they would've walked right in on her.

With trembling hands, she opened her car door, jumped in and spun off. So many things were racing through her mind as she drove aimlessly. But the one thing that stood out was the fact she had to hurry up and find out which Bank Mrs. Daye had her safe-deposit box before the police started investigating. If something of importance needed to be kept safe, then a deposit box was where a wise person would keep it. At least that's what Dinasia hoped was the current situation.

As Dinasia calmed down, she began to formulate a plan of action. Then, suddenly, she frantically reached inside her pocket, hoping in her haste she hadn't accidentally fail to retrieve the safe-deposit key or inadvertently dropped it as she fled the apartment. A couple of the keys fell to the floor as she sat a handful of them on the passenger seat. She hastily picked up one at a time while glancing back and forth between the road and the selected key. On the fourth pick, she saw it was the safe-deposit key. She expelled a breath of relief as she put the key inside her pocket. She was sure it was one of those particular keys because she had one herself.

Now, she needed a super fast way to get a listing of all banks near 711 Seagate Avenue and for some odd reason Dinasia couldn't seem to think of one single way to accomplish this task. Since Mrs. Daye was old and wouldn't do any extensive traveling, Dinasia knew if she could find the nearest Bank, she would likely hit the jackpot.

After considering her options for a moment, she reluctantly realized there was only one way to handle this. She looked at the next street sign, which said 29th street. She realized she was getting too far from the area and made a left turn at 28th street, heading back to Seagate Avenue.

There was no time to waste trying to figure out a better way than to simply drive around the neighborhood, find all the banks, go inside, pretend to be the daughter of Mrs. Daye, have them check to see if she had a deposit box in that particular Bank, and if so, hope and pray they would give her access to the safe, and most of all, that the tape was there.

*   *   *   *

Earlier, on Seagate Avenue moments before any shots were fired, the black and white guys in the Ford Escort were becoming impatient because the police were taking too long to arrive. When the two police cars pulled in front of 711 Seagate Avenue, they both thought: It's about god-damn time. As they observed the four police officers getting out of their vehicles, all hell was unleashed.

BOW! BOW! BOW! BOW! BOW! . . .

The sudden, massive gunfire caused the white and black guys to ducked behind the dashboard even though they knew the shots weren't directed at them.

"What the fuck was that!?" The black guy said. "Where the--Who the--"

The White guy snatched his binoculars, sat up, and looked down the street at the location where the police were returning fire. He quickly rolled the window down and put the binoculars in a position which enabled him to see, at the corner of the street about a block away from the police, a black man with a handkerchief covering his nose and mouth, firing a handgun; he looked like an out of place train robber dressed in urban attire. He moved the binoculars to the right and saw another man with some kind of mask on, standing in the middle of the street shooting at the police with a gun in each hand.

"What the fuck you waitin' for!?" The black man shouted. "Let's get the fuck outta here, man!"

"Relax!" The white guy knew he had to stay calm and was now concentrating to keep any hasty activities under control. "These are some bold motherfuckers here." He sat the binoculars down, started the car, and as he did an inconspicuous U turn, two stray bullets struck the car; one shattered the back door window while the other hit the front fender.

"Move this fucker, man!" The black guy shouted as he remained crunched down in the seat. "Fuck all that Mr. Cool shit!"

The white guy hit the gas pedal and breezed away from the area, hoping none of the cops noticed them pull away. Looking through the rearview mirror, he was certain they got away undetected because the cops' backs were turned and they were too preoccupied with the men doing all the shooting.

After they made a couple of right and left turns, the black guy spoke. "I know she got her ass up outta there. The second those shots went off, I bet you she ran right out the back door."

"What I wanna know is who were them motherfuckers shooting?" The white guy turned down Surf Street.

"Hey, where you goin'?"

"We're going back." The white guy said. "In the meantime, call him and find out how he wants us to handle this in light of this crazy shit that just happened?"

As the black guy spoke over the cellular, they cruised past the back alleyway of 711. The gunfire had apparently come to a stop and they didn't see Dinasia's car.

The black guy disconnected the line. "He wants us to follow her and get back with him before we do anything." He hissed angrily. "Now, we gotta find this bitch."

They drove around aimlessly, making a series of right and left turns that made their heads spin with confusion, aggravation and frustration. Five minutes later, the white guy spoke excitedly. "There she goes! Right up ahead."

Dinasia's blue rental car had made a left turn onto Neptune Avenue and was headed towards them.

"Easy," The black guy said as the rental car passed and a rapid U turn was being made. "Don't play her too close." He pulled out his gun and screwed on a silencer. "And whoever it was that started shooting, I can't help but get the feeling they were trying to divert the police before they entered that apartment building. They were helping her, no doubt about it. If they show up again, he wants us to take it to the next level."

The white guy smiled as he pulled his gun and sat it in between his legs. "That sounds like music to my ears."

Little did they know, as they followed Dinasia, an old blue Buick Regal containing two men followed them.

CHAPTER # 20

Tislam entered the basement of the Jay School area of the facility and waited for Cheops and Chico Rico. This was one of the places they frequently utilized to deal with unsuspecting prisoners targeted for a hit after they were lured to the area by means of trickery and enticement. C.O. Lane, who worked the area, was C.O. Carol's partner and would let them down in the basement for a small fee. The only stipulation was if someone died they would have to move the body to another area of the facility and all blood had to be cleaned up.

As Tislam leaned against the wall next to a huge steam pipe, thinking about what Cheops told him about this guy they were supposed to hit, he felt a nervous premonition as if something wasn't right. He struggled with the feeling and successfully swept it away with the help of a noise that came from the other entrance about twenty yards away.

"Cheops! Chico Rico!! That y'all?" Tislam called out as he strolled towards the other side. The heat from the boiler pipes and the musty smell were strong as usual. The buzzing sounds from the numerous electrical boxes were alive and kicking also. He now heard a lot of footsteps coming down the metal stairs.

When he saw the prisoner named Pus, the leader of the Crimson Cowboys, along with four of his soldiers whom all were brandishing store bought knives, Tislam thought his eyes were playing games with him. While instinctively stepping backwards, he pulled his homemade shank which looked like a sheer joke when compared to the weapons all five of them possessed.

"Ahhhh, come on, man," Pus said teasingly. "I just know you ain't gonna try to run from us. That's why I came prepared." He whistled.

Tislam heard footsteps come from behind him. He frantically turned and saw three more prisoners. They also possessed similar knives as those of the other five. Tislam knew he couldn't show fear because they would fed off of it like hungry hyenas. He struggled to sound fearless and firm.

"Since when have you mothefuckers got into the business of suicide missions? You can hit me, even kill me, but my crew'll kill not only you, but your families and any--"

Pus laughed. "Damn son, you dumber than I thought. You ain't figured this shit out yet?" He laughed again. "Well, if you can't see what time it is, then it ain't meant for you to see it . . .

As Pus went on about how he wanted Tislam to lay down and die without a struggle because there was no way out, Tislam felt like he was struck on the head with a sledge hammer possessing a rude awakening formula. It was evident Cheops and Chico Rico set him up. Looking at all those knives while trying to come up with a maneuver to survive this eight against one conflict, Tislam fought desperately to get out of his head the thought that this conflict was most likely the final scene in his life. He drew a nervous breath of air and decided if he was gonna die, he would most definitely go out with a bang, fighting all the way to the bitter end.

As the Crimson Cowboys eased closer to him, Tislam muttered. "God bless the child who can hold its own" and pulled up all the mental pictures of him and Dinasia. He found energy in the firm belief that they would be back together one day again. And he refused to believe it would be otherwise.

YYAAHHHH!!!

The first three inmates shouted as they charged at him and Tislam let the image of Dinasia's face be his guiding force.

*   *   *   *

Dinasia walked out of the Handover Trust Savings Bank on West 30th street and Surf Avenue on the verge of giving up completely. This was her third failed attempt. If it wasn't for the mental pictures constantly flashed inside her head of Tislam being dragged off of the Rikers Island visiting floor while pleading with her to help him, she would've thrown in the towel a long time ago. Also, their 'no other love' vow danced crazily in her mind and gave her superhuman strength to carry on. She learned to respect the power of love when she promised to get Tislam out or die trying.

Dinasia was, however, glad her little ruse was working quite well. Each time she entered a Bank, Dinasia went straight to the safe-deposit section, told the clerk she was Mrs. Elizabeth Daye's daughter and she needed to know whether or not her mother possessed a safe-deposit box in this Bank. If there was a need to explain why she wasn't aware of this information, Dinasia told them her mother was suffering from Alzheimer disease and forgot the Bank where she had a safe deposit box, and also misplaced or threw out all her receipts and other records. In an attempt to incite more sympathy, Dinasia told them her mother was currently in the hospital recuperating from a brain surgery and desperately needed the things inside the box. So far, all three clerks told Dinasia they had no safe-deposit box for a Mrs. Elizabeth Daye after checking their files.

As Dinasia headed for her car parked around the corner, she realized this particular Bank was the last Bank within reasonable distance from Mrs. Daye's home. The next one was over two miles from 711 Seagate Avenue and was the last one in the immediate area. The acid production in Dinasia's stomach from the permeating stress instantly sparked up.

She entered her car and pulled from the curb trying to swallow and digest the agonizing reality of defeat because she subconsciously knew an old lady wouldn't travel that far to handle her Banking affairs when several others were just a stroll of a walk from her home.

She stopped at the red light and looked at her watch. "Damn it!" She muttered loudly because it was already 2:45. She knew some Banks closed early and hoped this particular Bank wasn't one of them. When the light turned green, she put an extra heavy foot on the accelerator.

Three minutes later, she pulled into the Dimes Savings Bank parking lot on 17th Street and Mermaid Avenue, about a block away from Coney Island's amusement park, and found a parking space. As she quickly got out of the car, she saw a green car with two men inside enter the parking lot, the driver searching for a parking space despite the numerous empty spaces. She could've sworn she saw that same car before? She noticed it felt like one of those dejavu experiences, but then she suddenly wondered did she see this car at an early point in the day? She didn't have time to figure out if she was bugging or what, because the Bank might be closing any minute.

As Dinasia entered the Bank her nervous eyes seemed to take in the numerous rolls of Bank teller windows, the armed security guard, the customers, and the directorial signs all at a glance. The directory was on her right side and she went to it. A couple seconds later, the billboard told her what she needed to know. She turned and headed towards the blue section and saw there was a small line of six people waiting to speak to the teller. She joined them.

Dinasia nervously waited in line and noticed her anxiety was suddenly becoming profound and intense. The mere aspect of standing still made her think about all the bad things that could happen if she was caught trying to get into a dead woman's safe-deposit box. When it dawned on her there was a possibility this Bank could produce nothing, she knew she had to think about something else. About five minutes later, the teller called "next" and Dinasia stepped forward.

After Dinasia told the woman her story, she began searching her computer. The woman looked up from the keyboard with a smile and said, "Yes, she has a safe here, her box number is 52G. It's right over there to your left. Give the guard this paper." She handed the document to Dinasia and waited until Dinasia was out of sight before picking up the phone.

Dinasia struggled desperately not to show her excitement as she headed for the safe-deposit section. The guard let her inside and directed her to the area where the safes were located. With trembling legs she entered the huge room and saw there were two other people present; a lady and an old man, sitting at separate stalls, preoccupied with the contents of their safes.

She began reading the numbers on the boxes. She saw box # 52G and her heartbeat increased. Shaking like the Taco Bell Chihuahua, she pulled the key from her pocket and inserted it in the lock. She almost fainted when the key wouldn't turn. Hysteria was about to grip her. Swallowing hard, she noticed the key wasn't all the way in. She relaxed, corrected the problem and tried it again.

It opened.

Dinasia pulled the box from its sliding tray and walked with it to the table. She sat down, opened the lid and started rummaging through the box. There were a lot of papers, some jewelry and in the back there was a manila folder. She pulled the package out with a slight struggle and lit up with happiness because it felt like a videotape. She quickly opened the envelope and smiled.

It was a tape.

She started looking for anything else that might be of help, and a minute later, came across an affidavit. She couldn't believe this was happening. The affidavit described the whole videotape-recording incident in detail and Mrs. Daye had even notarized it. As a safety measure, Dinasia took a few more minutes to thoroughly check everything inside the box because it was obvious there was no turning back. Nothing else of importance was found and she was on her way out the door.

She gave the teller a smile accompanied with a head nod and approached the exit. Just as her hand touched the door she heard someone shouting.

"Hey, Mrs., wait a minute!"

Dinasia turned and saw the security guard running towards her. An indescribable fear took hold and her first instinct was to run. She listened to her inner voice and hastily opened the door, about to get knee deep into her frantic flee.

"Wait! You forgot your receipt."

Dinasia stopped and felt silly and embarrassed as she took the piece of paper from the guard. She exited the Bank.

With the tape in one of her coat pockets and the affidavit in the other, Dinasia headed for the car with a joyous sensation running through her veins. She couldn't wait to get home and view the tape. Afterwards she would then get it to a lawyer named Bruce Snyder, who assured her if she obtained evidence of Tislam's innocence he would get Tislam out of prison. Mr. Snyder sounded very sincere and was a self proclaimed expert in the field of criminal law with twenty years experience; he had a lot of connections in the Brooklyn Courts, won about 98% of all his post conviction motions, and the price range was very affordable. After meeting Bruce Snyder, she knew she didn't have to look any further for legal assistance for Tislam.

She inserted her key in the car door and suddenly saw the rapid movement from the corner of her eye. Her head snapped in that direction with a flinching jolt just as the white man spoke.

"Excuse me, ma'am, my name is Detective Sentowski. I would like to have a word with you . . .

CHAPTER # 21

"Don't back up!" Pus shouted from the sideline with a hunting knife in each hand, leaning on the staircase railing. He impatiently watched his soldiers as they moved towards Tislam, swinging and jabbing their knives at the moving target. "Take him down."

AEHHHHH!!

The Crimson Cowboy, who looked like a hound dog, screamed when Tislam stabbed him in the neck. The man stumbled backwards with his hand clutching his neck and went to his knees as all the fight was sucked clean out of him.

Tislam was officially in the maniac zone, and the blood gushing from the stab wounds to his lower back, right arm and his left leg served only to make him angrier.

No sooner than hound dog face hit the floor, one of the three cowboys in back of Tislam rushed towards him. Tislam swung his body around as his iron will to live enabled him to totally disregard the dizzy sensation caused by the lost of blood and provided the means for him to disarm this attacker. The Kung Fu maneuver was implemented so swiftly, the man didn't realize he was in trouble until it was too late. With his own weapon Tislam repeatedly stabbed the man into a state of triple darkness. When he fell to the floor, Tislam stepped on his chest and spring boarded into a flying reverse roundhouse kick and caught another Cowboy in the face. The kick catapulted him into a huge sewage pipe face first.

Now, with a knife in each hand, breathing extremely hard from the rage and fear, Tislam looked like a crazed bull on a suicide mission from hell. He saw the five remaining men were hesitant and none of them wanted to rush towards him. "You wanna fuck with me motherfuckers!!" Tislam charged at the group, stabbing, jabbing and swinging the shank and the store bought knife with ungraceful speed and sluggish force, almost as if he was drunk.

Pus was fed up with the games. He held back, expecting his soldiers would handle this matter without his direct intervention. But it suddenly didn't look like it was gonna be that kind of party. *If you want it done right you gotta do it your goddamn self.* With a smile, he held up his hand. "Alright, alright. That's it!"

His soldiers stopped and made way for Pus to get in front of them.

Pus got into a stance with a hunting knife in each hand.

Tislam nervously got in a stance as he and Pus sized each other up. The rumors of how awesomely good Pus was with a knife tried to inch its way into Tislam's head, but he shoved the thought away with a small struggle. Tislam swung the store bought knife.

"EEEAAHHHH!!"

Tislam screamed when he felt Pus's blades sliced through his chest and forearm. The white-hot pain caused him to drop the store bought knife.

"Ahhh, ain't that cute," Pus said smilingly. "Mr. Karate man sounding like a little bitch now . . . You didn't know I knew that shit too, huh?" He then psyched out Tislam with a fake move that looked like he was going to release a side kick, but suddenly turned it into a spinning wheel kick, which landed on Tislam's jaw.

Tislam stumbled backwards, hit the concrete wall with extreme force and noticed his head was spinning profusely. His clothing was now drenched, soaked through and through with blood. As he tried to get in a stance, Tislam noticed his movement was fatigued and totally uncoordinated. That voice inside his head spoke: *You're bleeding to death.*

Tislam struggled to get control over the impulse to panic, but his very diligent efforts seemed futile.

WHAM! BLAM!

Tislam blocked the two blows thrown by Pus and then threw a lazy jab at him, missing Pus by a mile.

"AAOOHHH!!"

Tislam hollered when Pus's blade slid across his stomach, unleashing a glob of thick blood. Instantly, Tislam spun, and with every drop of energy he had left in his body, he charged at the two soldiers standing in the pathway to the door he entered the basement. *Retreat! Retreat! Retreat! Run before it's too late!* Tislam's mind screamed as he frantically swung his blade, successfully moving the two cowboys out of the way. He ran and stumbled up the stairs with blinding speed, banging excitedly on the door. Simultaneously he noticed the stampede of footsteps behind him. He turned and kicked the closet cowboy back down the stairs, but received a stab wound to his ankle in the process.

It didn't take long for Tislam to remember C.O. Lane wasn't gonna open the door since Pus and his crew apparently paid him to open it only if a special password was uttered, which would indicate they were finished with their business. As the sleepy sensation began to firmly set in, Tislam tried desperately to ward off his attackers, kicking and swinging the shank valiantly, but he knew it was just a matter of time before he would either pass out or one of them would get in a fatal shot.

As soon as Tislam thought about the final blow that would put an end to it all, he felt the blade of the knife plunge through his upper chest, near the collarbone. The pain was so agonizing it not only cut off his screeching scream, but also sucked every drop of energy out of his body. He lifelessly fell backwards, hit the back of his head on the steel railing and lethargically curled up into a fetal position as several additional stabbing blows were inflicted all over his body, including the head.

Then, suddenly, as he faded into a state of unconsciousness, Tislam saw an angelic, mystical dream like image of Dinasia inside his head and he could hear her talking to him.

*   *   *   *

Sauntering leisurely along the Jay School corridor, Sergeant Brickle was doing his rounds a half hour earlier than usual. With all the corruption going on, and in light of the fact he was secretly working for an undercover internal affairs unit commissioned by Cemtral Office, he made it his business to alter his patterns to the point no one was able to pin down his schedule. He was the new white shirt on the block, and the hostility and mistrust from his fellow colleagues were unmistakable.

Brickle turned the corner, and when he made eye contact with Officer Lane, he saw a disturbed expression suddenly appear on the officer's face. *Now, that there is the look of something in the making.*

"Hey, Sarge, how yah doin'?" C.O. Lane said, meeting the Sergeant half way while trying to sound casual. "You're a little early today. I thought you were working in C-Block?"

"Yeah, you thought right," Sgt. Brickle scanned the area looking for something out of the norm. He went to the logbook and began writing. "Me and Sergeant Wilkins swopped areas. Plus, I needed a break from Jordan and his wacked out jokes." He saw C.O. Lane was now perspiring. "Are you all ri--"

Thump! Thump!

The noise caused Sgt. Brickle to spin around. The sound was low and a slight distance away, but audible enough to be heard clearly. "What the hell was that? Where'd that come from?" The commotion suddenly became louder and continuous, causing Brickle to rapidly move towards the basement door a few yards away from the desk.

"It's nothing, Sarge." C.O. Lane nervously cut in front of the Sgt. "It's probably just a few stray cats or something. Believe me it's nothing."

Sgt. Brickle politely moved C.O. Lane aside. "It don't sound like nothing to me," Brickle unlocked the door and snatched it open. When he saw the group of inmates stabbing another inmate, who was on the floor curled up into a ball, he frantically pulled the pin on his emergency alarm attached to his radio. "Stop! I'm giving you a direct order to stop right this minute! All of you drop those wea--"

WHAM!

The hunting knife thrown by Pus struck Sgt. Brickle in the chest, knocking him backwards into C.O. Lane.

Pus ran over to Sgt. Brickle, pulled the knife from the Sgt.'s chest and began stabbing him repeatedly in the same area. By the time the fourth carefully placed blow was inflicted, all life was expelled from the Sgt.'s contorted body.

"What are you doing!?" C.O. Lane's terror-stricken face was almost comical as he squirmed to his feet. "This wasn't supposed--"

WHAM! WHAM!

One of the Cowboys stabbed C.O. Lane twice; once in the head and the other in the throat, dropping him back to the floor. C.O. Lane then received multiple stab wounds in areas all over his body by the other Crimson Cowboys as they came from the basement.

Pus ran over to Tislam, pulled a handkerchief from his back pocket, wiped his prints off the handle of the knife dripping with Sgt. Brickle's blood and hastily put it in Tislam's hand. He actually didn't know why he was doing this since Tislam looked as dead as a door nail, and no one would believe he killed these police and then somehow killed himself, but he always wanted to do this because it was done that way in the Movies, Pus rationalized.

Pus turned his head, saw what his soldier named "Slow-gases" was doing, and hissed frustratingly. He pulled a single edge razor from his pocket and ran over to Slow-gases, who was still stabbing both Sgt. Brickle and C.O. Lane's dead bodies while he wallowed in a pool of blood like a happy hog in a barrel of shit.

Pus snatched Slow-gases onto his feet and almost slapped the man's teeth out of his head. "Didn't I tell you to be careful not to step in any blood!? Now look at yah! You're gonna leave tracks all over the damn place!" Before Slow-gases could utter a word, Pus slit his throat from ear to ear. Blood sprayed everywhere just as Pus leaped away, fully aware of the messy effects of a severed jugular vein.

Pus fled, leading his remaining four soldiers towards the law library, just as the riot squad's thunderous stampede could be heard coming from the Jay School corridor.

CHAPTER # 22

"Do you have any identification?" Dinasia asked the detective as she continued unlocking the car door with trembling hands. "A badge of some kind?"

"Yes, I do as a matter of fact," The man pulled a wallet from his back pocket, flipped it open and put it back in his pocket. "My partner and I would like to ask you a few questions. Our vehicle is right over there." He pointed to the green Ford Escort.

Dinasia turned, saw the car and realized she wasn't buggin' out when she thought she saw that same car when she was at the first and second Banks. She instinctively realized something wasn't right when she noticed the back door window of the car had a clear plastic bag taped over it. A sudden avalanche of other odd things came to mind; like when this detective failed to show his badge in accordance with universal law enforcement procedure and he flashed it so quickly it was obvious he didn't want her to get a good look at it. Dinasia knew this was a trick of some sort. She turned and spoke. "I'm sorry, but I'm in a hurry and I don't have--"

"Is that a videotape in your pocket?" The white guy said as he reached for it.

"Hey!" Dinasia shoved his hand away. "I beg your pardon, Mister. But you don't have the right to touch me like that. Now, if you don't mind, I don't wanna talk to you and I'm leaving, unless you got some kind of wa--"

The white guy grabbed Dinasia by the throat and slammed her into the car. "Sorry, but you don't get to choose with this one." He said as he took the videotape from Dinasia's pocket and put it in his.

Dinasia tried to pull away and was about to strike the man's face with her fists, but his grip was firm and had that no nonsense feel to it. The man's face was so close to hers, Dinasia could smell his foul, sour cigarette breath as he spoke. Ain't this a fine fuckin' time not to have the gun, she thought, cursing herself for leaving the gun in the car.

"Now, you can come the easy way," The white guy said as the cloud of smoke swirled from his mouth due to his breath hitting the cold air. "Or I'll drag your ass over there by the fuckin' neck. This is the part where you choose." When he saw Dinasia attempt to mumble the statement "all right", he pushed her in the direction of the green car.

As she stumbled, Dinasia instantly thought about running, but something told her these men may be the ones responsible for killing Mrs. Daye and probably had guns. Moving slowly towards the car, she saw the other man was black. She walked pass an old lady on a cane and a young white couple and wanted to scream for help. The thought of being shot made her change her mind.

Then, suddenly, Dinasia saw the black man's panic-stricken behavior as he frantically got out of the car. She quickly turned her head to see if there was something behind her causing all the excitement.

Just as she saw a man wearing a ski mask with a gun in his hand running towards her and the white guy, Dinasia saw the white guy's body jerk violently. She automatically thought the white guy was having some kind of epileptic fit since she didn't hear any gunshots. When she saw the blood oozing from the top of the white man's head as he collapsed to the ground, all her exposure to the Movie's told her the masked man was apparently using a silencer.

"Get the fuck outta the way!" The masked man yelled at Dinasia. "Duck! God-damn it! Get down!"

SZK! SZK! SZK! SZK! . . .

Dinasia dove to the pavement just as a barrage of silenced bullets started hitting the nearby cars and bouncing off the ground. Laying face down on the pavement next to the fallen phony detective, she turned and saw the black guy by the Escort was shooting. There were no loud blasts, but she could see fire sparks repeatedly bursting from the barrel of his gun.

She turned her head the other way to see where the masked man was and noticed he was behind a parked car exchanging gunfire with the black guy.

Dinasia's fear was so crippling, she didn't even realize she was crying until a tear dropped to the pavement. The eminent threat of death was so unbelievably real, it made her feel light headed, and since this type of situation was a first time experience, she recognized it had a way of hindering her thinking process. The hysteria was mounting and she concentrated not to let it cause her to fall apart completely.

AAARRRRHHHH!!

A blue Buick Regal came barreling into the parking lot and Dinasia thought the car was going to run her over. She closed her eyes, tucked her knees close to her chest while tensing up all the muscles in her body, waiting for the wheels to crush her. She heard the car come to a screeching halt no more than a couple of feet from her. Opening her eyes, she noticed the car stopped in between her and the black guy who was now shooting at the car.

"Woman, get your ass outta here!" Another masked man shouted from inside the car. The passenger window was rolled down and he yelled at the top of his voice. "Run! Go! Now!"

Dinasia thought she was having an illusion when she heard the man screaming for her to get outta here. She snapped into action. She was about to jump to her feet and flee, but she remembered the tape.

As Dinasia nervously dug into the dead white man's pocket, she heard police sirens. Pulling the tape out, she noticed people across the street were observing the conflict from behind cars and those who were inside the nearby stores could be seen peeking out of the windows.

Just as Dinasia frantically jumped inside her car, started it with one smooth turn of the key and breezed towards the exit, she noticed the Ford Escort was already racing out of the lot. She swerved around the dead white man and almost floored the gas pedal before she was out of the lot. As she turned right onto Mermaid Avenue, now flooring the gas pedal, she saw and heard a police car had arrived and was now tailing her.

"Pull it over!" A voice from the loud speaker of the police car said. "Pull Over!"

CCRRASSHH!!

Dinasia saw through the rearview mirror the blue Regal rammed the back of the patrol car. Logic told her to take advantage of this opportunity. She also knew if she was arrested that would end her fight for Tislam's freedom. There were two dead bodies laid stretched out on the sidewalk and in light of the racist, corrupt and malicious nature of the Court system, she knew they would find a way to hang her for these murders. If they did it to Tislam, they could damn sure do it to her.

She floored the accelerator, then made a series of sharp turns while pressing down on the horn, ducking and weaving cars and pedestrians. Her heart pounded vibrantly in her chest, ears and everywhere else.

After an indeterminate amount of turns, she looked at the mirror and still saw the police. Then, suddenly, she saw the blue Regal pull along side the police car and started side swiping it. When the police started shooting at the two men in the Regal, Dinasia flinched and almost hit a double parked car. Snatching the steering wheel to the left, she regained control and then looked at the rearview mirror again. She saw the Regal had pulled back, now trailing the cop car that pursued her.

Up ahead the street light at the upcoming intersection suddenly turned yellow. She pressed the gas pedal to the floor, locked her hand on the horn and prayed any on coming cars would hear her horn and not enter the intersection.

AAARRRHHHH!!! . . . BBBOOOOMM!!

Dinasia entered the intersection, almost struck a van, and caused another car to collide with the van. Once she was through the intersection, she hastily looked at the rearview mirror.

AAARRRHHH!!!---BOOOMM!!--BOOOOM!!--BOOOM!

The police car struck a small foreign car, bounced off that car, hit another car and flipped over. The Regal turned right. After making a couple of left and right turns, Dinasia sighed with relief as she let up off the gas pedal.

As she slowly began to calm down, it dawned on her. She had to get rid of this car. There was no doubt the police most definitely radioed in her license plates, the color of the car and the make. Every cop in the city is going to be looking for this vehicle, she realized, only seconds from hitting the panic button. *Relax. Don't lose your head girl. If you stay calm and think straight, you'll be all right,* she mumbled to herself while rocking back and forth, her grip so tight on the wheel her knuckles ached.

"What should I do? Where should I go?" Dinasia spoke out loud to herself as she nervously started chewing on her bottom lip. A minute later, a little voice in her head was telling her to get rid of the car immediately. That frightened her, made her hesitant despite the fact ditching the car was the logical thing to do. It was cold outside, she was a long way from home and the interior of the car gave her a false sense of safety and security.

The thought of the police chasing her again forced her to come to terms with reality. She frantically looked at the street signs to get a bearing on her whereabouts. She was on Ocean Parkway. A moment later, she stopped at a red light at the corner of Kings Highway, rolled the window down and spoke to the first person she saw crossing the street. The middle aged black woman was bundled up very snugly with a scarf covering her mouth. "Excuse me, Miss, where's the nearest train station?"

The woman hesitated, pulled the scarf from her face and said, "Go five blocks down and make a left." She pointed in the same direction the car was headed. "Then go about three blocks down to Bay Parkway. I think it's the D-train line. You can't miss it."

"Thank you," Dinasia said excitedly, watching the woman go about her way, wondering if her life was as crazy and screwed up as hers. The light turned green and she pulled away. She followed the woman's instructions. Two minutes later, she saw the underground subway station. Dinasia quickly found a parking space.

As Dinasia gathered everything of importance from the glove compartment, she heard what sounded like someone had turned a siren on and off very quickly. She looked up, observing the scenery in front of her and saw nothing. Turning her head, she heard the same sound again. When she noticed she couldn't see down the street in back of her because of the position the car was parked, she looked out the side view mirror, and a lightening bolt of shock struck her.

A police car was headed towards her.

Shock waves of terror, anxiety and hopelessness exploded inside Dinasia's mind. Trembling as if she was freezing to death, Dinasia did the only thing anyone in her catastrophic and unfortunate predicament would've done.

CHAPTER # 23

Cheops and Chico Rico were leaning against the wall near the E-Block windows staring at the yard door, waiting for Pus to return from the School. When a dozen Correction Officers came through the door, looking nervous as they started spreading out, circling the yard, Cheops and Chico Rico looked at each other with one of those knowing expressions.

The loud speakers all over the yard suddenly came to life. "THE YARD IS NOW CLOSED. ALL INMATES ARE TO REPORT TO THEIR CELLS IMMEDIATELY."

Neither Cheops nor Chico Rico had to be told there was a red dot in progress and it obviously had to do with the contract hit on Tislam. As they merged with the several dozens of other inmates, heading for their respective cellblocks, Chico Rico whispered. "This is fucked up, man. You know they don't shut the jail down unless one of them gets smoked."

Cheops was speechless with anger. He just looked at Chico Rico and gritted his teeth. A couple seconds later, he whispered to Chico Rico. "C.O. Carol's gonna visit me in another hour or two. We'll know soon enough."

"Hey Cheops," A prisoner with thick coke bottle glasses said as he quickly approached. "You heard what happened!?"

"Nah, what happened?" Cheops knew Paulie was like the facility Esquire, loaded always with gossip, rumors and info on all the latest news.

"Six motherfuckers got murdered in Jay School." Paulie whispered excitedly. "I heard it looked like a massacre, man."

Six!? Cheops was now trembling in his boots. "Who got murdered? Was it a C.O. or something?"

"They're shutting us down ain't they? It was that cool ass C.O. named Lane and they killed that new sergeant named Brickle. The other four were prisoners." He paused. "One of them was your man Tislam."

Cheops didn't have to pretend to be upset by the situation, which he knew Paulie expected him to be, and so he let the emotion be seen on his face. The death of two police is what actually shook him to the bone because that meant there was gonna be hell to pay. The heat wouldn't only come from in here, but would have its strongest impact from the outside because C.O. Lane was C.O. Carol's close friend, and since Carol had direct contact with the peoples, Cheops felt a terrifying anxiety growing in the pit of his stomach.

As Cheops entered the cell Block, he realized he had to find a quick way to deal with this crazy ass nigga Pus. Cheops figured if he was gonna take a hard fall for Pus's gross negligence, then Pus would have to get a piece of the pain and punishment too.

*   *   *   *

The black guy in the Ford Escort was on his cellular phone talking as he kept his eye on the road. He was traveling south on Kings Highway.

"Pete is dead, I told you . . . I saw it with my own fuckin' eyes. It was a head shot . . . Yeah, I saw him take the tape from Dinasia and then he gave me the eye signal saying it was a touch down . . . That's right . . . She took the tape after them dudes shot him . . . Yeah . . . huh . . . I saw it in her hand when she was getting in the car . . . If I had X-ray vision I would be able to tell you some shit like that. They had on masks for crying out loud. I don't know who the fuck they are . . . Tell Ronnie I need him to meet me at Church Avenue and Ocean Parkway . . . I don't wanna rub it in, but I told you I work better with my partner. I know Pete had that cop look and all, but people work better when they're comfortable . . . Listen, relax man. Me and Ronnie are gonna find her and that tape. If you got any extra guys you can spare, we could use them . . . Maybe seven or eight might do . . . Shit, if you got more than that send 'em all . . . She ain't got that many places she can go . . . I doubt if she goes there first, and even if she did, don't you got people over there as well? . . . She's gonna wanna see what's on that tape first, believe me, man . . . Yeah . . . huh . . . As long as you do your part, everything'll be fine . . ."

*   *   *   *

Dinasia rushed down the stairs of the Subway Station, bumping into people as she headed for the token booth. It wasn't hard to tell by the crowd of people entering and exiting the station that rush hour had just begun.

Moments earlier, when the police car approached, Dinasia crouched down in the front seat, hoping and praying the police would simply pass by without noticing her car. A couple seconds later, she noticed they didn't drive by and she peeked over the back seat and saw they had pulled over a group of teenagers who were drinking quarts of malt liquor. Dinasia hastily got out the car from the passenger door and almost ran to the subway station.

After purchasing a token, she went to the subway system map posted next to the booth and began mapping out her route back to Queens. While waiting on line to buy a token, she decided going home was out of the question; going to Keisha wouldn't be wise, and therefore that left one other place. Robert Sanchez's pawnshop. He had a VCR, and since right now the only thing that held any importance to her was seeing what was on that tape, the decision was the easiest one she made all day. Even food, and what she intended to do tomorrow, the next day and so on, didn't cross her mind at the moment. It took her two minutes to figure out how to get to Queens.

Five minutes later, she was on the D train and finally was able to think about other things besides escaping life threatening danger and arrest as she sat in the crowded train staring at the coat button of a woman standing in front of her. Instantly, the questions started raging wildly in her mind, competing with each other in an attempt to be answered first. There were so many things she wanted to know, but the main one was how could Shateek do something as wicked as kill an old lady?

He was behind all this madness, flinging his money and connections around like some kind of Big Willie. *He's trying to cover this thing up because he knows if it comes out, his ass might end up in prison forever.* Then it dawned on Dinasia: *That white man tried to rough me up.* This really touched her deeply and the thought almost pushed her over the edge because if Shateek loved her in any sense of the word, he would never allow one of his flunkies to physically abuse her no matter what the issue was. *That dirty trifling bastard!* She was fuming and inadvertently released a loud angry sigh, attracting the attention of the straphangers in her immediate vicinity.

Dinasia looked up and smiled at the woman in front of her. When she saw the woman's hateful eyes accompanied with an upside down smile, she turned away. What is wrong with this world? she thought, why are people so preoccupied with being mean when others are trying to show some love?

A second later, her mind was back at it again. Then the two masked men entered her head and that blew her away. Who could those men be? And why did they come to her aid? Were they the ones who diverted the police when she was in Mrs. Daye's apartment? It had to be. All the incidents re-enacted themselves inside her mind, and she knew this issue would certainly drive her mad as a hatter if she continued thinking about it because there was no answer to be found at this point. There was no telling what condition she would be in if those masked men hadn't showed up at the apartment and the Bank on Mermaid Avenue. She pushed the issue to the back of her mind, but wouldn't let go of the fact she wanted to thank them dearly.

As Dinasia got off the D Train at 34th Street in Manhatten and transfered to the R Train, she was still dazed and in deep thought, walking through the subway as if she were sleep-walking. By the time Dinasia exited the Northern Boulevard train station she was so anxious to see if this videotape was the real deal, she felt the urge to run all the way to Merrick Boulevard to Robert's pawnshop.

She flagged a cab, jumped in, told the driver the location, and several minutes later, she was getting out of the Taxi, trembling with anticipation. She rushed inside the Pawnshop and saw Robert was attending to a customer.

When Robert saw her, he smiled and gave her a head nod.   Dinasia browsed around the store looking at the items on display.

"Dinasia," Robert said cheerfully as the customer left the store. "How you doin'?"

"Not too good, Rob," Dinasia pulled the tape from her pocket. "Before I burn out your ear with all my problems, I need to use your VCR."

"No problem at all," He waved for her to follow him to the back of the shop. "It's always a pleasure to be of assistance to you. When I told you I'll always be in debt to you, I meant every word of it." He pointed to the VCR, which sat on a huge metal desk next to the T.V. "It's all yours." He turned and went back to the front of the shop.

Dinasia frantically turned on both the VCR and T.V., inserted the tape and pressed the play button. While the tape turned and churned, she quickly took her coat off, realizing for the first time just how lovely the heat was inside the shop. She pulled up a chair and got comfortable.

*   *   *   *

Moments earlier, across the street from Robert Sanchez's pawnshop, a man sitting alone inside a white Range Rover Jeep observed Dinasia get out of the cab and enter the store. He immediately dialed a number on his cellular and spoke.

"This is Fontaine. She just arrived at the pawnshop. No, she's alone . . . No problem at all . . . When y'all get here, I'll be waiting." He disconnected the line, put the phone down and continued observing the pawnshop.

*   *   *   *

The picture of the Pink House Project popped on the screen, and Dinasia's heart start beating with anxiety. When she saw Tislam and Kirk arguing, she shouted "yeah!" knowing this was it. She felt like she hit the Super Mega-Million dollar Lotto.

As she sat riveted to the T.V., the events unfolding just as Mrs. Morris had said, she felt a strong pain in her heart for Tislam. Her eyes

162

instantly became watery. She smiled when she saw Mrs. Daye pointed the camera at the man hiding on the side of the building. When he started shooting, Dinasia flinched despite already knowing the gunfire was forthcoming. Suddenly, the camera was pulled back so as to catch all the action. Then it turned some, landed on the shooter and then focused on him clearly as he started to leave.

"Oh, shit!" Dinasia rose from the chair, leaning closer to the T.V. The shock was mind boggling. "That was . . . Nah, it can't be." She sat back down and rewind the tape to the close up shot of the shooters face.

As she repeatedly scrutinized the same part of the tape over and over again, her mind started making the connections and that feeling of hate returned. The thought of shooting Shateek on sight was now becoming the only way to deal with him. She mumbled angrily to herself.

Robert entered. "Hey, you all right in here?" he asked, observing the television. "This must be some serious stuff, the way it got you in here talkin' to yourself."

Dinasia stopped the tape and rewinded it to the beginning. She needed Robert's help and was going to show him the tape during her effort to persuade him. "Rob, I'm not gonna beat around the bush. I need your help. What I'm about to share with you is gonna sound far-fetched, but it's the truth." It took Dinasia fifteen minutes to explain just about everything to Robert. She started from the day Prince was shot and worked her way up to the point when she decided to come to his store about two hours ago. "It's crazy isn't it?"

"Wow, this sounds like something right out of a movie script." He paused. "And you say your husband is behind all this? He's now trying to kill you? Well, let's go to the police--Oh, yeah, I forgot his brother's a big time cop. Well, I guess I put my foot in my mouth when I told you to come see me for anything." He giggled nervously.

"Let's watch the tape." Dinasia said, pressing the play button. "This'll help motivate you some. You're a very kind and moral person, and just seeing how they went about putting him in prison for the rest of his life should help boost your--"

"Hello, anyone here?" The voice came from the front of the store.

"I'll be right back," Robert quickly rose and went to the front of the store as Dinasia stopped the tape.

About two minutes later, Dinasia heard what sounded like sudden whispers commingled with temporary moments of ordinary talk coming from the front. This activated her curiosity. She walked closer to the entrance and for about a minute she strained to hear those short whispers again. There were no whispers. Just ordinary customer/salesman talk. When Robert said good-bye to the male customer, she scurried back to her seat.

"Okay let's see the tape." Robert sat down as Dinasia pressed the play button.

When the tape got to the part where the camera was focused on the shooter, Dinasia observed Robert's reaction to see if he knew the man. She saw his eyebrows slightly crunched up and he shifted in his seat. She couldn't tell for certain if his response was from knowing the shooter or because of the graphic nature of the shooting.

When the tape stopped, Dinasia spoke. "For starters, I wanna make a couple of back-up copies of this tape; we'll need another VCR."

"That's not a problem," Robert said, standing. "Mr. Walton next door will let me borrow his if he hasn't gone home already." He looked at his watch. "We might be out of luck. He closes at six. It's 6:32 now. He's probably gone." He headed to the front, looked out the door and then returned. "Yep, he's gone. I got a VCR at my home, but I'm a little apprehensive about taking you there."

Dinasia's eyebrows rose. "Why's that?"

"The safety of my children. What if you're being followed? I can't afford to have my children exposed to danger like--"

"I'm telling you, Rob, no one followed me. And whoever these people are, they wouldn't expect me to come here. No one knows I know you."

Robert paused, thinking. "Well, all right. But what are you gonna do after you get copies? I really would like to offer you to stay at my--"

"I'm staying at a hotel." She was actually going to ask to stay a night, but now that was a dead issue. "Tomorrow first thing in the morning I'll go to the lawyer's office. I just need you to assist me with getting copies of this tape . . . And I was wondering if I could borrow your car?"

"Consider it done, my friend," Robert said, good naturedly. After a moments pause he continued. "I can borrow one of my cousin's cars to get to work. It's an old piece of junk, but it runs . . . Are you hungry? From what you told me, I doubt if you had time to eat today."

Upon hearing something related to food, Dinasia's stomach exploded with hunger pains. "I'm so hungry, I could eat a restaurant into bankruptcy."

"We'll grab a bite to eat while on the way to my house. You can get yourself cleaned up." He pointed to the bathroom. "I'll start closing up the place and be with you in a couple of minutes." Robert exited the back room. He quickly and loudly began closing all the showcase display windows. When he heard Dinasia enter the bathroom, he rushed over to the threshold to make certain she was in the bathroom. He saw she was gone. He turned and hurried to the phone directly under the cash register.

CHAPTER # 24

At about the moment Dinasia was on the R Train, heading for Queens, the Dutchess County Hospital's emergency surgery unit was in an uproar. Two critically wounded male patients from the prison arrived alive and went straight into surgery while four other males were dead on arrival and went to the morgue.

In emergency surgery room # 3, two Doctors, Bill Evans and Richard Gibbs along with three assistants worked on Tislam's multiple stab wounds to his torso, chest and head areas.

Ten minutes into the surgery, the heart monitor assistant, with curly brown hair and a baby face, spoke excitedly. "He's going into cardiac arrest, doctor!"

Bill spoke excitedly. "Give him four cc's of--"

"He's flat line!" The same assistant shouted as the monitor buzzed loudly.

Bill grabbed the defibrillators as the female assistant sprayed an ointment on the two hand held instruments.

Tislam's body bounced violently when Bill sent the jolt of electricity through his chest.

"Again!" Richard said. "We got a flutter."

The defibrillators sounded like a stick hitting a cardboard box as it sent jolts through Tislam's chest.

Tislam's lifeless body bounced again, but nothing happened.

Bill tried it again and again.

Richard grabbed Bill's arm when he was about to try it a fifth time. "Let it go, Bill."

Bill shrugged frustratingly because he hated when death won. "He was doing fine the whole damn operation. I can never understand why--"

"We have another flutter!" The heart monitor assistant shouted. "He's trying to come back."

With lightening speed, Bill applied the defibrillators on Tislam's chest and released another electrical jolt.

The heart monitor started beeping loudly with a full heartbeat.

"All right!" Bill cheered calmly. "He just needed a little help that's all. Increase oxygen and stabilize all of his--"

"We're losing him again!" The assistant shouted.

"Shit!" Bill sighed.

"Flat line!" The assistant shouted. "He's flat lining!"

Bill hit Tislam four straight times with the artificial electrical current without his heart coming back to life. Bill was about to try it again.

"Bill," Richard grabbed him. "He's gone. Let it go, Bill. Even if he came back he'll be a vegetable for the rest of his life. With such an extended lack of blood flow to the brain, permanent full blown apoplexy will be inevitable."

Reluctantly, Bill sat the defibrillators on the sterilized tray, sighing as if he was exhausted. "Yeah, you're right." He was even more angered than before because it was like death was taunting him, almost as if it winked its eye and then spitted in his face.

"You want me to pronounce him, Bill? You look like you need a break."

"I'll handle it," Bill looked at his watch. "Jerry, I need you to mark the time on the--"

"Look Doc!" The heart monitor assistant shouted. "We got a strong vital! He's back!"

Bill was beyond shocked. He raced over, shouting orders with gruesome accuracy and then said, "I'll be damn if we lose him again. Apparently this guy doesn't wanna leave here . . ."

An hour later, Tislam's four major stab wounds were repaired. Bill and Richard were washing their hands in the Sterilization Unit about to take a short break.

Richard spoke. "You know this young man is gonna be a vegetable. Do you really think the State is gonna spend all that money to keep him alive on a life support machine? Expensive is not the word as you know. More like outrageously costly would be a better description. An inmate will never get such red carpet treatment. Since this is your patient, guess who they're gonna want to pull the plug? It might've been a lot easier if you had let him go when he flat lined."

Bill was sizzling with a mixture of anger, rage and disbelief. He wanted to haul off and knock the living shit out of Richard. But he restrained his urge to lash out because he knew Richard had an issue with Mr. Parker because he was black; old toxic Rich was just being himself, a genuine racist. "Rich, my man, unlike you, I'm an ethical surgeon. And I treat all my patients in accordance with my sworn oath."

Bill walked over to the hand-drying machine, hit the hot air button, and continued. "If the state gets a court order directing me to pull the plug, then that's what I'll do when that time comes . . . Until then, Mr. Parker will get the red carpet treatment like all other patients under my care."

*   *   *   *

When C.O. Carol appeared in front of the cell, he saw Cheops pacing inside the small cage and could almost feel the rage rolling off of his body.

The music from the nearby cells was loud enough mask any nearby conversations, but C.O. Carol still whispered. "What the hell happened?"

Cheops's tongue felt like it was tied in knots. "Tislam was family. We vowed never to flip once we took that oath. I had to get an outsider--"

"That was a quarter million dollar hit!" C.O. Carol wanted to shout, but kept his volume low. "With money like that, those little silly ass oaths are out the window. What are you? Outta your fuckin' mind!?"

Cheops was about to speak, but C.O. Carol wasn't finished. "Of all the crews running around here why the fuck you chose the Crimson Cowboys? You know Pus got a thing for warring with cops or anyone involved in law enforcement . . . Do you realize what happened here!? The people out there are already raising hell. This was the sloppiest run in the history of this whole god-damn prison."

"But at least the target is dead. It may have cost some extra causalities, but the mission was accomplished." Cheops didn't like the sudden look on Carol's face. "I heard all six of them are dead."

"Well you heard wrong," C.O. Carol hissed. "Everyone except the god-damn target is dead."

Cheops became weak in the knees and he had to sit down on his bunk. "How the hell is that possible!?"

"I don't know. But you better brace yourself because boy oh boy is the top man out there pissed off with you . . . But you got something working in your favor."

Cheops noticed Carol's silence was persisting beyond reasonable bounds. "What is it!?" He stood and went to the bars.

"The target is in a coma. I don't know if that qualifies as a score since it's just as good as being dead, but it's something they might take into consideration . . . Need I tell you they obviously want people to pay for this royal fuck up? And Pus and his crew gotta be dealt with?"

"No, you don't." Cheops was already rigging up extravagant ways to murder these lunatic niggas. "There's only one problem. This lock down might go on for the next month or more. I would love to deal with this as--"

"Tomorrow I'm working the gallery where Pus is housed. I'll make arrangements to have you transferred over. Need I say anymore?"

"No, you don't," Cheops smiled as C.O. Carol walked away. "Not at all."

CHAPTER # 25

Dinasia swallowed the last morsel of her seafood salad, savoring the tasty delicacy as if it was the best meal she'd ever eaten. Even the strange looking black man who had an unusually thick beard and mustache, who entered "Regina's Restaurant" located on Concord Boulevard shortly after she and Robert, couldn't distract her from enjoying the meal. The strange man sat a few tables away. All throughout the meal, Dinasia spied the man and eventually realized he wasn't paying her and Robert any mind, or at least it appeared that way.

"I'll handle the check, Robert," Dinasia raised her hand to get the waiter's attention. "It's the least I can do after all you've done for me."

"Ahh, come on, those things I did are nothing when people are true friends. Don't forget, you helped me when I was messed up pretty bad, and I still haven't repaid you."

"Don't be silly," Dinasia handed the waiter her credit card and he scurried away. "The deal you gave me with that gun was more than sufficient to clear this debt you talk about."

"Do you still have that thing?" Robert asked with a smile.

"I got it right here in my purse along with the tape," Dinasia patted the tote bag that sat on the table. She stood when she saw the waiter approaching with her credit card and a receipt. "Thank you very much. This was a wonderful meal."

"Thank you, ma'am," The waiter said smilingly. "Please come back."

Dinasia and Robert went to the coat rack, put on their coats, and were on their way out the door.

With her tote bag snuggled closely to her, Dinasia stepped out of the restaurant and instantly noticed a man with thick facial hairs standing in front of the establishment with a Salvation Army cardboard sign hanging around his neck, a beggar's cup in his hand and those eyes. The man had eyes that instinctively meant something to her even though they were a deep blue set in a white face surrounded by a salt and pepper beard and mustache. The man looked a little like a decrepit Santa Claus. But the way those eyes made contact with hers disturbed her deeply. Dinasia shook loose of the chill that grabbed hold of her as she led the way towards Robert's Toyota.

The car was parked smack dab in the middle of the parking lot and she still couldn't understand why Robert parked so far from the entrance, especially when there were closer unoccupied spaces. When they were about ten feet from the car, Dinasia saw the rapidly approaching cars coming from all four directions.

AAARRRRHHHH!! AAARRRRHHHH!!

The screeching car tires from the four cars and the white Range Rover Jeep that surrounded her and Robert launched Dinasia into a frantic flee. She reached for her 25 automatic while she spun around in a circle, noticing they were boxed in completely.

She pointed the gun at the black guy, who was the first person to get out of one of the vehicles. The cranberry colored Nissan Maxima looked new and she recognized it was the black man from the Bank parking lot. Another man got out the passenger side; he had on sunglasses and looked rather ridiculous, since it was nighttime and freezing cold.

The black guy spoke. "Now, what in the world are you gonna do with that little ass pee shooter against this." He waved his hand in the air as the 13 men got out of their cars.

Each one of the men pulled, cocked and pointed their weapons, ranging from Uzis and assault rifles to a spectrum of all sorts of handguns.

Dinasia saw all those guns aimed at her and Robert, and decided determinatively that if she lived to see another day, she was gonna shoot Shateek on sight. This was beyond an outrage.

The black guy continued. "First, drop the gun, Dinasia."

He knew her name and that was the clincher for Dinasia. She shrugged angrily. They knew her because they were apparently Shateek's boys. That low-life motherfucker, she sizzled inwardly as she dropped the gun.

The black guy came from around the open car door and headed towards Dinasia with the man wearing sunglasses on his heels. "We want that tape. Give it to me and we'll let you walk away without getting yourself hurt or killed. How that sounds?" He nodded his head nonchalantly.

Dinasia saw the man nodded his head while looking strangely at Robert and wondered what was that all about? Suddenly she felt Robert snatch at her bag, but she held on to it with a death grip. "Robert, what the fuck's wrong with you!?" She tried to jerk the bag from him.

"Please just give them the tape," Robert said to her with clinched teeth. The thought of not getting that ten thousand dollars Fontaine had offered him was making him crazy.

"That's right, Robby," The black man said smilingly. "Bring it to us and everything'll be just fine."

"You know them?" Dinasia was thunder-struck with surprise. "You back-stabbin'--"

"They threatened to kill my kids," Robert continued tugging at the bag. "They said they would kill them."

Dinasia and Robert fell to the floor. "Get the fuck off me!" Dinasia shouted, not wanting to even imagine losing this evidence of Tislam's innocence.

Suddenly, police sirens could be heard from a far off distance.

Ronnie took his sunglasses off and shouted. "Let's get this shit moving--"

BOW! . . . BOW! BOW!

One of the soldiers on the sideline shot at Dinasia's hand when she reached for the 25 automatic.

The black guy shot the soldier twice in the head, spraying blood and brain matter all over Foutaine's white Jeep. "I told you motherfuckers . . ." He was about to reiterate his order that Dinasia was not to be hurt, but held his tongue. Instead, he shouted. "Robert, you was supposed to have the fuckin' tape already--"

BOW! BOW! BOW! BOW! BOW! BOW! . . .

The sudden gunfire from the two men with thick facial hair startled everyone. Their bullets rained upon the area with prefect precision, knocking five of the soldiers, including Fontaine out of the picture with bullet-ridden bodies before they realized it was an ambush.

The remaining seven men who weren't gunned down jumped in their cars, while returning fire at the two men who were on either side of the circle of cars. They frantically drove off with tires screaming. The three cars barreled out of the restaurant parking lot doing close to 60 miles an hour, leaving the white Range Rover and one of the cars behind with their bullet ridden owners and operators sprawled on the pavement.

Dinasia and Robert were still on the pavement wrestling and tussling over the bag containing the tape. Suddenly, the bag ripped and the tape was flung as if it was a discharged missile, sliding under the white Range Rover.

Dinasia tried to go for the tape, but Robert grabbed her foot, tripping her back to the pavement. He started punching her in the back of the head. Dinasia rolled over and kicked Robert in the face. She sprung to her feet. "They're gone, Robert. Stop this foolishness and let me--"

Robert punched Dinasia in the face, almost dropping her back to the ground.

Dinasia clutched her mouth and decided she was sick and totally tired of playing games with Robert. Her martial arts tactics came back to her like a vivid flashback. First she unleashed three lightning fast and solid kicks to his head; a couple of right crosses to Robert's glass jaw came next and then a countless barrage of upper cuts to his flabby gut took the fight out of him. The coup de grace blow was an overhand right, which took him down hard, fast and forthright. He was out cold.

Breathing like she'd just ran ten miles, Dinasia noticed the sirens were now becoming much louder as she frantically spun around in a circle, searching for the tape. *They'll be here any minute*, the voice in her head screamed at her. *It's time to flee or get arrested*, the voice continued.

Dinasia got on her hands and knees and looked under the white jeep. She panicked when she didn't see the tape, but instead saw the black work boots of two men. She stood, went to the side of the vehicle and peeked at the old busted ass Santa Claus with the Salvation Army sign still hanging around his neck; instead of a beggar's cup in his hand he had a huge machine gun in one and the tape in the other. The other bearded man, the one who was inside the restaurant, was standing behind the Salvation Army beggar pacing back and forth with a gun in each hand. She could see a small stream of smoke oozing from the barrels of both guns.

Dinasia stood, headed for the men as if she was hypnotized, and the words flowed from her mouth as if they had a mind of their own. "May I please have my tape back?"

The Salvation Army beggar paused for a long moment and then tossed the tape to Dinasia.

Dinasia tried to catch it, but noticed it was deliberately thrown a manner not designed for her to catch it. She instinctively kneeled to pick it up while not once taking her eyes off the two strange men she knew had to be wearing disguises.

When she saw the blue eyed bushy face Salvation Army beggar raise the gun, pointing it at her, she screamed. "NOOO!!"

BOW! BOW! BOW! BOW! BOW! BOW! . . .

CHAPTER # 26

Shateek nervously peeked out his living room window to see if the blue car that was following him would reappear. After giving the two guys the slip, Shateek parked his Jeep two blocks away in front of a Novelty store, got out the vehicle, proceeded to the back of the store, leaped a few fences, entered his home from the backyard and strategically left the lights turned off while heading straight for the window.

As his eyes danced over the front area of his house, noticing nothing out of the norm, Shateek pulled his cellular and dialed the number.

A moment later, he spoke into the phone: "What the fuck happened!? I thought I told you I didn't want Dinasia hurt!? . . . Don't worry about that!? What the fuck is that, a joke? Oh, so now you wanna be a goddamn comedian, huh? . . . You stupid motherfucker that's my wife, that's why . . .That's too fuckin' close for comfort and I don't want any more close calls like that again . . . I heard about that, yeah . . . That's right . . . Now that was a smart move . . . Listen here, those two motherfuckers are the ones we need to stop fucking around with. We're gonna bring the noise to them and get this shit jumpin' the way it's supposed to be . . . Maybe if we get rid of them, we'll be able to get this thing under control . . ."

*   *   *   *

Dinasia laid in the hotel bed, slowly drifting to sleep. The second floor single occupancy room in a Hotel located on Spencer Place a few blocks from Nostrand Avenue, wasn't a top of the line hotel room, but it did have heat, hot water and was clean. However, Dinasia was upset because the room wasn't equipped with a VCR. If she had a car besides Robert's (which was hotter than fresh Volcanic Lava because the police was probably looking for it by now), she would've continued searching for a better Hotel.

She reflected on the events of the night and could still hear inside her head the voice of the bearded man, the one who was inside the restaurant with her and Robert. After he and the Salvation Army beggar shot the man who sprung to his feet and tried to shoot them, the man said to her, "These people are trying to kill Tislam. He's in a hospital right now. If he stays in there any longer, they'll eventually get him. Whatever you're gonna do, you better hurry up." The man's voice was very deep and had a strong southern accent. Then, the two turned and fled. She jumped in Robert's car and fled to Brooklyn.

Dinasia held the image of Tislam's face in her mind as she dozed off.
BUUUZZZ!!
The alarm clock rang.
The next morning felt like it came as quick as the snap of a finger.

Dinasia rose in a mechanical fashion, turned the alarm off and went straight to work. She hastily took a shower, got dressed, went to the store, ate a quick meal, got a pocket full of quarters and headed for the public phone booth. It took her two minutes of talking with the operator to obtain the number to the Green Haven Prison. After her past experience with the prison officials, she knew she had to pretend to be someone they would respect and give her the info she needed. Taking deep breaths to clear her head, she dialed the number.

"Green Haven Correctional Facility." The voice of a lady said through the phone.

"Hello, this is Captain Martha Jones of the New York State Police," Dinasia said into the receiver. "I'm investigating the incident that occurred yesterday. May I speak to the Superintendent, please?"

"Yes," The woman said. "Please hold."

As Dinasia waited, she crossed her fingers hoping and praying the State Police hadn't begun an in-depth investigation. Based on the books she read, the State Police normally waited until the county people got their stuff together before officially intervening. Please let this be the case.

"Hello, this is Superintendent Sterling."

"This is Captain Jones of the State Police, I would like to ask you a few questions regarding yesterday's incident. One of my subordinates visited your facility yesterday, but his account of the incident was somewhat inadequate and his report was missing a few important details. I need a brief run-down of what transpired."

And they call us incompetent, Superintendent Sterling thought and then said, "It appears there was a deadly conflict between two rival gangs. While they were engaged in a huge knife fight, two officers were killed when they tried to break it up. Three inmates died as well. There's a whole lot of in between information, but that's it in a nut shell."

"Were there any survivors?"

"Yes, one of the inmates survived."

"Where is he at this moment?"

"He's in the hospital, of course," Superintendent Sterling said in a tone that indicated she obviously should've known this.

"Excuse me, I meant what hospital is he in?" Dinasia said seriously.

"Dutchess County."

"And what is his name?"

"Tislam Parker."

Although Dinasia found what she was looking for, she asked several additional questions to make it look good and then terminated the interview. She hung up, dialed the operator, obtained the number to the Dutchess County Hospital and made the call. After a brief discussion with the telephone receptionist, the woman connected Dinasia straight to Doctor Bill Evan's phone line.

"Hello," Bill said.

"This is Captain Martha Jones of the State Police. I'm investigating the altercation that occurred at the prison and I was informed that you're Tislam Parker's physician. I have several very brief questions I would like to ask you--"

"I'm sorry, but I'm about to perform a surgery and I can't--"

"It's not gonna take long. I wanna know what is Mr. Parker's current condition? Is he able to be interviewed?"

Bill sighed loudly. "No, he's in a coma."

Dinasia almost lost her composure, but quickly got a grasp on her emotions. "Is he expected to survive this ordeal? This condition he's in, is it permanent?"

"Under the circumstance, I would say that's very likely," Bill sighed again.

"By next month would it be possible to communicate with him through--"

"At the rate it's going, ma'am, I doubt he makes it until next month. He's on life support and there's already talk of pulling the plug. I don't normally get into all this police stuff, but I was told this inmate is suspected of killing one of the officers and now the prison people want his head. I'm caught in the middle of all this madness."

"What do you mean, you're in the middle of all this?"

"Legal papers have already been filed by the Correction's Union to have the plug pulled. When the Court grants that order, which they most certainly will, I'm the one who has to pull that plug. It's a dam shame this poor guy doesn't have some kind of family member to intervene. This is really a big mess."

"About how long do you think it'll take this Court order to be handed down?" Dinasia struggled to hold back the sniffles. She wiped the runaway tear from her face.

Bill drew a deep breath and let it out. "I would say within the next two weeks, maybe even sooner."

"Two weeks!?" Dinasia repeated; her voice riddled with sheer devastation. Without saying another word she dropped the phone and raced out of the phone booth.

"Hello . . . Hello. Captain, you there?" Bill shrugged and hung up the phone.

*   *   *   *

Dinasia entered the law offices of Bruce Snyder looking like a nervous wreck. The second floor establishment was a hole in the wall set-up located in 134 Court Street, about six blocks from the Brooklyn

Supreme Court. She'd finally gotten the tears under control, but the nervous twitch was there to stay, at least until she found a way to neutralize the problem that caused the anxiety.

"Hello, Mrs. Wesley," Dinasia said to the secretary, who was writing something in a yellow steno-pad. "I need to see Mr. Snyder?"

"Do you have an appointment?" Mrs. Wesley looked up from the pad with an agitated expression on her face and a nasty tone in her voice. Her cat-woman glasses made her look like the epitome of a ball-breaker, ass-hole secretary.

Dinasia thought about the question. The possibility of not being able to see the lawyer made her lie with a straight face. "Yes, I do. Mr. Snyder told me if I have an emergency, to drop in anytime."

"I didn't ask you what you discussed with Mr. Snyder. Is there something wrong with your hearing? I wanna know if I look in this appointment book will I see your name?"

Dinasia was about to explode with anger. Mrs. Wesley's snotty attitude was working her last nerve in such a way she felt a rapidly growing urge to get hostile and assertive. Her eyes got chinky as she spoke. "Is Mr. Snyder here? Is he in his office?"

"Yes, he's in his office--"

Dinasia headed for the door in back of the secretary.

"Hey!" Mrs. Wesley sprung to her feet. "Where the hell do you think you're going!?" She rushed behind Dinasia. "You can't just barge in here like that."

Dinasia opened Mr. Snyder's door and saw him on the phone. When the secretary grabbed her arm, Dinasia snatched it away, turned and faced Mrs. Wesley. "You put your hands on me again and I'll break your fuckin' back BITCH!" Dinasia almost burst out laughing when she saw the woman flinch and cringe like a cold blooded coward and then scurried away as Mr. Snyder released a good hardy laugh.

Dinasia turned and spoke. "I have to speak with you. It's an emergency." She didn't wait to be offered a seat.

Bruce brought the laughter under control. "The way you handle my sentry that's not hard to tell." Bruce inched up in his seat. "Your name is Mrs. Whitman, right? I remember now, the innocent guy in prison. Yeah . . . Well, I'm all ears."

It took Dinasia five minutes to tell Bruce what happened. She started from the day of her last visit here at this very same office, working her way to the point when she made the phone call to Doctor Bill Evans. She was in tears and on the verge of hysteria by the time she finished.

"Take it easy," Bruce handed her a box of Kleenex tissues. "Please dry your eyes. If you have that tape with you I would sure like to take a look at it. Mrs. Elizabeth Daye did a remarkable deed if she was able to capture that moment."

Dinasia's alarms started ringing and the surprise literally shook her into a state of extreme caution. *How did he know Mrs. Daye's first name?* She was absolutely certain she never mentioned Mrs. Daye or Mrs. Morris's first names since she knew if she did it could imply she had a personal relationship with them, and therefore, she consciously used only last names. Her sudden change in attitude was done so abruptly, she realized the lawyer sensed it. "First, I wanna ask a few other questions."

"Be my guest," Bruce leaned back in his chair, got comfortable and then looked at his watch. "I have a meeting in twenty minutes. But this is much more important. I guess they'll have to wait."

"Can we get Tislam out of that place before they pull the plug?"

"I have to see the tape first," He said point blank.

"What's the usual time length it takes to present an issue like this to the Courts?" Dinasia wondered why the lawyer started acting like he was upset.

"I can't do anything without seeing that tape," Bruce leaned forward, propped his elbow on the desk and cupped his hands. "Do you have the tape with you?"

No response.

"I have a VCR right here." Bruce continued. "We can both watch it together. Then and only then will I be able to tell you what--"

"It's been nice talking to you, Mr. Snyder," Dinasia said as she rose and headed for the door. She turned the doorknob. It was locked. She turned, facing Bruce. "I would like to leave if you--"

"Have a seat, Mrs. Whitman," He gestured his hand toward the seat she sat in moments ago.

Dinasia pulled the 25 automatic and pointed it at Bruce. "I said open the fuckin' door!"

"Wow," Bruce appeared completely unnerved, almost as if this was the most natural thing in the world. "Is that a real gun!? It looks rather small, I might add. What caliber is that? Looks like--"

"You think I'm fuckin' around with you?" Dinasia rapidly and angrily moved towards Bruce with the gun aimed at his head.

Bruce raised his hands in the air. "Woooh, now, take it easy. I wouldn't do that if I were you. I think you better put that thing away before they enter."

KNOCK!--KNOCK!

The hard knock on the door stopped Dinasia in her tracks and made her wonder what Bruce meant when he said 'before they enter'? She heard commotion on the other side of the door, along with the sound of a key tinkering with the lock and then the door swung open.

Dinasia almost fainted when she saw the two police officers.

"DROP THE WEAPON!!—PUT IT DOWN!--NOW!!" The two police officers shouted frantically, pulling their weapons with incalculable speed.

Dinasia was petrified, but she quickly complied with their order. After dropping the gun, her hands shot up in the air, trembling like a certified alcoholic fiending for a hit of some hard liquor.

One of the police officers rushed over to Dinasia and put the cuffs on her while the other spoke to Bruce. "Does she have the tape?"

Dinasia was shocked when she heard the cop mention the tape. As the other cop spun her around, she saw the smirk on Bruce's face grow into a proud grin.

Bruce answered the cop's inquiry as he walked towards Dinasia. "Actually, I don't know," He began pat-frisking Dinasia, sneaking in a couple of perverted squeezes while in the process. "But we're sure about to find out." He smiled when he found the tape in her coat pocket. "Well, well. Bingo!"

The cop, who spoke earlier, continued as he picked up the 25 automatic from off the floor. "I guess this'll slow down our little Miss busy body." He headed for the door. "Let's get her over to Central Booking, Johnny." As his hand touched the doorknob, he turned and spoke to Bruce. "Give him a call right away and let him know everything's in order."

"You know something? You must be a mind reader," Bruce said sarcastically, but really wanted to say something along the lines of 'what the fuck you think I was gonna do?' "That was the first thing popped in my head. How did you know?" He smiled when he saw the cop screw his face up as he walked out the door.

As Dinasia was escorted out of the office and towards the front door, she saw the smile on the secretary's face and decided if the woman said one word, she would spit in her face. She said nothing and they stepped into the hallway, heading for the elevator.

The minute the cop's hand touched the elevator button, Dinasia heard the movement and just as her head turned right . . .

"Put your hands up!" The rapidly approaching masked man said venomously. As he hastily moved towards Dinasia and the two cops, he had both his handguns carefully aimed at the three of them.

"I wouldn't do that if I were you," Another masked man said with a strong southern accent, placing a double barreled shotgun to the back of the cop's head as his hand went for his revolver. "Let's try this again, gentlemen. Put your fuckin' hands in the air!" The rage in his voice was frightening.

Both police officers complied.

After both cops were bound, gagged and handcuffed to a radiator near the staircase and she was uncuffed, Dinasia spoke. "Who the hell are you guys and why are you always popping up--"

"Let's go," The man with the two guns handed Dinasia the 25-automatic and lead her down the staircase. "Tislam needs you. That's all you need to know."

"Wait!" Dinasia sounded terror-stricken. "I can't leave." She headed back to the office. "He took something from me." Dinasia's mind instantly went crazy with questions. The main one that nagged at her was how did he know Tislam? But she knew the moment was too intense to seek answers to these inquiries.

The masked man grabbed Dinasia's arm just as she was about to enter the office. He took the lead and stepped inside with both guns pointed at the secretary, noticing she was about to unleash one of those ear-shattering screams. "If a scream comes outta your mouth, I'll splatter your brains all over that pretty picture on the wall behind you."

As he handcuffed and taped the woman's mouth, the other masked man who had the shotgun rushed inside Bruce's office. He kicked the mobile serving tray and rack into the wall. It made a nerve-racking crash, shattering glasses and liquor bottles. The strong odors of various liquors instantly fumigated the entire office.

"Put your hands up!" He shouted when he saw Bruce hysterically reached for the draw. His southern drawl wavered from intense to almost non-existent. "Don't play yourself, motherfucker! Now, put 'em up!"

The masked man with the two guns, shouted at Dinasia. "What are you waitin' for!? Let's go!"

Dinasia didn't know what he was referring to since the crashing sound disoriented her. She looked truly panic-stricken and as confused as a lost child in a foreign supermarket.

"The tape!" The two gun masked man shouted. "Hurry!"

Dinasia ran into the room, came to a sliding stop and saw Bruce was tied up, laying face down on the floor.

"It's right there on the desk," The masked man with the shotgun pointed as he was placing tape over Bruce's mouth.

Dinasia wanted to stop and ask them how did they know about this tape? But everything was moving too fast. She also wanted to pull those masks off their faces so badly the temptation felt like one of those pestering itches that could drive the most disciplined Buddhist Monk insane. She could also tell the men were attempting to alter their voices when they spoke.

As Dinasia crammed the tape in her pocket, the masked man with the shotgun said to her: "I hope you can handle it from here." Afterwards, he ran out the door. With flinching speed, she rushed from behind the desk and followed. "Wait for me!" She shouted at the backs of both men as they disappeared out of the office. Dinasia was about to follow, but her curiosity along with the desire to go to the next location fully equipped and her belief that things were under control, dominated the rational part of her mind.

She stopped, turned, rushed back to Bruce's desk and started searching the draws and file cabinets.

Bruce mumbled and thrashed on the floor.

"Shut up, you back stabbin' bastard!" Dinasia shouted, now rummaging through the bottom draw of the file cabinet. She was looking for something that would tell her who Bruce was working for and hoped he had something laying around that specifically linked him to Shateek.

Time is running out! The voice in her head shouted. *Hurry up!*

Dinasia wasn't the least amazed by the fact Shateek and his connection's hands were able to reach into places she couldn't begin to imagine. This fiasco made it clear, she had to go someplace higher. With only days left, strong action was the only avenue of approach. If there was hard evidence inside this office, like documentary proof (consisting of handwritten notes mentioning Shateek or Mrs. Daye or reports or documents linking Bruce to the actual shooter), which could further support her position that this was a conspiracy to frame Tislam, it would be stupid on her part not to take advantage of this opportunity. She was now tossing papers all over the office floor.

She looked behind the small refrigerator and saw the safe built inside the wall. "Hey! Look what we got here." She kneeled and tried to open it, but the vault door wouldn't budge. She stood, turned, and saw Bruce had rolled onto his side; his knees were tucked close to his chest in what is known as the fetal position. "Bruce, we're gonna play us a little game called you either open this safe or lose a few fingers." She headed towards him.

Bruce mumbled and thrashed frantically.

"Look who's smilin' now, Mr. cut throat lawyer," Dinasia said to Bruce, who mumbled angrily in response. "This is for squeezing my behind and breasts!"

WHAM!

She gave Snyder a firm kick square in the ass. Upon impact, his legs shot out like a switchblade knife. "Now, are you gonna open this safe?" She kneeled beside him, couldn't tell what the responsive mumbles meant, but she sure liked the way the kick felt on the tip of her toes. Real cushiony. She instantly decided to give ole Miss ball-breaker Wesley a few swift kicks before leaving.

Suddenly, Dinasia heard screeching car tires out front down below and she frantically ran to the window.

"Shit!" She hissed angrily. The heart stopping shock immobilized her when she saw five police cars and the numerous cops racing towards the building she was in.

CHAPTER # 27

The cell door opened.

Cheops scooped up his shower gear and headed down the gallery. He was so cool, calm and collected he looked like he didn't have a care in the world. He'd done so many hits during his 18 years in the system he wondered would he ever experience that adrenaline rush he once felt just before a hit. Boy did he miss that feeling; it was what got him hooked in the first place.

He doubted that would ever happen again as he pulled aside the plastic shower curtain, entered the shower stall next to the one Pus was in, took off his brown terry cloth robe, laid it on the shower curtain pole and wanted to puke because the rap song Pus was trying to sing sounded truly sickening. Thanks to the pleasant smell of Pus's deodorant soap that was heavy in the air, Cheops was able to tame that urge to vomit.

"Rollin' with my niggas . . ." Pus's voice crackled with irritating force. "Blazin' bitches and snitches with the ease of a sneeze, break your seed's knees as graceful as a summer's breeze . . . Yo! Who that in the next shower?"

Cheops turned on the water and changed his voice. "It's P-Man."

Talking through the water that sprayed over his face, Pus said, "Never heard of you, dog."

"I just got here from Auburn," Cheops said with a smile.

"When this shit tones down a little," Pus turned the water off and grabbed his towel. "You come check me out. My name is Pus. Yeah, it's me. I know you heard of me because my name is ringing hard up north. Me and my crew got this whole camp in the smash. You roll with Crimson Cowboys, you'll live large, son."

Cheops stopped smiling as he pulled the 6-inch huge plastic straw and the hypodermic dart from the pocket of his robe. C.O. Carol said this stuff could explode the heart of an elephant upon contact with the blood stream and Cheops was itching to see if it really worked. The part he thought was a little over the top was C.O. Carol said this stuff would make the victim appear to have had a massive heart attack, thus, alleviating any allegations of foul play. Initially, Cheops wanted to do it the good old fashion, foolproof way, but C.O. Carol insisted it be done as clean as possible.

Cheops inserted the dart inside the straw and waited until Pus stepped out of the stall.

A few seconds later Pus stepped out.

WHOOSH!!

"Hey, what the . . ." Pus wobbled and collapsed to the floor. On his way down he banged his head on the side of the slop sink.

Cheops slid the curtain aside, calmly stepped out of the shower, leaving the water running to drown out the noise, pulled the dart from Pus's upper back and dragged him back inside the shower stall. After undressing Pus, Cheops placed a bar of soap in his hand and turned on the shower.

Cheops then took his shower and returned to his cell, bored half out of his mind.

*   *   *   *

As Dinasia ran at top speed towards the front door, she suddenly felt herself falling head first towards the floor. Her hands shot out in front of her to blunt the fall. Upon impact, the agonizing pain shot through her wrist with explosive force. When she saw it was the secretary who was responsible for tripping her, she sprung to her feet and was about to slap the woman into a state of delirium, but the life threatening seriousness of the moment catapulted her forward and out the door.

Just as Dinasia ran past the two handcuffed cops and up the stairs towards the roof, she heard the police coming up the stairs. Their radios and frantic comments told her they were approaching this matter as if it was a sheer emergency. Dinasia's heart felt like it was trying to beat itself out of her chest.

As her legs pumped up the stairs, Dinasia cursed at herself for not leaving when those two masked men basically rescued her. *Stupid! You should've been content with what you had, stupid!* But that safe! Something of great importance had to be in that safe. Her failure to get inside that safe was going to nag her senseless.

When she reached the roof she saw the door was cracked open. As she stepped through the door, she noticed a broomstick was wedged in the door and was apparently put there to hold it open. She grabbed the stick, allowing the door to close behind her. The lock sounded like it was activated, but she checked to make sure it was actually locked.

Dinasia sighed with relief when the door wouldn't open. She turned and ran towards the other roof stairwells, hoping and praying that at least one of them wasn't locked. All together there were three stairwells. When she reached the first one and tried it, the door wouldn't open. *Shit!* She murmured and headed for the next.

When she was several feet from the second stairwell, she heard a crashing sound. She turned and almost hyperventilated when she saw the police had crashed through the stairwell she entered the roof from. All five of the cops had their weapons in their hands as they ran towards her. She instantly increased her speed, now running as fast as she could. When she slammed into the door, it stopped her, but the impact hurt her other hand. She turned the doorknob.

It was locked.

Instantly, she headed for the next stairwell, tried it, but it was also locked. A heat wave of desperation and despair swarmed over her mind. The thought of Tislam dying snapped her out of the shock and she ran towards the railing. She looked over at the street below and she felt a slight ping of relief when she found what she was looking for.

The fire escape apparatus was about five yards from where she stood and she raced for it.

"Stop!" One of the rapidly approaching cops shouted. "I'm ordering you to stop right this minute!"

Dinasia quickly climbed down the metal stairs and eased past the fifth floor window; then the fourth, and when she got to the third floor, she noticed the apparatus stopped. When she saw the *out of order* sign she wanted to scream. With lightning speed she began banging on the third floor window. Breathing extremely hard, she shouted. "Please let me in! Is anyone home!?" She looked up and saw two cops descending.

SMAASSHH!

Dinasia broke the window with her elbow, unfastened the window latch and entered what looked like a studio. As she stepped through the window, she heard the man's voice.

"Hey! What the hell is this!?" The man ran for his desk, frantically rummaging through the top draw.

"I'm sorry for the intrusion, mister," Dinasia ran out of the room, searching for the main door that would let her out of this Art Gallery. There were pictures and statues all over the place. When she found the door and began unfastening the locks, she heard the man in back of her.

"Put your hands in the air where I can see them," He shouted nervously. The revolver trembled in his hand. He always wanted to make a citizen's arrest. Now he had his chance. "I'm warning you, I'll shoot!"

Dinasia ignored the man because she was too close to escaping this madness and there was no way in hell she was going to stop now. She frantically turned the last lock on the door and as she snatched it open.

BOW!

The bullet struck the door less than a foot away from her head. This close call had the effect of saturating her entire body with an adrenaline rush that was out of this universe. She raced out of the Art Studio with blinding speed. She hit the staircase like a runaway tornado, twice jumping down a whole flight of stairs. When she reached the ground floor, she instinctively headed for the back door. The people in the lobby frantically got out of her way as she quickly moved along. She saw the emergency exit sign and went for it.

When she hit the hand lever bar and the door swung open, an alarm ignited simultaneously. Resuming her frantic flee, she noticed when the door closed behind her the alarm stopped. She saw the exit of the alleyway just up ahead and wondered would a whole fleet of police cars be waiting there when she arrived? Decreasing her speed to a trot and then a fast walk when she was a few yards away, she knew if the police were waiting it would be the end of the line. A quick glance at her surroundings told her there were no other turn offs and all the nearby windows had security bars covering them. Obviously in a crime-ridden City like New York, it was unlikely any of these back doors would be open.

She nervously peeked around the corner of the building and could've screamed for joy when she saw no police cars. Just pedestrians, cars, commercial vehicles like trucks and taxicabs moved about.

She emerged from the alleyway and flagged the first empty cab she saw, waving her hand in the air excitedly as if her situation was of a sheer life or death nature, which is exactly what it was for her because she had already decided if Tislam died, so would she . . . But not without taking the guilty party along with them.

*   *   *   *

Moments earlier, the two masked men sat in the car down the block from Bruce Snyder's office watching the police and talking among themselves. They were unmasked and anxiously hoping not to see Dinasia being brought out in handcuffs because there was no way they would be able to save her this time.

"What the hell's wrong with that woman!?" The one who had the shotgun said, his accent not as heavy as earlier. "She was supposed to get the fuck outta the building right then and there!" He concluded with a very loud sigh.

"She went back for something," The man with the two handguns said. "I can't imagine her just hanging around waitin' for the backup police to arrive."

"Maybe we should've made her come with us," Shotgun said. "At least that way, we could've protected her from the most dangerous thing to her."

He didn't have to say what it was because they both knew it was from herself.

CHAPTER # 28

Dinasia jumped in the yellow cab, breathing heavily while speaking excitedly. "Take me to the FBI office."

The fat white guy was perplexed by the request; he turned around to see what Dinasia looked like. "Did you say the FBI Office?"

A nervous tension erupted inside her gut. "Yes, I did." Dinasia's hand involuntarily slid towards the lever on the door. "Is there a problem?"

"Not really," He turned back around and put the car in drive. "It's only about four blocks away." The car pulled off. "You could've gotten there a lot faster if you walked."

As they cruised past Court Street and the mob of police cars scattered all over the immediate area, she crouched down in the seat. Dinasia saw the cabby sneaking quick peeks at her through the rearview mirror and she wondered if he was thinking about turning her over to the police?

After the cab turned onto Cadman Plaza Dinasia relaxed a bit, but suddenly realized she felt self-conscious about going to the Feds, since this was (according to the streets) considered snitching. But, the more she thought about the situation the more she was convinced there was simply nowhere else to go to stop them from killing Tislam. And if a street code was going to be the cause of Tislam's death, then she had no choice but to say the hell with such a code without an inkling of a hesitation.

The two-minute ride felt like an hour. When the car came to a stop in front of the skyscraper, Dinasia asked, "Which building is it?"

"Right there," He pointed. "831 Cadman Plaza. That'll be five dollars, ma'am."

"Thank you very much." Dinasia gave the cabby a ten-dollar bill and hastily exited the cab, ignoring the cabby's comment about her change.

Just as she was about two feet from the revolving door of 831 Cadman Plaza, Dinasia put both hands in her coat pocket and not only did she feel the tape, but the 25 automatic as well.

Since she was already inside the revolving door by the time she realized she couldn't enter this place with an illegal weapon, she casually rotated around the door and back outside.

It took her a minute to come up with an idea to stash the gun. She strolled down the block, picked up a small brown paper bag, walked over to the window of an electronic shop, inconspicuously put the gun in the bag, headed for the half full trash can and dropped it inside. She didn't expect to be inside long and her only worry was the sanitation people picking up the trash before she finished her business here. As she headed back to the FBI building, Dinasia knew there were other safer hiding places, but time was something she couldn't toy around with.

She entered the building and went to the information clerk, who sat in the center of a circular counter equipped with all sorts of state of the arts monitors and other electronic gadgets. "I would like to report a crime."

The premature balding white man looked up from the console. "The local precinct is several blocks from here. The Federal Bureau of Investigation doesn't get involved in local criminal violations."

"This is far from local, sir. I have a videotape here which establishes a conspiracy." She pulled the tape and showed him. "Have you heard of a man named Darrel Mixon?"

The man smiled. "Of course . . . Who in this city hasn't?"

"Well, I have evidence of him performing a contract killing."

The man's eyebrows rose. "Really? Please excuse me a moment. I have to make a call." He spun around in his mobile cushioned chair, giving Dinasia his back and spoke on the phone for less than two minutes. He turned, facing Dinasia. "Someone's on their way down to see you."

A minute later, she saw a white man with sandy brown hair and a tall slim black woman, walking towards her. They both were dressed like corporate lawyers.

"Hi, my name is Special Agent Carl Winters," He extended his hand.

Dinasia shook it. "My name is Dinasia Davis."

"I'm Special Agent Tracy Dickinson." She shook Dinasia's hand. "We hear you have a videotape of Mr. Mixon engaged in a murder?"

Dinasia nodded her head.

"Please follow us," Tracy led her to a small room near the elevators. After a man waved a metal detector wan over Dinasia's body and Tracy conducted a perfunctory pat frisk on her, the three went to the elevators and boarded one of them.

About two minutes later, the three entered a fourth floor office. Before Carl took Dinasia's coat to hang it up, she quickly retrieved the tape and affidavit from the pockets. Dinasia inspected her surroundings, noticing the place looked like an expensive conference room used by executive board members of a huge corporation. The huge round table could easily seat 16 people, and the sliding window curtain was closed. The plants scattered about even looked real.

"Please have a seat, Mrs. Davis," Carl pulled out the seat at the head of the table for Dinasia while he and Tracy sat on either side of her.

Tracy pulled a small tape recorder from her purse and sat it on the table. "I hope you don't mind us recording this interview? It's standard policy."

"Not at all," Dinasia said, suddenly feeling a nervous tension growing.

"Please feel free to tell us whatever you like," Carl cupped his hands on the table, staring at Dinasia.

"There's so much---I, I don't know where to start."

"Well, normally the beginning is the best place," Tracy said with a smile and hit the record button. "Wouldn't you agree?"

Dinasia started from the day she first heard Prince was shot and killed. She worked her way up to the part where she pretended to be the daughter of Mrs. Daye, explaining how she retrieved the tape and the affidavit. She unfolded the piece of paper. "This is the affidavit." She handed it to Carl. "She's describing all the steps she took to record the tape and how she was threatened by some strangers."

194

As Carl read the affidavit and passed it to Tracy when finished, Dinasia continued with her detailed and painfully honest description of her journey.   When she reached the part about Tislam and his current predicament regarding the pulling of his life support plug, she burst out crying. The tears flowed in an involuntarily and uncontrollable fashion.

Carl got up, found a box of Kleenex tissues and handed them to Dinasia.

"Calm down," Tracy said softly as she caressed Dinasia's shoulder. "Take your time. Let it all out."

Dinasia picked up from the part when she left the phone booth after talking to a Doctor Bill Evans and went straight to Bruce Snyder's office. She articulated in depth what transpired with the masked men and what occurred thereafter. When she finished, Dinasia saw the two FBI Agents had that look on their faces that said, "Where's the rest."

Through sniffles, Dinasia said, "We have to do something or else they're gonna kill him. I came here because there was nowhere else to go. The Doctor said--"

"We have to look at the tape first," Tracy's heart went out for the woman, unable to imagine the pain she was experiencing. "If what you say is on that tape, we might be able to do something."

Carl stood, extending his hand. "I'll go take a look at the tape in the lab."

Dinasia stared at his extended hand as if it was riddled with scabs from a contagious disease. "Please don't take this the wrong way. But, after all the drama I've been through, I would greatly appreciate it if I could be present while this tape is played. It's not that I don't trust you or anything like that, but I got to--"

"No problem at all," Tracy stood. "We understand exactly what your concerns are and we're not offended in the least. Please follow us." She led the two out the door, down a blue carpet covered hallway and into a room 12 doors down from the conference like room.

Dinasia saw this room was much more than a lab. There was a mixture of all sorts of electronic devises, ranging from huge computers and televisions to consoles and countless other sophisticated gadgets she couldn't begin to guess what they were. She caressed the tape in her hand as they headed for a man who sat behind a desk on the far right of the room. There were several monitors and electronic boxes all round him.

Tracy spoke as they arrived. "Hey, Mike, we need to scan a videotape."

"No problem," He stopped typing on the keyboard.

Dinasia handed the man the tape and watched him insert it in an oversized VCR that had close to a hundred buttons and knobs all over it. *Super hi-tech stuff* she concluded as the screen lit up.

Suddenly, the image of an old woman popped on the screen. She was at a child's birthday party, cutting a cake with the numerous children cheering and shouting playfully.

Dinasia's heart felt like it stopped. Her eyes got wide with heart-rending terror written on her face. "It--it can't be . . . Fast forward it." She sounded hysterical since she knew this was useless because she scanned the entire tape at Robert's pawnshop from beginning to end and none of this stuff was on it. Procrastination just seemed like the only sane thing to do.

As the images on the monitor moved rapidly Dinasia saw the impatient gestures of the two FBI Agents and she desperately wondered if there was a way to convince them the tape was apparently switched? Bruce had more than enough time to do it. The hidden safe behind the refrigerator popped in her head. But despite the gut feeling the tape was at Bruce's office, she continued backtracking.

Then it dawned on her. The tape was out of her hands at "Regina's Restaurant" when the two bearded men saved her. *Could it have been switched then? Nah, the switch had to occur at Bruce's office. Bruce did it* she concluded just as the tape ended.

"Bruce—he--he switched the tape," Dinasia said to Tracy in a pleading voice, hoping her sad eyes would illicit some sympathy. "It was him. He. . .He switched it . . .

Long silence.

Dinasia nervously spoke again. "I saw that tape with my own eyes. Darrel Mixon, that hit man, shot my foster brother Prince, I tell you. It was him. Please, you gotta believe me. My husband has a lot of connections with people in high places and he and Mixon are behind this. But, but we can get it back." Her eyes suddenly got wide with hope. "If we hurry over to Snyder's office, we might be able to catch him. That bastard was alone with the tape long enough to switch it. And he's got a hidden safe in his office." She started pacing nervously. "Maybe if we move quickly we could get to his office before he goes--"

"Sorry, Mrs. Davis," Carl sprung to his feet. "That's not gonna be possible."

"You got that right," Tracy waved to another man on the other side of the room. "Because you're under arrest."

CHAPTER # 29

"Doctor Evans, please report to Director Stevens' Office as soon as possible." The woman's soft voice said from the Hospital's loudspeaker system.

Bill looked up from the surgery report. He sat his pen down on the desk and released a good tiresome stretch. *Why do they always wait until it's time to close out to start paging people?* He rose from his seat and was out the door.

When he entered Doctor Stevens' Office and saw the short beady-eyed man was on the phone, Bill invited himself to a seat.

A moment later, the Director hung up the phone and spoke. "Bill, thanks for dropping by. We have some unfortunate news." Scrambling through the scattered papers on his desk, he continued. "I just got this fax." He handed it to Bill. "It's a Court Order from Dutchess County Supreme Court."

After reading the Order, Bill spoke. "This is two days away. How on God's earth did they get this Order so quickly?"

"I guess some strings were pulled in some high places. Mr. Parker is suspected of killing a white Corrections sergeant. It's certainly not a difficult endeavor to convince a Judge to sign an Order under these circumstances . . . Especially when there's no opposition."

"Director Stevens . . . I want to ask you a question off the record. Do you think it was possible for this young man to have actually committed this murder, considering the fact he was just as fatally injured as all the others involved in this ordeal?"

Short pause.

"Well," The Director thought for a moment. "I believe I'm not in a position to say. Without being there to see what actually happened, it's hard to say. But looking at the facts placed before us, I would say it was emphatically impossible for Mr. Parker to have killed those men and then turned his own knife on himself."

"I have one more question," Bill paused, trying to structure his words correctly. "What is the penalty for refusing to obey this Court Order?"

Director Stevens leaned back in his chair; his mannerism now becoming stern. "Something you and this Hospital can't afford to fix our minds to even consider. However, if you want to go to prison, lose your license to practice medicine and be black-balled for the rest of your life, then I guess it could be an act worth considering."

"Hold up, wait a minute here. I'm not saying I was contemplating doing something as crazy as that. I was just curious. Plus, I got another kid on the way. I may be a moralist fanatic, but I am not stupid or suicidal . . ."

*   *   *   *

491 Carver Lane was as huge and as elegant as any standard multi-million dollar mansion owned by those classified as the rich and famous. But the seclusion and the peculiar Suffolk Long Island silence was the main reason Darrel Mixon decided to make this location his home sweet home. As the second in command of the third largest crime family in the entire State of New York, trailing only the Gambinos and Lucianos, Darrel and Eddie Mack had their hands into just about everything considered illicit activities. With a twenty-man security force guarding the grounds of his Mansion around the clock, Darrel very rarely, if ever, felt threatened. But tonight he felt far more than just threatened.

Darrel's 175-pound frame moved gracefully across the room as he paced. His facial structure, which usually had that confident G.Q. model look, was now twisted into a mask that resembled the grimace of a man waiting for a verdict in a capital punishment case. Darrel was new to this sort of high intense stress.

An hour ago, he got a call from Eddie Mack (the undisputed top man in their family), informing him that he was coming over to have an emergency meeting. *Why in the hell did he let Sha talk him into not killing this bitch?* He cursed himself constantly for taking such a stupid and dangerous risk. He knew it was his and only his ass that would catch the flames when the fire was turned up. As he brooded, he suddenly became perplexed by his willingness to let Sha play a bunch of crazy ass games with that tape.

Then it dawned on him. Eddie had said Bruce Snyder managed to get the tape from Dinasia. But what really bothered him was there was a likely chance Dinasia succeeded in obtaining copies of that tape. Robert had told them that's exactly what she was planning to do. And after those two masked motherfuckers put a monkey wrench in the plan at "Regina's Restaurant", she obviously had more than enough time to obtain those copies.

Shit! Darrel was at the boiling point now. *God damn it!* He had to calm his nerves. He fixed a glass of cognac and sat on the sofa sipping the strong liquor. The warmth caused by the alcohol hitting his stomach went straight to work.

The timing of this ulcer provoking dilemma came to mind again, flooding his thoughts with memories and reminders. After all of these years of getting knee deep in the trenches without once coming too close to the ledge of destruction, Mixon couldn't understand why all this shit had to happen now? Why now, just when he and Eddie were about to flip to the legal world!? And, on top of that, his ten-year-old daughter was admitted to the hospital two days ago, suffering from a potentially fatal bout of sickle cell anemia, and his ex-wife's lawyer just served alimony papers. When it rains, it pours was a perfect description of Darrel's current situation.

He reflected on all the things he'd done to help the black community and knew none of that would count. Even despite the fact his deeds were done surreptitiously (and without the intent of ever acquiring praise and recognition), he knew the bad things he'd done were and will always be the only things people saw and remembered.

Who would know (or even care) he had secretly provided the start-up funds for well over four hundred black owned small businesses all across the country with no strings attached? How many people knew (or gave a rat's ass) he financed the campaigns of approximately two thousand black politicians seeking to run for various political offices? Who was aware of the fact he donated hundreds of thousands of dollars to black colleges, sickle cell anemia research centers, non-for-profit community based organizations and a spectrum of all sorts of black owned institutions?

The answer certainly wasn't a difficult one: Nobody. Not a single soul.

Sure, there were so many things he'd done that would make even the most sadistic ruffian's stomach turn, but in war, there were very limited rules, and certain lines had to be crossed. Mixon crossed damn near all of them and would cross them again and again if that's what it took to get the job done. Shit, it didn't take a super genius to realize in wars, people had to die in order for others to live. Sacrifices were an intricate part of the game of war, and if someone could prove otherwise, Mixon wanted to meet this person so they could have a nice little talk; he was always willing to learn new, innovative tactics.

Darrel Mixon had a dream. It wasn't much different from the one Martin Luther King Jr., had. But the difference between Mixon and King was that Darrel Mixon wasn't afraid to take the type of risks that could make things happen almost overnight.

He wanted to see black folks unified, economically and socially empowered, intellectual and educationally intact, politically and diametrically connected, and most of all, respected as a collective race of people with first class citizenship in the very country they built literally with their blood, sweat and tears. And from Mixon's standpoint, there was only one way of attaining these things, and that was the good ole American way (steal, cheat, lie, kill, rob, deceive, use, abuse, and utilize anything that facilitates the end justifies the means concept).

At a very young age, Mixon realized it took money to get the wheels in motion to attaining this dream, and thus, began his life into the world of organized crime.

Two minutes later, there was a knock on the door and one of his security personnel stuck his head through the door and said, "Eddie just drove up."

A few minutes later, Eddie entered. His golden brown complexion had that unique shine as usual, but the business suit and tie made him look over-dressed for the occasion.

"Eddie," Darrel embraced his partner with a hug loaded with brotherly love. "I'm glad to see you, big bro."

"Same here, little bro." Eddie sat in the armchair and then said, "I just hate when it's to deal with shit that could spill-over into the business . . . So how's Shaquana holding up?"

"The doctor said it's gonna be touch and go for a couple of weeks, but her spirits are up."

"Tell her I'll see her tomorrow."

Darrel nodded his head. "You want a drink?" He went back to the bar to re-fill his glass.

"Nah, I'm cool. I didn't come here to party. I think you should have a seat before I tell you what I have to say." He knew this would jerk Darrel's chain and he looked for the nervous facial response. He smiled when he saw it.

Ah shit, Darrel thought as he realized this was far worse than he imagined. He quickly sat down on the sofa pretending to be in control of the anxiety. "Well, let's hear it."

"That fuckin' broad went to the Feds."

It took a few seconds for this dreaded news to soak in. Darrel was unable to maintain that calm look. "What!? The Feds!?" He rose and started pacing. "I knew it. Goddamn it. I knew I should've personally smoked that bitch the minute she started snooping around. Why all this shit had to happen now? In two more months all this'll be behind us . . . I'm just dying to hear how the fuck Sha is gonna explain this shit. She's gonna take his ass down along with--"

"Chill Dee! It ain't as bad as you think."

Darrel gaped at Eddie with wide-eyed amazement. "It ain't as bad as I think!? That's easy for you to say . . . That's my ass on that tape not yours."

"I spoke with Jamie and she said they arrested her." Eddie smiled when he saw Darrel stop on a dime and squinted his eyebrows as the confusion mounted. "Bruce switched the tape, remember. Here's the funny part. The broad was so stupid, she spilled her guts to the Feds, telling them about a whole shit load of all sorts of crimes she committed in the process of obtaining the tape. She talked about murders, burglaries, Bank forgeries." He giggled. "She apparently didn't have time to look at the tape after those guys in the masks helped her get it back. Lucky thing we had--"

"But what about copies? She might have copies of that tape?"

"She ain't got any copies. Jamie said she never mentioned any copies. If she had any copies, you can bet your ass she would've utilized them to avoid arrest."

Darrel became silent as realization took hold.

"Another piece of half-ass good news is I got Charlie to speed up the legal assassination of Tislam. Once they pull the plug on this guy, it'll make re-opening the case a lot more complicated . . . I also got an idea who those two masked men are. I spoke with Carol and he told me he had a conversation with one of our hitters in Green Haven. From the way it looks, it might be two cats that did time in that jail. They found a way to re-route Tislam's mail and this guy in the letter is saying shit that sounds like he's one of those masked men. The strange part is," He hesitated. "Carol believes these guys use to work for us. I'm still working on it. Hopefully, I'll have something solid soon."

"My man Ronnie should be able to help you with that since he did a nice stretch in the Haven. In fact, he just got home not too long ago. Shit, he might even know 'em personally."

Eddie nodded his head. "I'll talk to him when we finish with this . . . I think it's about time we start fixing up all those loose ends and I'm talkin' all loose ends. You know what I mean? The last thing we need is to get this far, only weeks from putting a close on all these years of struggling and planning, and start running into a bunch of brick walls."

With a smile, Darrel knew exactly what he was saying. "So, you reconsidered I see? This is the only way to handle it and I'm glad we're both on the same page now."

"There's simply too much at stake," Eddie sighed hard. "The run against Sha is gonna be a rough one." His face displayed his internal pain. "He was like a brother and a teacher, but we're almost at that stage we've been working towards too long and way too hard. And we can't let it all fall apart on the account of some pussy whipped cat who--"

There was a knock on the door.

"Come in!" Darrel shouted.

Bruce Snyder entered carrying his briefcase, looking like he was on his way to a courtroom. "Good evening, gentlemen. I guess we'll get right down to business." He sat next to Darrel and flipped open the lid of the briefcase. "Yes, I have the tape." He pulled it out with a smile and handed it to Darrel. "It came straight out of her possession."

Darrel hit a button on his pager. A minute later the door opened.

"What's up, Dee?" Ronnie said with his sunglasses on, his countrified accent toned down.

"Come put this tape on," Darrel handed Ronnie the tape and spoke as Ronnie prepared the TV and VCR. "Brucey my man, you just earned yourself one helluva bonus. We got a few minor things to take care of--"

CCCRRRSSSHHH!!!

The sudden loud distortion sound from the TV volume being turned up full blast startled the three men.

"Turn that damn thing down!" Darrel shouted as Ronnie nervously fumbled with the remote control.

Ronnie turned the volume down and then pressed the play button on the VCR. A moment later a picture popped on the screen.

"What the fuck is this!?" Darrel said to Bruce. "You tryin' to play me, man?"

"I—I—I took that tape straight out of her pocket." Bruce felt dizzy with fear and bafflement as the image of four little black boys playing with toy guns in a Park danced on the screen.

Everyone was speechless.

Darrel stood, gave Bruce a menacing glance and then said to Eddie. "I guess this is the part where we turn it up full volume, wouldn't you say?" When he saw Eddie's head nod, he turned. "Ronnie . . . Get the crew ready. I want every able body front and center in two minutes. Let everybody know, whoever takes that broad down, gets a 200 thousand dollar bonus. And tell Flipper I said I wanna see him right now. Let Manny know I want him and his crew to dee-up on Sha . . ."

*   *   *   *

"Come in!" Isaac Gilmore shouted in response to the knock on his door. He then resumed his phone discussion.

Special Agents Carl Winters and Tracy Dickinson entered their supervisor's Office and took seats when Isaac waved for them to sit in the chairs in front of his desk.

"I gotta go; I'll talk to you later, good-bye." Isaac hung up the receiver. "Well, what's so important that can't wait until tomorrow's briefing?"

Carl said, "It's the Mack and Mixon investigation. We have credible evidence linking them to Prince Shepard's death."

Short pause.

"Well let's hear what you got," Isaac said, leaning back in his chair. "I hope it's something of substance this time."

Tracy said, "A couple hours ago a woman named Dinasia Davis who claims to be the wife of Shateek Davis came here to the Bureau--"

"Is he the younger brother of that ah--ah Shaba--"

"That's right," Carl said. "Shabazz Davis."

Tracy continued when she saw Carl gave her the signal indicating his comment was completed. "As I was saying, this woman, Dinasia Davis apparently thought she had a videotape of Mixon shooting Prince. During the interview she sounded truthful, but when we observed the tape, none of those things were on it. Obviously she claims the tape was switched."

Carl spoke. "She insists the young man serving time for this murder is innocent and claims Mixon and her husband framed this man because the husband wanted to marry her, but had to get Tislam out of the picture. She gave us a detailed description of what she went through to get the tape, and in my opinion, I think she's telling the truth."

Isaac sighed hard. "You know something, this sure sounds familiar. If I'm not mistaken those were your exact words when that guy was caught at JFK with two kilos and said it was the Gambinos who killed Prince. Come to find out, he was a pathological liar, who was trying to escape imprisonment. How about the time when you thought Shabazz was the actual triggerman? . . . You're gonna always be biased since Prince was your personal informant and--"

"I beg your pardon, sir, but that's not the case here." Carl said in a respectful tone. "When Prince was murdered, Tracy and I were merely acting as assistants. It was Elijah's case. And at that time, we were almost ready to bring Shabazz down. We've always suspected there was a leak that caused Prince's death. What this woman revealed to us fits perfectly with what we've been saying all along."

Short pause.

Tracy spoke. "After we arrested her in order to gain some leverage, and because her confessions provided substantial probable cause, we did some checking and discovered she was Prince's foster sister . . . The story she told us about several homicides over in Coney Island and in Queens all checked out exactly the way she described them. She also claims they're trying to kill Tislam, the man convicted of killing Prince, in an effort to cover-up their involvement in the murder. Even that checked out convincingly."

Isaac sighed. "So, to make a long story short you want to re-open the Prince investigation and merge it with the current Mack and Mixon investigation?"

"Yes," Carl answered. "We believe this evidence provides more than sufficient grounds to proceed in this fashion."

"Well, I'm sorry to burst your bubble, but it's not enough." Isaac said, almost frustrated because he felt they were chasing a dead case, which couldn't be solved. "The only thing you've presented to me is a bunch of hearsay that could be coming from some woman who's probably seeking revenge against her husband, or is bored out of her mind and is trying to--"

"Read this, sir," Carl handed Isaac Mrs. Daye's affidavit. They were hoping they could've held back this piece of evidence until a later date, but that wasn't going to be the case.

Isaac took the paper and began reading.

When Isaac finished, Carl refused to let up on the pressure. "I have the audiotape of her interview right here." He pulled the small cassette player from his pocket, sat it on the desk and pressed the play button. "You can make your own credibility assessment."

Eight minutes later the tape came to a stop and the room became silent as the three stared at each other.

With a strained look on his face, Isaac leaned back in his chair and went further into deep thought. After a moment he spoke. "You got twenty days to come up with something tangible that connects Prince's murder with the Mack and Mixon Investigation. If you produce that evidence, at that point, I'll formally incorporate it with the case." He paused while drawing a deep breath and slowly letting it out. "There's a strong chance this tape is forever lost. If what Mrs. Davis says is true, then Mixon and Mack may already have the tape. And we all know what that means."

"Yes, we do," Tracy said. "But I think doing all we can to retrieve it, if it still exist, is well worth the effort, sir."

"How many agents will be at our disposal?" Carl inquired.

"How many do you think you need?" Isaac knew such an answer to that sort of question was a no no in this business, but that tape touched him deeply.

Carl and Tracy looked at each other realizing this was the first time the Director ever made such an offer. This was an invitation to acquiring more than adequate manpower.

"Twenty agents should suffice," Tracy waited for an objection. When none followed, she added. "Surveillance equipment and 24 hour access to the main frame computer would certainly help."

Isaac wrote down the items on a note pad. "What do you intend to do with Mrs. Davis? Holding her might not be in our best interest. Disgruntled folks are almost never cooperative at times when their help is needed the most. But then again, letting her go might not be in her best interest. We may have created a situation, which put her life in further danger."

"That's exactly what we want," Tracy said, and when she saw the confusion in the Director's eyes, she continued. "If Mixon and Mack is behind this and they get wind she went to the authorities, they'll want to kill her whether they have the tape or not. We'll put a tag on her, stay close by and see what happens."

Carl said, "Another plan of action is to force her husband to pay a huge bail, draw him out, keep an eye on him and see if he slips up. That's not much, but it is an approach."

Tracy said, "We figure since her husband was involved in this conspiracy to cover-up Prince's murder, and as a result, has actually caused several additional murders in an effort to facilitate a criminal organization, we could easily get him on a RICO charge."

"All those construction sites of his," Carl said. "And those sleek business offices can't possibly be totally legit. His brother is as dirty as a pigsty and I bet you so is he."

"Most important of all," Tracy said. "Too much valuable time, energy and money is gonna be spent on this investigation. It would be sheer madness to walk away empty handed."

CHAPTER # 30

Dinasia sat in the cell staring at the wall as if she was in a catatonic state. About twenty minutes ago, she'd stopped crying since it served no beneficial purpose to her main objective, which was to re-gain her liberty. But every time she thought of the two week time clock ticking on Tislam's life, it made her pace nervously. She simply refused to believe it was over and she repudiated the thought of giving up with such force, she felt a monster growing inside of her.

The image of Darrel shooting Prince constantly pranced crazily in her mind. She kinda welcomed those images because she noticed they made her stronger and more determined to save Tislam's life.

Earlier, as the agonizing reluctancy fiddled with her conscious, she loathingly decided to call Keisha. The Judge had set bail at twenty thousand dollars. It was an amount Keisha could come up with without considerable difficulty and on such short notice. Her gold credit card had a $50,000 limit and Dinasia intended to repay Keisha from the $120,000 stash of cash money she'd been accumulating to pay for Tislam's legal fees. Dinasia made Keisha promise not to tell Shateek, but she sensed Keisha wasn't going to keep that pledge. When it came to Shateek, Keisha would always be his flunky. For the hundredth time, she suddenly wondered if Shateek was having sex with Keisha or something? Keisha was so deeply under Shateek's control, logic dictated he had a sexual spell over her.

At this point, even that didn't matter. The only thing that meant anything to her was getting out of this place and finding a way to stop them from killing Tislam. The situation with the tape was obviously a dead issue, and after trying to come up with another way to free Tislam, it became evident things had reached a truly critical stage.

Dinasia felt the desperation rapidly setting in. She decided if she had to break inside the hospital and stand guard over Tislam's bedside with a machine gun, that's what she would do. Because if he died, she knew she would be forced to join him.

The way she abandoned him when he needed her most stayed in her mind and made it clear she wouldn't be able to live with herself. The Romeo and Juliet story came to mind and a new thought suddenly hit her. What if the time came and she couldn't do it? Unrelentingly, another question entered her mind. What if Shateek escaped punishment while she and Tislam perished?

No, that won't happen because I won't let it. She concluded resoundingly. He would pay, and that was as sure as day turns to night and night turns to day, she decided conclusively and would do whatever it took to fulfill that promise.

The sound of keys opening her cell door snatched Dinasia out of her trance like reverie. She looked up and saw the guard enter. His face was fat, red and could pass for the epitome of a red neck racist from the ultimate good ol' boys club.

"Looks like you won't be spending the night here with me, young lady," The guard said with chewing tobacco in his mouth. "You're on the bail out."

Dinasia rose from the bed and breezed out of the cell. After she was processed and her personal effects returned, she was escorted to the front gate. Keisha raced towards her.

Keisha's eyes were wide. "Dinasia! My God!? You, you look beat up pretty bad, girl. Did they put their fuckin' hands on you!?"

"No," Dinasia lead the way outside into the brisk night air, anxious to get as far away from this place as quickly as possible. "I'm just tired and worn out. Where's the car? Let's get outta here."

When they were inside Keisha's red BMW, Dinasia spoke as the turn of the ignition key brought the car to life. "I need you to make a stop near Cadman Plaza."

Keisha thought about the location with squinted eyes. "That's going towards Tillery Street." She pulled the car from the curb. "Ain't that in the wrong direction?"

Dinasia gritted her teeth, but held her temper in check. "Yeah. I gotta pick up something important. I hope you're not in a hurry?"

"Nah, I'm cool. Talk to me, girl." Keisha said happily. "I ain't see you in weeks. How the hell did you get arrested!?"

"Please Keisha, not now, please. I just need to think of something else right now."

Keisha smiled. "I'm sorry, you're right. We can talk about something else then . . . Why you didn't call me last week? I thought we were gonna do some shopping together? . . .

As Keisha rattled on and on about a bunch of mundane issues while Dinasia responded with insincere "Yeahs" and "Um huhs", Dinasia's mind was locked on Tislam.

About three minutes later, Dinasia spoke, "Pull over here. Yeah, park right there . . . Wait here, I'll be right back." Dinasia got out of the car, walked quickly to the corner, turned right and headed for the trashcan several yards away. She subconsciously suspected the gun would probably be gone, but she had to check to make sure. It was after nine and the streets were partially deserted.

As she approached the trashcan, Dinasia saw it looked in the same condition as she left it earlier. She dug inside and smiled when she saw the brown paper bag. Dinasia snatched it up, felt the weight and then the gun itself. She turned and headed back in the direction of the car.

Suddenly, Dinasia heard a car coming up behind her. It was moving slow, she instantly noticed. When the car reached her, she saw two figures inside and they both were staring at her. Dinasia inconspicuously took the gun out of the bag, stuffed it in her pocket and held it in the ready position. She increased her pace.

*   *   *   *

Two blocks away, Ronnie A.K.A. Spade and the black guy A.K.A. Flipper sat in a black Plymouth Skylark with infrared binoculars to their eyes, watching Dinasia walking back towards the red BMW. They'd been following Dinasia and Keisha ever since the two left the Federal Courthouse.

As Flipper put the gear in drive, Spade said, "I wonder why the hell she stopped here?" Spade's southern accent was smooth and firm. "I should've followed her. Whatever she did, she damn sure did it quick."

"I sure would love to know," Flipper said. "Because the FBI building is in that direction." He applied pressure to the gas pedal, following the red BMW.

"Man, I still say we should drive up alongside them at a red light and spray both them bitches." Spade sat the binoculars down and put his sunglasses back on.

Flipper cut his eye at his partner. "How the hell can you see with them silly ass shades on?"

"If you ask me that again," Spade drawled. "I'm gonna spazz out up in here. You know my eyes are fucked up. I got sensitive eyes."

Jokingly Flipper mocked him. "I got sensitive eyes. Nigga, you sound like a bitch!"

They both laughed.

"But on the real to real," Spade said. "I could sure use those 100 gees. If we blaze this bitch right now, we--"

"That ain't the plan, Spade. Relax. You know all that speed ballin' shit is what causes shit to go wrong. We play strictly by the plan on this one."

After a short silence, Spade said, "What's up with Tislam? Did he kick the bucket yet?"

"If he didn't, he's definitely days from it." Flipper started whining his voice up for another joke. "I sure wish there was a way to see his face after telling his crazy strung out ass we're gonna kill his sweet little Dinasia."

He giggled. "His eyes would probably fall right out of his head, like this." He demonstrated.

They both laughed.

When the laughter toned down, Flipper looked through the rearview mirror and smiled when he saw the blue car for the twelfth time.

*   *   *   *

Special Agents Dawson and Weinstein followed the black Skylark that followed the red BMW. The blue Ford Taurus they drove was an agency vehicle, and so they stayed as far behind and out of sight as possible.

Sitting in the passenger seat, Dawson was on the radio talking to Tracy. "Yes, we have the black vehicle in our view. We're currently on Atlantic Avenue traveling east. We'll let you know when they reach the destination. Over and out."

*   *   *   *

Directly behind the blue agency vehicle was a green Chevy Impala, driven by the man who brandished the shotgun at Snyder's Law Office. The man with the two handguns sat beside him in the passenger seat.

"Be careful, easy now," The two handgun man said when a car turned onto the Avenue and cut in between them and the blue FBI car. "Let's stay alert. The car Dinasia's in is out of our sight and therefore our reach. If those clowns in that black car decide to flip out, we better pray like hell these guys here will intervene quickly."

"Damn. I wish we could get a little closer," Shotgun said, still altering his voice to sound like a southerner, unable to get out of character. "But if we do that, we'll blow our cover."

The two-gun man said, "Would you lighten up on that silly ass down south voice. You making me think I'm in the car with my aunt Mae or some shit."

Shotgun spoke normal, "We need to think of a way to get in front of these chumps here without blowing our cover,"

"These Federal cats very rarely move alone. I wouldn't be surprised if our cover is already blown." He looked out the side view mirror, trying to find the car that kept popping up every couple of minutes. He saw nothing.

*   *   *   *

The red BMW drove into the driveway.

"Thanks Keisha," Dinasia reached over and hugged her. "I'll give you that in a couple of days." She started opening the door.

"You sure you don't need me to keep you company?" Keisha was already getting ready to exit the car. "All the lights are out, which means Shateek ain't home. After all you've been through, I don't think you should be alone. You know I'm there for you."

"Thanks, but that's exactly what I need: to be alone right now. I'll call you tomorrow morning." Dinasia exited the car and waved to Keisha as she drove away.

Dinasia rushed inside and frantically went straight to the phone. Just as she was about to dial the number to the Dutchess County Hospital, she realized she'd forgotten the last two digits. *Shit!* She hastily dialed the operator, retrieved the number again and then made the call.

"Hello, Dutchess County Hospital," A woman's voice said through the phone. "May I help you?"

"Yes, you can. My name is Captain Martha Jones of the State Police. I'm the investigating supervisor on the Tislam Parker case. And I would like to ask you a few questions regard--"

"Where is this patient, ma'am?"

"The last I heard he was in a coma. I assume he's in the Critical Care Unit."

"I'm sorry, ma'am, but that part of the hospital at this time of night is not open for the release of information. Maybe if you call--"

"Excuse me, who am I talking to?" Dinasia said firmly.

"My name is Sandra Rodriquez."

"I'm only going to say this once, Mrs. Rodriquez." Dinasia's voice became even firmer as the desire to know gradually turned into

214

desperation. "Doctor Bill Evans made it unequivocally clear, I could call at anytime to obtain information regarding the health status of this patient . . . Have you heard of a crime called interfering and obstructing a police investigation?"

"Yes, I have," Sandra said, terror-stricken. "I--I'm just following--"

"If you do not cooperate with this investigation, I will personally come down there and arrest you. Do you realize several men have been killed? Murdered!?" She paused. "Now, I'm gonna try this again. What is Mr. Tislam Parker's current health status? I wanna know any and all developments regarding this particular patient."

"Yes, okay," She typed on the computer keyboard in front of her and brought up all current information on Tislam Parker. "He's in the Intensive Care Unit. His coma hasn't subsided and . . . There's a court order instructing the hospital to terminate life support on December 3rd. I also see there's--"

"Did you say December 3rd?" Dinasia struggled to sound unemotional. "I thought it was scheduled for two weeks from today?"

"Well, this order was faxed to the hospital earlier today," Sandra said. After a moment's pause she continued. "The medication Mr. Parker is receiving--"

"Thank you, Mrs. Rodriguez. I appreciate your cooperation. Have a good evening." Dinasia hung up, found the nearest chair and sat in it.

Her head spun with fright, anxiety and a mixture of a thousand other agonizing sensations. The tears poured freely because there was nothing she could do in two days that could save Tislam's life. If she went to some important person, like a politician or Governor for help, that would obviously require time. And not only that, even if there was enough time, what would she tell them that would make them believe Tislam didn't deserve to die?

All was lost, she realized, as the tears oozed heavily from under her eyelids.

The sudden noise that came from a key opening the back door of the house jerked her into attention because she knew it had to be Shateek. No one else had a key, that's for sure. Angrily wiping her eyes, she went for her gun.

Shateek entered and instantly noticed the living room lights were on. After closing the door behind him and locking it, he looked around the immediate area and went to the living room. When he saw his wife with the 25 automatic in her hand, he spoke softly. "Dinasia, please, baby. Put the gun down. We need to talk. There's a lot--"

"You killed him! How could you? . . . Why? You paid that bastard Mixon to kill Prince and then made it look like it was Tislam. Don't lie motherfucker! I know all about it. I saw the tape. And you killed Mrs. Daye to cover--"

"Please listen to me, Dinasia. We need to sit down and talk--"

"Fuck you!" she shouted, bracing herself for the loud explosion. "Stop! Don't you come near me! I swear I'll blow your fuckin' brains out!"

Shateek ignored the threat and walked right past her. He knew she wasn't the type who would kill a person in cold blood.

Dinasia rapidly moved out of his way with the gun pointed, and noticed she couldn't pull the trigger. She actually tried it again and again, but her trigger finger felt like it died on her. She focused her attention on all the built up rage boiling inside of her, hoping the anger would guide her finger. But it was useless. She couldn't kill another human being. It simply wasn't in her no matter what the situation or circumstance was. Talking and thinking about it was one thing, but doing it was entirely something else she suddenly realized.

Dinasia dropped the gun and charged at Shateek. She punched him in the back of the head as he was fiddling with the TV. She couldn't shoot him because of the possibility of killing him, but beating him half to death with her hands and feet was something she knew she could do. When she saw Shateek stumbled sideways and almost fell to the floor it made her feel good.

"Please, Dinasia, hold-up baby," Shateek tried to grab her hands. "Let me--"

WHAM! BLAM!

Dinasia caught him with two solid right jabs; one landed on the nose, the other on the chin.

As Shateek stumbled backwards, crashing into the bookshelf, he shook his head to re-orient himself and then ducked and side stepped the next wave of punches and kicks. He didn't blame her for being in a rage as he blocked her punches, kicks and blows aimed at his head and private parts, but let her hit him in all other areas. He knew she had to vent and he let her do just that.

Finally, after five straight minutes of blocking and taking blow after blow, Shateek gently and carefully tackled Dinasia to the floor. He laid on top of her as she squirmed momentarily and then laid still. They both were breathing and sweating profusely.

"Get the fuck off me!" Dinasia tried to head-butt him in the same fashion as she did Kirk years ago, but Shateek weaved it. "How could you?" She said exhaustibly and started crying again.

Shateek got up off of her and went to his coat.

Dinasia just laid there, recuperating and getting her wind ready for another round. She was far from finished. She had to admit; she did feel a little better. Although her fists were throbbing with white hot, tear provoking pain. She stared at the ceiling while she heard Shateek turn the TV on. Then she heard a gunshot. When she hastily sat up to see what Shateek was doing, and why he turned on the television, her eyes bulged out of her head.

"Now, are you ready to listen to me?" Shateek said as he sat on the sofa with the remote control in his hand.

"The tape!?" Dinasia sprung to her feet and ran to the TV and VCR to make sure she wasn't dreaming or experiencing a mirage or an erroneous perception of reality. "But--but how!?"

*　　*　　*　　*

Meanwhile, on the outskirts of the Davis Home, the two FBI agents, Dawson and Weinstein, parked their blue car several blocks away from the black car they were following. They instantly locked their binoculars on the vehicle, scrutinizing Flipper and Spade's every movement.

After a moment of watching the two men, Special Agent Dawson got back on his communication device and spoke to the two other units that had been on the scene for almost an hour before he and Weinstein arrived. These two Units were positioned in the northern and western outskirts near the Davis house. Dawson said, "This is Unit one to Units two and three, come in please."

Both Units indicated they read him loud and clear.

Dawson continued. "We're on the eastern side of the house. From the way it looks, we might be stationery for a while. I want you guys to check in every ten minutes. Over and out." He sighed and put his binoculars back to his eyes. About a minute later, he laid the binoculars down and said, "I still don't understand why Dickinson and Winters want us to sit around waiting until these two creeps make a move before taking any affirmative action?"

"This is a huge investigation," Agent Weinstein said, still looking through the binoculars. He saw the two men were smoking something, *probably marijuana*, he thought. "From what I understand, they think Mrs. Davis has some concrete evidence that might assist us with the Mack and Mixon investigation--"

TAP! TAP!

The sudden simultaneous taps on both the driver and passenger windows startled Dawson and Weinstein. The two masked men both had guns pointed at them.

"Put your hands up!!" The masked man on the driver side shouted, stopping Dawson and Weinstein from reflexively reaching for their weapons.

Thump!

Another masked man jumped on the hood of the car with a shotgun aimed at Weinstein, who was behind the wheel.

SMMAASSHH!

The masked gunman on the passenger side broke the window with a crow bar as Dawson and Weinstein's hands touched the roof of the car.

The masked man then yanked Dawson out of the car by his coat collar, spun him around, handcuffed him with his hands behind his back, slapped some thick masking tape over his mouth and blind folded him while the other masked man did the same to Weinstein. Both agents were tossed in the back seat of the car.

Still standing on the hood of the car, the masked man with the shotgun waved to Mixon who was twenty yards away, hiding in a patch of bushes. He then jumped off the hood, got in the car and drove off as the other two masked men approached Mixon.

*   *   *   *

Meanwhile, Units two and three were undergoing the same exact thing that just happened to Dawson and Weinstein. The three incidents occurred precisely at the same moment and all produced the same outcome (The six agents were bound, gagged, blind folded and whisked away).

*   *   *   *

Mixon pulled his special made communication device from his inner breast coat pocket. The gadget resembled a cellular phone and was equipped with a state of the art scrambling system. Mixon pressed a button and spoke into the device. "Listen up, gentlemen. The two Feds on the eastern side are outta the picture. What's up with everybody else?"

"The western side is under control," The voice said through Mixon's radio. There was a slight pause and another voice said, "The northern Feds are out."

Mixon spoke into the device. "I want all groups to go forward with the plan. Once you're in place, I want you to contact me immediately. And keep in mind, we're not working with unlimited time here." He disconnected the line.

As Mixon and the two masked men got inside a green Jeep, the 25 hit men quietly began surrounding the Davis home. Each man within this professional doom squad had a weapon equipped with a silencer. Their firearms ranged from long-range infrared scope rifles to military style fully automatic assault rifles.

*   *   *   *

"You fuckin' bastards!" Dinasia shouted at Shateek. "You put Tislam in prison for the rest of his life for a murder he didn't do!" She had the tape in her hand, clutching it as if it was the world's most precious jewel.

"I had no idea Prince was gonna be murdered. When it happened I was probably more shocked than anyone."

"Why does that sound like bullshit to me!?" Dinasia sounded sarcastic. "I tell you why! Because I overheard Trigger and Watch Dog say it was you that set up this whole thing."

"That's probably what they honestly thought, since I didn't go outta my way to say it wasn't me until all this madness started with you and this tape." He paused for a long moment, pacing. "My fuckin' brother, Shabazz, was behind this shit. He set this whole thing up. After I told him about how I was going to get Tislam to shoot Kirk for what that perverted bastard did to you, he apparently sent Mixon out to do what he did. I had no idea--"

"But why would Shabazz wanna kill Prince? They were friends. And Shabazz was the one who helped Prince leave the drug game in the first place. There ain't no reason for him to wanna kill Prince after going through all that?"

Short pause.

"Yeah, you're right, they were friends." Shateek sat down in the armchair. "But your brother, Prince, was about to destroy Shabazz and his entire drug empire." He sighed. "Prince was an informant for the Feds . . . And he was about to testify against Shabazz at a grand jury. When Prince came home from college, and that altercation between Kirk and Tislam was about to go down, Shabazz apparently saw the perfect way to get rid

220

of Prince without focusing light on himself. Obviously, if he could make it look like Prince was shot and killed as a result of some family feud, there would be no way the Feds could link him to the murder."

"You knew Tislam was innocent all along! Why did you lie to me, Shateek? Telling me all those tales about Tislam was planning to kill Prince. And I know you had those crack-head women at the Shelter attack and harass me." Her tone became almost venomous. "How could you, Shateek? Those bitches were gonna infect me with some HIV tainted blood! And I bet you were the one who planned that shit!" Her tone suddenly became soft, but forcefully. "How could you? How could you do something like that to me?"

Long pause.

Shateek felt like he was an inch tall. "Because I love you." He let that heart-felt statement hang in the air for a moment and then continued. "I wanted you so bad, Dinasia, I would've done anything to win your heart. And I still feel the same to this day. I love you, Dinasia."

"How can you say you love me and allow my life to be threatened!? You sat back and did nothing while an innocent person's life was being destroyed. And you lied to me--"

"At that time I was young, dumb, full of come and as hot headed as a smoke stack . . . I admit, that was probably one of my worse youthful indiscretions ever . . . But I did it all for love. And my love for you hasn't wavered or diminished one bit . . . What I'm about to say may sound crazy, but I would die for you, Dinasia. I know it's the words to a song, but I'm dead ass serious when I say this. And everything I've done from the day I laid eyes on you proves it."

Dinasia wasn't moved by this heart-felt speech. "That still doesn't alter the facts. What if one of those women stuck me with that needle? And . . . and you apparently knew I was out here trying to find this tape. The hell I went through to get this tape, and all along you knew those men were after me and didn't lift a finger to--"

"I was the one who prevented those men from harming you. Over in Coney Island at Mrs. Daye's apartment when the cops were about to walk in on you." He saw her eyebrows crunched up. "Yeah, the Bank on Mermaid Avenue when those two men were going to kidnap you. That Salvation Army worker at Regina's Restaurant--"

"That was you!?" Dinasia sounded surprised as the image of the blue eyed Santa Claus looking man circulated in her mind. "Get outta here! That couldn't be you! The man had blue eyes and his skin was white."

"Have you ever heard of colored cosmetic contact lenses? And you'll be amazed at what you can do with that theater make-up." He smiled when he saw Dinasia's shocked facial expression. "Watch Dog and Trigger were the two at the lawyer's office, but even then I was right outside acting as a back-up. That's right, those masked men were me, Trigger and Watch Dog."

Dinasia's mind rewound those incidents. She didn't know if she should be upset, glad, angry or agitated. "Well, why didn't you just come right out and help me get hold of the tape without all the--"

"Dinasia, Mixon and this guy Eddie Mack aren't street corner clowns anymore. If it wasn't for Shabazz, you and I would be dead. He talked them into not hurting you and made them believe I knew absolutely nothing. If they even thought I knew what was going on, they would've sent a fuckin' army straight to our door step. The way I did it, it worked didn't it?"

Dinasia stared at him as her mixed emotions became more turbulent with every passing second. Then she snapped out of her semi-trance. "I have to get this tape to someone who can stop them from killing Tislam."

"Wait a minute, Dinasia," Shateek quickly went to her. "It's hard for me to say this, but I--I'll just—" He paused as he counted his thoughts. "If you turn that tape over to the authorities, it'll mean we'll be putting ourselves in extreme danger. Like I told you, Mixon is no longer some two bit, up and raising hit man anymore. He's got his own crime family that's connected with other families. And, if you turn the tape over to the

Feds, not only is Mixon going down, but so is Shabazz. They'll make the connection because Mixon was working for Shabazz at the time Prince was murdered and the Feds were investigating Shabazz. Mixon has some kind of mutual pact with a dozen or more other heavyweight crime families. Italians, Russians, Mexicans, Jamaicans. If he's arrested, they'll hunt down and kill the people responsible for his down fall, even from behind the wall."

There was a long pause as Shateek and Dinasia silently stared at each other with expressions that indicated they both understood the life and death nature of the situation.

Shateek continued. "That means we'll have countless men looking for us for the rest of our lives. Shabazz'll be the first they'll kill. With these people, even the famous Witness Protection Program wouldn't be a guaranteed way around them because they got people all over the place, especially in damn near all those Federal agencies. It'll be just a matter of time before they catch up to us."

Short pause.

"So, what are you saying?" Dinasia's anger returned with explosive force. "That I just let them pull the plug on Tislam? Is that what you're telling me?"

"I'm not telling you anything, Dinasia," He tried to caress her shoulder, but she pulled away. "I love you. And want to see you happy. If that means putting my own life on the line to guarantee your safety, I'll do it again and again at the drop of a hat . . . Whatever you decide, Dinasia I'm with you, even though I might lose you to him . . . I'm just spelling out the repercussions, so when we walk into--"

"Repercussions!?" Dinasia went for her coat and began putting it on. "The only repercussions I'm concerned about at this moment is the one that could cause Tislam to lose his life." She picked up the 25 automatic from off the floor and tucked it in one pocket while the tape was in the other. She then headed for the door.

"Wait!" Shateek shouted when he suddenly saw numerous red laser beams of light dancing across the walls and furniture. The one that landed on Dinasia's shoulder was what really got his attention.

"Get down!" He shouted as the terror-stricken, dreadful realization took control of his hysterical movement.

Dinasia turned and was truly startled by Shateek's sudden frantic change in his behavior. Just as she saw him dive in the air . . .

SZK! SZK! SZK! SZK! SZK! SZK! . . .

The silenced bullets suddenly rained all over the living room, savagely shattering, ripping, shredding and tearing at the windows, walls, furniture and anything in their path.

"AAEEHHH!!!" Dinasia screamed when she felt the burning hot pain from the bullet wound. The scream was unleashed just as Shateek collided with her.

As they collapsed to the floor, the bullets sounded like a deranged mob of pissed-off armor covered bees and hornets engaged in a delirious suicide rampage.

CHAPTER # 31

"Excuse me, Shabazz," The bodyguard named Martin said, after nervously bursting into the room. "We got a major problem. Mel's on the line. He said--He's on line number two."

Shabazz Davis had been waiting for this moment. He calmly reached over and picked up the phone. "What's up, Mel? What's happening?" He waved for Martin to leave.

"I gotta make this quick. Mack and Mixon is sending a hit crew up there to see you. They got a contract out on you, man." Martin said in a tone that sounded as if this was the most unbelievable thing he'd ever encountered in his entire life. "I'm still trying to find out the reason for the track. Rest assured, I'm on the job, Sha. They're coming with at least thirty and better hitters. I--I don't think you and the crew should wait around."

"Thanks, Mel. I'll get in touch with you when I get situated. I'll talk to you later." He hung up the phone.

As Shabazz rushed to the secret safe in the wall near the window, his thoughts were all over the place. He opened the safe and pulled out the knapsack he prepared earlier when he got word Shateek clipped the tape. The sachet was filled with stocks, bonds, municipal and mutual fund certificates, diamonds, emeralds and other priceless jewels. He knew Mack and Mixon were going to flip out like this once they found out they didn't have the tape, but Shateek was his baby brother, and blood would always be thicker than mud. He just hoped Shateek took his advice, which was to find a quick safe haven from Mixon's wrathful vengeance because it was definitely on its way.

In the back of the safe there was also a bulletproof vest. Shabazz pulled it out with a struggle. As he put on this special made vest that could stop Teflon bullets, he wondered how life was going to be in the UK?

The minute he found out Dinasia stumbled onto the tape, and after he began convincing Mack and Mixon not to kill his sister-in-law, Shabazz started making preparations to disappear. All his finances were transferred to the UK under a fictitious name (Stanley Raft). His wife Charmaine and son Shabazz Jr. were moved to their new mansion in the UK. The private jet along with all appropriate papers was put on stand-by. And he even found a way to sell his home at a decent price ($750,000) considering the short notice and the need for expeditious liquidation.

The more Shabazz thought about the current situation, the more he cursed himself for allowing that old big mouth woman Mrs. Daye to create all this chaos. How could he allow himself to believe she didn't have copies of that damn tape? Then he realized it wasn't that he believed what she said regarding the tape, but it really was because he was getting soft. Killing an old helpless woman wasn't something he could do and be able to sleep well at night. *Was it worth it?* This was the only question he repeatedly asked himself for years, and no answer seemed to come to mind until Mixon contacted him last week with the unfortunate news.

No, it wasn't worth it.

As Shabazz headed down the plush carpet covered stairs on his way to the stretch Limo, he literally hoped and prayed Shateek took his warnings seriously because whether he knew it or not, that tape was gonna be the root of a lot of people's down fall, including his own if he wasn't careful.

*   *   *   *

Special agents Tracy Dickinson and Carl Winters sat in their brown car watching Mixon's mansion with binoculars. The other two Units were on the southern and western regions of the huge multi-million dollar grounds.

Carl put his binoculars down and said, "I'm telling you, Tracy, something is wrong here. Those two aren't in there. Just because those Limos are parked out front, don't mean there's a meeting going on and Mack and Mixon are in there . . . Shit, if we could just get a fuckin' agent amongst these fucks, we'd have a half ass fighting chance. We'd probably have car loads of arrested--"

"You need some patience in your life," She said, watching the second floor window where several shadows danced on the drawn blinds. "Those are their vehicles. They always use them and why would Eddie have his Limo sitting out front unless he's in there . . . Give Dawson another call, maybe the radio transmission cleared up by now."

"Their failure to respond has nothing to do with a radio transmission and you know that, Tracy." He punched in the number. As it buzzed and buzzed without an answer, he said, "This whole surveillance is crumbling right before our eyes, and of all people, we're in the wrong place." He sighed after the tenth buzz and disconnected the line. "Nothing again . . . We're outta here." He turned the ignition key.

"Now, I have to agree with you," Tracy said. "Something has apparently gone terribly wrong." The thought of Dawson, Weinstein and the others possibly being dead almost caused her to lose control.

As Carl maneuvered the car out of their hiding place, Tracy said, "Give me the radio."

He handed it to Tracy and accelerated the vehicle onto the road and down the street.

"Units four and five, this is Unit seven," Tracy said into the radio. "Come in please."

Both Units answered their transmission.

Tracy continued. "Unit seven is disengaging from this surveillance. I want you two to maintain surveillance until further notice. We'll land mine you in twenty minutes. If you see any odd activities, please contact us before you proceed. Over."

*   *   *   *

"How bad is it?" Shateek was lying on top of Dinasia. He felt relieved she was only clutching her left forearm, cringing in pain. "We gotta get to the basement." He slid off her. "Can you crawl with that injury?" When he saw her nod her head, he quickly led the way. "Come on! Hurry!"

The intensity of the bullets striking all over the living room sounded like it increased as Shateek slid towards the hallway.

Dinasia rolled over onto her stomach and realized the fear of being shot again paralyzed her. She felt the bullet hole in her coat sleeve and noticed the pain wasn't as excruciating as she expected it would be. She also felt the warm blood oozing out of the wound and fought back the urge to take her coat off to see just how bad the injury really was. As she wiggled her fingers to make sure the bullet hadn't broken any bones, the pain exploded to life, but she was able to move them. She could feel it was merely a flesh wound.

"Let's go, Dinasia," Shateek whispered forcefully.

Crawling on her belly, Dinasia followed Shateek, flinching nervously every time a bullet ricocheted and struck the floor near her.

Just as they arrived at the basement door, the massive silenced gunfire stopped. Right outside the house running footsteps and excited whispers could be heard.

Dinasia quickly followed Shateek into the basement, stood up and, out of unconscious habit, was about to flick on the light switch.

"No!" Shateek responded as if a bomb was attached to the switch. He quickly closed the door, engulfing them in pure darkness. "They'll see the light and know where we're at."

"It's so dark I can't see my hand," Dinasia whispered. "How are we gonna see where we're going?"

"Grab onto my shirt," He found her uninjured hand, held it for a moment, savoring its softness and guided it to his shoulder. "Stay quiet. We gotta move fast." As he moved towards the back of the basement, bumping into things while on the way, he wondered why Mixon was moving so quickly? Something went wrong. He could've sworn he had a couple more hours before they would mobilize and send out a hit mob. "Where the hell is Trigger and Watch Dog? They should've been here by now!" He mumbled frustratingly.

When they stopped, Dinasia said, "I still can't understand why we came down here?" She let go of Shateek's shirt when he bent down and started tearing at the carpet. "We've trapped ourselves even further since the cellar door is useless to us. We can't get out this way. Those men are probably all over the place." She had to step to the side when he pulled the carpet completely off the floor and flipped it over. The loud clacking sound from the latches on whatever it was Shateek was tinkering with perplexed her because she never knew there was anything on this side of the basement. "What are you doing? What is that?"

No response.

A few seconds later, Dinasia felt Shateek nudge her with something hard and huge. *What was he doing?* She recoiled when sudden loud, rapid gunfire went off somewhere outside the house.

"Take it, hurry! It's an Uzi," Shateek waited until she had it in her grasp. He then turned and quickly continued rummaging through his secret arsenal. "It's about damn time." He mumbled to himself.

"I--I don't how to use this thing," Dinasia noticed the weapon felt like it weighed a ton and the handle was gigantic in comparison to the 25 automatic in her coat pocket.

"You were handling that automatic pretty well," Shateek smiled and noticed the gunfire outside came to a stop. "Don't worry, I'll show you." He flung the heavy clip belt along with the strap attached to the Heckler & Koch, MP5K submachine gun over his shoulder. He stuffed six 9mm clips in his pockets, grabbed two extra clips for Dinasia's weapon, temporarily tucked them under his armpit and turned. He grabbed the gun from Dinasia and spoke as he prepared the Uzi. "I'll fix the gun to where it's ready to shoot. All you'll have to do is aim and pull the trigger. When it runs out of bullets, I'll re-load it for you. These are extra clips to that Uzi. Here, let me put them in your pocket."

As he stuffed the two fifty round clips in her pocket with the 25, Dinasia said, "What if you and I get separated?"

"Don't worry I won't let--"

BBOOOM!! CRRAASSHH!!

The explosion ripped the cellar door off of the hinges as easy as a piece of lint blown away by a violent gust of wind.

Shateek hastily pulled Dinasia behind a weight box, pointed the MP5K and waited for the first person to walk down into the basement.

BOOOM!!! SMMASSHH!! CRRASSHHH!!

Another explosion from the battering-ram tore the basement door Dinasia and Shateek entered from clean off its hinges. The sudden sound of breaking glass along with the simultaneous hissing noise from the two tear gas canisters, and the smell of the noxious chemical, startled Dinasia and Shateek into a state of frantic desperation.

We're trapped! Dinasia's terrified mind was on the verge of sheer hysteria. *Oh, God, no! We're trapped!* Her nervous grip on the Uzi became slippery from the wetness of her palm.

Then, suddenly, the massive gunfire outside started up again and Shateek joined in when six men attempted to rush down into the basement from both the cellar and inner basement doors at the same time. The flames that burst from the muzzle of the machine gun lit up the basement as if a gigantic disco strobe light was suddenly turned on.

Through irritated eyes, ringing ears and blinding tears, Dinasia pointed the Uzi and was shocked she was able to squeeze the trigger. The rapid jerking motion from the gun felt like the weapon had a life of its own and was as angry as a violent hurricane.

*   *   *   *

At around the time the 25 hit men were surrounding the house, and Shateek and Dinasia were in the living room talking, Trigger and Watch Dog drove past the house for the second time, trying to come up with a plan.

"Whatever we're gonna do," Trigger said with his two guns setting in his lap. "We better make a decision." He pointed at the group of men wearing dark clothing, who scurried about with rifles and machine guns in their hands.

"I'm waiting to hear it," Watch Dog said with his Shotgun lying next to him. "You always like to call the shots when Sha ain't around, well get to calling."

Trigger chewed on his bottom lip and wondered if it was wise for them to go up against these men? When he thought of Shateek and Dinasia being trapped in that house only seconds from being murdered, he made his mind up. "Go two blocks down near that small wooded area. Hurry!"

After they parked the car on the side of the road, they hastily got out and went for the trunk.

Watch Dog opened the trunk. "You think these bullshit firearms are gonna be any good against that army back there?"

Trigger reached inside and pulled out one of the Tech 9's. "I guess it depends on how we approach this thing." He handed Watch Dog the other Tech 9 while stuffing three of the fifty round clips in his coat pocket and handed the other two to Watch Dog. He slammed the trunk and fled in the direction of the house with Watch Dog on his heels.

As they ran through the backyards and fields of the near-by homes, Trigger said, "Sha's gonna try to get out through the cellar door. As long as we keep the element of surprise along with a few guerrilla warfare tactics, we might be able to keep the upper hand."

About a minute later, they arrived at the house next to Shateek's. They both stopped running and instantly saw the hundreds of flashes, but didn't hear any gunfire. They didn't have to be told the men were using silencers.

Trigger whispered excitedly. "I need you to go all the way to the left over there." He pointed. "Get in position behind them, and when you hear me open fire, you do the same."

Watch Dog took off with frantic speed.

As Trigger waited for Watch Dog to get in place, the flickering lights from the guns came to a stop. He took several deep breaths, counted to three and rushed towards the six men who were crouched down behind a row of bushes with their backs to him. With the Tech 9 pointed, Trigger squeezed the trigger just as two of the men heard his rapidly approaching footsteps and was about to turn around.

BOW! BOW! BOW! BOW! BOW! BOW! BOW! . . .

The 9mm bullets struck all six men as Trigger waved the Tech 9 in a fast sweeping motion. Simultaneously he heard Watch Dog's gunfire join in the destruction of the night's silence with the explicit music of warfare. When the men were laid out, Trigger pulled one of his handguns and shot three of the men who tried to get up. The three headshots closed the book on those men as smoothly as the words 'the end'.

Trigger put his back to the wall and moved towards the backyard of the house. Suddenly, an explosion went off and, immediately afterwards, an enormous crashing sound similar to a wall being knocked down by a ten ton wreaking ball was heard. The sound of shattering glass followed.

When Trigger made it to the end of the house, he peeked around the corner and saw about eight men milling around the cellar door. He heard violent commotion inside the house, which prevented him from hearing the two men coming up behind him. By the time he heard the men in the back of him, massive gunfire came from what sounded like everywhere; inside the house, near the cellar and most of all in the direction he turned while aiming, diving and pulling the triggers on both the Tech 9 and handgun.

"EEEHHH!!! Shit!" Trigger screamed when the bullet hit him in the hip. When he hit the dirt, his fingers were still locked on both triggers. He saw one of the men went down as the other sought cover in the bushes. The gunfire inside the house and near the cellar maintained its continuous urgent flow.

Trigger dragged himself towards the yard of the neighboring house and saw someone peeking through their shades. He quickly inserted a fresh clip in the Tech 9. The gunfire filled the night and turned this quiet residential district into a battlefield.

The police sirens came to life.

Trigger's heart almost stopped because he knew with this injury he was as good as caught, but he still tried to flee, frantically dragging himself through the grass and toward the backyard.

*   *   *

Dinasia was amazed at how the men continuously tried to enter the basement, despite the fact their previous comrades were mowed down by her and Shateek's bullets. She also sensed the persons outside, who were shooting weapons without silencers, were doing major work to these attackers. The tear gas had a river dripping from her eyes and the nasal pain felt like a blow torch was crammed up her nose and turned on full blast. She coughed uncontrollably.

The muted symphony of police sirens faded into existence.

It took a moment for Dinasia to notice those sirens. The realization occurred only after she and Shateek ceased fire when the men took a break from entering the basement. Dinasia spoke excitedly. "Sha, do you hear it?" She coughed loudly. "It's the police." The thought of being arrested by the racist Nassau County Police Department freaked her out because the tape could possibly be deliberately mishandled or even outright destroyed if they found out it could save the life of a black man in prison accused of killing Correction Officers.

"Just relax," Shateek caressed Dinasia's shoulder, sounding like he had a head cold. "Once we get a signal from--"

"Yo, Shateek!" Watch Dog shouted as he stood at the top of the cellar door, reloading the Tech 9 while nervously scanning the terrain. The tear gas instantly began burning his eyes and nostrils.

"Let's go," Shateek tugged at Dinasia's uninjured arm, the one grasping the Uzi. "That's Watch Dog."

They ran towards the cellar door, jumping over the men sprawled out on the floor with gas masks covering their faces. The moonlight shun through the opening where the cellar door was once located and provided ample lighting for them to see.

When they reached the bottom of the stairs, Shateek hastily ushered Dinasia up the stairs. Suddenly he heard movement in back of him.

BOW! BOW!--BOW! BOW! BOW! BOW! . . .

Two shots rang out from one of the fallen attackers. Reflectively, Shateek spun the MP5K at the precise second he heard movement, spraying the area with bullets while increasing his speed as he ran up the stairs.

When Shateek bolted past the threshold of the cellar, he saw Dinasia heading towards the front of the house. "No! Dinasia! This way!" He turned and spit venom at Watch Dog. "When the fuck was you gonna stop her?! You know that ain't the way outta this shit!"

Before Watch Dog could respond, the three of them were running towards the fence leading to the backyard of the Bradford family's property.

While Shateek ran, he stayed in the back and repeatedly looked in back of him to make sure no one came up behind at them. When they were a few feet from the fence he saw the two men rush from around the house. "Duck! Everybody down--"

BOW! BOW! BOW! BOW! BOW! BOW! . . .

Dinasia dove for the grass the second she heard the word "duck!" She noticed the attackers were no longer using silencers. The bullets struck the fence in front of her with grueling force.

Shateek and Watch Dog returned fire while the Police sirens screamed louder and louder.

Dinasia was surprised when she saw the two men rush back around the house and out of sight.

"Watch Dog!" Shateek said excitedly "Go over first and make sure the other side is clear."

As Watch Dog climbed over the fence he wanted to tell Shateek, *why don't you take your black ass over first?* It was obvious, he could be walking into a trap, but he held back the comment because the moment was far too critical for bickering. He jumped to the ground and went into a sloppy combat roll. It took him a few seconds to conclude it was safe. "It's cool! Let's go!"

"Come on, Dinasia, you're next," Shateek grabbed her arm while his eyes were still riveted on the house.

As Dinasia climbed to the top of the fence, she wondered was Shateek playing games by the way he hoisted her up and over the top while firmly caressing her butt in the process. She hit the grass, went into a kneeling position and instantly noticed Shateek was not even seconds behind her.

As they raced through the Bradford's backyard heading for the street, Dinasia could hear the six police cars had arrived in front of what used to be her home. Her adrenaline levels were so high it made her feel light-headed. The sudden sound of a barking dog snatched her attention. She turned and almost panicked when she saw the dog galloping towards them with a vicious snarl on its face.

BOW!

Shateek shot the dog just as they arrived at the front of the Bradford's house.

Watch Dog peeked around the house and saw the coast was clear. "Everything look's alright, Sha."

"Let's keep it movin'" Shateek rushed into the street jogging in a fast pace with Dinasia beside him, heading for his blue Cherokee Jeep parked down the street near the strip of stores that were all closed. The last thing he wanted to see right now was any police because if they saw the three of them running down the street with guns in their hands, it would be either over for them or one helluva shoot-out. Just as they were only yards from the Jeep . . .

SZK! SZK! SZK! SZK!--EEAARRHHH!!!-- SZK! SZK! . . .

The silenced bullets came from across the street, striking Watch Dog twice; once in the side just below the rib cage and the other one shattered his jaw. The near-by car windows exploded into massive piles of glass cubes. The blood from the face shot splattered droplets of blood on Dinasia's face causing her to dive for the pavement.

As Watch Dog lied on the pavement cringing in pain, from behind the hood of a red car, Dinasia nervously pointed her weapon at the man across the street behind a small white car.

"Wait!" Shateek rushed over to Dinasia. "We can't shoot at them." He pulled her down. "It'll draw the police to this area!"

*   *   *   *

Earlier, just before Trigger and Watch Dog opened fire, Mixon along with his personal sidekick, Brass, sat in their separate vehicles watching the events unfold. They were parked two houses down from the Davis house in a position where they couldn't see the back areas of any of the houses. Mixon was in the driver seat of a green Jeep while Brass was in a beige van.

When the rapid unsilenced gunfire suddenly went off, Mixon's nerves were almost completely unhinged. He frantically grabbed his communication device, hit the send button and mumbled angrily to himself as he waited for someone to answer. There wasn't supposed to be any shooting without a silencer. Although he asked his inside man within the Nassau County Police to be on watch for any 911 calls from this area and to divert or outright ignore them, but he knew if shots were fired, it would be almost impossible for him to maintain a lack of involvement under these circumstances.

The gunfire intensified as if two automatic weapons were being fired, and now Mixon was on the edge of his seat. A minute later, the shooting died down and the high-tech cell phone sizzled to life.

"What's up, Mixon?" The voice said through the communication device.

"Who the fuck is shooting without a god-damn silencer!?"

Two explosions went off and terminated the transmission.

"Hey, come in," Mixon shouted into the device. "Come in, god-damn it!"

The unsilenced shooting exploded to life again, but this time it sounded like it was coming from inside the house. Mixon struggled to control his impatience. He continued shouting for someone to answer their communication device.

The police sirens blended with the gunfire and Mixon readjusted the frequency dial connected to Brass's communication device.

"This is Brass, what's up, Bro?"

"Let's circle the area. I got a strange feeling this shit is backfiring. If the cops get here before we find out what's up, at least we'll be in motion." He sat the device down.

Mixon started the Jeep and drove off. He drove three blocks down and made a right turn. Brass drove the van in the opposite direction.

Mixon's high-tech cell phone came to life. He picked it up and pressed a button.

"Mixon, this is Flipper." The voice said through the communication device. "The broad and Shateek are headed for the street in back of the house. I'm ordering everyone who ain't dead to--"

"Dead!?" Mixon thought Flipper had finally flipped his wig. "How the fuck could Shateek and a woman, who can barely shoot a fuckin' gun, kill some nig--"

"Two dudes came outta nowhere . . .

As Flipper spoke, Mixon raced the Jeep to the corner and turned onto the street in back of the Davis home. He realized the two men Flipper just mentioned had to be the same two who'd been protecting Dinasia. *Who the hell are these motherfuckers? And why are they always coming to Dinasia's rescue?*

The sudden flashing sparks up ahead instantly got Mixon's attention. "I'm on the back street, Flipper, and it looks like we got some action. If you can get here without attracting the police's attention, do it."

He laid the device down, killed the headlights, hastily parked the Jeep, found his binoculars and saw Shateek and Dinasia on one side of the Street and one of his front-line soldiers on the other. He noticed the three were engaged in some kind of standoff. It took a few seconds to figure out what was going on and what he should do.

Mixon picked up the cell phone. The binoculars were still held to his eyes and he saw who the soldier was. "Hey Sing Sing! Come in!"

"What's up, Mixon?"

"I want you to break out. Let'em leave."

"But I thought you wanted--"

"One more word out of you," Mixon's tone was almost as soft as a baby's bottom, "I'll have you strung up to a lamp post by your motherfuckin' nuts!"

"Sorry," Sing Sing said as he ran down the street at top speed.

Mixon pushed a bottom. "Listen up Brass and to anyone else available. I'm over on the street in back of Shateek's house. I need you to get over here quickly. They just got in a blue Jeep heading west. We're gonna follow them outta this area. When we're a good distance away, we're gonna put this shit officially to an end."

As Mixon followed the blue Jeep, he noticed not only did Brass join in the pursuit, but so did four other vehicles.

CHAPTER # 32

Dinasia was in the passenger seat of the Jeep nervously rocking back and forth as they moved rapidly down the partially empty Long Island Expressway on their way to Brooklyn. The comforting words of those two FBI agents before, during and after her arrest, made it clear they really wanted to help her, and now that she had the tape, the Brooklyn FBI Office was the only logical place for her to go. She just hoped they had people working at this hour of the night.

Every few minutes, Dinasia cut her eye at Shateek and couldn't understand why he looked a little too comfortable? It made her wonder if he was desensitized to all this madness? Watch Dog was a lifelong friend, for crying out loud. The way Watch Dog trembled violently and released a huge, loud breath of air just before he died, played itself over and over in her mind. This horrifying sight was enough to drive her insane with fear, sorrow and guilt because she, in essence, created all of this madness.

She felt something stronger than the urge to cry brewing inside her, and the inner feeling was so overpowering, it made her shiver uncontrollably for several straight minutes. Moments later, the thought of losing Tislam gradually faded into a feeling similar to the one a person gets upon accomplishing an arduous task. She repeatedly caressed the tape in her pocket realizing this act induced a drastic soothing effect on her emotion-ridden mind because this evidence was enough to save his life. This tape completely and unequivocally exonerated him, and since this evidence proved that Tislam shouldn't have been in prison in the first place, Dinasia knew it was evident that anything which happened after his wrongful conviction was the fruit of the poisonous tree and would have to be disregarded on the basis it couldn't have occurred without the gross injustice.

She smiled at the thought of him being freed soon. Even his current unfortunate condition with respect to the coma wasn't enough to disrupt her slowly developing optimistic attitude and good mood because she would take care of him, nurse him back to good health and be with him forever, every step of the way this time. With the force and power of love on her side, she knew she would find a way to make it through any ordeal flung in her path.

Dinasia's eyes grew when she saw a car on her side suddenly attempt to sideswipe them.

"Get down!" Shateek shouted and floored the gas pedal. He frantically reached for the MP5K sitting next to him. "It's them!" Shateek aimed the weapon at the car, completely oblivious of the fact the passenger window was rolled up.

BOW! BOW! BOW! BOW! BOW! .....

Dinasia felt faint as her ears screamed in pain while glass was scattered all over the inside of the car and her good mood and optimism vanished instantaneously. The shell casings from the MP5K rained upon her as Shateek's finger was locked on the trigger for a few seconds. She heard a huge crashing sound and knew it was the car colliding with something. Shateek laid the weapon next to her and increased the speed of the Cherokee. She rose to see what was happening in back of them. She saw a lot of headlights.

Suddenly, Dinasia heard and felt hundreds of bullets striking the back of the Jeep. She ducked down just as the gunfire started, bumping heads with Shateek. The back window exploded and so did the windshield. The wind gushed inside the interior of the Cherokee, sounding like it was in a savage rage. The temperature inside the Jeep plummeted and the gunfire didn't seem like it was ever going to stop.

Then, suddenly, the Jeep slowed down.

Dinasia spoke frantically. "What's wrong with the car!?"

"They shot the tires out," Shateek said, peeking over the dashboard periodically and then pulling back. "It feels like both of the back ones." He sighed angrily.

"So, what are we gonna do!?" Dinasia said, seconds from losing control.

Shateek peeked over the dashboard again before answering excitedly. "I'm gonna pull-over. We gotta get us another ride." He peeked again. "Get your gun ready. Hurry! The minute we stop, I'll jump out and start shooting. Slide outta the car through my side. Alright!?"

"Then what are we--"

The Jeep struck the curb, causing them to bounce violently as they entered a truck depot.

Shateek hit the brakes. The tires squealed as the Cherokee came to a full stop about 20 yards from a row of thirteen tractor trailers parked in a neat line. He shot out of the vehicle and began shooting at a car that already stopped about 50 yards from them.

Dinasia was out of the Jeep only seconds after Shateek started shooting and squeezed off a few rounds. As she and Shateek ran towards the 18-wheelers, Dinasia saw there were at least five vehicles following them. They quickly ran in between two of the huge trucks. When they reached the back and saw another row of trucks, they headed for them.

She saw Shateek increase his speed and mount one of the huge trucks with a frantic leap while waving for her to get in on the passenger side. Dinasia also noticed the truck was left running, and as she climbed inside, she saw a white man rushing out of the store screaming: "Wait! What the fuck are you doing! That's my rig!" Just as the truck began to move, she saw two of the attackers step from in between the same two trucks they came through moments ago.

Dinasia was surprised Shateek knew how to drive one of these monstrous vehicles. As they barreled out of the depot, the truck struck one of the pursuing cars. It went into a vicious spin as if it was a plastic toy car being mishandled by a belligerent child. Dinasia ducked down as a wave of bullets struck the truck. She sat back upright when they were back on the Expressway and zooming along.

A moment later, Shateek spoke while looking through the side view mirror. "Here they come again . . . With this trailer attached, it's gonna be impossible to out run them. If they start shooting at the gas tanks, we might go up in flames."

With terror in her eyes Dinasia spoke. "Then why did we get inside this death trap!?"

"Try ta figure that shit out yourself." He said coldly and then remained silent for a long moment while constantly looking out of the side view mirrors. His thoughts were all tied up with a myriad of painful emotions. He turned and saw the look on Dinasia's face. The way she looked, split his heart in half. "I'm sorry, Dinasia, I'm not trying to be sarcastic or anything. But . . . You know . . . I . . . All this pressure got me all--"

BOW! BOW! BOW! BOW!--OUCH!--BOW! BOW! BOW. . .

The machine gunfire ignited from the driver side, and a chunk of flying glass struck Shateek's face. He leaned away from the window as the blood dripped from the wound. He jerked the steering wheel to his left, ignoring the pain.

The truck struck the car, tossing it away with fearsome force.

When Shateek saw the rapid gunfire being directed at the gas tanks, he knew it was over. Even if the tanks didn't explode, the fuel would certainly leak until the tanks were empty. In a desperate attempt to ward off the cars on both sides, he zigzagged along the highway, hoping he would catch one of the cars under the back wheels of the trailer or possibly knock them off the road.

Each time a shot was fired at the tank, Dinasia flinched, expecting an explosion to follow.

"Whatever happens, you get out and run!" Shateek said as he brought the truck on the ramp leading to the residential streets. "We got about a minute of gas left. I'm gonna crash land this sucker in a place where you can get away. I'll stay behind and hold them back."

Dinasia's heart pounded with explosive force. She remembered the Uzi needed another clip. "I have to re-load this gun. I need another clip."

"They're all gone. Get ready! You see that--"

The police sirens and flashers burst to life.

After the truck and three cars roared past the intersection of Lafayette and Willington Boulevards, the two officers inside the patrol car, parked on the corner of Lafayette, snapped into action. The two officers were taking a late night coffee and donut break, and frantically gave chase while radioing for back up.

"I don't know if this is good or bad," Shateek said, referring to the sirens, and then made a right turn. "Get ready, Dinasia. Here we go!" He viciously jerked the steering wheel to the right while locking the back brakes of the tractor, causing the whole truck to jack knife.

CRRAASSHHH! SMMAASSHH!! BOOOM!! CRRAASSHHH!

The back-end of the trailer part of the truck crashed into the brick wall of a grocery store after tearing down a streetlight, a fire hydrant and a mailbox. While still in a jack knife position the front part of the trailer and the tractor flung around and smashed into a parked car, bringing the rig to a stop. The whole truck blocked the intersection and Shateek was amazed at how he succeeded in pulling off this intended feat.

As Shateek hastily got out of the truck with the MP5K in hand, he shouted. "Run! Dinasia, go!"

Dinasia pushed the door open, jumped on the roof of a car that was crushed under the wheels of the truck and just as she landed, she almost lost her footing. Waving her arms frantically to regain her balance, the Uzi slipped from her grip and bounced off the roof of the car, and of all the places in the world it could've landed, it went under the truck.

"Shit!" Dinasia muttered because the weapon was gone for good.

When her feet hit the pavement, they instantly went into a frantic running mode.

The gunfire was loud and continuous.

The police sirens stopped screaming, and she could instantly hear the gunfire from the police revolvers as it joined in with the automatic gunfire. She was able to distinguish which was which since one form of gunfire was rapid while the other was singular.

Dinasia ran so hard and so long, her lungs felt like they were on fire. She turned corners while completely oblivious of where she was or where she was going. Ten minutes later, she slowed down and started jogging. Thinking of her destination and how to get there, she felt blessed her body was in top shape. Then, suddenly, Dinasia realized she wasn't so lucky because there was no way she was going to get to Brooklyn on foot.

As she headed for the ramp of the Long Island Expressway, Dinasia knew if she walked on this highway long enough, she would be able to hitchhike a ride to an area which had an all night cab service or to the public transportation system. She had no idea where either one of them were located, since she always used her own car to travel, and was hoping and praying whoever gave her a ride would know.

After walking for ten minutes, and six cars passed without stopping; each one completely ignoring her hand waves as if she was invisible, Dinasia wondered if what she was doing would produce any results. But, still, she walked on.

*   *   *

Brass couldn't believe his eyes when he saw Dinasia standing in the breakdown lane, waving her arms for him to stop. He immediately pulled his gun and sat it in his lap, in between his legs. If there was enough time, he would've called Mixon, but this was one of those situations where jumping on the moment without calling in was the only way to handle it. He pulled the beige van over and opened the passenger door.

"Hello, Miss, can I be of any assistance?" Brass had a huge smile on his face.

"Yes," Dinasia said, not wanting to appear over anxious to get inside the van. "My car broke down a ways back and I need a lift to the nearest train station or cab service."

"No problem at all. Come on in."

As Dinasia got in the van, Brass was now glad he and Mixon stayed far away from the pursuit when they chased the blue Jeep and the truck. If they hadn't, she would've recognized the van. He pulled away and wondered if trying to squeeze her for information on the whereabouts of that tape was a good idea or was it better to just blow her brains out and deliver her dead body to Mixon? Since he had her by at least sixty pounds, he decided to have a little fun first, make her squeal and scream like the little bitch she was. He smiled as he cut his eye at her.

Already he was counting the 200 thousand dollars. He decided to get to a nice secluded location before taking care of business. In the meantime, he engaged her in a conversation to get inside her head.

"What is a pretty, young lady like yourself doing out here alone at a time like this?" He said without looking at her.

Dinasia wasn't prepared for this. She was hoping this would be one of those no talking sessions like most cab rides were. "Well, I was—ah--On my way to Brooklyn to—eh, visit a family member."

"My name is Jerry." Brass stuck his hand out for a shake. "Jerry Brass." When Dinasia shook it, he said, "What's yours?"

"Martha Jones."

"Nice name." He shook his head approvingly. "How long were you walking before I came?"

"Not that long," She sighed.

"Where's your car? I'm pretty good at fixing cars. What happened before the car broke down?"

"Well, it made a funny noise and then . . . just went dead." She was now feeling very uncomfortable talking because when she lied, it made her feel awkward and self-conscious, even when it involved trivial falsehoods.

"Sounds like a transmission problem. So, I guess it's fair to assume you live out here in Long Island? Nassau?"

"Yes," She was now becoming angry.

"Are you married or single?"

That's it, she thought. "Excuse me, Mr. Brass, I don't want to be rude or anything, but right now I'm going through a family crisis and I'm really not in the mood to talk. Please don't take it the wrong way. It's just--"

"No problem. I understand." Brass really wanted to say: "In the next minute or so, you'll find out what a crisis is, believe that shit sugar foot." But instead, he just smiled.

After about three minutes of silence, Dinasia saw Jerry Brass turn onto the ramp, leaving the Expressway. She couldn't help but get a nervous feeling something wasn't right because this exit led to a deserted area consisting of back roads and wooded land. She struggled to stay calm while pretending she was unaffected by what just happened. Her breathing increased drastically and she could've sworn she saw a smirk on Brass's face.

She spoke when the van made a turn down a dirt road, which had no street lights or any signs of civilization. "Is this a short cut or--"

The van came to an abrupt, head jolting stop.

Brass pulled the gun and pointed it at Dinasia. "No, it's not a short cut, Dinasia."

Dinasia was hit with a double whammy. The gun and he knew her name. When she made eye contact with Brass, she could've sworn she saw his face change into a skeleton head with blood dripping from the eye sockets and then flipped back to normal. She wondered if this was the image people spoke about when they claimed they stared death straight in the face? Or was it a sign telling her she was about to die?

She suddenly felt herself being viciously snatched by the collar from the seat and hurled to the back compartment of the van. She stumbled and hit the floor so hard it literally knocked every speck of air out of her lungs. She suddenly realized she couldn't breathe; at first she thought it was because of the paralyzing fear. Within seconds she realized it was because Brass was sitting on her chest and had the gun crammed in her mouth.

"Before I blow your brains out; I wanna ask you a few questions." Brass said. "What did you do with that tape everybody's all worked up over?" He took the gun barrel out of her mouth.

Dinasia started crying because she didn't want to die like this. Plus, she hoped the tears would elicit enough sympathy to enable her to pull the gun out of her pocket, or aim it at a vital part of his body when he shifted the aim of his gun.

Moments ago, as she was hurled to the floor, Dinasia stuffed her hand in the pocket where the gun was, but before she could pull it out, he pounced on her. His current seating arrangement restricted her arms from moving. She wasn't concerned about him seeing the gun because it was almost as dark as a windowless room. If it weren't for the light from the half moon and stars, it would've been as dark as when the eyes are closed shut.

"Where's that fuckin' tape!?" He shouted.

Dinasia flinched. "I—I—c--can't breathe," she squirmed. "I--I can't--"

"You just spoke, you dumb bitch!" He struck her face with the 357-magnum. "How the fuck you can talk and not be able to breathe at the same time?! It's either or, you dizzy, chicken head bitch!" He hit her on the top of the head and knew it made a deep gash.

Dinasia screamed as the warm blood oozed into her scalp as her cheekbone began to swell to the size of a golf ball. She squirmed harder while trying to point the gun at his lower back by twisting her wrist, but that wasn't gonna work because he was too far up on her chest.

"Well, I guess if you ain't gonna tell me," He placed the gun on her forehead. "I might as well--"

BLOOM!--BOW! . . .

Dinasia threw Brass off her chest just as he pulled the trigger. Upon feeling the gun touch her head, Dinasia got a sudden burst of super human energy. She had swiftly and violently turned her body to the left, and with blinding speed, her left hand grabbed Brass's wrist that had the gun.

Brass's head struck the side of the van and Dinasia was on top of him. She now had the 25 automatic in her hand.

BOW!

Brass pulled the trigger again. The thunderous explosion was far beyond mind shattering.

Dinasia and Brass tussled and wrestled with each other, their bodies slamming savagely against the sides of the van. The springs on the van bounced and the whole frame savagely shook, rattled and rolled.

Dinasia placed the 25 on his stomach and pulled the trigger.

Nothing happened.

Dinasia almost went into convulsions. If there was such a thing as an overload of terror-stricken shock, Dinasia felt it in that moment.

BOW!

Brass fired another shot. Dinasia felt the powder burn from the explosion on her face and hand that clutched Brass's wrist. She realized this particular shot was only inches away from hitting her. She felt like a rodeo cowboy the way Brass viciously flung her around while striking her face with his free hand. But she had a death-defying grip on his wrist.

Dinasia suddenly realized she hadn't hit the safety switch on the 25. She released the switch, but Brass began overpowering her and she saw the gun was now pointing at her leg.

BOW!

The shot was close enough to cause Dinasia to feel the heat through her pants from the flame that burst from the barrel. The bullet missed by a fraction of an inch and went through the floor.

Suddenly, they both crashed to the floor with Dinasia once again on the bottom and Brass on top.

Just as he slowly maneuvered the gun to the side of Dinasia's head with a straining effort, Brass said teasingly while breathing extremely hard. "I see you're one of them strong bitches . . . Let's see you get out of this." He strained as hard as he could and smiled when he realized the gun was in place.

Bow!--BOW--Bow! Bow! Bow! Bow! Bow!

The six rapid shots sounded muffled since the barrel was firmly placed on the body. Even after the weapon was empty, the trigger was still being pulled.

Dinasia had the gun placed on Brass's private parts, and each time a shot exploded, he responded as if he was having a monster ejaculation. Also, at the precise moment she pulled the trigger the first time, she shoved Brass's wrist upwards, and lucky thing she did because Brass was able to pull the trigger one last time before he was loaded up thoroughly with 25 caliber bullets that ricocheted off of his pelvis and lodged themselves all over the torso area of his body.

Dinasia rolled Brass's dead body off her and noticed her clothing was already soiled with thick blood. As she got up and sat behind the steering wheel, she pulled the tape out of her pocket to make sure it wasn't damaged. After concluding it was intact, she went to work. She dragged the dead body out of the van, laid him on the side of the dirt road and took Brass's coat off, using it to wipe up the blood. It took three minutes to complete this task.

Another ten minutes later, Dinasia was behind the wheel of the van and back on the Long Island Expressway.

*   *   *   *

The following day at around 10:00 a.m., Tracy and Carl were inside the Office of Director, Isaac Gilmore, trying to convince him to go the extra mile for Dinasia Davis/Whitman.

"She's not concerned about that," Tracy said, sitting in the chair in front of Isaac's desk. Carl sat next to her. "Her only concern is stopping that Court order terminating Mr. Parker's life support apparatus."

"Well," Isaac paused. "Like I said, I did everything within my powers to stop it. I personally spoke to the Judge who signed the order and so did the U.S. Attorney."

Carl was steaming with rage, but learned many years ago that venting anger in the way he wanted to do right now wasn't always the wise way to respond. So, he decided to remain quiet. But after hearing this, he couldn't continue to keep his mouth shut. "There has to be a way to stop this. That tape exonerates him, and if they kill him based on the assumption he might've somehow been involved in those correction officers' deaths, it would certainly constitute a gross miscarriage of justice."

"I agree with you 100%," Isaac said. "And that was the same argument I used to convince the U.S. Attorney to get involved. But that judge, in his discretion, can refuse to retract his order since the law says if an innocent person commits a crime while falsely incarcerated, he can and will be punished for that crime, even after it is discovered and proven the confinement was false. I'm sorry, but my hands are tied. I feel very sorry for this young man . . . There's nothing more we can do for her or him."

"I still say we should take this to Washington," Tracy said. "Go straight to the Attorney General or even the President. This man is about to die without a due process proceeding to prove he did anything. We all know damn well Mixon put a hit out on Mr. Parker to cover his tracks."

Carl interjected. "And we also know those killers hired to kill Mr. Parker apparently killed those officers in the process. This is as obvious as--"

"But what you're saying is not evidence," Isaac said. "If we had evidence that Mixon is responsible for this then maybe, just maybe, we would have a chance of swaying that Judge … I emphasis the word maybe because we also have to keep in mind, tomorrow they're going to terminate life support, and when you get right down to it . . . Even if we had evidence, it might be a lost cause anyway in light of the slow moving bureaucratic process, and that Correction Officer's Union is literally on a rampage. They're just dying to see Mr. Parker go down hard and fast. If we had a few weeks, it would make a world of a difference."

Carl stood, shaking his head with a defeated look on his face. "Thank you, Director Gilmore." He turned and headed for the door.

Tracy gave Isaac a short stare. "Thank you, Mr. Gilmore." She turned and exited the office.

*   *   *

Dinasia's knees gave in when Tracy and Carl broke the news to her. "No, no, NOOO!" Both of her hands went to her head as though she had a

250

vicious migraine headache. She fell backwards onto the wall, slowly slid down into a sitting position and cried.

"I'm sorry, Dinasia," Tracy kneeled and massaged Dinasia's arms, trying to comfort her. "We did everything in our power to stop it. But, we, it's. . .

Carl stood, staring helplessly. He hated to see women cry and he could never understand why it made him feel so extremely terrible. "Mrs. Davis, we're very, very sorry."

Dinasia wiped her eyes. Something snapped inside of her. And suddenly, her mind was made up. She stood, sniffling and breathing deeply. "I'm okay." She said softly to Tracy. "I just need to go outside and get some fresh air. I'll be all right after that." She headed for the elevator.

"I'm sorry, you can't do that," Tracy said, walking along side of Dinasia. "Mixon and Mack won't be arrested until the tape is presented to a Grand Jury. He probably has every man in his organization looking for you."

Carl said, "You have to be under 24 hour protection at all times from here on end, Mrs. Davis. A drastic restriction on all outside contact is an absolute necessity. The U.S. Marshals are on their way to pick you up and transport you to a safe house. This is for your own safety--"

"I'm going outside!" Dinasia said angrily as she pressed the elevator button. "You can send whoever wants to come along with me, if you'd like, I don't give a shit. But I have to get some air, god-damn it!" She was seconds from ranting and raving.

Tracy waved two agents over, Jamie Lewis and Nathan Howard, and met them halfway. She whispered to them. "I need you two to go with her and don't let her out of your sight. Bring her back here in an hour. No more, no less." Tracy walked over to Dinasia just as the elevator arrived. "Mrs. Davis, we can only permit you an hour and then you have to return. These two agents will go along with you. Are you going to return in an hour without any drama?"

"Yeah," Dinasia said unemotionally, stepping pass Tracy and then pushing the button to the ground floor. The two agents followed her onto the elevator.

*   *   *

Dinasia was doing some serious window-shopping while trying to come up with a plan to get away from these two agents. She noticed the woman named Jamie was acting a little nervous, looking around as if she was waiting for something to happen. Dinasia noticed she'd been like that ever since she got off her cellular phone about ten minutes ago.

As Dinasia stared at the mannequins in the window of a huge woman's clothing store, she figured out the perfect way to escape. She went inside the store and asked the clerk could she try on a dress. Dinasia made a special effort to let the agents see her utilize the stall farthest away from the entrance of the huge twenty-stall dressing room. As expected, the two agents checked all twenty stalls and the small window before allowing Dinasia to enter and then waited out front.

When Dinasia saw the agents leave, she went straight to work. She took off one of her socks and stuffed some tissue in it. She climbed one of the stalls and smiled at the woman in the stall next to her, who looked up at Dinasia with a startled facial expression. Dinasia tied the sock around the fire detection and sprinkler prong, lit the bottom of the sock with a match and then ran to the side of the door and waited.

Thirty seconds later the alarms all over the store went off, and all sprinklers were automatically turned on, spraying water everywhere. Dinasia smiled when she saw the two agents burst inside the dressing room and headed for the last stall in the back of the dressing room where they saw Dinasia moments earlier.

Dinasia rushed out of the dressing room and fled the store doing a twenty-mile an hour trot. It took her three minutes to get to the beige van.

As she cruised down Atlantic Avenue, Dinasia mumbled the quote Tislam used quite frequently, realizing it fit the moment just right: "God bless the child who can hold its own."

252

*   *   *   *

Tracy and Carl were seconds from hitting the ceiling when Nathan called and told them they lost Dinasia.

"Let's relax," Tracy said more to herself than to Carl. "We have to come up with a plan of action. First off, there's no question we know where she's going."

"We can't just take off and go upstate. Isaac won't allow it. He'll want to pass this on to one of the offices near the Dutchess County hospital."

"Who said we have to tell him?" Tracy smiled. "They're gonna pull the plug tomorrow morning. It's obvious she's gonna make her move before then. We'll catch her before then and bring her back before anyone notices."

"Well, you know my style. Ain't nothing like a good ole adrenaline rush brought on by the thrill of taking risks that could get yah ass fired. Let's go." He led the way out the door.

A half hour later, while they were cruising down Dutchess Turnpike, only minutes from the Hospital, the car's cellular phone rang.

Tracy picked up the receiver. "This is special agent Dickinson."

Isaac's voice came through the phone. "I got some really good news for you guys." He said cheerfully. "A correction officer named Glen Carol entered our uptown office in the Bronx, claiming the Mack and Mixon family made an attempt on his life. Apparently this guy was working for them and had some kind of falling out with them. He works at Green Haven and says those murders at the prison were Mixon and Mack's doing. He claims a group called the Crimson Cowboys picked up the track and basically attempted to kill Mr. Parker along with everybody in sight. This is the evidence we need to save Mr. Parker."

"Yes!" Tracy shouted happily. "So, are the bureaucratic wheels of justice in motion? Is the matter fixing itself or is it still in the early process?"

"Once the uptown agents get here, the U.S. Attorney and I will talk to that Judge again. If he attempts to play hardball, then an emergency federal injunction will be filed. However, based on the evidence, I doubt if we have to go that far. It's an open and shut situation . . . I would like for you and Carl to be present when these uptown agents arrive."

"Eh--we can't make it. We're—ah--in the middle of something very important that might help the case. Don't worry; go ahead without us. The minute we're finished, we'll check in."

"Well, if that's fine with you all, it's fine with me. Did you get any word on Dinasia Whitman, yet? The Marshals haven't." He chuckled. "You thought I didn't know, huh?"

Tracy was shocked. She thought they successfully concealed it from him. "Not a word yet, but that's what we're working on at the moment."

"Take care and contact me the minute you're finished."

"Hey Isaac . . . Thanks." She disconnected the phone.

It took her five minutes to share the news with Carl.

Carl spoke with a touch of doubt in his voice. "I just hope we get to this woman before Mixon and Mack does. Those bastards always seem to be several steps ahead of us." He paused for a moment while in deep thought. "Who do you think is the inside leak?"

*   *   *   *

At the time Tracy was on the car cellular phone, four vehicles pulled up in front of the Dutchess County Hospital. In the back of the Hospital three other vehicles positioned themselves in various locations. Three vehicles on each side of the building were scattered about. Present on the scene in the front of the hospital was Mixon. He was in a black Jeep with tinted windows. In total there were 28 men, each one equipped with weapons that all had silencers, and each one had a picture of Dinasia Davis/Whitman.

Flipper, Spade and two other men entered the hospital. All four of them were dressed in medical assistants clothing, and had tote bags flung over their shoulders. Flipper and one of the men entered through the front while Spade and the other soldier entered through the back door.

254

Mixon sat staring at the Hospital main entrance and fought with the doubtful feelings he had about this run. The Feds had possession of the tape and that meant his whole house was only days away from crumbling. He hoped Bruce Snyder was right when he claimed they still had a chance of preventing the tape from being used as evidence by killing Dinasia. According to Bruce, without Dinasia, a proper foundation could not be laid, and therefore, if she was unavailable, there was a strong possibility the tape would have to be suppressed. It sounded like a long, last shot worth taking, Mixon had to admit, and without hesitation, he seized the moment.

As he watched an old couple exiting the door (realizing Flipper and the soldier entered several minutes ago), he hoped special agent, Jamie Lewis, was right about Dinasia coming to this Hospital. When he realized Jamie never once gave them a faulty piece of information up to date, he allowed himself to relax.

*   *   *   *

As Mixon watched, so did the man in the green car that had been following Mixon and his fleet of cars ever since they left Long Island. Dressed like a bum with excessively thick and dirty facial hairs covering almost all of his face, the man sat patiently, watching Mixon through high-powered binoculars, waiting for the perfect moment.

CHAPTER # 33

The mental images were fuzzy, distorted looking and appeared at a distance. But the small figure inside the dream world was recognizable and he noticed it was a moment in time permanently engraved in his mind forever.

If someone held the position that those within a deep coma (one so deep that on the Glasgow coma scale every response [motor, verbal and eye] was well below the lowest possible point) had no neural appreciation or sensory perception, was 100% wrong. In fact, they were as wrong as the twisted theory that Columbus discovered a land occupied by millions of people. Tislam could not only hear and feel, but he could dream as well.

At the moment, Dinasia's small image danced in his mind. She was a child once again. The vision was through his eyes and he saw they both were at the Foster care institute. This was the day at the festival when they solidified their "NO OTHER LOVE" pact, which was a moment in time that would live endlessly inside Tislam's mind. Boy did he welcome this image and yearned for it since the mental picture made him forget about that frightening feeling of being paralyzed, buried alive and completely unable to force himself to awake.

He sometimes heard the voices all around him. The low pitched beeps of a machine, the constant hum of the fluorescent lights over head, scurrying feet that came from somewhere beyond. Even that damn pestering fly that buzzed around his head and would land on his face and hang out until it got bored or someone entered the room. Other noises rose and faded in the background, commingling into a muted symphony of squeaks, clicks and flutters that orchestrated everyday life of people at work.

He felt the people probing him with needles, touching him and putting things in places he would've never permitted if he weren't in this condition. The tubes inserted in his nose annoyed him, but the ones crammed up his ass and in his penis freaked him out the most. It didn't hurt, at least not all the time. Indeed, he normally experienced no severe pain, and it scared him because it felt almost like tranquility, and made him wonder if he was actually dead. They had him on drugs, he realized because his mind spun, his thoughts were cloudy and the stab wounds and head injury throbbed with a slight pain only at certain times of the day. They probably kept him loaded on the powerful shit like Demerol or Novocain.

Subconsciously, he knew he was in a hospital and was in terrible shape.

It had to be really bad or else he would be able to move when he wanted, and the feeling of being in a sealed coffin wouldn't exist. Many times, he tried to scream, knowing such a release would re-orientate him to the world of the living, but nothing ever happened. He could feel himself gradually going insane.

Other memories twirled about and were so chaotic, they made absolutely no sense and were outright absurd in most instances.

Yes, there were some recollections that did make sense. Pus and the Crimson Cowboys were inside his head constantly. And that day in the Jay School basement replayed itself over and over in his mind. The moment he received those stab wounds and the head injury, were the events he remembered most. They came and went with flashing intensity.

But, he wanted to awake from this deep sleep, and no matter what he did, he couldn't. The thought of being stuck inside this world forever made him wish for death. That horrifying and agonizing feeling of being in a coffin and buried alive without the ability to move a muscle was rapidly driving him crazy. Each and every moment he was able to appreciate his surroundings it was like an eternity of unspeakable mental suffering.

Thank goodness it wasn't all the time.

*   *   *   *

Dinasia got out of the old red Volkswagen and moved extraordinarily slow towards the hospital entrance. With a cane in her hand, old brogue-iron shoes on her feet, dressed in the most typical grandma attire, with a head full of sprinkling gray hair, and a fake rubber nose that made her look like a relative of Carl Malden along with the white latex skin to match, Dinasia saw the black Jeep, and her inner instinct told her who it was.

As she struggled up the long ramp, hunched over a little to give her disguise a realistic effect, her crippling fear and nervousness returned with excessive vigor. Her conscience started talking to her again, and what it was saying was something she didn't want to hear. That voice had been pissing in her ear ever since she decided to take matters into her own hands.

This is sheer madness! That voice said when Dinasia purchased bullets for the 357 Magnum and the 25 automatic along with several other items at a hardware store on Liberty Avenue.

You're gonna wind up dead or spending the rest of your life in a damn prison cell! This inner voice continued when she went to the theater costume shop over on Jamaica Avenue.

Think of another way to deal with this for crying out loud because what you're about to do is the ultimate extreme, girl! This is just too much, child! That same voice pleaded when she entered the car lot on Guy Brewer Boulevard and drove out with the Volkswagen on credit, using the van as a down payment.

They sure didn't lie when they said love will make people do some real crazy shit! The voice said when she called the Hospital and found out Tislam's room number, and the contact information of armed law enforcement personnel standing guard. During another phone call to the Hospital, she also found out the name of a patient on the same floor as Tislam.

Woman, you're signing your death certificate and don't even know if Tislam would do the same for you if the shoe was on the other foot! Her terrified, inner voice said repeatedly during the ride upstate.

Each and every time that voice opened its mouth, Dinasia's willpower grew stronger because once her mind was made up there was no turning back. The formula to this equation was so insanely simple: There were no other options available besides doing whatever it took to stop them from killing the man she vowed to love until death do her and him apart because if Tislam died, then so would she, but not without a fight.

Dinasia entered the entrance and went to the Hospital receptionist window.

"Hello," Dinasia altered her voice to sound hoarse, feeble and almost southern like. "My name is Susan Scott. I'm here to see my sick nephew. His name is Keith Scott."

The woman smiled and typed on her computer keyboard. Seconds later, she said, "He's on the third floor; room 321." She handed Dinasia a piece of paper. "This is your pass. The elevators are right over there." She pointed.

Dinasia took the pass and crept slowly towards the elevators. She pressed the button, and seconds later, the elevator doors slid open. She flinched upon seeing FBI agent Tracy Dickinson getting off the elevator. They briefly made eye contact as Dinasia's heart began to pound.

Tracy smiled politely and continued on her way.

From the way Tracy responded, it was unquestionable, she didn't recognize her, Dinasia realized with relief as she got on the elevator along with a middle-aged woman and a man dressed in doctor's whites, who looked very familiar. She pressed the third floor button.

Moments later, Dinasia stepped off the elevator. Her eyes instantly began taking in everything they gazed upon as the elevator doors closed behind her. People dressed in white doctor's frocks moved about; some with clipboards in their hands, others carrying medical instruments. The antiseptic smell was thick in the air. The arrow on the sign in front of her said the room she wanted was to her left. She stood staring at the sign with a dumbfounded look on her face for almost a whole minute and then shook loose of the daze.

She moved down the corridor, looking at the numbers on the doors. When she saw room #371, her heart thundered in her chest because Tislam's room would be just around the corner up ahead.

Turn back! It's not too late! That innate voice cried and screamed at her; *try another way! One less crazier than this approach, for god sakes! Please!* But Dinasia struggled forward, her legs trembling and her head spinning with a fear that made her feel light-headed, almost as if she just chugged a pint of liquor.

You don't want to do this and you know it! The voice shouted unrelentingly. With trembling hands she opened the tote bag; she was shaking so hard she had to stop walking as she inconspicuously pulled the 357 Magnum out and put it in one of her coat pockets. Looking around to see if any eyes were on her, she did the same with the 25, putting it in the other pocket. With a slight struggle she started walking again.

Dinasia turned the corner and her heart fluttered when she saw a police officer sitting in a chair positioned in front of room #352. *Where's the other one?* She wondered, maybe inside the room with Tislam or somewhere close by. The Nurse's Station, she saw, was a few feet from the room.

It's still not too late! The voice persisted, but Dinasia ignored it and the urge to procrastinate, telling herself for the thousandth time that after all the hell she'd been through, there was simply no way she could turn back now. It just couldn't be done.

She crept towards the police officer in a hypnotized fashion, her eyes locked on the target with unwavering precision, her heart beating lively. When she was about two yards away and still slowly approaching, she let go of the cane and pulled both guns as fast as a seasoned gunslinger. "Don't move!"

She saw the cop almost jump out of his skin while his eyes grew as wide as bus tires. "Stand up! Slowly." Dinasia shouted as the whole floor seemed to ignite into a state of pandemonium. "Take your gun out of the holster and drop it on the floor! . . . Now!" She had no problem shouting over the panic-stricken noise.

Several screams almost unraveled Dinasia. The crashing sounds from frantic fleeing nurses and other medical personnel, as they knocked over trays and other things, had Dinasia's eyes darting around every which a way to make certain it wasn't the other cop.

"Miss, please, calm down," The cop said with both hands in the air. He saw through the corner of his eye, his partner was peeking out of a room just beyond the Nurse's Station. "Whatever it is you're seeking, going about it this way is totally wrong!"

"I thought I told you to drop that fuckin' gun!" Dinasia shoved both guns at the cop and saw him recoil as if he was touched with a red-hot branding iron.

The second the cop reached for his gun, and Dinasia was about to move towards him, an ear shattering shout ignited.

"Dinasia! Mrs. Davis! Wait!" Tracy ran towards Dinasia with Carl along side of her.

"Stop right there!" Dinasia shouted, pointing the 25 at Tracy and Carl while keeping the 357 on the cop.

Tracy and Carl came to a sliding stop. Tracy spoke frantically. "You don't have to do this, Dinasia. Tislam is gonna be all right. We got evidence that proves it wasn't him. The Judge retracted his order. Tislam is saved. He's going--"

"You're lying!" Dinasia shouted, her emotions now mixed and confused. "I know the little games you fuckin' people play. Tell me what I wanna hear, disarm me and the show's over. Well, sorry, it ain't gonna work today."

"Please, listen to us," Carl said softly. "About an hour ago, a correction officer came forth who worked for Mixon and he identified the actual killers. I can call the Judge for you right now and let you talk to him yourself. Mr. Parker is gonna be all right. We would never do something as malicious and deceitful as lie to you regarding something as delicate as this. Mr. Parker. . .”

As Carl went on, Dinasia sensed she was caught between a rock and a hard place because they sounded sincere. But, she had read books on how police negotiated with people, and lying was standard operating procedure. Her mind was so preoccupied she forgot to continue looking around the area for the other cop, who was missing in action.

As Dinasia stood contemplating whether to trust the agents, the other cop was waiting for the opportunity to get off a few shots. Moments ago, he tiptoed out of the room and into the Nurse's Station the moment the agents started talking to the old woman with the gun. He peeked around the corner, noticing he was only several feet from the woman now. He took aim.

*   *   *   *

Mixon was becoming restless. Then, suddenly, his communication device came to life. He picked it up. "What's up?"

'Hey, Mixon," The voice of Flipper said excitedly. "The shit just jumped off on the third floor. It's Dinasia. You were right. She's dressed in a disguise, looking like an old white lady."

Mixon's whole body percolated to life. "Where are you!?"

'I'm in a stairwell," Flipper said, "Looking right at the situation."

'Did you disable the phones and electrical lines?"

'That's already taken care of. Ronnie was in the basement on standby. The second I heard the commotion, I told him to cut all phone cables. Sing Sing turned on the radio and microwave frequency scrambler."

'I'm sending in the others," Mixon said, and pushed the disconnect button and then another button. "This is it, big homies, Dinasia's on the third floor. The phones are dead and so is anything else that'll connect them to the outside. But that don't mean you can drag your feet. I want y'all in and out as quickly as possible." He disconnected and watched his soldiers jogging towards the entrance with guns in hand.

*   *   *   *

Doctor Bill Evans heard the screams and it rattled his nerves deep down to the bone. He was in his office preparing his daily surgery reports. He rushed out of the office and was shocked when he saw the level of mass hysteria.

262

"What the hell is going on!?" Bill asked a nurse named Nancy, who completely ignored him as she fled down the hallway. He ran to the corner where everyone seemed to be fleeing from, and when he turned it, he saw the root of all the confusion. There was a woman with a gun pointed at one of the cops in front of Mr. Parker's room. Bill pulled back around the corner. He raced back to his office and got on the phone.

Bill punched in 911. "What is this?" He muttered nervously when he realized the phone was dead. He frantically pressed all the buttons hoping it would provoke a response. Nothing happened.

He sat the receiver back in its cradle with trembling hands, rushed out of the office, and just as he neared the corner to take another peek at what was going on . . .

BOW! BOW! BOW! BOW! BOW!

Massive gunfire exploded, causing Bill to flinch so hard, his knees gave out and he went to the floor. Lying on his belly, he heard rapid movement behind him. He turned and saw two men wearing ski masks running towards him with huge weapons in their hands.

Bill frantically crawled towards the nearest room, stood and burst inside. It was Richard Gibbs office.

"What the hell is going on, Bill?" Richard said as he was pulling up his pants.

The first thing Bill saw was Nurse Kelder's huge breasts, and then the smell of sex. "I--I don't know. There's men with guns and--and the phones are--" He frantically grabbed Richard's arm. "Don't go out there! What are you, outta your mind?! They're shooting guns!"

Richard paced nervously.

Bill spoke calmly as he kept spying Nurse Kelder as she was getting dressed. "Let's just stay put, stay quiet and hide somewhere until this is over."

*   *   *   *

"No!" Tracy shouted when she saw the other cop take aim while at the same time a rapidly approaching masked man came up behind the cop shooting a weapon apparently equipped with a silencer. The flames burst from the barrel of the weapon like a furnace spitting stripes of fire.

SZK! SZK! SZK!--BOW! BOW! BOW!

Tracy dove to the side while screaming. "Dinasia! Watch out!" She saw the cop's body jerk violently as he frantically spun around, squeezing off three terribly aimed shots at the masked man while collapsing to the floor.

Carl dove the other way and entered the nearby room with his gun at the ready.

Dinasia felt a bullet whiz pass her face just as she heard Tracy scream "No!" Reflectively, she dove to the floor and hastily crawled into Tislam's room. The cop, who she had the gun pointed at jumped backwards inside the room the second he saw the masked man and heard Tracy's scream. She saw the cop had his gun in his hand. As she stood up, they both stared at each other for a moment. Both of their weapons were now pointed downwards.

BOW! BOW! BOW! BOW!

The gunfire from Tracy and Carl's un-silenced revolvers startled Dinasia. She looked pass the cop. When she saw Tislam's motionless body in the bed surrounded by all sorts of machines, the sight hurled her into a trance. She pulled the wig off, tossing it to the floor. Then she ripped off the latex mask that was professionally pasted to her skin and flung it. Damn that stuff made her hot, she sighed, relieved as she heard the cop display his surprise at the disguise. She slowly approached the bed in a mesmerized manner.

When Dinasia arrived at his bedside, she saw he looked so peaceful. It frightened her. If it weren't for the constant beeping sound from the heart monitor machine, she would've thought he was dead. "Tislam," she whispered, caressing his cold hand, as her mind was flooded with memories, both good and bad. She couldn't hold back the tears of joy.

Dinasia was so caught up observing the man she'd wronged and loved so dearly, and had went almost to hell and back for, she didn't hear the cop screaming "Get down! Watch out!"

*   *   *   *

Moments ago, while Tracy and Carl were shooting at the three men in front of them, and gunfire sounded like it was coming from other areas throughout the building, two men slowly eased up behind them. By the time Tracy saw the two men it was too late.

SZK! SZK!--BOW! BOW!--SZK! SZK!

One of the silenced bullets struck Tracy in the lower section of her back as she squeezed off two shots. One of her bullets hit the man in the neck, dropping him instantly. Tracy stumbled inside the room clutching her exit wound on her stomach.

"Tracy!" Carl yelled to her from the other room when he saw her enter the room. "Are you alright?"

"I'm hit!" She said through clinched teeth as she laid on the floor to reserve her energy.

BOW! BOW! BOW!

Carl rushed out of the room shooting while racing towards the room where Tracy was. He went to Tracy, quickly dragging her away from the doorway and kneeled down beside her. Just as he was about to assist his partner, he heard rapid footsteps outside the room. He turned with his gun aimed.

Whoever it was ran past the room.

BOW! BOW! BOW! BOW!

The rapid gunfire went off down the hall in the direction where Tislam's room was located.

Tracy said while cringing in pain, "The room. They're going for Dinasia. Go stop them. I'm okay. Go ahead."

Carl crept to the door, looked both ways and saw the two men on each side of the room door where Mr. Parker was. He drew a deep breath and stepped out with both hands controlling the aim of his weapon. When his targets were in his sight, he locked his finger on the trigger.

BOW! BOW! BOW! BOW!

The headshots were all a perfect bull's eye.

For a split second, Carl didn't know whether he should run down the hall to see what happened inside Mr. Parker's room or rush back inside the room and tend to Tracy. Obviously, his partner deserved his undying loyalty.

*   *   *

Twenty minutes earlier, as Mixon instructed his men to enter the hospital, the man who was sitting in the green car, dressed in filthy clothing, watched the events unfold and had his eye on the black Jeep. After he saw the men enter the Hospital, he got out of the car and headed for the Jeep. Now, the time had finally come, he thought smilingly.

He tapped on the window. "Hey, Mister. Can you spare a few coins? I'm so hungry, Mister. I ain't eat nothin' in three days."

Mixon rolled down the window while sighing in a frustrated fashion because the bum startled him. He reached in his pocket and pulled out a fifty-dollar bill. "Here! Take it and get--"

BOW!

Mixon's brains were splattered everywhere. The gruesome impact of the 44 Magnum bullet at point blank range was so devastating it literally blew off the top portion of Mixon's head from the mouth up. The entire inside of the Jeep looked like it was transformed from black to red in an instant.

While walking towards the hospital entrance, the bum stuffed the gun in his waist, reached his hand in back of his waist and pulled out an AK 47. He dug in his pocket, retrieved one of the seven banana clips, and slid it into the chamber. Moments later, he entered the hospital.

BOW! BOW! BOW! BOW! BOW

He gunned down the three armed men in ski masks that had their weapons pointed at the scared people who sat on the floor, huddling each other, terrified. The bum scanned the area and found what he was looking for. He headed for the Receptionist window. "Where's the person who handles this window?" He could hear massive gunfire coming from somewhere upstairs.

No one answered.

"I'm not gonna hurt you," The bum said politely. "I'm here to help. Those men are here to kill someone I wanna save. Please, I really need your help."

Suddenly, a white woman scurried from out of the crowd and entered a door several feet away and popped up in the window, trying to force a smile.

The bum smiled back. "I need to know where is a patient named Tislam Parker?"

The woman tried the computer first and saw it was dead. Then she pulled the computer readout sheet of all the Hospital residents from under her desk and scanned it. Within seconds, she found the name. "He's in room #352."

"Thank you," The bum turned, and just before he headed for the staircase, he said to the crowd. "I would seriously advise everyone to stay put. There's men out there with guns waiting for the first person to show his face." He then walked extremely fast to the staircase, hoping they went for the ruse because the last thing he needed was someone running to get help before he finished taking care of his business.

He entered the stairwell and ran up the stairs two steps at a time.

*   *   *

Dinasia snapped out of the trance when the policeman started shooting at the door. A silenced bullet breezed past her, and she panicked, realized one of the bullets could strike Tislam. She frantically rolled the bed toward the back of the room as the explosions sounded off. She noticed she had to push the bed a short distance and then the machines and IV rack. Little by little, she managed to get the bed and the machines and IV rack as far away as possible from the line of fire.

267

When she looked up at the threshold, she saw two men sprawled out on the floor.

*   *   *

Just before the bum reached the third floor, he heard men somewhere up ahead. He slowed his pace, peeked around the corner and saw two men with their backs to him about to enter the third floor. He stepped around the corner and aimed the AK 47.

BOW! BOW! BOW! BOW!

The bullets made the two men dance violently. Both men tumbled down the stairs and landed at the vagabond's feet.

The hobo stepped over them and continued up the stairs. He cracked the door and spied the area. He let the door close and changed the clip even though the one in the weapon had about five shots left. He opened the door and walked swiftly.

He put the AK 47 behind his back when he heard someone up ahead around the corner. When he saw three masked men turn the corner he acted scared.

"Hey motherfucker," one of the masked men said. "Didn't we tell you to sit the fuck down and don't move? Ohhh, I see you got a death wish, huh?" He aimed the weapon.

As the man spoke the hobo's eyes widened with delight because that was the voice of a person he wanted to give a very, very special treat to. *It's Flipper*, he thought with a huge smile. Through the corner of his eye, he saw a room was open and he lunged inside it just as the silenced bullets rained.

The men raced towards the room he dove inside, apparently thinking the hobo was unarmed.

The bum pointed the AK 47 and sprayed the hallway with bullets as he waved the fully automatic rifle. The hobo stuck his head out and saw all three were laid out on the floor. He quickly approached and inspected his magnificent work. Two of the men were squirming. He reached down and pulled the masks off each of the men.

When he saw Flipper's terror-stricken eyes, he smiled. "Hellooo. Well if it ain't ole Flipper dipper. Ahh, don't get scared now." He shook his head teasingly. "Boy, ain't it a small world." Just as Flipper was about to open his mouth the vagabond shot him in the forehead. Flipper's head disappeared. The other two squirming men received the same treatment.

He continued on his way toward room #352. He turned the corner. After taking about ten steps, he heard frantic movement behind him and spun around with his finger on the trigger assuming it was one of Mixon's hit men. When he saw his bullets mowed down a doctor, he felt terrible. "Ahh, shit!" He muttered angrily. "Why the fuck are you people moving around at a fuckin' time like this?" He said out loud, more to himself than to the fallen Doctor.

Doctor Richard Gibbs never saw it coming and regretted he didn't listen to Dr. Evans, who told him to stay in his office under the desk. The bullets ripped and tore through his chest as easy and swiftly as a red-hot razor cutting through a stick of butter. He saw stars exploded before his eyes from the horrendous impacts from the bullets. Two minutes later, he died.

As the bum neared room #352, his heart started beating a little faster because he knew Dinasia was in there. He entered, and as he suspected, she was in the room.

BOW! BOW! BOW!

One of the several bullets fired by the policeman and Dinasia grazed the hobo, forcing him to dive for the floor and scurry back out the room. Impulsively, he was about to return fire with the AK-47. He hesitated out of fear of one of his bullets hitting Tislam. He peeked inside the room.

BOW!

The cop shot at him again, forcing the vagabond to strap the AK-47 around his neck onto his shoulder, and pull the 44 Magnum from his waist so as to hit the target and only the target. He dove inside the room, did a combat roll while taking aim and opened fire.

BOW!   BOW!--EEAAHHHH!!--BOW!--BOW!   BOW--BOW!
BOW!

The cop's chest exploded as he let off two wild shots, crumpling to the floor. Dinasia fired her last two shots, missing the hobo only by inches.

The bum stood motionless, staring at Dinasia pointing her weapon.

In that moment, Dinasia thought it was Shateek and nervously hoped she hadn't shot him when she impulsively fired her weapon without looking to see who was trying to enter the room.

"Dinasia," The hobo said softly. "Why?" He shook his head pitifully. "Why do you cause so much pain? You were gonna cause me pain. Look at you? You were gonna shoot me!?"

After hearing the man speak, Dinasia realized it wasn't Shateek. An eye raising puzzlement grabbed hold of her because the man knew her name.

The bum walked past Dinasia with his gun pointed downward, heading for Tislam's bed.

"Leave him!" Dinasia tried to step in the hobo's path.

BLAM!

The vagabond slapped her across the floor. He went to the bed and stared down at Tislam. He touched his face. "He's suffering," He whispered softly. "This is crazy." He sighed painfully. "We have to stop this . . . Did you know being in a coma's like being buried alive. The level of mental pain and suffering is literally out of this world?"

Dinasia got up from off the floor as the hobo spoke.

The vagabond paused and then continued: "That's what the research says. Look at him, he's in great pain." The bum paused, in deep thought. He sucked his teeth as if he was disgusted. "If it was me laying there suffering like this, Tislam wouldn't turn a blind eye . . . I have to stop this." He pointed the gun at Tislam's head.

"Stop!!" Dinasia screamed as she rushed towards the hobo. "Leave him the fuck alone. You motherf--"

BOW! BOW!

270

The hobo spun around and squeezed off two shots to Dinasia's chest.

The two bullets catapulted Dinasia backwards, lifting her off the floor. Everything seemed to be going in slow motion as she glided in the air. It felt like it took an hour for her to complete the crash landing. The back of her head hit the floor, making a thunderous bang.

As Dinasia rapidly faded into a deep, permanent like unconsciousness, the sound of massive gunfire was the last thing she heard.

CHAPTER # 34

The seasons passed.

There is one thing in life that is an absolute certainty . . . And that is change. No matter how rich, poor, pretty, ugly, tall, short, skinny, fat, black, white, red, brown or yellow, going from one stage to another in a transformative fashion is an inevitable process, absolutely no exceptions to the rule.

Whether from bad to good or good to bad, or life to death or death to life, all conversions, alterations, modifications, variations and even all out transmutations, boils down to one thing and one thing only . . . And that is Change.

Although there are some changes so slight even the most trained eye could hardly detect while the grand scale ones are visible to all. However, they all have that magical thing in common -- Movement.

In the past year and three months since that day before Tislam's plug was to be pulled, there were a whole lot of changes going on.

Little Johnny Steele made the ultimate leap from life to death. On a dreary summer night in the Brownsville section of Brooklyn, he and two of his comrades attempted to rob a gambling spot, and all three were brutally gunned down by the overseers of the establishment.

Barbara Shepard died of a heroine over-dose four months ago, which caused her daughter, Valerie, to finally seek drug counseling. Valerie Shepard is now an in-house patient at the Dayton drug rehab.

Mrs. Rachel Morris remains a resident of the Pink House Projects. With the exception of her arthritis, she's doing reasonably well.

Robert Sanchez remains on the missing persons list. The last time Robert was seen alive was two days after the shoot-out at Regina's Restaurant when he was released from custody on bail. Robert is presumed dead by the authorities. His family plans to conduct funeral services if nothing happens within the next month.

Cheops and Chico Rico both were arrested, tried and convicted for conspiring to kill Sgt. William Brickle, C.O. David Lane and numerous other unsolved homicides. Both were transferred to federal custody and are now serving their natural life sentences in the Federal Prison System.

C.O. Glen Carol and his family were moved to Washington State after Glen testified in Federal Court against Cheops, Chico Rico, Eddie Mack, Jamie Lewis, and Shabazz Davis. As a participant in the Federal Witness Protection Program, his identity has been changed to Samuel Hartel, and he is employed as a state trooper in a small backwoods town in Okanogan County.

Eddie Mack retired from the Underworld after he was found not guilty of all charges in the Federal Eastern District Court in Brooklyn. After the IRS unsuccessfully attempted to charge him with tax evasion, Eddie invested his money into a multi-chain food conglomerate company and is currently doing quite well.

Shabazz Davis remains a fugitive of justice. After the Federal trial, Shabazz was found guilty of one count of conspiracy to kill Paul "Prince" Shepard and four counts of racketeering. In absentee, Shabazz was sentenced to 175 years imprisonment.

Bruce Snyder was found dead in his car, parked in the back of an abandoned bowling alley in Hoboken New Jersey. The cause of death was carbon monoxide poisoning. The autopsy also unveiled traces of a tranquilizer solution in his blood system.

Special agent Jamie Lewis was found guilty of obstruction of Justice, conspiracy to commit murder in furtherance of a criminal enterprise and racketeering. In complete disgrace to the bureau, Jamie was sentenced to 25 years imprisonment and a 250 thousand dollar fine was imposed.

Trigger moved to New Jersey after spending two months in Long Island Hospital for the gunshot wound to his hip. With a permanent limp, Trigger, his wife and two children currently reside in Patterson County.

Spade, AKA Ronnie Gray, escaped the fiasco at the Dutchess County Hospital unharmed. He is now the head honcho of a drug gang called

"Pure Pleasure", and has drug houses all over Brooklyn, Queens and the Bronx.

Keisha Anderson divorced her husband, Herbert, and married Shateek Davis, who is serving a 10-year sentence for reckless endangerment, attempted murder on a police officer, possession of military weaponry and resisting arrest. After Shateek crashed the 18-wheeler, he was arrested shortly thereafter when the police back up arrived on the scene consisting of a SWAT team and over fifteen police vehicles. Shateek currently resides at Green Haven Correctional Facility and ironically occupies a cell once utilized by Tislam Parker.

Doctor Bill Evans continues to work at the Dutchess County Hospital and was recently promoted to the Chief Surgeon. The proud father of a newborn baby boy, Bill is planning to put his extra money from the raise to use by purchasing a bigger and better home.

Special Agents Tracy Dickinson and Carl Winters both received awards for outstanding achievement for their work in the Darrel Mixon, Eddie Mack, Jamie Lewis and Shabazz Davis investigations. To this day, they remain partners and are currently assisting the DEA with their investigation and accumulation of evidence against the drug gang "Pure Pleasure."

Reggie Watson was laid to rest at the Evergreen Cemetery in Bushwick Brooklyn three days after Carl Winters shot him five times as he stood over Dinasia Davis/Whitman about to continue shooting her. After an investigation, which consisted of numerous interviews with Reggie's family and friends, it was discovered that Reggie and Tislam did time together in Green Haven. They also found out that Tislam saved his life and befriended him when no one else would.

Upon his release, Reggie kept heavy tabs on Tislam. Reggie hired an investigator, who found out Tislam's current situation. He also found a person who had strong ties with just about everyone involved in the Underworld, and to his surprise, Reggie not only discovered Mixon was trying to conceal the fact he was involved in Tislam's wrongful conviction while trying to kill Dinasia, but Reggie also discovered Mixon was the one who had set him up for the rape conviction. The combination of all the mounds of tragic information pushed Reggie completely over the edge.

Although Reggie never told anyone about the three times he was brutally raped while on Rikers Island, the way these permanent scars inadvertently showed themselves, most people, if not all, knew after his stay in prison, he would never be the same and had changed for the worst.

* * * *

Gloria Wallace was perplexed as she inserted the key in the bottom lock of the door of her red brick one story home.

A sudden noise came from behind her.

Gloria frantically spun around, leaving the key stuck inside the lock. Her eyes darted about, scanning the bushes while the reddish orange sunset on the horizon tried to steal her attention. When she heard the meow and then saw the little white cat that had three black feet that resembled black socks, Gloria sighed and giggled at the way she over-reacted. "Hey Sox, what are you creeping up on me like that for?" She kneeled and playfully rubbed the cat's head. "Did you eat today?"

Sox meowed again and Gloria took that as no.

She stood and her bewilderment returned because normally Alice, the home attendant, would have the door wide open by now. There was rarely a time Alice failed to greet her with an opened door the minute Gloria stepped foot out of the car.

Gloria unfastened the two locks and just as she pushed open the door, a noise came from inside the house. It sounded like footsteps, and Gloria thought it was Alice on her way to the door. "Alice, is that you? You sure must be busy." She entered the house.

No response.

When Gloria noticed Sox slowly entering while hissing with his back raised into a hump, she hastily reached inside her purse and pulled out her lucky 25 automatic. With the help of Agent Dickinson, she finally obtained a carrier's license for a concealed weapon and was now legally armed at all times.

Something was wrong.

"Alice," Gloria's heart pounded crazily in her chest and her whole body trembled as she got into a shooting stance. "Alice." She closed the door and activated the locks, instantly wondering was it wise to restrict her access to a hasty escape route?

The sudden realization hit her like a thunderbolt. *Oh no! They found us!* She ran towards the bedroom where Anthony was. Gloria crashed through the door with the gun at the ready. Her tension lightened tremendously when she saw Anthony lying in bed with all the health apparatuses in their usual locations. Breathing hard from the terror, she stepped back out, closing the door behind her.

Where the hell is Alice? Gloria repeatedly asked inwardly as she thoroughly checked all the rooms for an intruder; searching under beds, inside all closets, behind curtains and in anyplace where a person could hide.

There was no one besides her, Anthony and Sox inside the house. She also noticed nothing out of the norm.

With her hands on her hips, looking around the living room as if she was contemplating her next move, Gloria now had strong doubts about what she thought she heard. *What was that noise? Was it really footsteps? Or was she hearing things again?*

After pondering the matter for a few seconds more, she concluded it had to be her imagination since everything was intact. She giggled again, realizing ever since the Witness Protection Agency re-located her and Tislam to this hot, humid town in New Mexico with new identities, she'd been so jumpy and paranoid, it was a miracle she hadn't had a nervous break-down by now. She placed the 25 back in her purse.

As the magnitude of Alice's gross negligence (leaving Tislam unattended) sunk deeper into her mind, Dinasia became infuriated.

"Alice, you can consider yourself fired!" Dinasia said out loud as she stomped over to the phone and angrily snatched up the receiver, about to report Alice to the Nursing Agency. She punched in half the number and realized the place was closed for the day. Slamming the receiver back in its cradle, she went to the sofa, flopped down on it, and expelled a loud breath of air from her lungs.

She felt totally exhausted. Her new occupation was extremely taxing on her energy reserves and required a lot of serious mental aerobics. She was a consultant for a social planning agency. It wasn't the best paying job in the world, but it was employment she enjoyed, and it dealt with a science she had plenty experience with.

Then, it dawned on her. Alice wasn't the type to just up and leave. The woman was too professional to do something as stupid as that. After giving the issue too much thought, Dinasia pushed it to the back of her mind since there were no logical answers available at the moment.

I don't know if I can take this any longer, Dinasia said to herself, leaning back comfortably on the sofa. She massaged the temple areas of her head, hoping to ward off the migraine that was gradually coming to life. As she thought about once and for all throwing in the towel, the bulletproof vest hanging on the wall in a picture frame caught her eye. Her hand involuntarily went to her chest and massaged her scars from the two broken ribs. That day at the Dutchess County Hospital when Reggie shot her danced in her mind every time she laid eyes on the souvenir. As usual, the mental picture brought her back to reality and sparked a burst of energy, boosting her willpower.

Tislam's current condition took center stage in her mind. This evening he was scheduled to receive his acupuncture treatment. There was probably no treatment on the planet Dinasia hadn't tried on Tislam up to this point. The books Dinasia purchased and read were so numerous she had compiled a humongous library on the subject of comas. Unknowingly Dinasia had become an expert on the subject.

There were many times she sensed Tislam was fully aware of her presence. From the way he responded, it was obvious some of those natural treatments were working. But she couldn't understand why he wouldn't awake. The therapies consisted of herbal, amino acids, acupuncture, universal inner cleansing, homeopathy, a strict vegetarian diet, absolutely no sugar or dairy products and constant exposure to concentrated brain regenerative substances. Tislam's skin had a wonderful glow to it, his hair and fingernails grew lively, and amazingly she noticed he was now getting an erect penis when she playfully whispered sexual things in his ear.

Dinasia suddenly felt sexually energetic as she reminisced about the numerous times she had sexual intercourse with Tislam. She would whisper sexual things in Tislam's ear and would get him excited. She would say: "Come on out of that place so you can get a taste of some of this juicy stuff." And low and behold, Tislam's penis would stand at attention, pulsating extravagantly. Several times she treated herself to some fun when her hormones got too worked up and her juices over flowed. She would get on top and ride him sensuously, and when she would hit her climax, she noticed so would Tislam. It always baffled her when Tislam would ejaculate without his body moving spasmodically. The only noticeable response was his breathing increased substantially.

Her thoughts were taken back to the time she utilized the advise she had gotten from a book, which said music or a special melody that had significance in a coma sufferer's life could have a profound effect on the patient's transitional journey back to full consciousness. The song "I Love Your Smile" was the first thing came to mind. After making several dozen phone calls, Dinasia drove over 100 miles to a record store three counties away and purchased the CD. Dinasia played the song all day long and was heart-broken when nothing happened. She cried so hard and so long, she felt dehydrated because she truly believed this was the treatment that would finally work. For the six months that followed, she continued playing the song at least twice a day.

Dinasia released a huge yawn, cleared her mind and headed for the kitchen. "Sox! Come on Sox, it's time to eat." She smiled happily when Sox raced towards her from the back room.

After feeding the cat she snatched up her purse and headed for the bathroom to take a shower. She still felt a little edgy about that noise and wanted to keep her gun close by just in case. Her plans for tonight were to go to bed early. But first she would give Tislam his acupuncture therapy and treat herself and Tislam to a little sexual fun afterwards.

*   *   *   *

The sound of the shower filled the house.

It was time. He'd made her wait long enough. And, Tislam had satisfied himself. Dinasia was sincere in her claim that she would be with him forever this time, through the good and bad times. If she could withstand this ordeal, it was evident to Tislam there would be no other difficult or painful experience that would out-do this one.

As he lay staring at the ceiling, Tislam suddenly realized he felt a slight apprehension. He was really enjoying all this special treatment because it gave him great pleasure being pampered around the clock. He didn't want to give it up, at least not anytime soon. But, after thinking about the way he almost gave Alice a coronary when he sat up and started talking to her, he knew there was certainly no turning back now. It took some convincing to get Alice to leave before Dinasia got home, but after ten minutes of insisting it would be a romantic surprise, she eventually gave in.

Six months ago, Tislam faded completely out of the comatose deep sleep. He opened his eyes and sat up upon hearing the song "I Love Your Smile." The flood of memories brought on by hearing that song was like being exposed to a super-potent smelling salt. When Tislam heard Dinasia rushing towards the room to see if there was a response, he laid back down and pretended to be unconscious. He decided in that moment to hold out and see how long Dinasia would hang in there. He had to be certain before he opened up to her again, because if he lost her again, the pain would definitely kill him this time.

As he slid out of the bed, he felt truly alive. All that stuff Dinasia had been giving him did wonders to his body. With the exception of a little stiffness in various places, he felt marvelous. In the past six months, he'd been sneaking around the house at night when Alice was gone and Dinasia was asleep.

As his feet touched the floor, he realized if he hadn't gotten that small amount of exercise, at the moment, he would be pretty messed up. He was able to make this conclusion because the first time he attempted to walk, he collapsed to his knees, and not only did he almost hurt himself, but almost destroyed his charade.

Tislam released a bone popping stretch. He touched his toes, did a few upper body twists, rolled his head around on his shoulders a few times, and headed for the living room. He'd been planning this little surprise for the past month or so, and he went straight to the CD player. Shuffling through the stack of CD's, it took him a few seconds to find the song. However, it took him a few minutes to figure out how to operate the CD machine.

He heard a hissing sound and turned. It was Sox. He couldn't understand why that damn cat hated him so much. Even after he and Sox hung out together on countless late nights, and he fed him on numerous occasions, Sox would still hiss when he saw him. Ole Sox probably thinks he's about to steal every drop of Dinasia's attention from here on out, Tislam thought as he inserted the CD in the slot. Or maybe Sox was letting his male jealous tendencies get the best of him. *Can't blame him because no man in his right state of mind is gonna let another man take what's rightfully his without a fight.* The male hormone known as testosterone simply won't allow it.

He counted to three and hit the play button on the CD player. The song began. He turned up the volume, re-positioned the chair so it was facing the hallway leading to the bathroom, and then he sat in it. When he imagined Dinasia's shocked and happy facial expression, it brought a huge smile to his face.

*   *   *   *

Dinasia almost hyperventilated when she suddenly heard the CD player blasting the song "I Love Your Smile." She panicked, realizing an invader was apparently inside the house. She rushed to her purse on the dirty clothes hamper. With lightening speed, she pulled the 25 automatic and hit the safety switch. She paused for a moment, trying to hear if the intruder was right outside the bathroom door.

She quickly turned the water off, and stood motionless, dripping water as she realized there was no movement outside the door. She nervously threw on her terry-cloth robe and then the Super Ninja necklace, her good luck charm. With nervous hands, she opened the door very slowly and stood in the threshold of the bathroom, the bone chilling fear saturating every crevice of her mind.

"Who's there?!" She tried to shout over the music. The fear ran so deep through her veins it made her forget to breathe. Trembling, she tiptoed towards the end of the hall, planning to hit the corner and start shooting wildly.

*   *   *

Tislam smiled and began clapping his hands to the beat.

*   *   *

The palm of Dinasia's hand that held the gun started to sweat as she eased closer to the end of the hall. The handclaps told her the intruder was in the living room, near the CD player, and was apparently trying to taunt and tease her. She wondered if rushing around the corner and opening fire would catch the intruder off guard?

When she was a few feet from the corner, she hesitated and then said, "Whoever you are, I'm warning you, I got a gun. And I'll use it if you don't leave right now!"

281

Tislam heard Dinasia say something, but the music drowned the words out. He started happily humming the melody, really getting into the song.

Dinasia shouted as she took two steps closer to the corner. "I swear, I'll shoot you!"

On the count of three, Dinasia told herself as she stood at the end of the hallway, about to jettison around the corner and open fire. *Here we go*, she said to herself as she positioned her grip on the weapon. *One ... two . .* .

Seconds earlier, Tislam realized Dinasia was standing right at the corner and had said something; it sounded like she said 'shoot you.' He reached over and turned down the volume just as she began counting. "Dinasia, why would you wanna shoot the man you promised there would be 'no other love'? After all we've been through?"

Dinasia was about to spring around the corner with her finger squeezing the trigger until she heard the intruder speak. The voice instantly made her slam down on the breaks. If she were in a car, the abruptness of her action would've caused a screeching sound. Her eyes lit up with realization and dread. *Those words. That voice.* She was hurled into a vicious state of shock at the thought of how close she came to pulling the trigger.

Dinasia frantically stepped around the corner, hoping this wasn't a dream. When she saw Tislam sitting in the armchair with that unique smile of his, she hit the safety on the gun and sat it on the nearby table. "Tislam! Oh, God, I can't believe it's really you?" In a delirious fit of sheer shock mixed with exhilarating joy, she rushed to him as the tears of gratitude sprang from her eyes. "I knew you would come back!"

When the two collided with each other it was like an electrical explosion of pure love had ignited inside the room.

As the Super Ninja necklace dangled from Dinasia's neck, they kissed, hugged, caressed, embraced and made passionate love with a vigor and urgency not of this world.

In the years that came and went, the numerous changes in Dinasia and Tislam's relationship displayed a boundless, mutual, prolific passion that grew into an indescribable love that was truly like 'no other love'.

THE END

About the Author

Divine G is the founder and owner of Divine G Entertainment. He is a four-time PEN American Center award winning writer and the winner of the 2008 Tacenda Literary award for best play. He has been quoted by the United Nations and the New York Times.

Divine G recently produced, directed and starred in his debut short film consisting of a scene from his novel, *Enigma of Love*, which is currently being entered into various film festivals internationally. The film's trailer can be reviewed at
http://www.imdb.com/video/demo_reel/vi69708057/

He was employed as a carpenter for Lil Wayne on his 2013 AMW tour and is also hosting his own Internet Radio (The Divine G Show), which can be reviewed at
http://www.spreaker.com/show/the_divine_g_show.

Discover Other Titles by Divine G:

The Canarsie Connection - www.**amazon**.com/**Divine-G**./e/B001RZYN1Y

Enigma of Love - http://www.amazon.com/Enigma-Love-Divine-G-ebook/dp/B00C1Y13AY

Money Grip - http://www.amazon.com/Money-Grip-1-Divine-G-ebook/dp/B00BWEU92W

Money Grip 2 - http://www.amazon.com/Money-Grip-2-Volume/dp/1481924451

Baby Doll - http://www.amazon.com/Baby-Doll-Divine-G-ebook/dp/B00D55MZYQ

Upcoming Novels from Divine G

TGONG
(In bookstores Spring 2014)

Rayhiem Jones loved his community (Nubia Gold) so much he was willing to do whatever it took to clean it up. But he never thought his efforts to rid the community of drugs would cost him ten years in prison for a murder he did not commit. After finding out Jose Rodriguez (J.R.), the leader of Supranova, a vicious drug gang, had framed him for the murder, and upon his release from prison, Rayhiem is unable to simply put an H on his chest and handle it. Driven by a series of incomprehensible, reoccurring, life-long dreams, Rayhiem formulates a group that specializes in shutting down drug houses called . . . TGONG.

TIME-JACK
(In bookstores Spring 2014)

Calvin Thompson spent countless years mastering the field of Time Travel Technology and just when he is finally about to become the first official time traveler, a jealous co-worker, Eric Seabright, sends him back in time to the year 1831 in the deep south at the height of slavery.

With 4 months to make it to a Backlash zone (a safety component within the Time Machine that may transport him back to the future), Calvin struggles to overcome slavery, futuristic hit-men, and the demons inside of him that will not allow him to love and appreciate the people who are indispensable to his survival, his humanity and the victory of his journey.